KISAENG

Song had been toughened by army service in South Vietnam and Korea. With his indifference to the principles of right conduct he'd taken to the intrigue, brutality and corruption of military life as a duck to water. He also possessed considerable training in *Taekwan-do*, Korean karate, and *keupso chirigi*, the art of attacking vital points on the body.

A year ago when an American Secret Service agent working undercover tried to penetrate his organisation Song had killed him with a kick to the throat. More recently a brashly cheerful Italian from Interpol had attempted the same ploy, only to be strangled to death by Song who'd then covered the corpse in concrete and added it to the floor of a Hong Kong warehouse.

About the author

Marc Olden is the bestselling author of six powerful and chilling novels: *Giri*, *Dai-Sho*, *Gaijin*, *Oni*, *Te* and, the most stunning of all, *Kisaeng*. He lives in New York City.

Kisaeng

Marc Olden

NEW ENGLISH LIBRARY
Hodder and Stoughton

British Library C.I.P.

Olden, Mark
  Kisaeng.
  I: Title
  813.54[F]

ISBN 0-450-53743-9

Printed and bound in Great Britain for Hodder and Stoughton Paperbacks, a division of Hodder and Stoughton Ltd., Mill Road, Dunton Green, Sevenoaks, Kent TN13 2YA (Editorial Office: 47 Bedford Square, London WC1B 3DP) by Clays Ltd., St Ives plc.

For my beloved mother, Courtenaye,
who told me believe in the magic of my dreams

Kisaeng — *Korean geishas. The literal meaning is recreational creatures.*

It is not beauty that traps a man, but himself.
Chinese

Use a thorn to draw a thorn.
Thai

1

Laughing Boy, the counterfeiter, flew home to Seoul on a cold December morning. He brought with him from Hong Kong a Shar-Pei puppy and ten million dollars in cash.

The puppy, whose breed dated from China's second century Han dynasty, was for his mistress, a fourteen-year-old Austrian named Elana whom he'd acquired in London eight months before in exchange for a Fabergé silver and translucent clock worth fifty thousand pounds.

The ten million was for Colonel Cha Youngsam, the mournful-looking, forty-nine-year-old head of South Korea's CIA. Nicknamed "the Razor", Youngsam was ruthless, manipulative and fanatical about squirrelling away cash. Laughing Boy owed him thirty million dollars and had three weeks to pay it all or be killed.

Time had never been more valuable. In a week he would be off again, commencing a ten-day trip to Europe and America, where clients were waiting to pay him twenty-three million dollars for counterfeit bonds, securities and American currency. With luck he'd have enough to pay Youngsam and turn a three million dollar profit.

There was the unexpected, of course. Like the flow of water, a man's future was uncertain. Everything was the will of heaven and the world did not belong to any man. Still, Laughing Boy expected to reimburse Youngsam then return to the world of those who were happy.

Laughing Boy's real name was Park Song and he was in his late thirties, a slim, sharp-chinned Korean with slick dark

1

hair, small eyes and a white-toothed smile. He'd acquired his nickname because of a constant and often untimely giggling. Those who believed that laughter sprang from the mouths of fools were easily taken in by Song's cheery exterior which hid a powerful ego and a ferocious cunning.

He counterfeited travellers' cheques, foreign bonds, securities and passports. His preeminent product, however, was the American hundred dollar bill. It was a work of art into which he'd put all his aspirations and dreams. He prided himself on being able to approximate the loops, crosshatching and intricate whorls that made American paper money the hardest currency to copy. Whatever else he did imperfectly Song created dollars well.

His sizable profits had gone into such investments as Hong Kong real estate, Taiwanese flea markets, a small Bordeaux vineyard and a Manila shopping mall. He'd also treated himself to a course at Le Cordon Bleu in Paris, where he'd spent twelve weeks learning to prepare classical French cuisine. Money brought him freedom and luxury. It even allowed him to buy love.

It was snowing when he cleared customs at Kimpo Airport without a baggage inspection, found his waiting limousine and settled in the back seat. He ordered David Mitla, the bearded thirty-five-year-old former Israeli paratrooper who was his bodyguard, to put the Shar-Pei's travelling case on the front seat.

The Korean chauffeur, a judo silver medallist at the 1984 Olympics and sometime bodyguard, stacked the luggage in the trunk. He received no help from Mitla. The Israeli positioned himself with his back to the car, a hand on the Uzi beneath his Burberry topcoat as he scanned crowds entering and leaving the terminal.

From Kimpo the limousine headed east along the Han River towards downtown Seoul. Song poured himself cognac from the bar, drinking while he stared through tinted glass at gingko and willow trees whose bare branches were chalky with snow. He finished his third drink as the limousine passed Nanji Island. He began to tap nervously the empty glass with

2

a thumbnail when the car neared the pine-forested mountains just outside the city.

Yesterday in Hong Kong he'd sold four million dollars in fake American hundred dollar bills to a gnomelike Irish provo with a ratty moustache who claimed to have planted the bomb which killed Lord Mountbatten and his grandson. Laughing Boy had remained indifferent to the Mick's appeal for admiration and worship. Any fool knew that boasting and lying were the same thing.

The hundreds had gone for thirty-two cents on the dollar, a good price though the total was far short of what Laughing Boy needed to stay alive. With no time to quibble he'd been forced to sell choice Hong Kong investments at bargain prices – his floating restaurant anchored off Aberdeen, a seat on the Hong Kong stock exchange, a twelve-storey chalet on Chi Ma Wan Peninsula and the three Kowloon motels that catered to prostitutes. His once financially secure future had disappeared, leaving him bitchy and depressed.

The ordeal with Youngsam was beginning to consume Song. It disturbed him to discover that being clever was no guarantee against setbacks. His possessions were dwindling which was ghastly, but not as ghastly as seeing the deadline approach full tilt. He could always buy more property but he couldn't buy another life.

Until recently he'd enjoyed the Razor's protection. Youngsam had shielded him from arrest, prevented his extradition to the West, furnished him with a KCIA passport and found buyers for his fake money. He'd also covered up crimes involving Song's sinister obsession with the domination and sexual abuse of women.

In turn, Song had served Youngsam as forger, informant, money launderer and assassin. Two weeks ago something had gone wrong with the money laundering, costing Youngsam millions and leaving Song facing extinction. Could anyone survive the Razor's ill will when it came to money? A fish had a better chance of climbing a tree.

"To assure me of your good intentions, you will make a

down payment on your debt," Youngsam had said. "An immediate down payment."

A pain started in the small of Song's back and moved to his groin. "Immediate? You gave me three weeks to raise the money."

"I insist on a show of your good faith. You will hand over ten million dollars at once."

"I don't understand."

"It will indicate your seriousness with respect to settling the debt. If you don't make this down payment, you will lose one finger a day until you do."

A tingling sensation in Song's hands and feet began to spread along his limbs to his body. When he spoke his voice was thick and almost incoherent. "Immediate, you said."

"I'm not unreasonable. You have two days before the loss of your fingers becomes an issue. As for the rest of the money, you still have three weeks to settle your account in full."

Song clenched his fists to stop his hands from shaking; he also experienced difficulty in swallowing. There was no running away from this new complication in his life. To leave Korea would only mean eventual extradition from his new home to face murder charges in America and Italy. That his potential executioner was also his protector was an irony not lost on Laughing Boy.

But if raising thirty million dollars in three weeks was difficult, coming up with ten million in forty-eight hours was almost impossible.

Until this second ultimatum, with its threat to his fingers, Song had reason to be confident and upbeat. He was an excellent counterfeiter, running his affairs with a minimum of waste and a tenacity of purpose. The Youngsam episode, a costly one to be sure, marked that rare occasion when he and not someone else had been the sheep thrown to the wolves.

His troubles with the KCIA chief had originated with Song's desire to own a bank, an idea which had persisted in his head for years and remained a fixation he could not control. In the past the timing hadn't been right; either he'd lacked the money or been unable to secure the proper locale and front man. But three months ago these elements had finally joined together and Song had rushed forward boldly to realise his life's dream. At last he was going to own the rainbow.

In September he had opened a bank in the Cayman Islands. His partner was Gerard Petrus, a plump fifty-two-year-old Frenchman and fellow Bordeaux vineyard owner for whom he'd twice counterfeited US Treasury bearer bonds. A banker with years of experience in handling covert accounts, Petrus also knew the importance of keeping secret banking information to himself.

Song saw Petrus as being gifted with a calculating mind and no end of forceful willpower. Both planned their moves well in advance, hid their true feelings and used people to their advantage. Petrus was the constant schemer, never allowing his brain to be at rest while being careful about what he said. Song admired these traits, although he sometimes found it difficult to predict the Frenchman's next move.

The two knew people in need of financial secrecy. Cocaine cowboys, tax evaders, gunrunners, Intelligence agents, businessmen dodging creditors, husbands dodging wives, Third World politicians foreseeing early retirement. The demand for financial secrecy had never been greater.

Both agreed that the Cayman Islands were an ideal home for hot money. Located four hundred and seventy-five miles south of Miami in the Caribbean, the islands' secrecy laws were more protective than those of Switzerland. Bank employees who dared admit the existence of a secret account faced two years in prison. Access to account information or identities of depositors was forbidden without a court order, which was rarely granted. What one was not informed about one could not inquire about.

While Petrus had more banking experience Song himself knew a thing or two about secret assets, bribery, tax evasion and shell companies, the usual fiscal skulduggery consistent with offshore banking. His own villainy had prepared him for the world of secret money, where those who were able to handle hidden assets and keep information to themselves

5

could become very wealthy indeed. Song and Petrus had only to open shop, remain mute and grow rich.

They formed a company, TransOcean-Caribbean, and agreed that Petrus should be the front man. The Frenchman had the more acceptable business profile, so why not leave the everyday running of the bank to him. Song, hidden behind shell companies registered in Panama and Luxembourg, would be the silent partner. Both would recruit depositors.

In the bank's third week Petrus telexed Song about customers he'd signed up, one of whom had made a half-million dollar deposit with a promise of more to come. Song himself had secured a couple of impressive clients. One was the head of a Philippines tear gas company who'd made millions as a result of a surge in violent protests against Corazon Aquino's government.

The other was Cha Youngsam, in need of a hiding place for bribes received from drug dealers and corrupt military contractors. Youngsam also wanted to conceal funds embezzled from his rich and very trusting wife. The KCIA chief's attitude towards Mrs Youngsam was simply an extension of behaviour considered acceptable in government.

If Song was committed to keeping the Razor as his benefactor, then assisting the spymaster in his hour of need was only realistic and far-sighted. Besides it made one feel important to do favours for powerful men. Helping the penny-pinching Youngsam to hoard his wealth would always ensure Song a kind welcome, or so he thought.

Then two weeks ago Youngsam telephoned him at his Seoul home to ask if Song knew that TransOcean-Caribbean money was being invested in Petrus's private business endeavours. Certain depositors, Youngsam among them, had their doubts about these ventures. Because of these doubts the KCIA chief wanted his money back at once.

Song had known nothing about Petrus's secret ventures. The news caught him completely by surprise, leaving him panicky and with abdomen pains as he envisioned Youngsam's reaction if his money wasn't returned.

Like all miserly men the KCIA chief viewed humanity with

6

distrust, making him paranoid concerning his own fears and suspicions. It was no surprise when he charged Song and Petrus with conniving to rob him. In fact he ordered his money, thirty million dollars, returned at once and threatened to kill them if they didn't do so.

Song had been toughened by army service in South Vietnam and Korea. With his indifference to the principles of right conduct he'd taken to the intrigue, brutality and corruption of military life as a duck to water. He also possessed considerable training in *Taekwan-do*, Korean karate, and *keupso chirigi*, the art of attacking vital points on the body.

A year ago when an American Secret Service agent working undercover tried to penetrate his organisation Song had killed him with a kick to the throat. More recently a brashly cheerful Italian from Interpol had attempted the same ploy, only to be strangled to death by Song who'd then covered the corpse in concrete and added it to the floor of a Hong Kong warehouse.

But for all his unsavoury and savage ways he could never hope to match Youngsam for villainy. The KCIA chief was Korea's most powerful man after the president, allowing him to commit criminal acts on a grand scale and get away with it. And since Youngsam wasn't inclined to wait out his enemies, this made him even more dangerous.

As expected Petrus's business ventures were in serious trouble and so was the bank. The Frenchman, being in the Caribbean, appeared to be beyond Youngsam's reach. Song, however, had the misfortune of residing in Seoul which placed him near enough to be pulled in whenever the spymaster saw fit. And it was during one such encounter following the bank fiasco that Song was told to make good Youngsam's losses or suffer the consequences. Song needed little reminding that he was looking into a dark future.

The bank's failure was his worst nightmare come to life. All telexes and telephone calls to Petrus went unanswered. Adding to Song's uneasiness, Youngsam had him under surveillance and was probably tapping his phones. Song was ready to charter a plane to the Caymans, to confront Petrus and beat

7

the shit out of him when he learned that the Frenchman was heading for Haiti on a Cessna jet packed with gold bullion.

That same afternoon TransOcean-Caribbean Bank closed its doors permanently.

More bad news from Youngsam whose spies were always at work: Cayman authorities had requested Song's immediate extradition and Petrus was continuing to victimise Song at every turn. The Frenchman had let slip Song's full criminal history, colouring it somewhat with the claim that Song had conceived the bank fraud. Petrus added that his felonious partner, as he called Song, had grabbed the lion's share of bank proceeds for himself.

Being a congenital and unrepentant liar, Song rarely told the truth. But he was as straightforward and aboveboard as he'd ever been when he told Youngsam he'd never taken a penny from the bank. Sad to say, the KCIA chief had less interest in claims of righteousness than he did in getting his money back.

After one particularly chilly telephone call from the Razor, a tense Song snatched a blanket, raced to the nearest bathroom and locked the door. Wide-eyed with fear he slumped to the floor and tore at the blanket with his teeth, vowing to kill Petrus on sight.

Laughing Boy the deceiver had himself been deceived. And in the process he'd almost had his manhood destroyed by the goddam Frenchman. Never before had life seemed such a fucked-up, stinking and treacherous game.

He learned that Petrus had surfaced in Paris to meet with attorneys and influential government friends who were being asked to intercede with Cayman authorities on Petrus's behalf. Through Youngsam, Song also learned that Petrus and his supporters had cut a deal with Cayman authorities, one that amounted to little more than a slap on the wrist. Petrus would voluntarily return to the islands to face prosecution, with the understanding that he receive not more than four months in the local jail, a fairly easy place to do time, it was said.

Worst of all, Petrus wouldn't have to make restitution of any kind. The Frenchman's intermediaries successfully repeated the argument that Song had walked off with almost all the money, so let him reimburse depositors. At this point Song's frustration became so unbearable that he vomited and lost his appetite for days.

Because Cayman authorities wanted to protect their banks from public scrutiny, Petrus would be allowed to keep the insignificant sum he claimed to have pilfered. As for Laughing Boy, to whom could he complain? His sordid history had branded him a villain; any claim of innocence on his part was a joke.

From the Frenchman's point of view it had all ended happily. Song, on the other hand, was furious at being blamed for something he hadn't done. The stress was such that he was unable to sleep at night without several cognacs.

At noon two days ago he'd received a telephone call ordering him to KCIA headquarters at once. Trembling and sweating he obeyed, hoping his sphincter muscles wouldn't give way in front of Youngsam. But instead of ending Song's days on earth, the spymaster handed him a telex to read.

Yesterday morning, according to the telex, caretakers had discovered two large suitcases in the Bois de Vincennes on the southeast edge of Paris. Because of nearby bloodstains police were called to the scene. The suitcases were found to contain most of the remains of a middle-aged white male, whose body had been cut into pieces and wrapped in plastic garbage bags.

His skull had been crushed and the neck of a broken bottle shoved up his rectum. All of his fingers had been sliced off.

The remains were identified as those of Gerard Petrus who'd been missing since leaving his attorney's office on Quai des Tuileries twenty-four hours before. Three Asians had been seen removing two large suitcases from a blue Toyota still parked near a Bois de Vincennes entrance. When police searched the car they found a bloodied length of pipe used to club Petrus to death. They also found his fingers which had been wrapped in tinfoil and hidden in the glove compartment.

Song felt cold sweat trickle down his spine. His heartbeat

was suddenly irregular and the abdominal pains started up again. A quick glance at Youngsam, who sat poker-faced behind his desk, then Song silently resumed reading the telex. Seconds later he stopped, unable to concentrate.

Youngsam said, "Petrus's punishment guarantees that he will not repeat his crimes. Call it a perpetual fine imposed for his arrogance in thinking he could get away with what he'd done. He offered to return the money, but you see I no longer trusted him. Therefore, he was of no further use to me.

"He was surprised at how much we knew about him. We knew, for example, that he'd paid large sums to certain French officials to intercede for him with Cayman police. He'd also paid off several outstanding debts and been quite generous with his attorneys. Much of the stolen money was no longer in his possession and the rest, I've learned, is sequestered in numbered accounts in four different countries. Recovering it would be difficult if not impossible."

Youngsam's abnormally deepset eyes bored into Song. "I want my money back," he said, "and that is the only reason you are still alive. Now let us take up the matter of your down payment."

Fifteen minutes later Song left Youngsam's office, waved his chauffeur away and began walking Seoul's streets in a daze. There was a tightness in his chest and he felt so restless that he almost ran. Despite the December chill he was perspiring. He cupped his face in both hands; his skin was hot and sweaty.

Removing his hat and topcoat, he dropped them on the sidewalk behind him and pushed into the lunchtime crowds, knocking an old, blind man to the pavement. The old man cried out as he landed on the base of his spine. Song never looked back.

How was he going to give Youngsam a ten million dollar down payment in just forty-eight hours?

Forty minutes later a weary Song found himself in Chongmyo, a forested park located in the centre of Seoul and the site of several traditional temples. Stopping in front of one shrine he bent over, hands on his knees, and breathed deeply. Then using his right fist he massaged the area over

10

his heart. In minutes his breathing and heartbeat became normal.

He approached the temple, eyes on the evil-repelling symbols, dragon, tiger and phoenix, carved into the beams and doorways. While the temple was closed – it opened only on special ceremonial days – worshippers had left offerings of wine, pigs' legs and an ox's head on the front steps. In the December chill Song's nostrils flared at the smell of still warm rice cakes.

Eyes closed, he stood alone in front of the temple, arms outstretched and fingers extended, fingers which Youngsam had just threatened to cut off. He swayed from side to side, barely hearing the distant buzz of traffic. Suddenly he opened his eyes.

He knew how to get the down payment. Simply sell off some of his Hong Kong property.

Another thought had come to him in front of the temple, namely how to get back at Youngsam.

He began to giggle.

2

Park Song lived in an exquisite pavilion within sight of Seoul's Kyongbok Palace where in 1895 Japanese assassins murdered Korea's Queen Min, stabbing her, then burning her with kerosene. An enthusiastic gardener, he'd planted many of the flowering lilac trees, giant pink lotuses and miniature maples within the arabesque walls surrounding the low one-storey building.

Recently he'd added a temperature-controlled wing to house a collection of Hollywood memorabilia which included costumes worn by midgets in *The Wizard of Oz* and rocks from California's Mount Lee, site of the legendary fifty-foot-high *Hollywood* sign. He delighted in Hollywood movies of the thirties, musicals in particular. A boundless admiration for Fred Astaire had led him to embrace tap-dancing as a hobby.

In fond imitation of Joan Crawford his kitchen was carpeted in white and a bedroom panelled entirely in Viennese mirrors. His homage to the actress also included eating the breakfast she had consumed for years: soda crackers with mustard and a coddled egg, no salt, no butter.

Two hours after arriving home with Youngsam's money Song stepped into a huge sunken bronze tub modelled after one in Tom Mix's Beverly Hills mansion. Placing a T-shaped straight razor on the tub's edge he then lowered himself into the jasmine-scented water up to his neck and sighed with pleasure. A hot bath was that rare innocent pleasure which didn't bore him.

He'd just completed the last of several telephone calls, this one to a customer in New York guaranteeing that $1.5 million in counterfeit Brazilian Treasury bonds would be delivered on time. The first step towards becoming businesslike was to appear businesslike.

In other telephone calls Song had cracked down on associates in Seoul and abroad. Paper needed for the final currency printing hadn't arrived from America, and while Song's printers insisted they were blameless, he'd made it clear he wasn't interested in excuses. He'd been even more abusive with his American paper suppliers, threatening to have them killed if the paper wasn't in Seoul tomorrow morning.

No sweat, they'd said in that loose American way he'd come to despise. The paper was absolutely, positively on its way and should arrive at any moment. Song had never made such a large request before and it wasn't easy to come up with so much paper at short notice, know what I mean? Song was unforgiving; when you forgave people they took advantage of you. The paper was to be in Seoul no later than tomorrow morning or there'd be hell to pay.

He hadn't explained why he needed such an enormous amount of paper this instant. But nothing was harder to keep than a secret so you could bet the truth would emerge in short order. The best he could do was pay Youngsam as quickly as possible and close this nasty chapter in his life. Any delay would only add to Song's pain and distress.

Youngsam was pressing Song, but the counterfeiter was too brutal for others to amuse themselves with jokes at his expense. Conscious only of himself, he had little tolerance of slurs and verbal jabs. He demanded and received respect from co-workers and associates, Youngsam being the one exception to this rule. The hand you cannot bite, you kiss.

Committed to retaining his fingers Song had telephoned Youngsam from Hong Kong, confirming that the down payment would be made on time. Later this evening Youngsam was having his men collect the ten million and bring it to him at the home of his mistress, a former beauty queen whose film career he was sponsoring at no small cost.

The KCIA chief was also investing heavily in copper shares, believing that the spread of AIDS in Zambia and Zaire, source of much of the world's copper, would devastate the skilled work force and produce a global shortage. When it came to seeking out profit Youngsam moved faster than a scalded dog.

In the tub Song patted his face with a large damp sponge. He'd just left an exuberant Elana next door in the master bedroom where she was holding a one-sided conversation with the Shar-Pei. The beige, long-faced dog was nervous and moody, which Elana saw as being sensitive. Song, somewhat more discerning, viewed the puppy's behaviour differently; like any purebred the dog was simply inclined to follow its own selfish whims.

Older women possessed this same selfishness which is why Song preferred adolescents in whom he could infuse certain knowledge and skills. He schooled each girl in the passionate feelings, manners and attitudes of a *kisaeng*, the most delightful lover a man could wish for. Song's affairs ended when time had ended love. Then he would select another girl and begin training her. Great emphasis was placed upon sexual submissiveness.

Song revered Korea's ancient traditions, particularly the tradition of the *kisaeng* which he saw as the most beautiful custom of them all. It had begun almost a thousand years ago when the court of the Koryo kingdom chose adolescent girls for their beauty, charm and talent then trained them to be singers, painters, musicians, dancers and story-tellers. This training produced the most highly educated women in the country, women who became the companions of kings, nobles, scholars and artists.

They were known as *kisaeng*, recreational creatures.

They were also known as "the perfect woman".

Tourists and foreign businessmen visiting Korea still had the opportunity to attend a *kisaeng* party at luxury restaurants where they were fawned over by female escorts who sang, danced, played traditional musical instruments and wrote calligraphy with brush and ink.

14

But as Song knew only too well today's *kisaeng* was merely part of a sex industry aimed at male tourists from America, Japan, Europe and Australia. What else could one say about women who'd undergone a state training course, the two main components of which were a commitment to anti-Communism and a study of the sexual positions preferred by Japanese men.

He wasn't fooled by government attempts to pass these females off as replicas of those highly cultivated artistes of past centuries. Today's *kisaeng* was a whore hired to entertain tired businessmen each of whom paid plenty for the privilege of being swindled. The favours of these pseudo *kisaeng* did not come cheap.

Song's knowledge of "the perfect woman" was far from shallow. He owned rare books and age-old records on the subject, including antique scrolls describing a sixth-century group called *wonhwa*, original flowers. The group, which predated *kisaeng*, was composed of beautiful young women chosen to serve as role models for the country. It was disbanded, however, when one of its two female leaders killed the other in a jealous rage.

To a great extent Song had succeeded in instilling much of the true *kisaeng* tradition in Elana, who was bright, manageable, and eager to please. The best tutors had been hired to teach her poetry writing, story-telling and Korean music, which she considered out of tune because it was not based on the tempered scale of the Western tonal system.

Song himself had handled some of the training, teaching her calligraphy and the royal court dances which he had her perform wearing the traditional costume and tiny flower crown. He'd also taught her folk-dancing with its graceful uplifting shoulder movements and slow rising and sinking movements of the knees. And he taught her how to pour his drinks and place morsels of food in his mouth as *kisaeng* had done for centuries.

She mastered *hangul*, the relatively simple Korean alphabet which consisted of only ten vowels and fourteen consonants. However, she had trouble speaking Korean, often forgetting to put verbs at the end of a sentence as required in proper speech. But with English words frequently appearing in Korean conversation Song didn't demand that Elana perfect the language. She was young and inexperienced; to be too critical would dampen her enthusiasm for learning.

As an orphan Elana had come to him without a penny to her name and with only the clothes on her back. Security, therefore, was important to her. Because a stable homelife mattered more than an unknown future she submitted to Song's demands. She was something of a patient plodder, but by letting her develop at her own pace he'd managed to get the best out of her.

She'd been a virgin who'd turned out to be marvellously sensual and under his direction an excellent lover. Sexually she did whatever he wished, no matter how shocking or forbidden. With her passion came a possessive streak that he sometimes found annoying. To avoid impregnating her Song bathed his testicles in warm water before intercourse, inducing temporary infertility while giving himself an exciting pleasure-pain sensation.

He had created his own perfect woman, one who wasn't for sale to a foreign businessman with a fat wallet. She was Song's personal property, trained solely for his gratification and indulgence. In knowing that other men could never have Elana he had enjoyed her even more. When he'd told her there'd never be another man in her life, she'd thrown herself into his arms and wept with joy.

Song was extremely generous to women and Elana was no exception. The return he got from such kindness was a contented and joyful young lover. Each gift, he told her, was a portion of himself.

Last month he'd given her a ten thousand dollar Honda Gold Wing motorbike outfitted with AM/FM stereo, on-board trip computer and rider-passenger intercom. He treasured photographs of the slender, blonde teenager posed on the motorbike, dressed in French bra and panties which left her nipples and vagina exposed.

On the trip to Hong Kong he hadn't forgotten Elana,

left behind in Seoul to overindulge in her favourite foods, Coca-Cola and chocolate cake. At the exclusive Landmark shopping mall he'd bought her two Claude Montana leather jumpsuits with shoulders extending six inches on either side. She was currently wearing one of the jumpsuits which had been tarnished to a degree when the Shar-Pei peed on her thigh.

In the tub Song lifted a leg from the water and examined a calf muscle hardened by dancing and the martial arts. After soaping the leg he shaved it with the straight razor, using long, sure strokes. A leg like this could kick Youngsam's balls through the top of his head. But this was fantasy and fantasy was the result of a weak mind. Song was far from weak. He'd get Youngsam in a more subtle way.

He giggled. Now was as good a time as any.

He was getting an erection. Looking over his shoulder at the master bedroom he called out, "Elana, come here. Now."

The door opened and the teenager entered the bathroom, the puppy in her arms. She stopped several feet from the tub, kissed the dog's snout and waved one of its paws at Song.

He lifted a watery hand in greeting. "Leave him in the next room, pretty one, then take off your jumpsuit and get in the tub. Lock the door so we won't be disturbed."

"I've decided to call him Springsteen," she said.

"What's wrong with calling him Mr Wee-Wee?"

"That was an accident. He didn't mean to mess up my nice new clothes."

"Perhaps he'll atone for his bad manners by sending you flowers. Now put him in the bedroom like I told you and hurry back."

Face pressed against the dog's head, she left the bathroom humming "Born in the USA". Two minutes later she returned, nude and smiling, a gold chain around her waist. She was slender and small-breasted, with green eyes and shoulder-length golden hair parted in the middle. Her nails were painted green and her pubic hair had been shaved off.

Elana climbed into the tub and slid into Song's embrace. Without a word she licked his nipples, gently pulling at each

17

one with her full lips. One hand went between his legs. Then ducking her head under water she took his erect penis in her mouth. Her hair darkened as it floated on the water's surface. Eyes closed, Song leaned back in the tub. He found her flickering tongue maddening.

Seconds later she came up for air. Using both hands she pulled wet hair away from her face and smiled at Song. He returned her smile, remembering to nod his approval. He'd taught her well.

He said, "Are you happy with me, I mean really and truly happy? Please speak the truth. I'll know if you're lying."

Placing her head on his chest she gently circled his right nipple with a small forefinger. "I love you. I want to stay with you for ever."

"That's not what I asked. I asked if you are happy, really and truly happy."

"I am. I have everything I could want. And I really do want to stay with you for ever."

She looked at him, sodden hair framing her small face. Her full mouth produced a trusting smile, one indicating a total reliance on his character and integrity. Song kissed her eyes, tasting the water and feeling her lashes gently flutter beneath his lips. She'd never looked more alluring.

She tongued the outside of his ear and began to writhe against him. Her voice was a compelling and carnal whisper. "I always want to be as happy as I am now."

Song brought a length of her hair to his lips and kissed it. His fingers massaged the back of her neck. "Now you're worth killing," he said.

He picked up the straight razor and quickly slit both sides of her mouth. A second later he sank his teeth in her right shoulder. Elana screamed, splitting open her face. Song giggled. Leaning back in the water he locked his legs around her waist, squeezing until she couldn't breathe. Her shrieking was instantly reduced to a pathetic gasp, then nothing.

Opening his legs Song placed his right foot on Elana's stomach and contemptuously pushed her away from him. She landed face down in the water and began floating towards twin faucets fashioned in the shape of wild horses raised up on their hind legs. Still clutching the razor, Song dived into the blood-darkened water after her.

Lifting his head out of the water, he rose quickly, Elana's watery and bleeding corpse in his arms. Rushing forward he slammed her back against a wall, forced his penis into her and ejaculated instantly.

Spent, he let the dead girl slip from his hands and fall into the water. Then eyes closed, he stood trembling with his forehead pressed against a bathroom wall made of paving stones taken from D. W. Griffith's driveway. He felt an unspeakable joy. The tension that had been with him earlier was gone. His mind was now clear and calm.

He could not fully satisfy his sexual instinct without killing. For this unique erotic experience he needed a woman without equal or equivalent, a woman surpassing what was common or usual. He needed one with recognised similarities to his mother yet formed with his distinctive needs in mind.

Song needed his own *perfect woman*. He'd often found her and he'd killed her each time.

Three hours later he was tap-dancing on the polished black granite floor of his living room in front of a fireplace flanked by bronze Art Deco lions, when a bow-legged, white-jacketed servant interrupted to tell him that three men had arrived for Youngsam's money. Song, dapper and white-tied, was dancing along with a Fred Astaire and Ginger Rogers video cassette of *Swing Time* now airing on an oversized television screen.

He continued to dance while talking. "Tell the gentlemen the suitcases they want are sitting outside this room. They can just take the cases and go. No need for me to see anyone."

When the servant closed the door Song smiled, thinking, Youngsam, my friend, you're in for a surprise. On screen Astaire had just finished "Never Gonna Dance", and with Ginger was about to go into "The Way You Look Tonight", Song's favourite number in the movie. It gave him goosebumps every time he saw it.

Humming along with the music he smoothly duplicated Astaire's every move.

Youngsam was forgotten.

In the study of his villa behind Seoul's only Anglican Cathedral Cha Youngsam squatted in front of five leather suitcases on the carpet facing his desk, remembering the evil omen which had foreshadowed his loss of thirty million dollars. Youngsam, a heavily built, fiftyish man with hooded eyes and an unpleasant nasal voice would never have admitted to being superstitious. But Korean spiritual traditions believed in prophecy, something he accepted without question.

The omen, a recent one, had appeared on Buddha's birthday, on the eighth day of the fourth lunar month. That night he'd joined the crowds at Chogye-sa Buddhist temple in downtown Seoul where he'd purchased a paper lantern and a candle. After writing the names of his family on a tag beneath the lantern he inserted a candle in the lantern, lit it, then hung the lantern from one of several wires stretched across the temple courtyard.

In the darkness around him row upon row of flickering candles brightened the courtyard. Youngsam bowed and prayed that Buddha's grace be upon him and his family. He also prayed for continued help in stockpiling money. The process of accumulating wealth made him happy and assured him of a more pleasant life when he had accumulated it.

Money would also allow him to make a timely exit from Intelligence work rather than stay too long and fall victim to one more pushy military strongman. With money he could escape his enemies.

Suddenly a blast of wind tore at his lantern, sending it dancing wildly on the wire. A second later the lantern caught fire and burned. *An evil omen.* Youngsam knew it and so did the horrified devotees around him. A burning lantern promised ill fortune for the year to come.

As luck would have it misfortune sought him out immediately. Shortly after the lantern incident his wife suffered a mild stroke and his eldest daughter, now in her first year at a

Boston medical school, lost a leg in a motorcycle accident. His twenty-four-year-old mistress, a competitive little bitch who lacked the patience to learn anything properly, had begun an affair with a Japanese film director in hopes of advancing her movie career.

Finally, there'd been the catastrophe with Park Song's bank and its threat to Youngsam's hopes for a cushy future. The loss of thirty million dollars made his other problems seem trivial by comparison. Even a government edict to crack down on student demonstrations favouring the unification of North and South Korea failed to command his full attention. A ruthlessly determined Youngsam gave little thought to anything except recovering his money.

He lost no time in pressuring Park Song. Youngsam wasn't interested in explanations, justifications or alibis of any kind. Song had talked him into making deposits at TransOcean-Caribbean, which made Song accountable for subsequent events. Youngsam, whose enemies claimed his pockets were sewn tight to make handing over cash a physical impossibility, was lethal when he felt cheated out of money rightfully his.

To hell with bad omens. He was going to squeeze his thirty million out of that bastard Laughing Boy. Forget what they may have done for one another in the past. It was the weight of the present, with its loss of Youngsam's money, that was pressing down upon the KCIA chief.

In his study he pulled a suitcase towards him and stroked it with trembling hands. Cheap leather, broken clasps, a loose handle. Probably picked up in a Hong Kong flea market, but no matter. What mattered was the contents, nothing else.

Opening the suitcase, Youngsam stared at the money and felt his chest tighten. His breathing became rapid and shallow. He was staring at a mass of American hundred dollar bills, a wondrous sight. His temples throbbed as he patted the money. Everything he needed for his wellbeing and happiness was in this suitcase. *Everything*.

He would count the money, of course. Trust only yourself and no one else would ever betray you. When the count was complete, the money would be wired to banks in Macau,

Hungary and Lichtenstein – banks thoroughly checked out by Youngsam so there'd be no repetition of the disaster he'd just experienced with Song and the Frenchman.

Were there any counterfeit bills in these suitcases? Youngsam doubted it. Song knew the consequences of handing over a single bogus note.

Youngsam had been wise to let him live. Scare him a bit, yes, but keep him alive because if anyone could raise thirty million on short notice it was Song. Laughing Boy was so vain he probably enjoyed the smell of his own farts. He could also be as loony as a March hare. But few men were as clever and resourceful.

Scooping stacks of hundreds from the suitcases Youngsam placed them on his desk. Minutes later he had emptied the suitcase and begun unloading a second. He'd almost cleared this suitcase when he saw it. Tucked between two stacks of hundreds. A tinfoil packet the size of a small envelope. Chances were good that Song didn't even know it was missing.

Youngsam picked up the packet, peered at it through wire-rimmed spectacles then weighed it in his hand. If it contained anything of value Mr Song was out of luck because anything in these suitcases belonged to Youngsam.

He unwrapped the packet, delighted at putting one over on Laughing Boy. And then he saw the contents. Stunned and disgusted, he let the packet fall to the carpet.

Youngsam stepped back, away from the tinfoil and the things it had contained. His neck muscles tightened and he had trouble breathing. He was close to vomiting.

Scattered at his feet were several human fingers. Blood-stained fingers with green-tinted nails.

Though brutal and cold-blooded, Youngsam had an intense aversion to touching dead flesh. He avoided physical contact with his torture victims, particularly after their demise, preferring to leave such grisly details to his subordinates. It was a lifelong revulsion dating from that morning when as an eight-year-old in a dirt poor family he'd awakened to find a younger brother lying in his arms dead from starvation.

A queasy Youngsam tiptoed around the strewn fingers and stepped to his desk, to be hit by a sudden shortness of breath. Palms down on a spotless green blotter he waited until his breathing returned to normal. Then with a trembling hand he pulled the telephone towards him, picked up the receiver and began dialling.

In his living room an exhausted Song flopped down onto a shell-back sofa, loosened his white tie and watched *Swing Time*'s end credits. Humming "The Way You Look Tonight", he dried his face with a small hand towel. On a low rattan table a telephone rang incessantly.

Song removed his tap shoes and made a mental note to have new taps put on the soles and heels. Closing his eyes, he massaged his feet. The telephone, which his servants had been told to ignore, continued ringing.

Finally, he stood up and stretched, then walked over to the rattan table. Smiling at his reflection in a mirrored wall, he removed an opened bottle of Moet et Chandon from an ice bucket and filled a glass with the chilled champagne. One sip and he sighed with pleasure. A second sip then he picked up the telephone receiver. "Yes?"

"You little shit. I'll see you dead for this."

Song held his champagne glass up to the light and eyed the bubbles. "Colonel Youngsam. So good of you to call. I trust the down payment's been delivered safely. Ten million dollars as promised."

"You're a sick bastard and you're not getting away with it."

"Get away with what? I don't understand." Song bit his lip to keep from giggling.

"You killed her didn't you, you fucking pervert?"

"Oh her? Elana, you mean? Well, yes, as a matter of fact I did. Now how did you know? It only happened a couple of hours ago —"

"I said I would cut off your fingers if you didn't make the down payment. Well, you've made the down payment and I'm going to remove them anyway. Each and every one. Play

23

your disgusting games with young girls if you will, but not with me. *Not with me.*"

Song couldn't stop smiling. "Colonel, will you please tell me what you're talking about?"

Anger made Youngsam more nasal than usual. "You thought sending me that girl's fingers would be amusing, didn't you? Well, the joke's going to be on you."

Song raised his eyebrows. "Ah, I see. You're saying I deliberately sent – "

Suddenly the counterfeiter turned apologetic. "Colonel, Colonel, please forgive me. What happened was this: I wrapped the fingers in tinfoil, then I mislaid the package. It's as simple as that. I would never send you such a gift. Never."

"You're a liar."

Song said, "I put the fingers on a table with the money. You see, I was transferring the money to less expensive suitcases and at the same time I wanted to save the fingers as a keepsake. She was a wonderful girl with truly lovely fingers. I wanted to hang on to those fingers for a while. You get more sentimental about some girls than others."

Looking into the mirror Song used a forefinger to stroke his eyebrows. "I was in a hurry, you see. Your men were coming to pick up the money and I wanted to be ready when they arrived. I guess the fingers *accidentally* ended up in one of the suitcases. I'm truly sorry for any inconvenience. You weren't too upset, I hope."

Song thought, I hope you heaved your guts out, you greedy scum.

Youngsam said, "You expect me to believe that little fairy tale?"

"By the way," Song said, "would you do me the usual good turn and send someone over to remove her body? I don't know what I'd do without your help at these times. She's upstairs in the bathtub. Tell your men to wear gloves and not to touch anything. The last time someone left bloody handprints on the door jamb – "

"You're lying about the fingers and you know it." This time there was doubt in Youngsam's voice.

"Colonel, why would I do such a thing?"

"Because you think you're clever. Because you know — "

Youngsam stopped, loath to admit that others might know of his distaste for corpses. How could Song have possibly learned about his little brother's death? In truth the counterfeiter knew all about Youngsam's horror of touching dead flesh. This incident, among others, was in a detailed report on the spymaster which Song kept on file and updated periodically.

Youngsam said, "So now that you've proven you can raise the money, you think you're free to do as you please."

Song said, "It's criminal the way these student riots are embarrassing our country. Who cares if one of their leaders died last week after your men took him in for questioning. What was the cause of his death? Oh yes, a heart attack."

Song finished his champagne and refilled the glass. The student hadn't died of a heart attack. He'd died when one of Youngsam's thugs had placed the tip of a ballpoint pen in his ear and stamped on it three times, driving the pen into the student's brain.

News of the student leader's departure from this life had only increased the rioting. At the same time his followers had accused Youngsam of the student's murder and demanded his resignation. The Razor might weather the storm and he might not. Should he be forced to resign, it was better to do so as a rich man.

More than ever Youngsam needed Song and the counterfeiter knew it.

"Colonel, believe me when I tell you it was an accident. I was so intent on having the money ready that I probably knocked the fingers into the suitcase and never noticed it."

"I still say you're lying."

"Colonel, I've got my printers coming over later. They're working around the clock to get our products ready for my trip. I'd really appreciate Elana's corpse being removed before they arrive."

Youngsam exhaled. "If you ever send me anything like this

again I'll personally put a bullet through your head. I'll have the body picked up before your printers arrive."

After a short silence he said, "Her fingers instead of yours, was that it?"

"Colonel, really, I – "

"That's your sort of joke. Well, my friend, why don't we wait until you've repaid the thirty million then we'll see what sort of joke I can play on you."

He hung up.

Song burst out giggling. A wonderful joke. A marvellous joke. Look for Youngsam to have a few sleepless nights in the near future.

Song picked up a file folder lying beside the ice bucket and opened it. An eight by ten colour photograph lay on top of several typed pages. It was a picture of his next perfect woman.

Song studied her face. A truly beautiful girl, one of the most beautiful he'd ever seen in his life. Blonde hair, no physical imperfections and no history of mental illness.

He'd pick her up in New York, his last stop, and bring her back with him to Seoul to begin her education as a *kisaeng*. She would want for nothing. Her brief life with him would be a golden one.

He had reviewed her resumé and records every day for the past week.

She was thirteen years old.

3

Manhattan, December

At four thirty-two in the afternoon Detective Sergeant Manny Decker entered an almost vacant Mexican restaurant on Columbus Avenue and stood beside a woman who sat alone at the bar, her back to a picture window full of small cactus plants. He watched her finish a Margarita, reddened eyes closed as she drained the glass. She'd been weeping.

After placing the empty glass on the bar beside an eelskin purse she picked up a half-smoked cigarette from an ashtray, took a quick drag, then stubbed it out. She looked at her watch and was taking a pack of Marlboros from her bag when she sighted Decker. Forcing a smile she slid off the bar stool and into his arms.

As Decker held her close a thousand sleeping memories came to life. Her name was Gail DaSilva and they'd once talked marriage. But that was before he'd returned from Vietnam a very different man from the one who'd left America as a young Marine with clean hands and a pure heart.

He'd seen a lot and remembered too much. Shit, he'd come back feeling as though he were a thousand years old. A disappointed Gail had married someone else.

"Eight years," she said. "Eight long years. Can't believe it's been that long since we've seen each other."

"You're looking good, Gail."

"You're lying but that's all right. Lying compliments are preferable to sincere criticism. God, you're as solid as a rock. Still doing your karate?"

"Still doing it. Karate, clean living and the power of prayer have made me what I am today, whatever the hell that is. My old man thought exercise was a waste of time. Said if you're healthy you don't need it and if you're sick you shouldn't risk it."

"Wise fellow, your old man. I was so afraid you wouldn't show," she said. "Thanks for coming."

Burying her face against his chest, she wept silently. The detective closed his eyes. Being a cop for any length of time left you colder than a gravestone in winter. Decker wondered if he had any concern to give. He couldn't weep for everybody, that's for sure.

Gail DaSilva, however, was a different matter.

Two days ago she'd telephoned him at the precinct and begged his help. The preceding day Tawny, her teenage daughter and only child, had gone off as usual to attend a private school on Manhattan's West 73rd Street. That evening she'd failed to return. A frantic Gail DaSilva wanted Decker to find her.

Manny Decker was in his mid-thirties, slim and muscled, with dark brown hair, moustache and a smile that made him seem congenial, which he wasn't. The first two knuckles on both hands were calloused from years of hitting the *makiwara*, a karate punching board. A broken nose had much to do with his good looks. He'd acquired the cosmetic fracture while on a US karate team competing in the Pan-American games, when an opponent, a free-swinging Mexican postal clerk, had failed to pull a face punch.

Decker had earned his detective's gold shield in less than two years. In addition to precinct duty he was secretly attached to the Internal Affairs Division which had recruited him as a field associate directly out of the Police Academy. Field associates reported police misconduct to department headquarters, making them the most detested people on the force. Discovery meant being ostracised, harassed and even physically attacked by fellow officers who insisted that FA stood for "fucking asshole". The job was hazardous and at times downright dangerous. Decker liked it.

To reduce risks to themselves field associates maintained

only one headquarters contact, a lieutenant or captain. Code names were used and meetings were held in out of the way places. Decker had insisted that he and his contact, known simply as Ron, never met. Better to get a tin beak and peck shit with the chickens than be seen publicly with headhunters from Internal Affairs. Decker and Ron communicated by phone, with Decker initiating all calls.

Decker was a loner, unable (unwilling his ex-wife said) to commit himself to anybody. He viewed himself as an observer, living a life free of commitment, a man on a stopover between womb and tomb, who fulfilled himself training alone in the *dojo* and who was blessed because his life permitted him to create his own laws. That's why he'd become a field associate, a fucking asshole. He'd wanted to make the laws himself.

In the Mexican restaurant Decker dropped his hat on the bar beside a Christmas wreath slated to be hung on the front door, and unbuttoned his topcoat. He had to work at catching the eye of a young, hook-nosed bartender who was busy changing channels on a television set near the cash register. After electing to go with *Love Connection* the bartender turned his attention to the detective who said, "Two coffees, black."

Gail DaSilva took Decker's hands and pulled him onto the bar stool beside her. Petite and dark-haired, she was in her mid-thirties but looked older. She wore a smart black suit and white running shoes which Decker had come to recognise as the uniform of professional women in Manhattan. He didn't care for the look, finding it as ugly as home-made soup.

He'd last seen Gail DaSilva on a chilly April afternoon at the Metropolitan Museum of Art when he'd bumped into her and hubby at a Van Gogh exhibition. She'd married Max DaSilva, a chunky accountant who also owned a mail order jazz record company. Decker remembered him as a man who seemed pleased with himself and displeased with everybody else.

In the telephone call about Tawny's disappearance Gail had also clued Decker in on a life which was undergoing some changes. Shortly before their child's disappearance Max had asked Gail for a divorce. As he put it, he was nearly forty and

29

it was time for a spiritual rebirth, a reawakening of interest in life. It was time to expand his soul, to increase his ability to give and to receive.

Gail said, you're talking shit, Max. Get to the point.

The point, as Gail told Decker, was that Max was banging a female client, which is how he'd developed a taste for psycho-babble. His new love, a Swiss designer of costume jewellery, had pushed him into hypnotherapy as a means of bringing repressed feelings to the surface of his consciousness. As a result Max learned he'd wanted a divorce for years but simply lacked the balls to go for it.

Now that he was in touch with himself, he wanted to end his marriage to Gail and marry the woman with whom he wanted to live while he was alive.

Gail had a surprise for Max; she was as bored with him as he was with her. Truth is, both of them had been cured of love simultaneously. All they'd done the past few months was discover each other's faults, she told him. The magic was definitely gone. It was time to end the happiness and misery of something that had become more miserable than happy.

Gail's response to Max had stunned him, proving he'd always underestimated her pluck. Then again so had Decker and on more than one occasion.

Max had agreed to give Gail everything she wanted. Money, maintenance, a piece of the record company. Gail could have custody of Tawny. Max preferred a clean break. Gail could even have their three-bedroom co-op located directly across from the Philippines Consulate on East 66th Street. As divorces went this one appeared to be hassle-free.

Eliminating Max from her life would allow Gail to concentrate on her job with a children's books publisher where she'd been a secretary for almost five years. She enjoyed the work, the money was good and she was about to be promoted to executive assistant. That's when she'd be getting her own projects, none of which would include secretarial duties. The future was looking so bright Gail was going to have to wear shades.

Another bonus. Life without Max would mean peace and

tranquility at home because he and Tawny didn't get along. Max was easily agitated, supercritical, and before therapy, believed in keeping his feelings to himself. Tawny was impulsive, restless and quick to speak her mind.

Decker hadn't met Tawny but he liked Gail's description of the kid's independence. If he hadn't been so unhinged after Nam, Tawny might have been his daughter. A photograph sent to him by Gail revealed a blonde girl-woman of extraordinary beauty, who also seemed to have a touching combination of defiance and uncertainty. Decker saw her becoming the kind of woman who did nothing she didn't want to do.

According to Gail her daughter had taken news of the upcoming divorce badly, running sobbing to her room and slamming the door. Max had barged in after her, provoking the latest in a series of nasty quarrels between the two. It ended with him slapping her and Gail slapping Max. The next morning Tawny went off to school and hadn't been seen since.

In the Mexican restaurant Decker said to Gail, "Have you received any ransom notes?"

"No. I wish I had. At least then I'd have something to hold on to, something indicating she was alive."

"I've been in touch with police runaway units, hospitals, morgues. No one fitting Tawny's description has turned up."

"What about the FBI? You mentioned something about contacting them."

"I did," Decker said. "But unless a missing person case is interstate they won't touch it. Right now, we don't know where Tawny is. Let's hope she's still in New York. Gives us a better chance of finding her. An FBI guy promised me they'll post a missing person's notice on her in their Washington headquarters, but that's all he can do."

"I don't want excuses, I want my daughter back."

"Gail, listen. The FBI guy says we have a problem. There's no proof Tawny's been kidnapped. No ransom note, no telephone calls, no witnesses who saw her being abducted. He says all we can do is work with local cops and hope for the best."

31

Decker massaged the back of his neck. "Look, I work vice – drugs dirty money, and some things I'd rather not go into. I don't know that much about finding missing children and my informants don't either. But I'm willing to give it a shot. I'll make what contacts I can, fall back on some old ones, and just get out on the street and try to make it happen. I'm saying we need all the help we can get and that includes the cops in your precinct."

Gail's chin dropped to her chest. "Max is out doing things on his own. He's been to her school, telephoned her friends, their parents. So far, nothing. He says he feels guilty for having hit her. I'm trying hard not to blame him for what happened, but it's not easy. It is not easy."

Decker put an arm around her shoulders. "Ninety per cent of missing kids return within twenty-four hours. I know it's been a couple of days but Tawny could be on her way home right now."

He didn't tell her that most runaways who return will have been sexually molested. Or that thousands didn't return because they were murdered in a growing wave of ritual occult homicides or by serial killers who preyed on kids.

Gail placed her clenched fists on the bar. "I want my daughter back. I just want her back."

She looked at Decker with red-rimmed eyes. "Max is Jewish and I'm Catholic, but we celebrate Christmas because Tawny likes it and we get a kick out of seeing her happy. I was planning to shop for her presents this week. She wants leather pants and a pair of shoes from Sacha. She always did have expensive tastes."

"Go shopping," Decker said. "Keep a normal routine if you can."

"I told the police about Tawny like you said."

"I know. I checked in to let them know I was involved as a friend of the family. They said, no problem. Just keep them informed. They'll check her school to see if she's staying with friends and they'll ask around the neighbourhood to see if she's been seen since her disappearance."

Which as Decker knew was just about all Gail would get

from her precinct. For the most part police were approachable and friendly. But the city's high rate of street crimes had resulted in a police force that was overworked, burnt out and, after years of seeing humanity at its black-hearted worst, very cynical. Fighting crime in this town was like trying to run a marathon with one foot.

Decker knew why cops didn't view Tawny's disappearance as urgent. Urgent was finding eight dead Dominicans in a Washington Heights apartment, the youngest six years old, the oldest eighty-three, all dead because one had burned the wrong people in a drug deal. Urgent was a twenty-two-year-old cop shot in the head while guarding the home of a Queens drug witness because drug lords wanted to send a message to the community about the dangers of cooperating with police.

Urgent was not a spoiled brat who didn't come home from private school yesterday, but who might very well come home when she was hungry enough.

Decker had suggested that Tawny's fingerprints be sent by computer around the country and matched with those of unidentified dead girls her age. The answer he'd got was, we're really busy right now, Sergeant, but if anything develops we'll let you know. Fuck off, in other words.

Gail said, "It was Max's idea to run two classifieds on the front page of *The Times*, which we're doing starting tomorrow. One says 'Tawny we love you and want you back.' The other offers a twenty-five thousand dollar reward for her return, no questions asked."

Decker took a sip of black coffee then pressed the cup between his palms to warm his hands. "The money will draw crazies, nutcases claiming they have information when they don't. But that can't be helped. Drink your coffee."

"I'd like another Margarita. Remember when I used to work here as a waitress, back when I thought I was a better singer than Judy Collins? A Margarita cost ninety cents. Now it's almost six dollars."

Placing a hand on Decker's arm, a tearful Gail turned to stare through the bar window at a young Hispanic couple outside on the sidewalk eyeing the restaurant menu. Decker followed her gaze. The man, small and tough-looking, wore a green wool cap, matching down jacket and stood gripping a newly purchased Christmas tree a foot taller than he. The woman, lean with a huge mouth, pulled a fake fur collar tighter around her throat and pointed to the menu. She said something to the small man who ignored her.

"First week in December," Gail said, "and already they're selling trees on every other street corner. I started seeing Christmas ads in August."

She looked at Decker. "I've never been the victim of a violent crime in my life. Had my purse snatched once and my behind grabbed on the street a few times, but that's it. I don't know what it's like to have someone you love murdered. But it can't be any worse than having that person disappear and not knowing what happened to them. Jesus, I'm sitting here and I don't know if my daughter's gone for ever or what."

Neither did Decker. Tawny could already be dead, an accident or murder victim. She could even be a suicide. Or she could be at home raiding the fridge while thinking of an alibi for her vanishing act. She could be at a girlfriend's house watching MTV. Or she could be chained in a cellar on Staten Island where some geek was doing things to her that would shake the toughest cop.

The bottom line: the longer Tawny remained missing the less chance she would ever be found at all.

Recently the press had gone crazy with a story about a twelve-year-old Queens boy who'd been missing three weeks. His corpse, minus the head and hands, had been found in Long Island Sound by clam fishermen. Since trapped gases caused a corpse to float the killer or killers had slit the boy's stomach.

So far there'd been no arrests. All the cops knew was that a middle-class white kid had gone alone to a tough black neighbourhood in Queens to buy crack. Crazy, but when you're a druggie you've lost the power to think. Decker asked Gail if Tawny did drugs; if so, she wouldn't be the first kid her age to run into trouble while making a buy. Gail said, you're not talking about my daughter. Tawny would never touch drugs and Gail was willing to bet her life on that.

Decker caught the bartender's attention and pointed to Gail's empty glass. Nodding, the bartender picked up a clean glass, wet its rim with a section of lemon then placed the glass upside down on a plate of salt. But not before changing the TV channels. Apparently *Love Connection* wasn't doing it for him.

Decker sipped black coffee, thinking it might be wise to grab something to eat while he had the chance. Maybe a beef-filled taco or a bowl of chili and some nachos. These days he ate on the run or not at all.

His precinct commander, the monosyllabic Deputy Inspector Allan Huda, didn't mind him looking for Tawny DaSilva providing it was on Decker's own time. Words to live by since Huda, Ayatollah Huda-Fuck to the troops, had breath that stank like cat shit and a disposition twice as nasty when crossed.

So Decker put in a full day then hit the bricks to show Tawny's photograph to Transit cops working Port Authority Bus Terminal; to shivering kids gathered in Central Park's Strawberry Fields to remember John Lennon; to scared runaways living in city garbage trucks among the trash on the West Side Docks. On "The Deuce", 42nd Street and Times Square, where runaways gravitated by the hundreds, he showed her photograph to black teenage pimps, three-card monte dealers and managers of adult video stores. Downtown it was bouncers in skinhead clubs, organisers of cockfights, a pair of Hell's Angels, and owners of homosexual bookstores.

He came up empty.

No sightings, no rumours, no rumbles from any quarter. Apparently no one had seen or heard of Tawny Joanne DaSilva. On one level Decker could deal with it. After all nobody wins 'em all. On the other hand he was competitive; there was a side of him that never liked losing and rarely accepted defeat.

Karate had taught him to be unwavering, to persist and remain constant in his purpose. He was slick enough, though, to appear casual in his tenacity; he rarely made anyone feel arms were being twisted even when they were. His problem was an inability to let go after situations were no longer feasible.

He was operating out of righteousness, so why in hell couldn't he find the kid?

In the restaurant Decker stood behind Gail, helping her on with a lambskin jacket as she reached for a pair of Isotoner gloves lying near her purse. Both stared at the television screen where the top story on the five p.m. newscast was the crash of a Pan Am jumbo jet in West Germany. Two hundred and thirty-three passengers and crew had died when the plane exploded in midair shortly after takeoff.

Gail said, "I know it's selfish, but I can't think of anything right now but Tawny. God forgive me, but I can't. *God*. How can anyone believe in God with all this insanity going on? Hundreds of people dying in a plane crash. My only child missing. Manny, please tell me she's alive."

"She's alive," Decker said, wondering if he'd done it again: lied to her as he lied to others in the course of being a cop. His ex-wife had refused to buy the argument that his job called for deceit, contending instead that lying of any sort was a corruption of his manhood. She was no longer in his life, leaving Decker free to lie under any and all circumstances.

A minute later he was looking through the bar window at Gail who was now outside on the street attempting to hail a cab. She'd invited Decker to her place for dinner this Friday. Max would be there. Maybe Decker could give him hope as he'd just done for her. Would he please come?

The detective thought, it's her final act of love for the guy. He accepted the dinner invitation, hoping he wouldn't have to tell Gail and Max that kids were on the street because home was hell.

Meanwhile, he was still hungry. Calling the bartender over Decker ordered nachos, chimichangas, a small house salad with avocado dressing and more black coffee. He was tired and would like nothing better than to eat, then stretch out on the bar. Sleep would have to wait. He'd committed himself to at least an hour on the Deuce tonight looking for Tawny.

Was he pushing his career to the breaking point? Maybe he'd bitten off more than he could chew with this Tawny thing. He had other cases. Jesus, did he have other cases. One in particular was a bitch. If Decker wasn't careful it could ruin his career or get him wasted.

For the past ten days he'd been investigating the murders of two undercover cops who'd been killed while working separate drug investigations in Manhattan. Like Decker one officer, twenty-four-year-old Willie Valentin, had been recruited directly from the Academy. The other, twenty-five-year-old Frankie Dalto, had been deliberately kept out of the Academy.

They were outsiders, strangers to drug traffickers and virtually the entire New York police department. On the surface you couldn't find more ideal candidates for undercover work. Willie Valentin was assigned to infiltrate a Colombian cocaine ring, Frankie Dalto was to get close to a major black dealer working out of Harlem.

These weren't the usual buy-and-bust operations built around an undercover team: one cop making the drug buy, a second, "the ghost", watching nearby; and if possible the field team, five backup officers, within view of both undercover cops. Valentin and Dalto had been assigned to bring down the fat cats, to work from deep cover where you couldn't have backup. There was no more dangerous way of making a drug bust.

The department had given Willie Valentin and Frankie Dalto the best training possible, but in the end it hadn't been enough. Both dead cops had been found in Decker's precinct, the area from West 59th to West 86th, and from Central Park West to Riverside Drive. Valentin's corpse, with two bullets in the left temple, had turned up in Riverside Park at West 79th Street. Frankie Dalto, shot three times in the face at close range, had been discovered in a trash dumpster on West 83rd Street and Broadway. Both had been taken out with a Hi-Standard 22, the handgun of choice for pro shooters.

Decker had been especially angered by the death of Willie Valentin, a stocky Puerto Rican with warm brown eyes and a passion for chess. A few years ago Willie had been one of his karate students, a seventeen-year-old with a spinning back kick he threw at bullet speed. Decker had encouraged him to be a cop, not that Willie needed much persuasion.

Willie's father, also a cop, had been relaxing off duty in a Bronx bar when a hired killer shotgunned him to death after mistaking him for someone else. At Willie's request Decker had attended the funeral, sitting in St Anthony's Catholic Church in the Bronx with the elder Valentin's widow and eight children, each of them crushed by a great grief. Five years later Willie had been inducted into the police department wearing his old man's badge. Three months later he was dead.

Decker had initially concluded that Willie and Frankie, both young and inexperienced, had got careless. They'd made a mistake somewhere along the line and paid the price. It was also possible they'd been executed by thugs who'd decided these two young "dealers" were worth ripping off for their drugs and money.

Word on the street, however, said the two had been given up. Given up by cops and killed by cops. *Killed by cops.* Which is why nobody was willing to come forward and say more. Police officers had power which they carried around in a holster. Combine this power with a badge, and you had a man who could kill you without fear of punishment.

Rookie cops as well as older officers were now having second thoughts about going undercover. Had a police nightmare finally come true? Had drug traffickers penetrated the department's most secret operations?

Murder belonged to the Homicide squad. Vice, Decker's territory, wouldn't catch this one. But because of Willie, Decker wanted in and was prepared to be a hard-ass on the subject. He foresaw two roadblocks.

First there was Homicide's paranoid pixie, the sad-faced

Lieutenant Barry Pearl who had more hair in his nose than on his head, and who'd rather battle over turf than breathe. And of course there was the Ayatollah Huda-Fuck, who'd rather stick his nose in a dog's ass for twenty minutes than tolerate over-achievers, especially one who lived life as recklessly as Decker had been known to on occasion.

Surprise, surprise. You're on board, said Pearl and Huda-Fuck when Decker asked to join the Valentin-Dalto investigation. Decker encountered no resistance to his request nor did the term over-achiever come up.

Pearl and Huda-Fuck were not acting out of benevolence and good will. Decker's expertise was needed. His reputation was built on making drug cases and these two murders were decidedly drug related. He'd gone after Colombian and black traffickers in the past, and while Willie's assignment had kept them apart, Decker knew more about him than did anyone else at the precinct.

The top brass down at Police Plaza didn't like unsolved cop killings. Ayatollah Huda-Fuck and Barry Paranoid had careers to consider; at this point in their lives Decker was a gift from God. But if he didn't come through his future was as dark as a stack of black cats.

He began with a telephone call to Ron.

"So far we've managed to keep this thing out of the papers," Ron said. "Valentin and Dalto means we've lost three undercover guys. First time it's Fleming, a black kid who could have made the NBA if he didn't hurt his knee. We said, OK, it happens. I mean you win some, you lose some. We didn't like it, but we weren't looking over our shoulder understand? Second, third time, well, I'm telling you there was a shitstorm around here. Internal Affairs is convinced there's a leak and until we plug it the entire undercover programme's in danger."

Decker said, "Some people at the precinct aren't buying the leak theory. You know the drill. Protect the brotherhood at all costs. Bury your head in the sand. To hell with the smoking gun even if someone giftwraps it and drops it on your doorstep. Anyway, don't count on keeping this thing out of the press for ever. Sooner or later somebody's gonna talk to reporters."

"We've got to plug the leak before that happens," Ron said. "Nail the bastard who's giving up our people before the press taps into what's going on. Let's face it, public confidence in the police isn't at an all time high, especially when it comes to drugs."

"That's for sure."

"It has to be coming from inside. We catch the son of a bitch, then we put our own spin on this thing. Let everybody know we can clean house ourselves. Manny, if we can't put people in deep cover, we're fucked."

"I'm concentrating on Willie," Decker said. "Who he made buys from, who he partied with, who his enemies were."

"Start with his reports," Ron said.

"Good idea."

"You need anything on this, I mean anything, just sing out. One more thing."

"Yeah?"

"The person or persons you're looking for could be sitting at the next desk, hear what I'm saying?"

"I hear you."

"Don't trust a fucking soul."

Decker said, "I wouldn't trust my mother on this one, and she's been dead fifteen years."

4

The morning following his reunion with Gail DaSilva, Decker entered DEA Headquarters on West 57th Street and Twelfth Avenue, a neighbourhood made stagnant by abandoned passenger ship piers, outmoded automobile showrooms and timeworn taxi garages.

He'd come to check out DECS, Drug Enforcement Cooperating System, a clearing house set up by federal drug agents to avoid duplication of effort in New York narcotics cases. All city, state and federal cases were logged in these files. DECS acted like a traffic cop, keeping the different investigations from covering the same ground.

Decker was interested in any profile sheets Willie Valentin had filed with DECS. Profile sheets contained a trafficker's physical description, family and criminal histories, aliases, and list of known criminal associates. Some cops mailed the sheets to DEA, others personally brought them in. But all local or federal narcs, whether undercover or working openly, were required to turn them in.

Before getting down to business Decker made his social calls. Which meant schmoosing with agents, cops and secretaries to learn who'd been transferred, who was retiring to become security chief for a television evangelist who was planning to breed Akitas in his spare time, who'd nearly lost a finger in a drug raid by reaching into a dealer's mouth to retrieve cocaine needed for evidence.

Biggest laugh: recalling the sentencing of a Pescia family underboss taken down two years ago by DEA and Decker on drug charges. The judge had buried the mob guy. First count: thirty years. Second count: fifty years. Third count: thirty years, and so on for ten counts, the total coming to three hundred years, causing the underboss to say to the judge, "What do you think I am, a sequoia?"

It was forty minutes before Decker reached the DECS file room. He hugged and kissed Susan Scudder, the waiflike thirty-three-year-old woman who collected the profile sheets and recorded them. In the last five years she'd stockpiled quite a few from Decker.

There was a naive charm about Susan Scudder that he found appealing. A breathy little-girl voice made her foul mouth emerge more erotic than offensive. She was a hard worker, twice divorced and had a reputation for worrying too much. She fell in and out of love easily, usually with black agents or black cops.

Susan loved to travel. A bulletin board on the wall behind her desk was covered with photographs, postcards, and travel folders from Caribbean cruises, skiing trips to Aspen, package tours to Las Vegas. When things were lax at the office she wasn't above taking a daytrip to Miami or Bermuda. Decker found her to be a talker, a steady source of gossip and hearsay.

Decker was about to ask her for Willie Valentin's profile sheets when Alicia, Susan's pop-eyed young Hispanic assistant, said she had a phone call. The raised eyebrows on Alicia's thin face, indicated that the call was personal. With a quick *excusez-moi* Susan hurried to her desk, seized the receiver and pushed down a blinking button.

As she removed a clip-on earring and brought the receiver to her ear, Susan Scudder became another person. Her femininity and sensuality intensified. One small hand gently brushed both breasts and her face softened. Turning her back to Decker and Alicia, she whispered into the phone then laughed, a lusty sound that made Decker want to drop his pants and whip out the lubricating jelly.

Decker said to Alicia, "She still going with Russell?"

"You know it. Too bad you can't get no more shoes from him."

Decker nodded. Too bad indeed. Russell Fort was in his mid-thirties, a shaven-headed, black ex-cop with a crooked smile and a sly, drawling voice. He'd retired on partial disability eighteen months ago after getting chewed up by a Doberman pinscher when he'd tried to separate the dog and a woman who'd been behaving in a very improper manner with it in Sheridan Square Park.

Fort had then gone into business, opening a running shoes shop among the glistening boutiques and restaurants of yuppified Columbus Avenue. In addition to pricey footwear he offered headbands from LA, sweatshirts from Milan, and striking looking Navajo Indian jewellery. None of it was cheap. As Susan Scudder told Decker the only people who could afford the stuff Russell sold were what she called wine and cheese assholes.

Nevertheless she'd steered Decker to the store, first arranging for him to get a twenty per cent discount. Decker liked Fort's shoes but he found the ex-cop a bit hard to take. One minute Fort was hitting on female customers, the next he was cursing the teenagers he'd hired at minimum wages. He saw himself as brighter than most people, a guy who gave you answers before you finished asking the questions.

Recently Decker had gone to the store only to find it empty and a notice on the padlocked door saying Fort's Fast Track had been closed for non-payment of state and city taxes. This time Fort had got chewed up, not by a passionate pooch, but by life's all-time ballbuster, the taxman.

In the DECS room Susan Scudder continued her breathy and apparently indecent telephone conversation. Decker and Alicia were ignored. "I have a life to live," Decker said to Alicia. "How about running off copies of Willie Valentin's profile sheets?"

He and Alicia spoke briefly about Willie's death and how tragic it was, and when Alicia went into how cute Willie had been and how she'd wanted to go out with him Decker politely cut her off, saying he was in a hurry.

Minutes later Alicia handed him a Manila envelope with the copies he'd requested just as Susan Scudder abruptly squealed with delight and yelled, "Oh, wow. We're getting the *stretch* limousine this time? Far fucking out. I'm so excited I could wet my pants. I've got my things with me. What time should I be downstairs?"

Decker thought, what we have here is one very turned-on lady. Folding the envelope he stuck it in a pocket of his topcoat. "What's that all about?" he asked Alicia.

Alicia's bulging eyes protruded even more as she prepared to channel a secret into the world. Whispering from behind her hand she said, "Russell. He's taking Susan to Atlantic City for the weekend. They go there a lot. She's always telling me about it. I mean she wants people to envy her, you know? Russell loves the shows, the gambling, and I guess she does, too. She's always running off somewhere. That's Susan, right? They're leaving after she gets off work today."

"Nice."

"The hotel always sends a free limousine for Russell. He likes it when they make a fuss over him."

Decker's eyes went to Susan then back to Alicia with imperceptible speed. He tried to sound casual. "You wouldn't happen to know the name of their hotel?"

Alicia frowned. "Hmmm, I think it's Gold's Castle. Yeah, that's it. Wait here, I'll check with Susan to make sure."

Decker gently placed a hand on Alicia's wrist, keeping her in place. She shivered involuntarily; Decker's touch made her think of Julio, the married Puerto Rican agent who was screwing her two afternoons a week in a motel four blocks away. Like Julio, Decker had eyes that removed a woman's panties.

The detective grinned. "Don't bother. It's not important. I was curious, that's all. Tell Susan I couldn't wait. Thanks for the copies."

Decker had reached the door when Susan called his name. He turned in time to see her blow him a kiss, then laugh at something Fort said on the other end of the line. The detective smiled and touched the brim of his hat. A second later she spun around to face her bulletin board. She never saw Decker's eyes harden.

44

One of the good things about being a cop was the unlimited power you had over people. You could tear their lives into little pieces and mail each piece to a different state in the union. And you could do it legally.

Decker immediately set about trashing the lives of Susan Scudder and Russell Fort.

After leaving DEA he gave Ron a buzz from a public telephone booth on the corner of 57th Street and Ninth Avenue, telling him about Russell Fort's failure in the shoe trade, Fort's relationship with Susan Scudder and their upcoming trip to Atlantic City with a free limo provided by Gold's Castle.

Casinos gave free transportation only to highrollers, to people who could afford to gamble big. Russell Fort's store had just gone belly-up. So where was he getting the bucks to while away the hours in Atlantic City? Inquiring minds wanted to know.

Decker also wanted to know the source of Fort's rent money. Commercial rents on Manhattan's West Side were steep. Fort's place had been small, but it was prime real estate and as the monkey said when it pissed into the cash register, this could run into money. Figure the monthly rent at five figures minimum.

Decker saw Fort as having only one visible asset: a girlfriend with access to the kind of information drug traffickers would pay anything for. And speaking of girlfriends, was Fort faithful to Susan Scudder or was he, as Decker suspected, wetting his wick elsewhere?

Thirty-six hours later Decker was told that Gold's Castle was furnishing Russell Fort with more than a free limo. He was getting meals, drinks, passes to all shows and a suite overlooking the boardwalk. He also had a fifty thousand dollar line of credit and the use of a car while in Atlantic City. The highroller treatment was his for the asking. All this for a man who didn't appear all that solvent.

Fort was a compulsive gambler. Two months ago he'd spent fourteen hours at Gold's blackjack tables, walking away with a hundred and ninety thousand dollars. The next night he returned, only to lose every dollar plus an additional fifteen thousand. Gambling also made him a loser in the marital sweepstakes. A former wife complained in a divorce petition that Fort had forced her to have sex with two men as payment for a poker debt he owed them.

Fort had opened his shoe store with money from Li-Mac Associates Inc., a New Jersey realty company dealing in commercial property sales and mortgage financing. Li-Mac was a mob front; the Pescia family, operating out of New York and Jersey, used it to launder proceeds from drug trafficking and illegal gambling.

"Business tax records show Li-Mac took over the store," Ron said.

Decker said, "Which means Fort borrowed money from Paulie Pescia and couldn't pay it back. The bastard's lucky he had something Paulie wanted. Otherwise he gets his eyes shot out."

"Li-Mac put more cash into the place. I've got copies of bills for new paint jobs, new rugs, new cash register. Paulie probably thought the family had another laundry for its dirty money."

Unfortunately, Fort was a gambler and gamblers didn't know when to quit. He'd skimmed store funds to feed his betting habit, his final act of looting being to wager the store's tax money on the losing Mets in the National League Playoffs. His life shouldn't have been worth dried spit.

Decker said, "So why's he still alive? Why isn't he buried under a Queens trash dump or crammed inside the cornerstone of a teamster union hall?"

"Because he's being protected by a man neither you nor anybody else wants to fuck with. Pescia's people, the other four families, nobody wants to take on this particular individual. I'm talking about Ben Dumas."

"I don't need this shit," Decker said. "I really and truly do not need this shit. Jesus. Ben Dumas."

Ben Dumas was a big, fortyish man who'd been a smart, tough cop until he'd left the force under a cloud. He spoke in a whispered monotone and was unfailingly polite. On the force he'd made big bucks by shaking down drug dealers, operators of after-hours clubs and the owners of gay bars, people in no position to complain. Complaints would have been risky, since Dumas was a vicious psychotic who would kill without hesitation or pity.

His law enforcement career ended when he was charged with attempting to sell an eight-year-old Puerto Rican boy for fifty thousand dollars to a Belgian businessman who belonged to an international pederasty ring. Dumas didn't fall all the way on this one. He avoided prison when the boy and his mother disappeared, presumably having fled to South America, and the Belgian jumped or was pushed from the twenty-eighth floor of a London hotel. No witnesses, no case. Dumas, however, was finished as a cop.

Currently he ran Ben Dumas Associates, a company calling itself personnel advisers. Decker knew it as a private detective agency with a suspect reputation. Dumas hired only rogue cops, men who like himself had been kicked out of law enforcement for breaking the rules. Decker hadn't been surprised to hear that Dumas and his goons were suspected of being hit men for the underworld.

Dumas was a mystery to most people, Decker included. He'd racked up a handful of commendations for bravery, made his gold shield in a drug shoot-out that cost his partner's life, and supposedly had an above average IQ. Yet how could you explain his motiveless viciousness? Was it insanity, sadism or just plain boredom?

Decker rated Paulie Pescia as the toughest of New York's five Mafia bosses. Paulie had started out as an illegal immigrant and worked his way up to *capo di tutti capi*, boss of bosses. And he'd done it in a field where life expectancy ranged between short and brief.

He was a man of respect but let him touch Russell Fort and Dumas would show up at Paulie's house, ring the bell and shoot him when he opened the door. To trespass against Ben Dumas was unsafe. He killed for a reason or he killed for no reason at all. Which told Decker nothing about the man except that he was a hardcore psychopath, unbelievably dangerous because he was uncontrollable.

Ron said, "I don't have to tell you to be careful around this guy."

"Tell me anyway. I need to be reminded."

"I've got a man undercover with a hijacking crew working Kennedy Airport. They're Pescia's people. My man tells me Fort's making payments on what he owes Paulie. Looks like Dumas bought Fort some time. If Dumas is Fort's rabbi, you can bet there's a reason behind it."

Decker said, "Suppose that Fort is getting the identity of undercover cops from Susan Scudder. He then sells this to Ben Dumas who turns around and sells this very valuable information to people who could use time off for good behaviour."

"It's possible. You think Dumas smoked Valentin and Dalto?"

"Maybe. Ben's a whacko so who knows? Or he could have identified the undercover officers and let the Colombians do their own dirty work. One thing's for sure: show a dealer a way of identifying undercover drug cops and you can name your price. By the way is Fort a chaser?"

"Is a pig's ass pork? His lady friend should only know. Last month he checked into Gold's with a black girl. Maybe he wanted to change his luck."

Ron snickered but Decker's mind was elsewhere. This was no time to be lacking in due care or concern for one's own life.

Ben fucking Dumas. Jesus.

At five p.m., ninety minutes before his scheduled dinner at the DaSilvas', Decker put himself through his first *dojo* workout in four days. He was alone in the West 62nd Street karate club located around the corner from his one-bedroom apartment. Formerly a small hat factory, the club was now an airy hall with a shiny floor, high ceilings and windows looking down on the schmaltzy pastiche of Lincoln Centre. Four days away and Decker had missed it.

Only in the *dojo* could he find peace. Here he did not have to reason; he only had to do. For that reason he found karate not savage, but serene.

He wore one of two *gis* he kept in the club. His right knee, twice seriously injured in karate matches, was protected by an elastic and steel brace. A sprained left elbow and right wrist were encircled by smaller elastic braces.

Class began at six, meaning the club was his for an hour instead of the usual two hours he would have preferred. For the past four days Decker's heavy case load had forced him to abandon his daily morning practice. Late hours looking for Tawny meant sleeping late, which barely gave him time for a quick first light run in Central Park, followed by a half-hour's karate practice in the park's vacant bandshell. Then it was haul ass down to the precinct.

At six Decker planned to leave for that rarity in his life, a home-cooked meal. Gail had promised him the best scampi he'd ever tasted. Definitely an improvement over cold pizza and fudge ripple ice cream.

With today's *dojo* training limited to an hour he cut his warmup to fifteen minutes. In that time he stretched his spine, hamstrings, trunk and arms. He rotated his neck, ankles, then pulled and twisted his fingers, wrists. Then he high-kicked twenty times with both legs front and back. Finished, he sat on the floor and massaged his feet to increase his energy.

After rising, he closed his eyes and took five deep breaths. Ready to rock and roll.

Battles were won during training, so Decker went all out in practice. Even against an imaginary opponent he held nothing back. Punches, blocks, kicks were delivered with speed and power.

Today he chose to work on in-fighting, nullifying his opponent's attack by stepping into it. Stepping in also reduced the number of techniques an opponent could use. In-fighting demanded short punches, knee strikes and low kicks. Above all it demanded speed.

Decker attacked the head: bridge of the nose, eyes, chin, throat, temples, back of the head and neck. He used hook punches, uppercuts, elbow, forearms and knee strikes. Then he went for his opponent's ribs, heart, abdomen, groin, again

49

using elbow and knee. Finally he attacked the inner and outer thigh, knee, foot and ankle.

He attacked as he defended, defended as he attacked. He looked for flaws in his opponent, pulling or pushing him off balance to make his opponent's position poorer. Each time he attacked from the side, never facing his opponent head-on.

He perspired heavily, despite an unheated *dojo* and an eighteen degree temperature outside. The hour ended all too quickly.

He was showering when a student, a middle-aged bearded Hassidic, came in to say there was a telephone call for him. Which is how Decker learned there'd be no home-cooked meal with Gail and Max DaSilva tonight. Instead he was to go to a meeting in the US Treasury Office on Church Street in lower Manhattan. The feds had entered his life again. This was not good karma.

In a direct order from police headquarters, those very prominent folks down at #1 Police Plaza, Detective Sergeant Manfred Decker had been commanded to assist Treasury Agent Yale Singular until further notice. This association was to commence at once. Do not pass Go. Do not collect two hundred dollars.

Said additional duty was not to interfere with Decker's regular case load.

When he'd called Gail to cancel he'd found himself speaking to a very worried woman. Max claimed he was being followed. Maybe it had something to do with Tawny's disappearance, maybe it didn't. Max had been relentless in searching for Tawny, bugging homeless people, thirteen-year-old drug dealers, homosexual prostitutes, anybody and everybody. Some hadn't appreciated having him question them for any reason. Max had frequently been told *get the fuck outta my face or it's your ass*.

Gail also had to wonder if Rashad Lateef Quai had anything to do with Max being followed. Mr Quai, a black Muslim, was a postal worker who claimed to be a jazz-poet and who'd submitted a tape featuring himself reading his own poetry while backed by himself on flugelhorn, sitar and bass. In returning the tape Max had called it the worst piece of shit he'd ever heard. Mr Quai hadn't taken kindly to rejection. He'd threatened Max with mail stoppage, personal and business, as well as with a serious *whupping*.

Gail was on the verge of tears and Max was jittery. When could they see Decker? Tonight, he said. He'd show up after his meeting with the Treasury people. Tell Max to write down everything he could remember about whoever was following him. Age, race, clothing, any peculiarities. Have it ready for Decker when he arrived.

He heard Gail tell Max, heard Max in the background say, "I'll get on it right now." Gail thanked Decker and reaffirmed her promise about delivering the best scampi. She'd been cooking for hours especially for Decker. It was the least she could do. Decker said he was looking forward to it and hung up. Time to meet Treasury Agent Yale Singular, whoever he was.

Decker had worked with the feds before, rarely willingly, and each time he'd got screwed. They were experts at taking the credit for cooperative investigations which turned out successful, plus they had more money and power than local cops, and never let you forget it. Because of that power Decker would now have to eat reheated scampi.

Yale Singular was in his early forties, a huge, heavily jowled man with a thick neck and wide nose. He appeared to weigh at least seventy pounds more than Decker who was one seventy five. Three-quarters of Singular's bulk looked to be muscle. By sheer girth alone he dominated the room.

He wore a three-piece suit of tanned wool lined with black silk, a black bow tie, dark brown cowboy boots, and a red silk pocket handkerchief. His eyes, under bushy brows, never blinked. He was said to have been the best linebacker in Texas A&M history, this in a state where football was a religious experience. Decker also found it interesting to note that Singular sported a Phi Beta Kappa key on his watch chain.

Singular did his talking perched on the edge of his desk, Styrofoam cup of coffee in hand, often punctuating his soft

Texas drawl with a chuckle. Decker thought it was one of the better acts he'd seen lately.

The Treasury agent was interested in Decker's investigation of Ben Dumas. Singular said, "I hear you're out to tie that boy's ass in a knot."

"We're working on it, yes." Decker had a bad feeling.

"I like the way you're going about it. Yes sir, seems like you got a bunch of country smart people kicking this thing around. Am I correct in sayin' that DEA don't know what you're up to as yet?"

Decker shook his head. "No they don't. Right now we're focusing on Ben Dumas and Russell Fort. Something tells me you know this."

Yale Singular grinned. "Don't go frothing at the mouth, pilgrim. We know what we know and let's leave it at that. Which brings me to why you and me are having this little encounter. Now I'm not here to stop your investigation. I'd simply like to establish certain guidelines for you in connection with something we at Treasury got going. Let's say that we don't want you to overwind your watch."

Decker said, "Two undercover cops have been killed. We think Dumas may have had something to do with it. Is Treasury trying to stop a Homicide investigation?"

Singular held up a huge hand. "Rest your features, son. Just hush up for a mo'. Nobody's stoppin' you from exposing Mr Dumas's wicked ways. No siree. You just proceed on course. We'd also like to see Big Ben get what's coming to him."

Singular said that Ben Dumas was suspected of supplying information to a certain counterfeiter wanted by the Treasury Department. This information was obtained in various ways, one of which involved tapping into police computers, something very hard to prove. The counterfeiter in question bragged of having a sixth sense about his customers and the police. But this so-called sixth sense was really information supplied by Ben Dumas.

Dumas was also suspected of coming up with the paper that made the counterfeiter's hundred dollar bills the best on the market. Yale Singular wanted Decker to continue digging into Dumas, sharing whatever information he dug up. Singular was big on eye contact. Decker got over the problem of holding his gaze by staring at the bridge of the Treasury agent's nose.

All the while Decker listened quietly, waiting for the other shoe to drop. It did.

Decker was to stay away from the counterfeiter who was expected in America very shortly.

Looking up at the ceiling, Singular rubbed the back of his meaty neck. "This oriental trader in funny money is an old acquaintance of yours. Two of you had a run-in over in Nam, where I believe he tried to punch your ticket. Name's Park Song. Aka Laughing Boy."

To control his anger Decker began massaging his left forearm while taking deep breaths. Then he looked at his fingernails and chewed a corner of his mouth. Finally he left his chair, walked to the window and looked down at the traffic of Chambers Street.

Run-in. In Vietnam Park Song had tried to murder Decker. When that failed the Korean then tried to have Decker convicted in a US military court on false charges of theft. Laughing Boy had come within a hair of having him sent to a federal prison for twenty years. The detective's hatred for the Korean remained one of the most violent of his life.

Yale Singular said, "We had an agent undercover but Song took him out. Probably with information supplied by Ben Dumas. Before that happened we did learn a few things. Ben Dumas is Song's eyes and ears in this country. He keeps the little gook posted on everything and I do mean everything. Customers, police, Dumas delivers information on 'em all."

Singular was now standing beside Decker, saying, "Hated to lose that agent. He was a good old boy. We got Song and Dumas down in our books for that one and believe me when I tell you, we do intend to collect. Before he died our man gave us the names of a few of Song's customers. That's how come we know the gook's planning a humongous sale of the queer in our beloved country. His customers look to be buyin' big. For sure they're gettin' their money together and heading in our direction. Gonna happen here in the east, New York, New Jersey, we don't know for sure. But we do know it's goin' down in this general area."

Decker looked at Singular. "And you think I'm going to mess things up by going after Laughing Boy. I'll kill him or scare him off, right?"

Singular looked down at his pocket handkerchief. "Let's just say we've heard you're the sort who exceeds his capabilities. This and the fact that you have a long memory could present problems. Laughing Boy is mine."

The big man's eyes became smaller. The smile had disappeared. "I understand you are one of those martial artistes. You 'sposed to be able to put a man away with a touch of your finger, shit like that. My way's more direct, not that I'm sayin' I disbelieve in your skill or anything, but when I played football what I did was, I rushed into the backfield, scooped up everybody in my two little arms, then tossed them all aside until only the quarterback was left. No finesse, you understand, but it got the job done. That's me. No finesse."

He put a thick hand on Decker's shoulder. "Seems you ain't havin' much luck in findin' that little girl. Maybe you ought to forget about her, at least for the time being. Just concentrate on Ben Dumas and those two dead undercover officers and see if you can clear that up. 'Course, you will keep me posted. Christmas is comin' and you probably ain't done your shopping yet. You ought to get on to that. Same old shit every year, ain't it? I mean you end up buyin' cheap soap for people you don't know, ain't that how it is?"

Decker said, "Aren't you forgetting something?"

"Such as?"

"When do I get sworn in?"

"Say what?"

Decker told him. He insisted on being sworn in as a deputy US marshall. Experience had taught him it was the only way to survive working with the feds. As a deputy US marshall Decker could serve federal warrants, subpoenas, and pursue investigations across state lines. He could carry a gun interstate and onto a plane.

54

And should complications arise, the feds wouldn't be able to screw Decker quite so easily. Working with the federal government was like being a fly on a toilet seat. Sooner or later you'd end up getting pissed off. The feds didn't like giving these powers to local cops. Yale Singular didn't appear to be an exception.

Not that Decker cared whether Singular was happy or not because he was sure of one thing: Singular wasn't telling him everything.

"You ain't being asked to invade Grenada," Singular said. "Just stay in touch with me and mind your ps and qs when it comes to Laughing Boy."

"Either I get sworn in or you'll wait a long time for any reports."

"A mite testy, aren't we?" Singular's eyes were slits. He didn't like being pressured.

Decker pulled away from the big man's hand and walked towards the door.

"Nine thirty tomorrow morning," Singular said. "US Attorney's office. And Sergeant Decker?"

The detective turned to look at him.

Singular grinned. "I do not like being forced into a course of action. You just went down in my book as a strut fart, a man too aware of his own importance. In the future I want you to remember that it was you who set the tone of our relationship. Stay well."

On East 66th Street Decker stepped from a yellow cab that had come to a stop behind two blue and whites parked in front of Gail's building. In the lobby dominated by a large Christmas tree decorated entirely in blue lights he saw a uniformed policeman and policewoman talking to two Filipino women wearing nurses uniforms under winter coats. One of the nurses shook her head, saying I live on the same floor and it's so sad what happened, especially at this time of year.

Decker walked over to the uniformed doorman, a squat light-skinned black who smelled of gin, had a boxer's thick ear, and wore a torn cap with the tackiest-looking gold braid

Decker had ever seen. The detective asked for the DaSilvas' apartment number and froze because the black's eyes said it all. Decker had been a cop too long not to recognise that look.

Shield in hand he pushed his way between the nurses and identified himself to the two uniforms.

Decker already knew what he was going to hear.

The female officer, young and black, her lips greased against the cold, said, "Yeah, it's the DaSilvas. They're both dead. Gun was in his hand. Shot her then did himself. Fifth floor. I guess it's all right to let you go up."

5

For the past six months Ben Dumas had been a partner in the discothèque P.B. which was four floors of an old slaughterhouse on West 14th Street facing the West Side Highway and the abandoned piers bordering the Hudson River.

The desolate, rundown area housed New York's meat-packing industry while also offering the dangerous sex of various leather and S&M bars. Here a lease could still be had at bargain rates, a rarity in Manhattan where landlords viewed rent gouging as a sacred trust granted by God.

Dumas had long held a bargain to be nothing more than an exchange in which each participant walked away thinking he'd cheated the other. The lease for his club, however, proved an exception to this rule. Commercial space in Manhattan ran as high as four hundred dollars a square foot. P.B. was paying fifteen dollars a square foot on a ten-year lease. If anybody had got burned on the deal it hadn't been Ben Dumas.

P.B.'s main dance floor was a former gay bathhouse now decorated as a high school gymnasium complete with basketball hoops, vintage jukeboxes and bartenders dressed like school-crossing guards. The second floor hosted live bands while the third floor offered upcoming experimental artists in live performances which included video, poetry, dance, film and conceptual art. The fourth floor, once site of the meat-freezing chamber, was the VIP lounge.

Whether Dumas would open the lounge tonight depended on how soon he concluded his business with Russell Fort.

Dumas was waiting for him now in the VIP area which was closed to the public in order to afford the two men privacy. Fort was twenty minutes late, not unusual for a man who was rarely on time.

Dumas was forty-three, a long-jawed, hulking man with receding sandy hair and a wolfish smile which hinted at his compulsion to manipulate and connive. Forceful and intense, he preferred his own standards and habits of behaviour to any authoritative direction. If provoked or offended, he went all out for revenge no matter what it cost him. Having little interest in the welfare of others, he felt no inclination to curb a deep-rooted and cold-blooded violence.

His disco, private detective agency and a gay bar he owned on Bank Street were all profitable. His game, however, wasn't money but total mind control over those associated with him. Club life allowed him to set a stage where he could watch the actors – employees and customers – perform under his direction.

In the spacious, mahogany-panelled VIP room Dumas sat peacefully in a white wicker armchair and listened to baroque lute music coming from a tape deck sitting on a pool table several feet away. Two empty wicker chairs were within reach. Resting on the nearest one was a hinged flat wooden box which when opened became a backgammon board.

Dumas sipped black coffee, smoked Lucky Strikes and watched his dog eat a large platter of raw hamburger mixed with chopped egg. The dog, named Oscar after Oscar Wilde, was a three-legged Great Dane and black Labrador mix, a huge genial animal which Dumas had acquired the day after resigning from the police force. Oscar, Dumas had decided, was a liberal because he wanted to please everybody.

Dumas and Fort were going to talk money. Despite his successful businesses, Dumas was in desperate need of cash. Almost everything he earned went towards the medical expenses of his lover, a slender forty-two-year-old Japanese psychiatrist named Ken Yokoi.

A year ago Yokoi had contracted AIDS, not through his homosexuality, but because of acupuncture treatments he'd received to ease severe bursitis. His insurance covered some costs, such as AZT and doctor visits. But it was Dumas who was paying sixteen hundred dollars a day to have private nurses serve Yokoi in eight-hour shifts.

The ex-cop's love for the dying Japanese knew no bounds. His loyalty to him was fanatical which is why he'd murdered the acupuncturist whose needles had fatally infected Yokoi. Dumas had shoved an ice pick up the acupuncturist's nose and into his brain, killing him instantly. Finding no evidence of violence, a coroner had concluded that the deceased had perished from natural causes, namely a cerebral haemorrhage.

Presently Dumas's bank account contained less than two thousand dollars while a dwindling stock portfolio was worth only four thousand dollars. He drove an eight-year-old Honda Civic, owned two suits and lived frugally in the Village, in a one-bedroom Hudson Street apartment facing the hundred and seventy-year-old Church of St Luke-in-the-fields. He was comfortable with a Spartan existence and could easily have lived this way for the rest of his life.

His love for Ken, however, demanded that Dumas make all the money possible. He had to be rich in order that Ken lived a little longer. Dumas had always been a resourceful man, but when it came to Ken's illness there were things he couldn't do, things that could only be done through money.

P.B. was successful because Dumas had taken Ken Yokoi's advice and instituted a door policy favouring Asians. Japanese businessmen, tourists and local residents were the biggest spenders on New York's club scene, Ken said. These days it was the east which begat money.

The idea of catering to Asians at his club appealed to Dumas who'd always found them charming and attractive. He took his lover's suggestion one step further by hiring Asians as half of P.B.'s work force. At times he found the delicacy and fragility of their beauty overpowering. Having them at P.B. was like owning a cage of beautiful birds.

In the VIP room Oscar looked up from his meal and eyed the tape deck, seemingly commending guitarist Jakob Lindberg for his work on Roncalli's Sonata in C Major. Dumas blew a smoke ring towards the ceiling, recalling how Ken had introduced him to baroque music saying it had been written in more cultured times and wasn't smeared with the shit of modern life.

Oscar returned to his dinner only to stop eating seconds later and swing his oversized black head towards the entrance to the VIP room. As the dog stared at the door someone on the other side of it tried the knob. Finding the door locked a male voice said, "What it is, what it is. Ben, you there?"

Dumas left his chair, walked to the door and looked through a peephole. Then he unlocked a dead bolt, opened the door and with a slight movement of his head motioned Russell Fort inside. The two men shook hands as a smiling Dumas said, glad you could come. He pointed to the wicker chairs.

Why, Dumas wondered, did black men feel compelled to dress like pimps. Tonight the chunky, round-faced Fort wore a purple velvet jumpsuit dotted with metal studs, a gold earring and grey lizard skin boots. A beige vicuna coat hung from his shoulders and he was decked out in enough gold to cover the altar of a Mexican church. His eyes were hidden behind amber lens Ray-Bans and his shaven head gleamed like the moon. There was a slight Caribbean lilt in his voice, a reminder that the first twelve years of his life had been spent in a Kingston slum.

Dumas noticed the drink in Fort's hand. Apparently Mr F had stopped at the bar downstairs, probably charging his liquor to Dumas who also wondered how many women Mr F had hit on downstairs before keeping tonight's appointment.

No, Dumas was not blind to the shortcomings of this African-American. Mr F was addicted to pleasure, making him unreliable in Dumas's book. He put good times, gambling and women in particular, before everything else. His life was immediate gratification. He wouldn't wait an hour to be happy, something Dumas found true of black people in general.

In front of a wicker chair Fort drew the vicuna around him, sat down and put his feet up on a nearby butcher's block that served as a coffee table. Dumas returned to his original seat.

His right hand came to rest on the backgammon board in the chair beside him.

Fort lifted his drink to Dumas in a mock toast. "Little toddy for the body, my man. Too much to drink isn't nearly enough, I say."

"Surprised you didn't fall in love downstairs on the dance floor," Dumas said. His whispered monotone was not unpleasant.

Fort sipped his Scotch then chuckled. "Ain't looking for love, amigo. But, dig, I am always in the market for a little L.W.P. Lust With Potential, that is. Danced with a cute little Korean gal. Fine young thing around eighteen. I was planning on showing her my two inch dick."

"Two inches?"

Fort giggled. "Two inches from the floor, my man."

"I see."

"Anyway, we're dancing when some Korean dude hustles over and drags her away. I was ready to throw down on the man but I see he's got his crew with him, so I chill out."

"You do complicate your life."

Fort grinned. "Can't fuck all the ladies in the world, but at least you can try. Meanwhile, I'd like that dude who interrupted my dance to get it up the ass on national TV. So, let's talk about the money I'm going to make. I notice you got your raggedy-assed dog with you."

"Oscar's birthday is day after tomorrow. He'll be four."

Fort grinned. "Four years old with three legs. Be better the other way 'round. Like, three years old with four legs, know what I'm saying?"

"I think I've got the gist of it, yes."

Dumas lit another Lucky and blew smoke at the ceiling. His eyes were slits; a vein throbbed in his left temple and he gnawed at his lower lip with large, yellowing teeth. Jesus, if Fort only had a brain. You had to wonder if his mother still bought his clothes. Dumas exhaled, put a smile on his face, and eyed the black man.

He stared at Fort for several seconds. Dumas's smile, still in place, was icy. His unblinking eyes held a dangerous glint. On the backgammon board the fingers of his hand clenched into a fist, squeezed hard, then unclenched before slowly forming a fist again.

Had Fort observed Dumas more closely he might have been more alert to danger. But behind his Ray-Bans the black's eyes were closed, so he missed any warning signal. He was wired, Jack, riding a fast train through a Peruvian snowstorm and feeling warm with joy and pleasure. Having soothed his soul with some dynamite flake, Fort was not afraid to deliver his black ass into the presence of Mr Ben Dumas. Man had to be anxious around a dude who not only killed people but who'd once strangled a drug dealer's pit bull to death with his bare hands.

Fort had a gambling Jones to feed else he wouldn't have been in the same city with this cold-blooded faggot, let alone the same room. It was a natural fact that Dumas had an inadequate understanding of what it meant to be human. Dumas had a big head, people said, in order to get all the mean in. His street name was "Hitchcock" because everybody recognised that he was a stone psycho.

Scariest thing was, you couldn't kill the dude because he was dead already.

Opening his eyes Fort looked over his shoulder at the tape deck on the pool table. "Don't know what you call that shit, but it ain't music. You're in a disco, so you got to get on the good foot. Real music is all way to the right of the dial, where they keep the black folks. Gonna put some dip in your hips, some glide in your stride."

Snapping his fingers and humming Michael Jackson's "Smooth Criminal", Fort rose unsteadily from his chair and stepped to the pool table. Unnoticed, his vicuna coat slipped from his shoulders and fell to the floor.

Dumas also got to his feet. After stubbing out his cigarette in an ashtray on the butcher's block he yawned and stretched his arms overhead. Then he picked up the backgammon board and followed Fort to the pool table. When Fort reached for the radio tuner Dumas lifted the backgammon board overhead and brutally clubbed Fort on the right forearm, breaking it.

Clutching his damaged arm, a screaming Fort dropped to his knees. Dumas swung the backgammon board again, striking Fort on the head, back and shoulders, tearing his jumpsuit with the sharp end of the board. Fort now sat on the floor, clinging to the pool table by one hand and calling out to Jesus. His pleas for Dumas to stop the beating were ignored.

Hitchcock was really putting the hurt on him. Fort had never been worked over like this in his life. The pain was everywhere – in his shattered arm, shoulders, even his brain. He felt as if his eyes had been ripped out. He was on fire.

No more. Jesus God, no more. He struggled to breathe as his brain asked a pertinent, and at this point, somewhat overdue question: *What the fuck had made him think Dumas wouldn't find out?*

By way of underscoring this timely query, a wide-eyed Dumas threw the backgammon board aside and kicked Fort in the stomach and ribs. After several seconds he stopped his attack, spat on the semi-conscious black, then kicked him once in the spine before backing off. Fort released his precarious grasp on the pool table and slumped to the floor.

Inhaling deeply, Dumas sat in his chair and stared at Fort who was curled into a foetal position and coughing up ugly fluids. Oscar, his tail wagging furiously, looked at Fort as if to say, could I play too?

"That was to encourage your comprehension," Dumas said. "If I didn't need you, I'd've dropped the hammer on your ass here and now. Did you actually think you could get away with it? Yes, I suppose you did. You have an unlimited capacity for being stupid. Sit up. I don't like talking to a man's back."

Teeth gritted, Fort slowly rolled over to face him. It was seconds before he could speak. "Needed the money, man. Needed it bad."

His Ray-Bans hung precariously from one ear; his chin was wet and there were dark stains on his jumpsuit. Under the pool table Oscar, drooling copiously, sniffed at a gold chain torn from Fort's neck during the attack.

"He needed the money," Dumas said. "Now that comes as

a surprise. Boys and girls, what we have here is a man who's in so deep he's travelling by submarine. I don't know why you gamble and I don't care. But I do care if your gambling costs me money. You tried a little hustle to finance that nasty habit of yours and as you may have guessed by now I'm not in favour of it."

Dumas leaned forward, forearms on his knees. "Because of you I had to whack Tawny DaSilva's parents."

He saw Fort's glazed eyes widen. Dumas also saw something else: Fort had correctly determined that hearing about Ben Dumas's compelling impulse to act in a certain way was not the same as experiencing it first-hand. Dumas found this exceedingly satisfying.

"*You* killed them?" Fort whispered. Eyes closed, he braced himself against a wave of pain. He took several deep breaths before speaking again. "Press said murder-suicide. Husband did her then himself. Jesus, my arm."

"Suck on this," Dumas said. "Gail DaSilva told Manny Decker that her husband was being followed through the streets by some jungle bunny. Now an hour or so before the DaSilvas got iced this same jungle bunny phoned them and said he could get their daughter back. For a fee, of course. Three guesses as to the identity of this mysterious spear chucker. The first two don't count."

Fort remained silent.

Dumas said, "All the DaSilvas had to do is point you out and Decker would have taken it from there. My guess is he'd have pounded your balls into veal patties if you didn't do the right thing. How long would it have been before you told him I've got Tawny DaSilva? One second? A second and a half?"

"How'd you find out 'bout me and the DaSilvas, 'bout them mentioning me to Decker?"

"Dumb question."

"You bug their phones?"

Dumas rubbed the back of his neck with a beefy hand. "I'm about to put you in the big picture. I went upside your head just now because this scam of yours to bamboozle the

DaSilvas could have ruined a nice payday for me and Mr Fox. I've already told you that Mr Fox and I intend to sell Tawny DaSilva to Laughing Boy. What you didn't know is that we're getting a hundred and twenty-five thousand apiece. Two hundred and fifty K total. I'm sure you know why I need the cash."

Fort said, "I know."

Dumas lit a cigarette. "I had a choice. Either waste you for attempting to screw me out of money Ken needs very badly, or waste the DaSilvas, thereby keeping Decker away from you, me and the girl."

Dumas tapped cigarette ash into an ashtray on the butcher's block. "Hear me. This thing's personal with Decker. He ain't about to let it go. You're still alive in this kinder, gentler America because Tawny DaSilva is worth 125 K and because that DEA tramp you're fucking can deliver certain information."

Fort painfully raised himself to a sitting position. "You don't have the facts of what was going on. I swear on my mother I wasn't going to tell the DaSilvas nothing. I was running a game on them, nothing more."

"I'm conversant with what you were trying to do. You were going to take the DaSilvas' money and give them nothing. That's the sort of thing we've come to expect from lawyers and television evangelists."

"Dig, Susan told me about the girl, okay? Decker comes to see her and he tells everybody at DEA he's looking for Tawny. I mean it ain't no secret. Also there was this ad in the newspaper offering a reward."

"Nail these words to your skull, Russell. I don't need another hand on the steering wheel. Tawny DaSilva is my business, me and Mr Fox. I can just see the eyes pinwheeling in your head when you heard there was a reward for the kid's return. A couple of phone calls to the DaSilvas and suddenly you're among the affluent. And I'd never find out, right? Just grab the money and run. Russell, I think medical science will have to open up your ass to find your head. I really do."

Removing the Ray-Bans from his ear Fort dropped them

on the parquet floor. "I owe, can't you understand? Not Paulie Pescia but another crew. Had some bad luck on the NFL playoff games."

"There are times," Dumas said, "when I doubt if you can count past ten without taking off your shoes. I help you with Paulie Pescia and a minute later you're in hock to some other maggot. Russell Fort. A man who hits bottom then finds a hole in the bottom. Let's hear about your new creditors."

Fort wiped tears from his eyes with the back of his hand. "Guy's name is Spindler."

"Ruby Spindler. Loansharking, bookmaking and the fencing of stolen goods. He's with the LoCasio crew in Brooklyn."

Fort said, "Spindler's with LoCasio?"

"Russell, please. You were a cop once, remember? We both know the greaseballs control gambling in New York. Spindler couldn't operate unless he had an arrangement with some dago. Don't look so uptight; it's just the whole world watching your life go down the tubes. Now here's what I'm going to do. You're into Spindler for how much?"

"A dime."

"Ten thousand dollars? Russell, if I didn't know you I'd swear you were unintelligent. All right listen up. I'm giving you ten K which you're going to give to Spindler. You pay him off and that's all you do. Lose it gambling and I'll make you sorry you were ever born. I won't kill you, Russell, but you'll wish to God I had. Am I getting through to you?"

Fort nodded.

"Terrific. Since there's no free lunch, you're going to pay me back. I have another job for you. Do this and we'll call it even. You have a problem with that?"

Fort sighed. "No problem, no problem."

"Good. First, you're going down to Washington and pick up some more paper for Laughing Boy. We sent him a pile, but he wants more waiting for him when he arrives. I understand he's turning out a ton of hundreds so he's hungry for all the paper we can lock up. You leave tomorrow evening."

Dumas said, "Follow the same routine you always do on a paper run. You stay overnight in Atlantic City, gamble a little and the next morning you go on to Washington where you visit your old diabetic Aunt Lorraine on H Street. Spend at least three hours with her. Everything must look righteous, remember? Before you leave town you pick up Laughing Boy's paper. It's waiting for you at the usual place."

"My arm's killing me," Fort said. "Got to get to a doctor."

"I'm not finished. Take Slutty with you. As long as she feels loved she'll stand by her man. I'll front you two thousand for gambling and expenses. Don't piss it all away at the blackjack table."

Rising from his chair, Dumas walked to the pool table and squatted down beside Oscar who lay licking his genitals. Dumas scratched Oscar's neck and spoke to Fort without looking at him. "One more thing: I want Slutty to give you copies of all reports Decker files with DEA. Any requests for files, information, whatever. I want to know everything and I mean everything."

Fort said, "I'm telling you right now, man, Susan ain't going to do it. The woman's scared. She knows Decker got copies of Willy Valentin's profile sheets to learn who maybe gave him up. She didn't know those two cops were going to get smoked. Right now she don't want to give me nothing."

"Maybe she didn't know, Russell, but you did."

Fort closed his eyes.

"Can't put the toothpaste back in the tube," Dumas said. "Valentin and Dalto are history. We survive in this world by lying to ourselves and pushing on. Lie to her, Russell, and tell her you didn't know they were going to die either."

"Susan won't give me shit, I'm telling you."

"Russell, Russell." Dumas's voice was soothing, undisturbed by anxiety or agitation. He rose, smiled down at Oscar and patted the dog on the head. Then placing both hands on the pool table he stared at a dartboard on the wall across the room. A vein throbbed on his left temple.

Suddenly he grabbed a pool cue, broke it on the edge of the table and shoved Fort to the floor. One knee came down hard on the black man's chest while a hand pinned the screaming

Fort's head to the ground. Instantly the sharp end of the broken cue was less than an inch from Fort's left eye.

Dumas whispered, "You like music, so I'll tell you what. How'd you like to be a singing eight-ball like Ray Charles or Stevie Wonder? Or how about we play Sammy Davis, Junior and go for one eye. What do you say?"

A terrified Fort tried to wrench his head from under Dumas's hand and failed. "Don't, don't."

Dumas stood up and dropped the broken cue on the pool table. He was calm, as if nothing had happened. "Russell, can I count on you to convince Slutty to do the right thing?"

"I'll make her do it, I swear I will."

Dumas began rolling pool balls into corner pockets. "I sell information, Russell. I sell to drug dealers who want to know who their customers really are. I sell to CEOs who want to know who's stealing from the company. I sell to a husband who suspects the old lady's spending afternoons in a hot sheets motel spreading her legs for her dance instructor."

He turned to look at Fort. "I sell to a woman who wants to know if her fiancé really has money or is just some loser with mental trouble and a bad credit rating. But you see, Russell, before I can sell this information I must first collect it."

Folding his arms across his chest, Dumas sat on the edge of the pool table. "It's a fascinating field, Russell, this business of collecting information. As a cop I worked with police Intelligence units which really got me hooked. I also did a few things for the FBI and CIA. Lot of technology in this business, Russell. I use computers myself to find out a lot of things, but you know something? There's no substitute for what we call *humint*."

He smiled down at a snivelling, beaten Fort. "*Humint*, Russell. It means human intelligence. What you might call person to person. You find out something, then you tell me. It's as simple as that. No computers, no microchips, no satellites, no space stations. Just one human being to another. And that's where you and Slutty come in.

"Forewarned is forearmed, Russell. That's how I stay in business. I tell people like Laughing Boy everything they want to know about their customers and in turn they pay me well. That's why I need your help from time to time. Otherwise there'd be little point to our relationship."

Dumas stood up and stretched. "Got to mind the store, Russell. Time to go downstairs before the bartenders steal me blind. You really should have that arm looked after."

Fort leaned against a leg of the pool table. "I don't know if I can travel, man. I'm hurtin' bad."

A smiling Dumas said, "As soon as you have Laughing Boy's paper I want you to call me at the office. Use the prearranged code. I might want to set up a different meeting place. There's a chance Mrs DaSilva called Decker from outside her home and told him about the mysterious black man following her husband. Which means Decker could know more than we'd like him to know."

"You mean he could know about me and this counterfeiting thing?"

Dumas shrugged. "If he's sniffing around Slutty he might already be on to something. We shall see, we shall see."

Fort shook his head. "Hey, man, prison ain't part of our deal. You get popped for counterfeiting and you're talking federal time. You're talking Atlanta and Leavenworth. Real shitholes where people die. Where cons are always killing each other over gambling and – "

Fort caught himself in time. He'd almost said *faggots*.

Dumas smiled. "I know all about federal prisons, Russell. You just leave Decker to me. You keep Slutty happy. And next time when you tie her to the bed, shove something in her mouth besides your joystick. The woman howls more than Lassie."

"How'd you know about that?"

Dumas chuckled. "I love it when you whine. Don't ask any more questions, your mind can't stand the strain. I think you can use a drink. I'm buying."

6

London, December

The cablegram annoyed Mrs Rowena Dartigue because it forced her into a last minute change of plans.

Park Song's wire arrived at her Georgian brick house in Chelsea's elegant Cheyne Walk at six ten p.m., not long before she was to attend the opening night of Mozart's *The Magic Flute* at Covent Garden. Having wrapped up his business in Rome and Paris the Korean was now in London. He'd arrived twenty-four hours ahead of schedule.

Mrs Dartigue was to meet him at once. A telephone call, to be expected momentarily, would inform her of the time and place.

He'd signed the cable "Taps". If Mrs Dartigue heard a buzzing sound in her ears it was most likely Fred Astaire spinning in his grave.

She read the wire a second time before dropping it on a small glowing pine log in the fireplace of her oak-panelled bedroom. Then she told Maureen Costello, her thin-lipped seventeen-year-old Irish maid, that she didn't wish to be disturbed. Mrs Dartigue desperately wanted to attend the Mozart gala – the Prince and Princess of Wales were honoured guests – but disobeying Park Song was out of the question.

Wearing a delicately floral caftan, she stood in front of the fireplace and sipped jasmine tea as she weighed the possibility of ignoring the Korean's wire.

There were two points to consider.

Point one: in meeting him a day earlier she would collect her one hundred and twenty-five thousand dollars from him that much sooner.

Point two: defying Park Song was unsafe. To put it mildly he had a violent antipathy to being snubbed. Meeting him as requested was the smart thing. It had the ancillary dividend of also being the right thing.

She telephoned Lord Jasper Kinsman straightaway and broke the news to the overweight seventy-year-old political has-been who was to have escorted her to the Mozart gala. "Sorry, darling," she said, "can't make it. You'll have to go on without me."

His lordship made no protest, being as shallow and spineless as they come. He was, after all, the man who'd inherited ten million pounds at age twenty-one and frittered it away by age twenty-three. For Mrs Dartigue, Lord Kinsman's appeal lay in his aristocratic lineage and avid willingness to accommodate her every whim and caprice.

Rowena Caroline Dartigue was in her late fifties, a slender, long-faced Englishwoman who looked years younger as a result of twice yearly sheep cell injections in Switzerland, dyed blonde hair and alert, grey eyes that rarely rested on one object for more than a few seconds. Unusually intelligent, she could sense a person's most vulnerable spot in the blink of an eye. She was ruthless when she wanted anything and viewed most people with distrust. Behind a charming facade she remained on guard, showing little of her true self.

She owned Rosebud, a fashion clothing and accessories shop in fashionable Beauchamp Place which had become a successful showcase for young design talent from Britain and abroad. Many of the designers were fresh out of college, permitting Mrs Dartigue to pay them a much smaller commission than she would have given established designers. Still, her prices to customers remained outrageously high.

"It's snob appeal, darling," she told her husband, Michael, a strapping American twenty-three years younger than she and for whom she had an intense if misguided love. "True

71

snobs have this enormous appetite for overpaying then boasting about it. Such people should be overcharged, don't you think?"

Michael himself was overcharging Mrs Dartigue, a practice which served as the foundation and justification for their relationship. The couple's marriage of six months was a trade-off: he'd married her for her money and she'd married him for his sexual prowess. Her most recent gift to him had been a new Mercedes 560 SL equipped with telephone, stereo, fridge and Fax machine. In return he'd promised to spend at least weekends with her for the next two months.

At thirty-five Michael Dartigue was still athletic, a big agile man with sleepy eyes, large nose and blond hair worn in a small ponytail. He was charming, amusing and bursting with can-do, the sort of American whose energy instantly endeared him to Englishwomen tired of cold and unresponsive Englishmen. Winsome traits aside, he'd failed at everything since his glory days as a basketball hero at the University of Miami. In his own words, he'd left school and hit the ground crawling.

He'd failed as a restaurateur, real estate salesman, film producer, rock concert promoter and drug dealer. No surprise since even Rowena Dartigue was forced to admit that her husband was shallow, unethical and had as much insight into the human condition as a walnut. Ethical sensitivity was not Michael Dartigue's strong suit.

As he saw it, the onus for his misfortune was not on him. He did not, he protested, have his finger on the self-destruct button. Instead he blamed his failures on a refusal to compromise, bad financial advice, betrayal by trusted associates, and on politics. "Ain't my fault I'm getting fucked over," he told Rowena. "You get knocked down once and the world won't let you up again. Wasn't for bad luck I wouldn't have no luck at all."

In the area of his sexuality Michael's confidence knew no bounds, an assessment happily shared by Rowena Dartigue. She'd never been with a man who'd given her more enjoyable orgasms or done a better job of keeping up with her sexual demands. His erotic exuberance was dispensed as a reward for her financial generosity and she couldn't have been more satisfied. Michael made her feel young; he gave her back the days when life had wings, something for which she was willing to spend any amount of money.

As for Rosebud it was not Mrs Dartigue's primary source of income. The shop allowed her to show the taxman legitimate earnings and to travel abroad, presumably in search of new designers. It also permitted her the appearance of respectability while concealing her secret life and the true origin of her sizable income.

Most of Mrs Dartigue's money came from white slavery. Using the pseudonym "Mr Fox" she sold sexual slaves — teenagers and young adults — to wealthy buyers from all over the world. Once a year she held a human slavery auction where her most attractive slaves were auctioned on the block for big money. The next such auction was scheduled for New York in less than three days.

She'd taken over the Lesley Foundation, a small charity designed to assist runaway and abused youngsters. Like her clothing shop the charity was used to launder her proceeds from white slavery. Among others who used the charity to conceal large amounts of money was Park Song.

The Lesley Foundation also provided Mrs Dartigue with human slaves. If charity was appreciated by mankind it was appreciated even more by Rowena Dartigue. Charity was a mask which allowed her to be useful to others while turning a profit.

She'd kept this part of her existence secret from Michael, who was not in her life because of his powers of thought. Only saints kept secrets and Rowena's husband was no saint. As far as he knew she made her living from the shop. Her travels abroad were to find new design talent and to sell Rosebud's products to foreign buyers.

After the telephone call to Lord Kinsman she walked to a bedroom alcove where curved shelves displayed a collection of antique bracket clocks. A non-bracket clock stood alone on the top shelf beside a small blue vase of yellow tea roses. This distinctive timepiece – a silver and translucent Fabergé clock – was worth more than all her bracket clocks combined.

Park Song had given it to her some months ago in exchange for an exquisite young girl from Austria. Mrs Dartigue couldn't recall the girl's name but given Song's wild enthusiasm for bloodshed one could be certain that the little dear, whoever she was, had long since expired. The Fabergé, meanwhile, had doubled in value and that made it money in the bank. Money didn't buy happiness but it did permit you to purchase the misery you preferred.

She'd asked Park Song to bring her a certain expensive item from Rome, to be applied towards the cost of a teenage American girl he planned to buy from Mrs Dartigue and her American associate, Ben Dumas. The girl, called Tawny, was currently in New York and being guarded attentively by Dumas. Photographs revealed little Miss Tawny to be a cool, blue-eyed beauty with golden hair and a teasing appeal which certain men found absolutely irresistible.

Copies of those photographs, air-expressed to Song in South Korea, had excited such lust in him that in a telephone call to Mrs Dartigue he'd been nearly speechless. On Mrs D's part it required no abundance of intuition to realise she had Laughing Boy by the short and curlies on this one.

"A quarter of a million dollars," she'd said to him. "Seize the moment, darling, or Tawny goes to auction."

"I want her. Sell her to me this instant." The Korean was practically in heat, no surprise from one dedicated to the fulfilment of highly unsavoury cravings.

"Gladly, dear boy. Two hundred and fifty thousand smackeroos and she's yours."

Song's voice shot up an octave higher. "Are you mad? I give you one hundred thousand which is more than I've paid for any of your girls."

"Something close to physical pain hits me whenever an individual attempts to bargain because it means an effort's being made to cheat me."

"One hundred twenty-five thousand. I want this girl."

Mrs Dartigue said, "Darling, you remember General Abuja,

that rather dwarfish and pushy Nigerian who spent a small fortune attempting to introduce bull-fighting into his country? You've done business with him, I believe. Well, he's been after me for months to uncover a little titbit like Tawny. As has a certain Italian prince with terribly close ties to the Vatican. And do I have to tell you how many wealthy Arabs would love to devour this sweet child? Allow me to put it this way: should she go to auction I intend to *start* the bidding at two hundred thousand. Under these circumstances, I'd say you're getting a bargain."

Park Song said, "And I say you're being quite ungenerous in this matter. You seem to forget you've made a lot of money with me in the past."

"I wouldn't have made this money you speak of if I hadn't produced a service worth having. You're not being forced to deal with me, you know. No one's holding a gun to your head, dear boy. Feel free to choose other alternatives."

The Korean was quiet. Finally he said, "You're a genius at getting people to believe you've got something they want. All right. Two hundred and fifty thousand dollars."

"Darling, nothing cheap is worth having. Half the money when we meet in London, the other half when Ben hands you the girl. Oh, when you're in Rome there's something I want you to pick up for me. Just apply it against the price of the girl."

"You know, I believe you'd sell shit out of your ass if you could. You empty a man's pockets and make it seem as though you're doing him a favour."

Rowena Dartigue's face reddened. She was about to say something unkind, something extremely brutal, but she remembered to whom she was talking, and closed her eyes.

"Harsh words, darling," she said. "But then no one's ever accused you of having a tender heart. You seem to forget who introduced you to Ben Dumas, the same Ben Dumas who furnishes you with that notable paper which is such a crucial factor in your counterfeiting endeavours."

Park Song snorted. "Forget? You won't let me forget."

"The same Ben Dumas who investigates the backgrounds of

your potential customers, thereby saving you untold hardship and suffering. Slander me if you must, but pay me you will."

The Korean chuckled. "You're a bitch."

"Thank you for the compliment, darling. Now here's what you're going to pick up for me in Rome."

Rowena Dartigue left her home and entered a waiting radio cab shortly before seven p.m.

Maureen had ordered the car which turned out to be a shoddy Ford with torn seat covers, full ashtrays and a back door containing a mysterious rattle. Being obsessed with cleanliness Mrs Dartigue's reaction to the vehicle's appearance was to flare her nostrils in disgust.

The driver was a pudgy, fifty-year-old Sikh in an orange turban and full length down coat, an illegal alien experiencing his first London winter and not pleased about it. Speaking Punjabi he cursed into a hand radio, relaying Mrs Dartigue's destination to the dispatcher along with an obscene opinion of a freezing rain which had slowed traffic all over London.

In the back seat Rowena Dartigue, eyes hidden behind dark glasses, sat with a large envelope handbag on the seat beside her. Designed by a seventeen-year-old Belgian girl the bag was made of deep purple calfskin lined with purple silk and a big seller at Rosebud. It complemented Mrs Dartigue's fur coat, a black ranch mink worn despite animal rights activists who weren't above hurling paint on women bold or foolish enough to wear furs in public. Rowena Dartigue, who despised any restraint on her freedom, wore fur whenever she felt like it.

The Sikh's fussy driving infuriated her. He obeyed speed limits to the point of madness and stopped at every pedestrian crossing, even when no one was there. Rain-slicked streets and backed-up traffic only added to the problem. Mrs Dartigue finally went to her bag for a Valium, washing it down with a sip of mineral water from a small silver flask.

It took the Sikh thirty minutes to drive from Chelsea to Parliament Square, the approach to the Houses of Parliament, and one of the busiest traffic roundabouts in London.

Here weather and traffic forced the Ford to creep along at a snail's pace, past bronze statues of Disraeli, Winston Churchill and a tall, rumpled Abraham Lincoln. Byron was right, Mrs Dartigue thought. The English winter ended in July, to recommence in August.

From Parliament Square the Sikh turned onto the Victoria Embankment, following the River Thames and encountering only light traffic all the way to Waterloo Bridge. A right turn onto the bridge and Mrs Dartigue, growing increasingly tense, was heading towards the South Bank. Not her favourite part of London, to be sure. Beggars living under bridges in makeshift cardboard shanty towns, London's uglier public buildings, deserted streets and sleazy pubs. It was absolutely Dickensian.

Just minutes off the bridge the Sikh pulled into Waterloo Station, stopping at the main entrance. He'd been a wretched driver and since Mrs Dartigue didn't believe in rewarding incompetence she tipped him a meagre twenty pence on a fifteen pound ride. Tips were wages paid to other people's hired help, a practice she avoided whenever possible.

She walked into the station, passing underneath the entrance arch which served as a memorial to staff killed in the First World War. The station, Britain's largest, was nearly empty; it was hard to believe that nearly two hundred thousand people passed through it daily. Mrs Dartigue walked briskly, eyes straight ahead, the envelope bag tight under one arm.

She shunned newsstands, bookstalls, fatigued baggage handlers and weary Jamaican ticket collectors on duty at the gate entrances to trains. Ticket windows were also ignored, most of them having closed for the day. Instead she continued walking until she reached the Waterloo Road entrance and stepped outside the building, stopping several yards away from a rank of black taxis.

The station overhang shielded her from the rain but failed to protect her from the damp chill. She trembled under her black mink; why in God's name hadn't she worn thermal underwear? It was cold as a well-digger's arse and getting worse.

77

She detested the rain. It had been raining that night in Capetown when a man dressed as a priest had shot her first husband Roger to death for working with anti-apartheid forces. And it had been raining the morning she'd left South Africa and returned to England carrying Roger's ashes. She'd adored Roger so much that for months after his murder she'd slept in his bloodstained shirt. Damn the rain. She'd shed too many tears in the rain ever to find it beautiful.

Rowena Dartigue walked to the rear of the taxi rank, then past it, stepping from the kerb onto the rain-wet driveway. Several yards ahead and to her left a pair of headlights flicked on and off, once, twice, three times. Pulling the collar of the mink around her face, she walked faster.

A taxi turned from the street and into the driveway entrance, heading towards Mrs Dartigue. To avoid it she hurriedly flattened herself against a damp wall until the taxi passed. Then she quickly walked towards a limousine parked with its engine idling, the privacy within protected by smoked glass windows. Opening a rear door she entered the car and sat down beside Park Song.

The Korean lifted a flute of champagne to her in a toast. "Well, I suppose we can get started," he said. "David?"

David Mitla, in the front seat with Song's Korean chauffeur, mumbled to the chauffeur sitting beside him and the limousine rolled away from the wall. Seconds later the limousine stopped alongside the first cab in the rank and the chauffeur blew his horn. Three short bursts, a pause, then two more.

Switching on his engine the driver and his empty cab pulled away from the line. His For Hire sign was off.

The limousine followed him out of the station.

On his London trips Song followed rigid security precautions. For their mutual protection he refused to meet Mrs Dartigue at her home or shop. Instead they met at night in a hired car and transacted their business while driving about the city. Because Song's chauffeur didn't know London a local cabbie was hired to precede the Korean's car.

"You look fantastic," Song said to Mrs Dartigue. "I'd

78

say marriage agrees with you. Yes, it most definitely agrees with you."

"A happy husband makes a happy wife," she said. Bit of a lie, this.

Yes, marriage had brought her immense sexual satisfaction but Michael didn't seem to be overelated with the legal union of husband and wife. He continued to drink, use drugs and stay out long past curfew. All of this while pissing away her money with the enthusiasm of a drunken sailor on leave. God alone knew where Michael was tonight. He wasn't at home, that's for sure.

Song's limousine crossed Westminster Bridge, following the vacant taxi past the Houses of Parliament and St James's Park then onto Constitution Hill which ran through the middle of Green Park. An excited Song pointed to Buckingham Palace on his left, calling it magnificent and wishing his own country were united under a king and queen. Being snobbish he revered royalty, the British royal family especially.

"It's too dark for me to see," he said, "but would you know if the royal standard's flying over the palace? That's an indication the queen's in residence, you know."

"Really? Yes, I seem to have heard that somewhere. Well now, come to think of it the queen's flag has been waving over Buck House this week."

Mrs Dartigue was lying again, having no idea where the queen was and caring even less. Her little fib, however, made Song feel better. He seemed overjoyed that he and the queen were in London at the same time.

After leaving Green Park the limousine crossed Piccadilly, and passed Wellington Museum before entering Hyde Park. On the park's South Carriage Drive a solitary jogger, ominous in a grey-hooded tracksuit, ran towards the car then disappeared in the darkness behind the vehicle. Song said to Mrs Dartigue, "Champagne?"

"Please." Unzipping her bag she reached in and handed him two sealed white envelopes, both of which were letter-sized. As he opened one she sipped her champagne which was dry and chilled, an excellent vintage aged to perfection. Laughing

Boy's hold on reality may have been fragile, but he certainly knew the difference between good wine and moose piss.

He removed three sheets of paper from the envelope and began reading. Rowena Dartigue gave him a few seconds then said, "Per your instructions Ben faxed that to me this morning."

Song nodded and returned the refolded pages to their envelope. Coded information, as Rowena Dartigue knew, to be deciphered privately. This was a last-minute report on the people in London and New York to whom Song was planning to sell his counterfeit currency, bonds and securities.

He insisted that Ben Dumas run two investigations on the background of potential customers, to include personal, professional and financial history. The first was a preliminary examination when clients or business associates approached Song. The second occurred forty-eight hours before he met these same people to conclude a transaction.

Ben Dumas produced reports which allowed Song to appear almost clairvoyant. Forewarned by this information the Korean seemed to know things out of the natural range of human perception. Such knowledge had its price. Park Song was paying Dumas plenty for keeping him out of harm's way.

The second envelope. No coded information here. Just a one-page update on the health and wellbeing of Tawny DaSilva as requested by Laughing Boy. Rowena Dartigue allowed him to read in silence.

Finished, the Korean smiled and casually stroked the page with the back of his hand. "Time to pay the piper."

Opening a small refrigerator door he reached in and removed bundles of American hundred dollar bills, giving each one to a smiling Mrs Dartigue.

"Cold cash." He chuckled at his pun. "Very cold cash. Fifty thousand dollars. First instalment on the down payment for Tawny."

"A thousand thank yous, darling."

His hand went back into the fridge. "And the rest."

He gave Rowena Dartigue a flat book-sized package covered in black velvet. Eyes closed, she took a deep breath and pressed the package against her chest. As she unwrapped the parcel her hands shook.

"You dear boy," she said to Song. "You dear, dear boy."

She opened it quickly and removed the contents, an Egyptian-style necklace made of gold, rubies, diamonds, seed pearls and turquoise. The necklace came with a matching pair of earrings. Rowena Dartigue had never seen anything so beautiful in her life. The warmth in her bones and blood was nearly sexual.

Necklace and earrings, both over a hundred years old, were the work of the Guiliano family, Italian immigrants who'd become nineteenth-century London's finest jewellers. Rowena Dartigue was mad for this jewellery which had been inspired by the European Renaissance, specifically Hans Holbein's paintings. What pleased her most was the subtle chromatic sense, the use of stones for their colour rather than their value.

The previous owner of the jewellery had been the wizened seventy-year-old Prince Stefano Cosenza of Rome, he of the Vatican ties and passion for blonde adolescent girls, whom he half killed before passing on to a brothel in Tunis. Needing money to cover stock market losses he'd sold the jewellery, his wife's, to Mrs Dartigue for seventy-five thousand dollars.

She'd learned that Park Song had business in Rome and pressed him into service, asking him to acquire Princess Cosenza's treasures for her. And while Laughing Boy had acted with less than joy and a whole heart, in the end he'd done as she'd asked.

To guard against burglars and opportunists such as her beloved Michael, she kept her Guiliano collection in a Shepherd Market safe depository. It was open three hundred and sixty-five days a year, twenty-four hours a day and offered excellent security. It also provided freedom from banking restrictions and the taxman. Only Rowena Dartigue could get near her safe deposit box which she did by matching her thumbprint and a photo ID with those on file at the depository.

Two keys were needed to gain access to the box. She had one

81

and the depository had the other, listing it not under her name but under a three-digit number changed every other month. Among other items she kept here were cash, personal papers and records on the money laundering conducted through her charity. She also kept listings of customers and their preferences in sexual slaves.

Reaching into her envelope bag Rowena Dartigue removed a pen flashlight and jeweller's loupe. As Park Song giggled she pushed her dark glasses atop her head, fitted the eyepiece to her eye and switched on the flashlight, training its beam on the necklace. Necklace and flashlight were brought up to the loupe.

She smiled. "Orgasmic, darling. And decidedly genuine. You can just about make out the Giuliano mark on the back of the enamel. The necklace is signed C and A.G., which would be father Carlo and son Arthur. The mark's somewhat unclear, an indication that it's authentic. As are the stones. Positively orgasmic."

She examined the earrings, also pronouncing them authentic. Removing the loupe she kissed Song on his cheek and again called him a dear, dear boy.

"Shall we conclude the rest of our business?" she said.

She watched the Korean pick up a small suitcase from the car floor and place it on the seat beside her. Opening the case he turned it round to allow her to view the contents. The case was bursting with American hundred dollar bills.

"Eight million dollars," he said. "All genuine, I assure you."

Plucking a bill from the suitcase Rowena Dartigue fingered it for several seconds, then eyed it through the loupe. She did the same with four other bills taken from the bag at random.

"Right you are," she said. "All genuine."

She locked the suitcase which contained Song's proceeds from his sale of counterfeit cash and securities on the continent – a sale aimed at saving his life.

He'd remained mum regarding his troubles with the Razor, but Ben Dumas had learned about them and passed the news on to Rowena Dartigue. Ben Dumas who knew everything about everybody, whom she found rather likable in his primitive way, who enjoyed listening to her English accent and treated her with a certain deference merely because she was English.

Rowena Dartigue would launder Song's eight million through her Lesley Foundation and be generously rewarded for her trouble. The smell of profit was in the air and she found it sweet indeed.

Ostensibly a certain Hong Kong real estate company was advancing the eight million to her charity on a short-term loan. She would deposit the money with the Lesley Foundation's bank in the Channel Island of Jersey. Later the bank would arrange for the Hong Kong company to receive bank drafts and guarantees against which it could borrow. Result: clean, untraceable cash for Laughing Boy.

Song's eight million dollars would yield at least eight hundred thousand in interest, to be divided equally between the Lesley Foundation and Rowena Dartigue. She would make the necessary payoffs to certain bank personnel.

"Drop me off at my depository," she said to Song. "I want to lock up my lovely gems for safe keeping. And secure your cash as well. Tomorrow morning the money will be off to the Channel Islands. And do have the taxi driver wait for me at the depository."

"What about papers confirming my 'loan' to your charity?"

"Should be in my hands late tomorrow afternoon. Ring me at the shop around three. You're leaving England when?"

"Assuming Dumas's information checks out and all goes well, I should be leaving the day after tomorrow. I'll let you know if I'm taking my profits with me or leaving them here with you."

Rowena Dartigue thought, you silly little man. Do you really think I don't know? Leaving England with his profits or leaving them here with her weren't the only methods of getting his money out of the country. There was a third way, one he'd mistakenly believed he'd kept secret from her.

Laughing Boy never travelled with his counterfeit wares. The goods came and went by a separate route, one so safeguarded and dependable that it appeared unlikely he'd ever lose a shipment to competitors or police. Should he be arrested outside of South Korea the lack of evidence would weaken any case against him. Separate routes for Song and his wares also forced his enemies to spread their manpower thin, weakening all efforts to stop him.

Ben Dumas had warned Rowena Dartigue never to repeat this information to anyone. Even he wasn't supposed to know about Laughing Boy's mysterious smuggling route but somehow he'd found out. Passing this news around could get you killed, he told her. While Rowena Dartigue promised to tell no one, she did keep a note of this astonishing news in her private safe deposit box.

Meanwhile what Ben had told her would remain a secret, words spoken in darkness and never to be revealed in light.

In the limousine Song said, "Still leaving for New York on schedule?"

Rowena Dartigue held up the Giuliano necklace. "Whenever you keep people waiting, darling, they tend to pass the time by speaking ill of you. I leave for New York the day after you do. My auction's scheduled the night I arrive. No chance to unpack, really. Feel free to attend. I expect the customary rich and debauched consumers of human flesh to be on hand. Michael's been told the usual untruth, which is that I'm going to New York to interview young American designers and to see about opening a New York branch of Rosebud."

Song lifted an eyebrow. "How is Michael these days?"

She returned the necklace to its box. "How is Michael? Working on another scheme to get rich, I would imagine. Ask me what it is and I couldn't begin to tell you. He's not seen fit to confide in me, you see. He's dropped hints of having an iron or two in the fire but nothing specific. Oh, before I forget, I have a little something for you."

Laying the jewellery box aside she reached into her bag, removed a brown Manila envelope and handed it to Song.

Opening it, the Korean removed a black and white photograph. For a few seconds he was speechless. Then he whispered, "Impossible. I don't believe it."

He held an eight by ten glossy of Dick Powell, Ruby Keeler, choreographer Busby Berkeley and director Mervyn Le Roy taken at the wrap party of the film *Gold Diggers of 1933*. Each of the four had autographed the photograph.

Song's voice was hoarse with emotion. "Priceless. Where did you get this?"

"From a young Frenchman who designs for me. He collects Hollywood memorabilia and came across this in some tacky Carnaby Street shop. He was quite pleased with himself."

"And you bought it from him?"

"Especially for you, darling." One more lie. She'd stolen the photograph from Georges who'd carelessly left it lying about the shop. Little Georges was heartbroken over the loss of his treasured relic, being a fan of movie queens and something of a queen himself. Anything that pleased Laughing Boy, however, could only advance Mrs Dartigue's cause.

An awed Song couldn't tear his eyes from the photograph. "I can't tell you how much this means to me. I worship these people."

"My pleasure, darling. It was no trouble, believe me. My first husband always said we are made kind by being kind."

The Korean tapped the photograph with a forefinger. "Their films will live for ever. For ever. Like you and Michael, perhaps."

For ever. The sadness came on Rowena Dartigue without warning. Turning from Song she stared through the tinted glass at the Serpentine, Hyde Park's artificial lake, where a strong wind sent dockside boats crashing into each other.

Michael. For ever.

She whispered into the darkness:

> Sigh no more, ladies, sigh no more,
> Men were deceivers ever;
> One foot in sea, and one on shore,
> To one thing constant never.

As Rowena Dartigue proceeded towards the Shepherd Market depository, her husband lay on a sagging bed in a two-room Soho flat and sucked the toes of Nigella Barrow, a leggy twenty-six-year-old English croupier whose dark eyes were filled with dancing lights. A cassette player atop a nearby night table featured Smokey Robinson's sweet tenor caressing "Tracks of My Tears".

From an adjacent closet a burly, forty-six-year-old Scotsman with a bristling red moustache peeked at the couple through a cracked door. His name was Bernard Muir and he wore the uniform of a London policeman.

Pausing, Michael Dartigue removed a bottle of advocaat from the night table and swallowed a mouthful of the thick, yellow Dutch liqueur made from egg yolks and brandy. Then he poured the liqueur on the inside of Nigella's thighs and began licking it off. Whimpering, she pulled his head towards her with hands tipped with multicoloured nails. As he sucked hard on her clitoris she pushed to meet his tongue, screaming as she lifted her pelvis from the bed.

Eyes glazed, she collapsed back on the bed in a pleasurable stupor and whispered, "You're rough. That's what I want. God, that's what I want."

Michael wet a foot in the liqueur on the bed and rubbed it over her pubic area.

"The saga continues," he said.

"I want to be on top," she whispered.

They traded places, she riding him in a frantic rhythm

consistent with her animalistic sex drive. "Twist my nipples," she said. "Harder. *Harder*." He did as she ordered, wringing the flesh painfully. "That's good," she whispered. "Ooh, that's good."

She climaxed first, screaming before biting his ear. When she clawed at his chest he quickly grabbed her hands. "Careful," he said. "My wife."

A winded Nigella hurriedly apologised. "Sorry, love. I keep forgetting. Forgive me."

Later they lay still, Nigella on top of Michael with her long, auburn hair covering his chest as she listened to his heart beat. Then she said, "Just a few minutes more, love, and we'll be finished."

Two minute warning. Except this wasn't basketball, but a bigger game with a different kind of championship on the line. Two minutes to win or lose it all. Chump or champ in one hundred and twenty seconds. Michael's heart was pounding. Too late to back out now.

Nigella said, "We're out of grass, but there is a bit of coke left. Like to do a few lines?"

Eyes covered by a muscular forearm Michael turned towards the wall. "Let's just get it over with, okay?"

She slipped out of bed and turned down the cassette player. As if on cue the closet door opened and Bernard Muir, small truncheon in hand, entered the room.

At the bed he licked his small round mouth and stared at Michael.

Muir tapped his palm with the truncheon. "Well now, young sir, what have we here? I'd say we've been more than a little indecent. Should detain you for this sort of thing, but I'm a fair man. Fact is, I'm in rather a forgiving mood. Let's do a deal, then. A bit of fun for myself and I'll forget about what I've witnessed in this room. Well?"

A silent Michael refused to look at the Scot.

Muir whacked his palm harder with the truncheon. "I said *well*?"

Michael whispered, "Please officer, I'll do anything but don't arrest me. Please don't arrest me."

Placing the truncheon on the bed Muir removed his dark blue trousers and a pair of white boxer shorts, dropping them on the floor. "So, you want me to do something to you, is that it?"

"Yes, I want you to do – " Michael's voice faded.

"Well, if that's what you really want."

Reaching into a breast pocket of his police jacket Muir removed a condom, tore off the wrapper and slipped the condom into his mouth. On the cassette Smokey Robinson held a high note on "Ooo Baby, Baby".

Wearing the police jacket and helmet a half-nude Bernard Muir crawled onto the bed and took Michael Dartigue's limp penis between his lips. In seconds his tongue had expertly fitted the condom over the American's sex organ. As Muir began to fellate, Michael, face to the wall, attempted to ignore what was being done to him. Fucking get it over with, he thought. Finish this shit before I throw up. I have no choice. Have to go along with this shit, but Jesus –

Shivering in revulsion a disgusted Michael slid from under the Scot. Sullen and still naked he rushed to the bathroom, leaving Nigella Barrow to sit on the bed beside Bernard Muir. Cupping Muir's square jaw in one hand she turned his head around to face her. Her dark eyes caught pinpricks of light from a red candle on the night table. "Did you enjoy yourself, Bernie?"

The chubby-cheeked Scot grinned. "Indeed. Absolute bliss. Now allow me to keep my part of the bargain."

Taking his trousers from the floor Muir pulled a small blue notebook from a back pocket. He smiled at Nigella, teasing her by gently waving the notebook in front of her face. Heart pounding she watched him hungrily, resisting the temptation to snatch the notebook from him. It was only after he'd torn out the first three pages and handed them to her that she realised she'd been holding her breath.

Three pages from a cheap notepad. Muir's payment for his just concluded fling with Michael. Three little pages containing information worth millions of dollars.

Thanking Muir she kissed him on the cheek and offered him a cup of tea, knowing it would be refused.

The Scot looked at his wristwatch. "Wish I could but I'm due at work in forty minutes. Going to have trouble getting there as it is. Not easy traipsing about in this weather."

"I understand. And we'll send your share to Liechtenstein as you asked."

"Wouldn't look right if I suddenly came into a large amount of cash here in Britain. The money will be quite safe in Liechtenstein."

Suddenly Muir seemed less amiable, less good-natured. Eyes narrowed, he spoke to the ceiling. His voice hardened. "Eddie Walkerdine's giving me a chance to get my own back and I intend to make the most of it. My employer, stinking wog bastard, says I'm too old. Says he has to sack me because these days guarding money has become a young person's game. The man's an unsurpassed Indian swine."

He looked at Nigella. "I'm still fit, you know. Work as hard as anyone, and it's been years since I've reported in sick. But that isn't stopping Mr Ravi Sunny from getting rid of me. First of the year and I'm out on my arse. No pension. Haven't been there long enough to qualify for one, he says. Know what that bastard's giving me after twelve years of faithful service? A cheque for one hundred pounds. And a plaque, of course. A bloody plaque. Christ all-fucking-mighty."

He rose from the bed. "Well, let him discharge me, but I'll be leaving with a damned sight more than a bloody plaque. Bet on it."

Nigella watched Muir walk to the closet, remove an empty suitcase and carry it to the bed. Into the case went the policeman's jacket, helmet, trousers and truncheon which Nigella knew had been rented. Back at the closet Muir reached in among her clothing and removed a grey suit, matching topcoat, dark brown cap.

Dressed, he picked up his umbrella and suitcase then looked round the room. "I believe I've got everything," he said to Nigella. "No time for a wash, I'm afraid. My regards to Mr Walkerdine. Those notes I've just given you should solve his problem. If he needs anything else he knows where to reach me. When I check my Liechtenstein bank in two weeks I expect to find my share on deposit."

Nigella said, "Thank you again, Bernie. Your money will be there as promised. Eddie's a man of his word."

Touching the umbrella handle to his cap in farewell Muir turned to leave then stopped. "Goodnight, Michael," he said in a loud voice, "I had a lovely evening."

From the bathroom came the sound of breaking glass then Michael shouted, "Fuck you, you sperm brain dickhead!"

Muir said to Nigella, "It's his musical use of the language which I'll miss the most."

Eddie Walkerdine was a small, forty-two-year-old Englishman with receding dark wavy hair and a gap-toothed, demonic smile. He wore a tuxedo with a white carnation in the lapel, black Gucci loafers and a gold pinky ring containing a star-shaped sapphire. Clenched in his front teeth was a small black cigar.

He and Nigella Barrow were seated on her bed when Michael Dartigue, freshly showered in grey slacks and white turtleneck, stepped from the bathroom. At the bed Michael sat down beside Nigella who took his hand and kissed it. Both watched as Walkerdine silently inspected the information received minutes ago from Muir. Humming tunelessly the little Englishman studied the pages with an aggressive slit-eyed stare.

Two months ago he'd begun work on a plan to acquire money for his permanent move to Marbella, the most glamorous and chic of Spain's Costa del Sol resorts. His plan, if successful, would yield ample funds to meet fixed expenses – alimony and child support to two ex-wives, a yearly allowance to another woman whose eight-year-old son he'd fathered, the expense of private nursing care for an ailing mother.

There'd also be enough to buy a restaurant on Marbella's marina, a small hotel near the casino complex of Puerto Bancus, and a block of new flats just outside the resort. The properties were everything Walkerdine had ever wanted and thought he'd never get. The thought of owning them was the sweetest emotion he'd felt in some time. Here was the prize he'd been chasing from birth and it was within reach.

From the moment he'd learned the properties were for sale he'd burned with a need to own them. At present they belonged to Ned Clegg, the hollow-cheeked forty-year-old Australian newspaper proprietor who needed cash to expand a four hundred-horse stable. Two months ago he'd offered to sell his Spanish holdings to Walkerdine for twenty million dollars, slightly under market value. The catch: Walkerdine must pay the full price in cash and no later than the end of December.

Done. Walkerdine would have the money, every penny, and on time. He avoided financial particulars, which was just as well since to acquire the money he intended to rob the Shepherd Market depository of some fifty million pounds, give or take a few million.

He saw no reason why he shouldn't pull it off. Energetic and shrewd, he planned his moves carefully, showed strength when challenged and prided himself on knowing when to walk away from a losing cause. A one-time bus driver who'd never known his father he'd clawed his way out of London's oppressive East End by expertly playing up to the weaknesses of those who could advance his ambitions. Despite a simianlike appearance women found him clever, forceful and erotic.

Walkerdine managed the Riviera, a Leicester Square discothèque which he'd turned into one of London's most successful clubs by catering to prosperous blacks. Unwelcomed at up-market clubs where non-white faces were greeted with "members only", affluent blacks also avoided clubs patronised by lower class blacks, places that were often rowdy if not menacing.

Whites were welcomed but the Riviera's primary patrons remained moneyed blacks, some of whom were African and Caribbean millionaires. Visits by blacks celebrated in American entertainment and sport had even given the club a certain cachet. Walkerdine and Dartigue had met when the American had dropped in with black friends who were professional basketball players in the States and Europe.

Walkerdine earned eighty thousand pounds a year. And what he skimmed, provided him with an annual income of over a hundred thousand pounds. The skimming was a response to the club's owner, a skinny Lebanese with ties to the Amal militia, who'd broken his promise to make Walkerdine a partner.

In September Walkerdine had married for a third time. The bride, who hated England where she suffered endless colds, was Gina Branchero, a twenty-five-year-old Spanish model born in Marbella and who longed to return there because it supplied more sun in a day than London did in a month.

Walkerdine had met the voluptuous, brown-eyed Gina while on holiday in Marbella, where she'd been the mistress of a resident Arab sheik who was a major arms dealer and owner of the largest yacht in the marina. The sheik was glad to rid himself of "Miss Sangria 1986", having become irked by Gina's demands that he dump his twelve wives and marry her.

Gina wasn't alone in wanting to chuck England's filthy weather for life in the sun the year round. Walkerdine's asthma was getting worse, aggravated by England's cold, damp climate. Last spring a Harley Street lung specialist had warned him that inhalers, pills and injections were no longer enough for his respiratory problems. Unless Walkerdine moved to a warm, dry climate he'd eventually suffer an asthma attack which might prove fatal.

And there were the effects of Walkerdine's working in discos, bars, private clubs and restaurants for twenty-five years. He was tired of it all: the eighteen-hour days, the conniving club owners, the villains demanding protection money, the bent coppers out for payoffs, the witless food suppliers and the pre-dawn knife fights between drunken patrons.

Walkerdine was also tired of dealing with drug overdoses in the ladies' room, with arrogant rock stars and their thuggish bodyguards, with employees who took off for Majorca without a by-your-leave, with bartenders who sexually molested waitresses and stole liquor by the case. Most of all he was tired of working for other people.

For years he'd vacationed in Marbella where his wit and arrogance had made him a popular figure among expatriate Brits, wealthy Arabs and film stars living in tax exile. He enjoyed sipping champagne and charming the pants off the truly rich while tanning himself on their huge yachts moored in the marina. Nothing would make him happier than to live there with Gina for the rest of his life.

He owned a small villa behind Marbella's Puerto Bancus casino and a marina flat, both of which he rented out for most of the year. Income from these properties, alas, would not cover Walkerdine's fixed expenses and also allow him to live the good life among the resort's fat cats. Income from Ned Clegg's properties would, however.

Two months ago on a Tuesday night Walkerdine's future, in the form of an inebriated Bernie Muir, had staggered into the club. Tuesday at the Riviera was "Gay Night", when homosexuals took over the club and frolicked among themselves. Nothing too wild. A bit of dancing, silly contests of one sort or another and a chance to relax without incurring the wrath of intolerant straights.

The idea had been Walkerdine's, his way of boosting business on what had been the slowest night of the week. He'd given gay groups a good price on food and drinks, allowed them to bring in a gay disc jockey and promoted the evening in several gay publications. He'd even permitted the club to be used for AIDS fund-raisers. As a result Tuesday nights had become extremely profitable.

Bernie Muir had been a "Gay Night" organiser. Walkerdine didn't particularly care for him, finding the Scot a moody loser who always picked the wrong lover and couldn't wait to tell the world about it. Muir also drank too much; he'd had a skinfull when he'd bitched to Walkerdine about being chucked out. Muir spoke of getting his revenge for being unfairly sacked and Walkerdine dismissed it as whisky talk.

He had even made a joke out of it. "Rob the place," he said. "Let's team up and rip off every single safety deposit box at the centre." Both of them could use the money.

"Good idea," Muir said, then told him how to go about it.

After spending a sleepless night reflecting on Muir's words, Walkerdine sought him out the next day. Both men took that night off from work and talked for six straight hours. This time there were no jokes.

Walkerdine's life was more than half over. He was sick of waiting for circumstances to make him rich. It was time he created those circumstances himself.

Walkerdine, seated on Nigella Barrow's bed, crushed his small cigar in an ashtray resting on a crumpled pillow then stood up. Scratching his chin with Muir's notes, he smiled at Michael. "You look none the worse for wear, sunshine," he said.

Michael rubbed the back of his neck. "I'm cool. I weirded out when Muir finished, but I'm OK now. Fucking guy's dippy. Dressing up like a cop. Jesus. If you ask me, the man's going through life with his headlights on dim. Anyway, what can you say about fags that hasn't been said about haemorrhoids."

Walkerdine grinned. "That was the deal, sunshine. We get information on the security at the Shepherd Market deposit centre and he has his way with you. That was Bernie's price. Your manly body plus two hundred thousand pounds. Sex and money. Makes the world go round, doesn't it?"

Walkerdine tapped Michael on the shoulder with Muir's notes. "Say what you will, the wanker kept his word. It's all here in black and white. Location of closed circuit television cameras, perimeter alarms, cipher locks. Number of guards on duty after midnight. Important thing is we now know that the telephone lines are connected to perimeter alarms. Cut one, you cut both. No calls in or out. No distractions."

Nigella fingered Michael's ponytail as he said to Walkerdine, "You say when the telephone lines are cut no calls go in or out. Fine. Now suppose we're in there punching all those boxes when somebody phones the guards and can't get through. Seems to me that's when the shit hits the fan."

Walkerdine shook his head. "You're not in America now, cowboy. We Brits are a bit more relaxed in certain areas and security, fortunately or unfortunately, is one of them. We lack your crime and therefore we lack your paranoia. Over here your American security is as out of place as testicles in a convent. Muir says security's lax, to put it mildly. Things are pretty dead around the depository at night. Clients rarely drop in after ten and there's never more than one or two after-midnight calls a week."

"How about the guards?" Michael said. "If there's going to be shooting I'd sooner stay home and listen to my own farts."

"Let me repeat: you're not in America now. Don't dwell too much on receiving a bullet in your irreplaceable backside. The guards don't have guns. Theoretically an alarm has to go off *then* the security company sends over armed guards. But when we cut the wires there isn't going to be any alarm. As luck would have it, the security company's located on the other side of London, meaning under the best of circumstances it takes a while before they arrive at the depository. The centre relies on strong locks, strong doors, alarms of course, and on the fact that it's never had a robbery in its history. It's a juicy apple ready to be plucked and I say we do the plucking."

A click from the cassette player signalled the end of the Smokey Robinson tape. As Nigella rose to change tapes Walkerdine lit another small cigar and blew smoke at the ceiling. Then he stared at Michael a while before speaking. The American struggled to hold his gaze.

"No backing down, sunshine," Walkerdine said softly.

Michael rose from the bed. His face was red and his temples were throbbing. "I don't take shit. I don't give shit. I'm not in the shit business. Where the fuck do you get off saying I'm going to wimp out?"

Up went Walkerdine's hands in an apologetic gesture. "Sorry, guv. Sorry. Didn't mean to offend. It's just that I'm in too deep, as the bishop said to the actress. You haven't met the two men who'll be working with us, but trust me when I say they don't take kindly to broken promises. Should we cancel our little adventure between now and Thursday, well, I'll have to explain things to this pair of villains, who in turn may demand a further explanation from you. Hard men we call them over here. From the East End of London where crime isn't just one way of life, it's the only way of life. They're the type who'd stick a glass rod up your granny's arse then tie her to the back of a lorry and drive off into the country, making sure to hit every bump in the road."

A grinning Michael scratched one eyebrow with a pinky finger. "You want to try and do this thing without me? Want to fence what's in those safety deposit boxes all by yourself? Speak up, I can't hear you."

"You know bloody well I daren't get rid of the stuff in this country. That's why I had to bring you in."

"No more phone calls, we have a winner. Fast Eddie ain't as dumb as he looks. You're the one who tells me we're apt to find everything from gold bars to false teeth when we hit the deposit centre. But you fence so much as a paperclip and Scotland Yard or whoever the fuck it is will tie your asshole in a knot. You might as well wear a tee-shirt saying you pulled the job. And that's where Big Mike comes in. I know how to get rid of the stuff. You don't. I got contacts in New York who can fence what we heist. You don't. I know how to make things disappear. You don't. Am I getting through to you?"

Walkerdine forced a smile. "No disrespect intended, Mike. Only two days before we do this thing. Got a slight case of nerves, I guess. We shouldn't, either of us, get our bowels in an uproar. If I've offended you, I apologise."

As Marvin Gaye sang "Give It Up" Nigella walked from the night table and stood beside Michael. Taking his hand in both of hers she said to Walkerdine, "You can count on Michael. He'll do his part, believe me."

Walkerdine's smile lacked any affection. He thought, a soft answer turneth away wrath even when it comes from a bimbo like Nigella. Her intervention gave Walkerdine a moment to calm down. Getting into a shouting match with Dartigue was a waste of breath. Why tell this cretin that robbing the safety deposit box belonging to his own wife would be the only way he'd ever get enough of her money? Walkerdine was not one for saying the wrong thing at the wrong time.

Not a bad girl, Nigella. Had a few brains which she rarely bothered to use, unfortunately. Half the men in London, Walkerdine included, had screwed the arse off her. Had she not really fallen for Dartigue and if so, why had she involved herself with this spoiled, overgrown child who had the attention span of a two-year-old?

As usual she'd let some chap sell her a bill of goods. This time it was Dartigue who'd laid it on thick by promising he'd chuck his wife after the robbery and take Nigella to the States with him. He'd also gone on about his intention to set up Nigella with a hair salon in Miami. Talk about being feeble-minded.

Walkerdine didn't believe Dartigue gave a hoot in hell about Nigella. The bugger was only using her to snatch his wife's money. Walkerdine was willing to bet his lungs that after the job Dartigue would hit the gas getting away from Nigella. She was better off when she'd been selling it to rich Arabs at one hundred quid a time. At least she knew where her next meal was coming from.

Taking his topcoat and hat from a chair Walkerdine said, "Duty calls. You lovebirds coming to the club tonight?"

Michael shook his head. "We have a few things to go over. Maybe tomorrow."

Walkerdine slipped into his topcoat. "Tomorrow then. Oh, when you drop by the club you must try our new drink. We call it the Afro-disiac. Rum, grenadine, vodka, bitters, bit of mango, fresh limes, fresh cream. Absolutely sensational. Guaranteed to put lead in your pencil, believe me."

After Walkerdine had left, a silent Michael and Nigella stood with their arms around each other, eyes on the door. She spoke first. "Eddie's too clever by half," she said. "He's what you call a bit tricky. Sneaks up on you, he does. Chips away at you. Bit here, bit there and before you know it, he's got you. Eddie's only out for Eddie, remember that."

Michael nodded. "I hear you."

He looked at her face, seeing the love which had nurtured him the past two months, a love that sometimes turned him into a fool who didn't know what he was saying, and which made everything about her precious. It was a love he'd tried to resist, which had finally overwhelmed him and was now his master. It was a love which had made him stronger than he'd been in years while leaving him vulnerable and afraid of losing it.

An uncertain Michael said, "I've got a lot riding on this and you know it. You also know Fast Eddie better than I do, so you make the call. Do I pull out or do I go through with it?"

Nigella dropped her eyes. "He's a first-class manipulator, Eddie is. We just have to be on our guard, that's all. You're the only thing that matters to me in this whole thing. I can do without the money if I have to. I can also do without Eddie and his little schemes."

She stared up at him. "You really can't just walk away, you know. I don't think you could live with yourself if you did and we both know it has nothing to do with Eddie. I think you should do what's important to you."

Michael shook his head. "I'm Florida white trash and that's about all I'll ever be in this life. The one thing I had going for me was basketball which I learned from blacks, which pissed off my parents since they hated blacks with a passion. My father especially got all bent out of shape over my choice of friends. He was a Baptist minister, the Ayatollah of his day. Gave me some fundamentalist bullshit about how I'd violated divine law because blacks were cursed by God and could never enter heaven. Nigger only gets to heaven, he said, if God makes him white."

Michael sat down on the edge of the bed and stared at the floor. "Man was out of his mind. One day I'd had enough of his racist bullshit, so we just went at it. I swung at him and he went upside my head with his cane. I really freaked out then and knocked his ass into the goldfish bowl. Funny as hell, him lying there and goldfish flopping all over the rug.

Would have killed him if my mother hadn't pulled me off. Don't forget, I was a big kid, tall for my age. Ended up with them kicking me out of the house. Told me to move in with my nigger friends. I did. I was sixteen."

"Andres's family, they took me in. Talk about poor. They didn't even have a bathroom. Had an outhouse out back. You bathed in a washtub set up out in the backyard. Cold weather, you put the tub in the front room. What little they had they shared with me. Good people, especially his mom. The best, bar none."

Michael smiled. "Me living in a rundown house in Liberty City with eight spooks. Had to sleep on the living room floor but I didn't mind. When our sneakers wore out, me and Andres would tape them together because we didn't have ten bucks to buy new ones. Wintertime, we wore pyjamas under our pants to keep warm. Great times. Fucking great times. We got recruited for the University of Miami the same day. Same day. His mom came to every home game. Should have seen the looks when she pointed me out on the court and said 'that's my son.' Whatever I know about the game, Andres taught me. His family was my family and he was my brother. Andres is the best. Period. End of discussion. I fucking love that man. Fucking love him. Can't walk away from him now. I just can't."

Nigella sat down on the bed beside Michael and took his hand. "Do the job," she said. "Do it for your friend, not for Eddie Walkerdine. Do it for Andres."

For Andres.

Eight days ago on a mild November morning Michael and Andres Valentino had met at Florida State Prison where Andres was doing ten to twenty for manslaughter. It had been three years since Andres had used a screwdriver and hammer to jam a couple of cash machines on Collins Avenue in North Miami Beach. When two bank guards showed up to service the machines Andres pulled a sawn-off shotgun from a shopping bag, took twenty-two thousand dollars from the guards then shot them. One guard had died, the other had lost an arm.

Prison was a long way from the University of Miami where

Michael and Andres had both made second team all-American. Only Andres had got a shot at the NBA. Drafted by the Detroit Pistons on the eighteenth round he'd been cut in training camp. Too slow. Michael hadn't even been drafted. Not big enough, read the scouting reports. Not fast enough, not tough enough.

As a pro he'd played a year in Italy, averaging twenty-six points a game for Milan and being a party animal until word had got around about him and Marisa Algeri, wife of the team's owner. Michael was alive today only because friends had bundled him into a car bound for Switzerland minutes before three men with guns had kicked down the front door of his Via Pontaccio flat.

In the prison visitors' room he sat and stared at his reflection in the glass barrier separating guests from inmates. Getting lines in his face. Getting grey, too. And there was *that sound* – steel gates slamming over and over, a sound echoing in his head since he'd set foot in this place. For days after each visit Michael would hear that sound in his dreams. Sometimes it was so scary he'd wake up with colitis.

To his right was a plump, middle-aged Haitian woman who spoke into a house phone to a convict on the other side of the glass, a slender, twentyish youngster who Michael assumed was her son. Both had tears in their eyes. Feeling he was eavesdropping, Michael looked away.

A family of Cubans moved noisily into the seats on his left. One woman, heftily built and barely out of her teens, held up a newborn baby, bringing it near the glass. Michael watched as a stocky, dark-skinned Cuban inmate in his mid-twenties, telephone receiver to his ear, pressed a palm against the glass, smiling as he "touched" the infant.

Pointing to his own eyes the inmate said something which made a grey-haired, big-nosed Cuban woman at the other end of the phone throw back her head and laugh. Michael thought, how the hell can anybody laugh in this shit hole? The room reeked of sadness, bad luck, and time wasted.

The women visitors appeared to be taking it the hardest. Weeping, some rose from their chairs and leaned as close to the partition as possible. A young, pregnant Jamaican woman bare-legged in a green dress and straw sandals, became hysterical. Shrieking, she began beating on the glass with both fists, fainting just as two guards rushed to her side. Tearing herself apart over something already done and which could not be recalled.

Michael wanted a cigarette, but there were no smoking signs around the room. He was searching his pockets for gum when he saw Andres Valentino enter the visitors' room accompanied by a balding, paunchy corrections officer. A tall, flat-nosed thirtyish black with a large, friendly face, Andres allowed the CO to guide him by the elbow to the empty chair between the Haitian and Cuban inmates.

Andres wore an orange jumpsuit, grey Reeboks and a green knitted skull cap over a shaven head. A black patch covered his left eye and fresh stitches ran down the left side of his face and neck. He sat only after the CO signalled him to. *Andres Valentino, the most daring point guard in the history of Florida collegiate basketball waiting to be told he could sit down. Jesus.*

Ignoring Andres's cut face Michael picked up the phone. "Hey dude, good to see you."

"Ain't much good in my world, but I thank you for coming."

Andres spoke with an inmate's awareness of the importance of words. Words determined one's very survival in a situation as unsafe as prison. His speech, therefore, was guarded, the words carefully chosen.

Michael said, "How you living?"

"Twenty-four and seven, my man. Twenty-four hours a day, seven days a week in the place where you don't pay no rent and there ain't no rules. You looking good. Your lady treating you fine, I see. I dig that jacket."

Michael touched it. "Suede. She's got connections in the fashion business. Gets a discount on everything."

Andres chuckled. "She treating you well which means you still gettin' the most out of your dick. Dick takes you where your brain never could. Then you always was a man who made himself available towards people of the female persuasion."

Both chuckled.

Michael said, "Your face, man. What happened?"

Andres touched the patch with long, brown fingers whose nails had been bitten down to the quick. "Least I be able to see out of my eye. Ain't gonna be like it was but I still got it. Gonna have them scars, too. Ran into some trouble with one of the Jamaican posses in this place. Dudes carry razor blades in their mouths. Spit them out then cut you faster than a cat can lick its ass. Had a discord with a Jamaican who said I paid his boyfriend to suck my dick. Didn't have to pay that fool at all."

Andres sighed and began biting his nails. "Anyway, this fag's lover, he jealous and he tries to shank me. I stomped his butt good. Wasn't the end of it. Last week his Jamaican friends come at me in the yard. Muslims stopped them from killing me, but not before I get my face cut up."

Michael shook his head. "Man, I am sorry."

"What goes round, comes round. People be waiting to see what I do about it. Got to do something. Can't let a dude put his mark on you without no payback. Next thing you know, the idea gets around you weak. If I want respect I'll have to make a move on the brother who threw them niggers on me."

Michael thought, I could be sitting on the other side of this glass, some of the shit I've pulled. Selling steroids, sinking boats for insurance, passing bad cheques, promoting fake rock concerts, selling fake time-shares, raising money for films that were never going to be made. Only thing he'd been lucky at was keeping out of jail.

Michael leaned towards the glass partition, anxious now to tell Andres why he'd taken time away from his business in New York to fly down here. "That lawyer you told me about last time I was here. Cuban who used to be on the parole board. He still around?"

Andres studied Michael. Then, "You mean De Laquilla. Yeah, he still around. Still in business but the man is very expensive. Charge you for breathing the air in his office. Heavy dude. No sense going to him unless you got a great big piggy bank. A big one."

"You said he's connected, that he can get you an early parole or put you in a work release programme."

"Seen it done. Guys with money, had eight, ten years to go, they hired De Laquilla. Before you know it they get paroled or ended up on the outside, living in some halfway house and working a nice civilian job. But it costs. Fifty K, maybe more."

"I can get the money. Is De Laquilla righteous?"

"Your old lady, she give you the bread?"

Michael snorted. "No way will that woman help me get some spook out of jail. She loves herself more than she could ever love anybody else. Buys me what I want, but getting cash out of her is like pulling teeth. Got to come to her every time I want something. Pisses me off which is why I'm dumping her. No, there's another way to scare up the bread."

Andres laughed. "You just got married and you quittin' the bitch? You a man of angles, Jack. Definitely a man of angles."

Michael told Andres about Eddie Walkerdine's plan to rob the Shepherd Market depository. When he finished Andres scratched his head and nodded. "Sounds cool. One thing, though. Why he bring you in? Like, why didn't he do it with his own people? He got his inside man, so why he need you?"

Michael held up a forefinger. "He has this little problem, which is fencing the stuff. Doesn't want to do that in England. Remember when I had that restaurant down here in West Palm Beach?"

"Seafood place. You was fronting it for some people from New York." Using a forefinger Andres pushed the tip of his nose to one side.

Michael nodded. "Yeah, I know. You don't fuck with these greaseballs, not twice anyway. Long as you kept your word, though, they weren't too bad. At the time they were expanding out of New York. They were the first mob people to make contact with certain Cubans down here and have them reach out for Castro. Had this crazy idea about getting him to let them reopen the casinos in Havana."

Michael grinned. "Fucking Castro almost went for it, but the Russians made him turn it down. Didn't want the Americans getting back into the country. Anyway, these clowns, these olive oil salesmen, they wanted to expand in Florida and one thing they needed was a local name to front a restaurant. Seeing as how I'd been a hoops star in my college days, I got the gig. These guys also paid me to be a mule. Carried cash and pharmaceuticals to New York, Atlantic City, Montreal, London. That's how I met Rowena, my wife."

Andres grinned. "Pharmaceuticals. I like that. Pharmaceuticals is what got me in here. Crack makes you paranoid, man. I smoked some rock before I hit the bank so I thought them two guards was going to kill me. They weren't, but I didn't know that. Anyway, I'm listening."

Michael said, "After we hit the depository the greaseballs will fence the stuff. But they ain't doing it for free. Whatever cash we rip off, they're only giving us fifty cents on the dollar. Everything else they take forty per cent off the top. When I get my share I'm buying you out of this place."

Andres squeezed the bridge of his nose with forefinger and thumb. "Man, I can't allow myself to even dream about that happenin'. If you can pull that off . . ."

He waited until he had control of himself. Then, "Momma ain't doing so well. Ain't been out of bed since the stroke. You did good sending her the bread – "

"Hey, nigger, don't give me that shit. Momma V's the only mother I got. Besides, it wasn't all that much. When I get a few bucks, Mom always gets a taste. You know that."

Andres nodded. "I know, man. I know."

"Left something in your prison account. Money, cigarettes. Anyway, listen up because I don't have much time. I flew to New York to wrap up things with the Italians. Got to check in with them before I go back to London. They don't do business over the phone. Told them I had to fly down here to see my family, which is true."

Andres said, "Man, you 'bout the only one who ain't forgot I'm here. My own blood don't want to know from me any more. All I got is you and thinking about what it was like back when we was in school, back when all we did was play hoops and chase pussy. After we leave school everything turn to shit."

"I hear you," Michael said.

"Hoops keep me alive in here, but it ain't like playing when you free. I go up for a rebound and for a few seconds prison ain't under my feet, know what I'm saying? For a few seconds I got no contact with this place 'cause I'm flying. Then I come down and I'm still here, man. Still here. Don't get no easier. Hoops ain't no good unless you free and I ain't free."

Michael said, "On our mother, man. I swear on our mother I'll get you out. I swear it."

He watched Andres reach inside his jumpsuit, which had no pockets, and remove something which he held up to the glass for Michael to see. For Michael the sight of it brought on a sadness too great to hide. What he saw was a newspaper clip, a photograph of the University of Miami basketball team shot during a game in his and Andres's senior year.

The photograph, taken the night the team had won the NCAA semi-finals by a point, showed the five starters huddled together during a timeout. Every Florida newspaper had carried it on the front page. The shot had also run in sports pages across the country.

Uniforms dark with sweat, their faces animated with joy, pride and fatigue they clung to each other, five against the world, Michael in the middle with his arms around the necks of Glenn, Ahmad, Jon and Andres, Michael the only white in the photograph. Two days later they would play for the national championship and lose by ten points. But the photograph from the semi-finals had been taken on the greatest night in their lives, bar none. *This* had been the best game they would ever play as a team.

As Andres watched from behind the glass Michael tried to stop the tears, but couldn't. He bit his lip, blinked to clear his eyes. The sadness was overwhelming. Right hand on the glass, he covered the photograph. Soon the tears made it impossible to see.

8

Park Song had checked into a fifteen-storey French chateau-like hotel on London's fashionable Piccadilly. He was registered under the name Harry Yue Lan, with a passport describing him as a Chinese stockbroker born in Taiwan and now living in Macao. This was one of several aliases he used on business trips to the West which numbered three or four a year.

Delighting in an occasional bit of nonsense, Song had chosen this particular alias as a private joke. The Festival of *Yue Lan*, the hungry ghosts, was celebrated in Hong Kong every July. On this day hungry ghosts wandered the earth and could only be appeased by paper money, fruits, food and other gifts. Song's mind was always on money so why not travel the world as Mr Hungry Ghost.

The hotel on Piccadilly had an exterior of Portland stone, a marbled entrance hall with gilded ceilings, an arcade of exclusive shops and a life-sized bronze sculpture of a half-nude woman in its Art Deco lobby. The woman was a nineteenth-century Irish courtesan who had built the hotel with the three hundred thousand pounds she had charged an East Indian diplomat for the privilege of spending one night with her. Song was amused to learn that she had died when a young actor had asked her to marry him and she laughed, provoking the actor to strangle her on the spot.

The hotel's French restaurant overlooked a private garden, boasted thirty-one champagnes on its wine list and served the finest smoked salmon soufflé Park Song had ever tasted. His enthusiasm for good food was no pretence. To think, to love or to do anything well one first had to eat well. Given the choice he'd rather die of too much food than too little.

At six forty-three on the morning after his meeting with Rowena Dartigue he entered the oversized sitting room of his hotel suite and switched on an overhead chandelier then a pair of Art Deco bronze lamps. He wore a black tracksuit edged in white, a yellow headband and rice straw slippers. He carried a pair of tap shoes and a small cassette recorder. A towel hung from his neck.

He planned an hour's *Taekwon-Do* practice and a bit of tap, followed by breakfast with bodyguards David Mitla and the judo-adept chauffeur Han Choi. Then he would get on with the business of selling counterfeit money and securities. By tonight he should be out of this country where it never stopped raining. Then it was off to New York, the final stop on his desperate excursion to stay alive – New York, where he would collect the big money and the American girl he'd bought from Rowena Dartigue.

At a damask-draped window Song placed tap shoes, cassette recorder and towel on the sill then looked down over the Buckingham Palace garden wall twelve storeys below. Nothing to see, unfortunately. His vision was eclipsed by darkness and rain. Nor did it help to know that the queen had landscaped the garden to ensure privacy. Since the garden was as close as Song had ever come to seeing the royal family in person he stared at it for several minutes. When you couldn't get what you loved, you had to love what was within your reach.

Breathing deeply he peered through the window and vigorously massaged the base of his skull with both thumbs. Then with the bottom of his fists he lightly pummelled his arms, torso and legs. His skin tingled and he felt a bit warmer. The cold, damp English weather chilled the blood. He needed to get his blood stirring again.

Song crossed the room to an Italian marble fireplace where he placed his towel, tap shoes and cassette recorder on the mantelpiece. Kicking off his sandals he began jogging in place, knees high, arms moving rhythmically. Five minutes later he stopped, circled his neck then swung his arms. Warming up wasn't enough. *Taekwon-Do* was basically a kicking art. A practitioner had to be limber enough to kick head high.

Gripping the edge of the mantelpiece with both hands Song began stretching. He lifted his right leg, easily placing his heel on the mantelpiece which was level with his chin. When he'd stretched the leg, thigh and hip on one side of his body, he turned to the other. In *Taekwon-Do* it was leg flexibility above all. Flexibility equalled speed and speed equalled power.

He stretched carefully, allowing his muscles to extend of their own accord, doing everything smoothly, without force or unwarranted pressure on joints and ligaments. In Seoul his private gymnasium included the latest body-building equipment plus simple pulleys and ropes. By looping one end of a rope around his foot and pulling on the other end Song could raise his kicking leg to any height. For power he had a pair of large training bags which allowed him to practise full-impact kicks as well as flying kicks.

Stretching completed he immediately began foot sparring, a form of training in which hand techniques were forbidden. Using front, side and back kicks he attacked an imaginary opponent, first the head then the body. Next he switched to roundhouse and hook kicks, striking with speed, accuracy, and above all, power.

Finished, a tired Song collapsed in a tapestry-upholstered chair, soaked with perspiration. The strict mental and physical discipline of *Taekwon-Do* was very demanding. But the reward for practising this martial art whose roots went back one thousand five hundred years was increased bravery and an unyielding spirit. *Taekwon-Do* gave Song the confidence to cope with life's problems.

After drying his perspiring face and neck he laced on his tap shoes. Then he left the chair, stepped to the fireplace and turned on the cassette recorder. As Fred Astaire began to sing "Too Marvellous For Words", Song started a slow-time step on the slate hearth. Dancing relaxed him. It was also when he did his best thinking. Closing his eyes, he let Astaire's voice warm him. He wasn't tired any more. His weariness evaporated. Life's problems and fears no longer disturbed him. Dancing was one of life's sweetest moments. He began to hum along with Astaire.

When travelling abroad Song usually did business at his hotel, taking care to withhold its location from customers until the last minute. On the day they were to buy from him, clients were ordered to sit by the telephone until he called and ordered them to come round at once. It was madness to count on anyone to protect you but yourself. Nature may have been indifferent to Park Song's survival but he wasn't.

As he tap-danced he made a mental rundown of the day's schedule. *Pick up the counterfeit money and securities before his customers arrived. Decide whether to leave the money from these sales in England with Rowena or send it back to Seoul. Get the loan papers from Rowena covering the eight million dollars he'd given her last night. Get David Mitla to confirm their flight arrangements from London to Montreal.*

From Montreal they would make their way to New York by rented car, crossing the Canadian-US border away from any customs agents or border patrol. Giggling, Song clicked his heels together. All roads led to the beautiful little girl named Tawny. She might be bitter at first but in his hands she'd eventually become as sweet as honey. In time she'd come to feel love as he did and live only for that love.

Today he expected to make four million dollars from just two customers. One was a seven-foot tall Nigerian with tribal facial scars who ran a travel agency on Thurloe Street when he wasn't occupying himself with insurance and credit-card fraud. The other was an Indian couple who arranged marriages for a living while indulging in a bit of gold, diamond and drug smuggling on the side. While Song had never dealt with either buyer before, both had come highly recommended.

Rowena had endorsed the Indians who had occasionally found an Asian child for her when a customer had requested one. As for the Nigerian, Song knew him slightly, having met him two years ago at a party in Rome hosted by one of Song's customers. Ben Dumas had checked out the Nigerian and the Indians, finding nothing to make Song reject either buyer. Song was now free to engage himself in commercial pursuit, to go forth and haggle in the marketplace.

With each hour, however, his schedule became increasingly tighter. He had only four days to raise the rest of Youngsam's thirty million dollars or fall victim to the Razor's wrath. Song would make the deadline but only by a hair, one day to be precise.

In New York, his last stop, he had arranged sales which should yield him eleven million dollars. This, plus sales made in Hong Kong and Europe, plus what he expected to make today, should put him over the top. He'd have Youngsam's thirty million and a three million dollar profit besides. But for the next ninety-six hours fortune had to be on his side or he was finished.

The sweetest part of this deal was the three million dollars profit. This money would allow him to stop counterfeiting for a few months, work on his tap-dancing and devote himself to shaping his little American girl into the perfect woman. Only through money, his heartbeat, could Song live and be happy. Anyone who believed money wasn't crucial to survival should try raising thirty million dollars in three weeks while under a death sentence.

Daylight was creeping through the hotel window when David Mitla, barefoot in a short terrycloth robe, entered the sitting room yawning and scratching his balls. Ignoring Song he flopped down on a tufted sofa, reached for a telephone on a fruitwood coffee table and ordered breakfast for three. Self-confident and outspoken, the former paratrooper didn't hesitate to mock Song's breakfast of coddled egg and soda crackers. After hanging up the phone Mitla said, "Your Joan Crawford special is on the way."

At the hearth Song did a three hundred and sixty degree turn, clicked his heels together three times and spun round again. On the sofa Mitla lit his first cigarette of the day, blew smoke at the chandelier then asked what time should he and

Choi pick up the goodies, Mitla's name for Song's counterfeit currency and securities.

"Nine thirty," Song said. He was now dancing to actor James Stewart's unique vocalising on "Easy To Love". "Gives you and Choi an hour and a half to eat breakfast and get dressed. I've telephoned and you're expected. Everything's ready and waiting. Is Choi up?"

Mitla snorted. "He's up. And he's got both windows wide open. Ice was starting to hang from my nose, so I left the room."

Song giggled. He had a private room while Mitla and Han Choi had to share, annoying the Israeli whose calm never revealed his true feelings. Even those who thought they knew the slender, bearded Mitla in the end found him as elusive as quicksilver.

He'd led a dangerous life, one of action and intrigue, one he'd never spoken of to anyone, including a wife back in Israel who ran their small software business from a cliffside home overlooking Haifa Bay. She also managed his other investments, which included a movie theatre on Haifa's Hanassi Street and citrus orchards on the Sharon Plain.

But Mitla, secretive by nature, told her nothing of his role as a mercenary who fought other people's wars for money. She knew that he possessed an insatiable lust for warfare, that he'd fought in combat all over the world since he was fourteen, that he couldn't count the number of people he'd killed. She also knew there was a chance he'd return to her in a coffin or simply vanish, never to be seen again.

Mitla was being paid a small fortune to bodyguard Park Song, more than he'd made training bodyguards and assassins for Colombia's *los magicos*, the name given the Medellin drug barons who appeared to have got rich as if by magic. Which is why, putting a bent for privacy aside, he'd accepted rooming with the brawny, twenty-six-year-old Choi who could bench press over five hundred pounds and had once broken a man's back for stepping on his foot in a discothèque.

Each morning the rigid and hard-headed Choi, who carried his judo silver medal in its original case with him everywhere, did two thousand pushups followed by several minutes of duck walking to strengthen his legs. Then he meditated in front of an open window for ten minutes, freezing weather notwithstanding. If the window was sealed, Choi would turn the air-conditioning up to high.

Mitla, who considered Choi a bit deranged, rated his own martial arts skills as good but nowhere near good enough to take on the Korean in a fight. Should that day ever come, Mitla, no stranger to trickery, intended promptly to shoot Choi even if it meant shooting him in the back. Since Choi preferred settling arguments using his judo skills, taking him on bare-handed was the equivalent of rushing to your death.

Song said, "After the pick-up you and Choi return here straightaway. No stops, no detours. While you're gone I'll set up appointments with my buyers."

The pick-up.

Song's counterfeit dollars and securities were waiting at the Korean Embassy on Palace Gate which was a street of grand houses located a stone's throw from Kensington Palace. The "goodies" travelled by diplomatic pouch, courtesy of Colonel Youngsam who was amply compensated for his assistance. Thanks to the avaricious Youngsam and his Intelligence agents at embassies around the world Song's property was safer than it would be in a bank vault. So long as greed remained the Razor's absorbing passion Song had a friend at court.

Mitla said, "I have to wire money to my wife."

"Do it before you go to the embassy, that's all I ask. I don't feel comfortable having you and Choi stopping anywhere while carrying the product. I'd like to leave England tonight which means everything has to run on schedule. I also have to allow for the possibility of a rain delay at the airport."

Mitla stubbed out his cigarette and stood up. "Whenever we come here it's always pissing down outside. I hate this grey country, hate the cold weather, hate the cold people. If I had to live here, I'd go crazy."

Song stopped dancing and towelled his face. "I hear New York's very cold so make sure you have your woollies."

Mitla jammed both hands in the pockets of his robe. "Speaking of New York, how's our friend Dr Yokoi doing these days?"

Song tossed his towel onto the mantelpiece then resumed tapping. "You should hear Rowena. Poor dear's terrified of catching the disease from Ken. Doesn't want him anywhere near her. Not to worry. We won't be dealing with Ken who in any case refuses to see anyone except his precious Ben. We'll be dealing with Mr Dumas. Oh, and Rowena, of course."

Mitla knew what Song did with little girls like Tawny DaSilva and he dealt with it by simply ignoring the matter. Other than being a bit too competitive at times the Korean was not a bad guy to work for. In any case how long would Mitla stay a mercenary if he turned down a job just because the offer came from a man who had a few loony ideas about women? He'd been around long enough to know that powerful and influential men in Africa, South America, Europe and the Middle East committed sex crimes and ritual killings daily. A mercenary's very livelihood depended on disregarding the inadequacies of such people. It had yet to occur to Mitla that a love of war had contaminated him.

Experience had taught him, however, that people were little more than wolves gnawing on each other. Even Machiavelli, Mitla's favourite writer, had called the people a wild beast. Big Mac was right. In any case morality was a luxury mercenaries couldn't afford. A soldier of fortune wasn't hired because he loved Christ.

Mitla accepted the fact that his job had him doing things no orthodox rabbi would say a *brocha*, a blessing, over. What mattered was the rush of adrenalin whenever Mitla went into battle. What mattered was the excitement. Except for his wife Messalina everything else in the world was nothing.

At thirty-eight she was three years older than he, the widow of a fellow paratrooper and now two months pregnant with her and Mitla's first child. He hoped she wasn't working too hard while he was gone, but Messalina was a *Sabra*, a native born Israeli, energetic and stubborn, and inclined to do as she pleased. He'd fallen in love with her because she was the strongest, most outspoken woman he'd ever met.

The tap-dancing Song broke into the Israeli's reverie by saying, "Wake up, Mr Mitla, time is money." Mitla snorted then walked towards the room he shared with Choi.

Behind him a cheerful Park Song added his adenoidal whine to Gene Kelly's husky tenor in "Singing in the Rain".

Shortly before one in the afternoon Park Song, in a red silk robe and matching slippers worn by Nelson Eddy in *Naughty Marietta*, concluded his first sale of the day in a hotel suite now darkened somewhat by the December downpour.

The customers were Mr and Mrs Prokash, a jovial Indian couple who exchanged two and a quarter million dollars for eight million dollars in fake hundreds and Hong Kong securities. A grey-haired, meaty woman in her early fifties Mrs Prokash wore a pink and yellow sari under a ragged cloth coat and did most of the talking. Her husband, a slender fiftyish Bengali with a durable smile, deferred to her but occasionally removed the pipe from his mouth long enough to say, "Veddy good, veddy good."

The couple had been accompanied by their two eldest sons, one in a three-piece suit, the other in jeans and a Chicago Bears sweatshirt. Both quietly sat down in front of the counterfeit money stacked on the fruitwood coffee table which they eyed in awe and wonder. Song thought, no woman will ever bring you two lads greater joy than that which you now see before you.

It was Mother who prodded her sons into reaching in their jackets for the pocket calculators, notepads and ballpoint pens needed to tally the counterfeit. As they counted, the sons packed the fake money and securities into five suitcases carted along by the family. At no time did Mrs Prokash's small dark eyes leave the money passing through the hands of her two offspring.

If there's trust among thieves, Park Song thought, it doesn't extend to this crew. Mother didn't trust her children nor did she appear to have much respect for hubby who was left to

114

stand around with his hands in his pockets while turning the air blue with pipe smoke. Mr Prokash, poor bastard, had married a tsar, not a wife.

At Mother's request Song had allowed her sons to be present at the buy. They were needed, she said, to carry home the counterfeit notes and securities. Rather than lose a badly needed sale, Song agreed. Nothing in the Prokashes' background had indicated the use of violence in their dealings. Still, Song insisted that both sons be unarmed, a fact confirmed by Mitla's thorough body search.

Firearms, Mrs Prokash said, frightened them all no end. Minus bodyguards or weapons of any kind they'd taxied to the hotel and planned to taxi back to their flat on Lady Margaret Road in Southall, London's largest Asian quarter. Song's reaction was to whisper to Mitla, I hope I never become that adventurous.

Song and the Prokash family made their respective counts in silence. To speed his tallying Song used a counting machine borrowed from the embassy, a device which amazed the Indians but not enough to switch from counting by hand. "The old ways have always worked well for me," Mrs Prokash said, "so why change at this point?"

Mitla, meanwhile, moved restlessly about the room with a silenced 9mm fifteen-round Taurus in his right hand, an Uzi dangling from one shoulder and a .357 Magnum tucked in his waistband. An air of menace clung to the Israeli, discouraging the Indians from speaking to or even looking at him. His eyes flicked from them to the door, from there to the house phone then back to the Prokashes. Like a snake, Mitla, even when calm, hinted at a swift, unpredictable violence.

Choi, sombre in dark suit and white socks, stood with his back to the door, arms folded across his massive chest as he too eyed the Prokash family. In contrast to Mitla he never moved, never blinked. Even his breathing was all but imperceptible. The only sound in the room was that of rain and wind against the windows.

The tallying concluded, a gracious Park Song shook hands with the Prokash family then escorted them to the door. They were as eager to depart as he was to be rid of them. Song, however, remained cordial and well-mannered while refusing to indulge in extended pleasantries or artificial social courtesy. No time for such rubbish. The Nigerian was due shortly, and after doing a deal with him it was off to America.

On the way out the Indians smiled nervously at Mitla and Choi but were ignored by both bodyguards who stared through the Indians as though they were made of glass. When one uncomfortable Prokash son dropped a suitcase at Choi's feet and tripped over it the muscular Korean simply backed away before resuming his watchful position. It was Park Song who extended a helping hand to the fallen son then wished the family a safe trip home.

The Prokash family gone, a smiling Song thrust clenched fists in the air. He felt like dancing and why not. He was richer than he'd been one short hour ago which was certainly cause for rejoicing.

He looked at the Mickey Mouse wristwatch he wore, a souvenir of his trip to Florida's Disney World three years ago. Twenty minutes until two. Twenty minutes before Katsina Jonathan, the gargantuan forty-two-year-old Nigerian, appeared with $1.8 million dollars for Song's coffers. Events were proceeding on schedule. Men might see him as lucky, but what the world reckoned as luck Song called hard work and smart thinking. In any case his destiny would be decided by him, not by Colonel Youngsam.

Mitla and Choi had finished carting the Prokash money to Song's bedroom and were seating themselves in the sitting room when there was a sharp knock at the door. "*Police. Open up.*"

A wide-eyed Song leaped from the sofa. His heartbeat immediately went out of control. He felt a severe chest pain and began to suffer a shortness of breath. In a vain attempt to stop a sudden headache he pressed the heels of both hands to his temples. "No," he whispered. "*No, no, no.*"

On the other side of the door a male voice spoke in a cockney accent. "Mr Henry Yue Lan, we know you're in there. Kindly open the door. We would very much like you to help us with our inquiries, if you please."

Song paced wildly back and forth. Stopping suddenly he pulled a red silk handkerchief from a robe pocket and tore at it with his teeth. He didn't see Mitla step to the house phone, pick up the receiver and listen. Near the Israeli a silent Choi rose from the sofa, face impassive as always. Eyeing Song, he awaited instructions.

Slamming down the receiver Mitla said, "Line's dead." He jerked his head towards the door. "They're not police. This is a hold-up."

Song stopped chewing the handkerchief. A small piece of cloth clung to his wet chin. "How can you be sure? *How?*"

Mitla slipped his Magnum into a pocket of Song's robe. "How can I be sure? Because I'm suspicious that the house phone's been cut off just when you come into two million dollars. Because with your record the police put a gun to your head *then* they announce themselves."

Song looked at the door. "What if you're wrong? What if those guys are real police?"

"We'll find out soon enough."

Mitla whispered into Song's ear. As the Korean listened he beckoned Choi to his side. Seconds later Mitla raced across the room and into Song's bedroom, leaving Song hurriedly to relay instructions to Choi.

"Mr Yue Lan, sir. Don't make it hard on yourself. We simply want to ask you a few questions."

Song said. "I'm coming now, Officer. Yes, I am."

His deferential voice was misleading. Gone were all signs of fear and dread. A calm, cold-eyed Song watched Mitla close the bedroom door then shifted his gaze to the suite door. His hatred of anyone attempting to rob him knew no limits. If the "policemen" calling on him were thieves Song proposed to crush them completely.

Choi, meanwhile, was excited at the prospect of a fight. He felt the icy hatred emanating from Song and knew how explosive the counterfeiter could be. Song was a generous

117

man to work for, but he was also a proud man who didn't like being insulted, tricked or cheated.

Followed closely by Choi, Song walked to the door. When he opened it his smile was straightforward and heartfelt.

"Good afternoon, Officers. I'm Henry Yue Lan. What can I do for you?"

"You can begin by standing aside and allowing us to enter your premises. How's that for starters?"

The speaker was a stocky, thirtyish cockney with small features set in a large red face. He was flanked by two younger men, faces half-hidden by police helmets. All three wore dark ponchos over navy blue uniforms.

Hands in the pockets of his robe Song backed into the room, followed by the three policemen. The red-faced leader and a tubby, buck-toothed man strolled casually past him, taking in the posh surroundings. The third policeman, a worried-looking thin man with a drooping moustache, stayed just behind Song and Choi.

Keeping his back to Song the red-faced cockney said, "I'm Constable Fowler. Like to discuss a bit of passport difficulty with you, if I may." Eyes on the chandelier he turned round to face the two Koreans.

Song's smile never faded. "Is there something wrong? I thought my passport was in order."

Fowler took another slow look about the room. "Before we go into that, I believe there's a third gentleman travelling with you. Would you, by any chance, know where he can be found?"

Song nodded towards his own bedroom. "At the moment he's taking a hot bath. I think he's coming down with a cold. He's not used to this sort of weather."

Fowler blew into his cupped hands. "Know what you mean. Filthy weather, this. Bucketing down out there and the cold's enough to freeze the balls off a brass monkey. Pleasure and pain, we calls it. That's cockney for rain."

"Really?" Song said. "I never knew that."

Fowler sighed. "You say your friend's having a bath. Well, they tell me cleanliness is next to godliness, though you

118

couldn't prove that by me mother-in-law. What a foul creature that one is. Allow me to compliment you on your choice of slippers. Red with gold braid. Matches that robe nicely, it does. Very nicely. Don't see much of that where I come from. I suppose the more sensitive little birdies appreciate proper dress more than the rest of us."

As the moustachioed constable near Song and Choi snickered the tubby, buck-toothed man stepped behind Fowler and whispered in his ear. Fowler nodded. Then jerking his head towards the bedroom the cockney said, "Constable Quillan here will look in on your friend just to make sure he's washing behind his ears, after which we'll get down to business. Constable Quillan, do your duty."

Buck Teeth swung his hands from under his poncho and produced a sawn-off shotgun. Song showed no reaction. His smile remained in place.

As Buck Teeth walked towards the bedroom Fowler addressed the two Koreans. "I'm sure you gentlemen won't mind remaining here with me and Constable Dawson until Constable Quillan returns with a report on your mate. Dawson?"

Backing towards the fireplace the moustachioed Dawson brought his own sawn-off shotgun from under his poncho, training it on the Koreans.

Song said, "I thought British policemen didn't carry guns."

A grinning Fowler folded his hands, the backs of which were tattooed with eagles and roses. "Oh, but we do, sir. In special cases we most definitely do."

"And this is a special case, I take it."

"Oh, indeed, sir. Indeed it is. Which reminds me. If you don't mind I'd like to scrutinise the pair of you for weapons. Just a formality, you understand."

He took the Magnum from Song and a fifteen-round Czech CZ75 pistol from Choi. "For shame, for shame," he said. "Going about England armed to the teeth like bloody pirates. Have you no faith in our policemen?" He placed both pistols on the mantelpiece then resumed his position by the sofa.

"Never liked guns meself," he said. "More likely to shoot yourself than the other fella, wouldn't you say?"

Removing his helmet the balding red-headed Fowler wiped his forehead with the palm of one hand then returned the helmet to his head. A bloody joke him dressing up like a copper. Him who'd spent three of the last four years inside for assault, theft and fraud. The same Reginald Emmett Fowler who'd been a boxer and a bookmaker and not very good at either, who was about to heist more cash than Ronnie Biggs and his thirty villains had in the Great Train Robbery of 1962. Reginald Emmett Fowler who appeared to be a formidable copper but who had to hide both hands under his poncho because he had the bloody shakes.

At the bedroom the buck-toothed, overweight Patric Quillan used the barrel of his shotgun to push open the door. Millions of dollars and we're in for a fat share, Fowler had said. Us and the individual what sent us. They'd be going after a slitty-eyed little bastard who was sitting on a pile of real lolly and a good amount of the fake stuff besides. No worries about genuine coppers either. In Fowler's words, Mr Henry Yue Lan was not exactly God's most noble work so don't look for him to reproach us for our sordid behaviour.

Quillan took three steps into an empty twin-bedded room lit by a single lamp on a night table. Three steps before he stopped dead and stared unbelievingly at the money. "Cor Blimey!" he whispered. He heard water running in a bath across the room, but his mind was closed to everything. Except the money. He couldn't believe his eyes. Spread across one of the beds was a beautiful big pile of American money. Quillan thought, Christ all-fucking-mighty, I'm a rich man. I've died and gone to heaven, I have.

Patric Ian Quillan had finally got lucky. No more drug dealing with the Yardies, the Jamaican gangsters who'd as soon shoot a man as look at him. No more teaming with Dawson to go debt collecting for loan sharks who were for ever demanding you break some poor bugger's kneecaps as a "Please Remit" notice. This rainy day in Piccadilly was the best day of Quillan's stinking life. Glory be to God, it was.

Images of a better existence raced through his mind. To start with, his own string of long-legged greyhounds and a new trailer to travel around in so's he could race at the best dog tracks. And women. Lots of those, mate.

This daydreaming consumed only seconds. But they were seconds in which he had forgotten why he'd come to the bedroom. Seconds in which he'd become distracted from the task at hand.

Reluctantly moving away from the money, he looked at the bathroom where the door was slightly ajar. The sound of running water indicated that the bloke inside preferred a full tub. On a stuffed chair near the bathroom entrance someone had left what Quillan thought were ballet shoes with steel taps. He snickered. Probably belonged to that wog in the red slippers who had to be taking it up the arse from the other two. Tightening his grip on the shotgun a confident Quillan walked towards the bathroom. Nothing to fear from this crowd of nancy boys. Nothing at all.

His mind, however, was still on the money. Should he tuck a few handfuls under his poncho before reporting to Fowler? A pleasant enough thought and why not. Every man for himself in this world and don't ever doubt it. At the bathroom entrance he stood beside the stuffed chair and gently pushed the shotgun against the door, the money very much on his mind.

Preoccupied, he never saw Mitla rise from behind the stuffed chair and with one hand grip the shotgun by the barrel, simultaneously pressing the silenced Taurus against the helmet strap under Quillan's jaw. The Israeli fired twice, holding onto the shotgun as Quillan went limp and crashed into the bathroom door. The door swung open and Quillan landed on the tiled floor, knocking the bloodied helmet from his round head.

In the sitting room Fowler raised his voice. "Constable Quillan, would you kindly tell us what's going on in there?"

Mitla stepped into the doorway of Song's bedroom and aimed his Taurus at Fowler's head. "Quillan can't come to the phone right now," the Israeli said.

Fowler froze momentarily, staring at Mitla for the space of several heartbeats. Then he yelled, "Get him, Dawson!"

An apprehensive and wide-eyed Dawson stepped away from the fireplace, thinking, I can't hit the bugger from this range. Shotgun's for close work. A wee bit nearer's what I need then I'll have him. In his excitement he forgot Song and Choi. He took two steps towards Mitla and in doing so he placed his back to the Koreans.

Moving quickly Choi seized Dawson from behind, pinned his arms to his sides and lifted him from the floor. As Dawson yelled, *put me down*, Choi tightened his already ironclad grip and broke the slender Englishman's arms. The shotgun fell harmlessly to the rug. Seconds later Choi dropped the shrieking Dawson to the carpet and sat on his chest. Then crossing both hands at the wrist Choi seized the lapels of Dawson's jacket, tightened the collar around Dawson's neck and choked him to death.

Mitla, gun still pointing at Fowler's head, slowly entered the sitting room.

Song raised his hand. "Don't shoot! I want him alive!"

Fowler looked at the entrance, seeing only Song between him and the door. Get by the wog, he thought, and I'm as free as a bloody bird. Tough on you, Henry Fuck Yue Lan. You and your red slippers.

Fowler didn't need a gun; they'd said they weren't going to shoot him, hadn't they? Therefore his fists ought to be enough to hang this scrawny little queer out to dry. A tiny punch-up, then Fowler would quickstep down the hall and put this disaster behind him. Let Dawson and Quillan fend for themselves.

Tearing off his helmet he hurled it at Song who ducked, the helmet passing harmlessly over his shoulder. As Song kicked off his slippers Fowler, fists held shoulder high, rushed him. Song waited two seconds then quickly spun round, and back to Fowler, kicked him in the face, firmly driving a callused heel into the cockney's nose.

Arms flailing, Fowler staggered backwards, a throbbing pain spreading throughout his head. Blood gushed from a crushed nose. His vision was blurred. Worse, he was seized by confusion and had lost all sense of direction.

Feet apart, he shook his head to clear it. Damn this bastard who'd got in a lucky shot. One lucky shot. Fowler could take him. He bloody well could.

He stumbled forward, forearms in front of his damaged face for protection. He saw Song take two steps to the right, wait, then take one to the left. Maybe Fowler was more cautious but he wasn't all that impressed. He was going to reveal some fancy footwork of his own and in the process he'd push Mr Yue Lan's yellow face through the back of his yellow neck.

But the hurt in his head wouldn't go away. Again he shook his head to clear it and that's when Song kicked him again, driving the edge of his right foot into Fowler's ribcage. The kick knocked the wind out of Fowler who felt as though he'd been hit by a car. Breathless, he panicked. Turning his back to Song he looked for an escape and found none.

Stepping closer Song kicked him in the spine, dropping the stricken Fowler to his knees. The instant the cockney touched the carpet Song, showing no mercy, moved in to finish him. Leaping forward he punched Fowler behind the left ear, knocking him unconscious and into the fruitwood coffee table.

Mitla sighed. "Nice, but I thought you wanted him alive. In case you're interested his friends are history."

He walked over to Fowler and felt his neck pulse. "Well, what do you know. He's still with us. Hope this doesn't mean a certain tap-dancer's losing his touch."

Song, who'd been calm during the fight, now raised his voice in anger. "How did they know we were here?"

"Your presence in London isn't exactly a secret. Rowena, the Prokash family, Katsina Jonathan, Colonel Youngsam, Dumas. They all know you're here."

Song held up his clenched fists. "Damn it, everything was going smoothly. Now I'm caught in a shit storm, a fucking shit storm. I don't like it. I don't care what it takes, I'm going to find out who betrayed me and I'm going to deal with them.

I won't have the bastard walking around knowing my plans. I will not have it."

Mitla said, "My money's on the Nigerian. Rowena and the Indians aren't cowboys. Rowena doesn't have to lift a finger to get your money. You hand it to her, remember?"

"If I'm dead she doesn't have to return it."

Mitla nodded. "Good point, but if Jonathan doesn't keep his appointment I'm betting he's our man."

"If he is I'm not leaving England until he's dead. He's not getting a second chance to fuck me. At the moment I intend to devote my attention to Constable Fowler or whoever this bastard is."

Mitla snorted. "Look, can't you put off having your fun just this once? You want to get back at him. I understand that, but I don't think we have the time. Give me two minutes and I can have Fowler singing in Hebrew. He'll talk, believe me. Then we terminate him, we get out of here, and we let your embassy clean up this mess. Whoever sent these guys knows where we are. I don't like that. I say we find another hole and crawl in it and do it fast."

Song spoke in a whisper. "Everything happens in threes. It's a law of nature. This business with these 'policemen' was the first setback. I will suffer two more, you mark my words."

He held up three fingers. "Three men they sent after me. Three. It's a sign. I'm telling you, it's a sign."

Mitla said, "I know what you're saying. But you're forgetting something. You survived this blow. I say it means you'll survive the others as well."

Song looked at him appreciatively. "Do you really think so? Do you really think I can survive the other blows?"

Mitla thought, if you don't then there goes my money. Therefore a bit of flattery is definitely called for. Aloud he said, "I see no reason why you can't achieve what you set out to do."

Smiling, Song placed a hand on the Israeli's shoulder. "Thank you my friend. At least you didn't dismiss my fears as Far Eastern mumbo jumbo. I'm on shaky ground and I

124

don't like the feeling. I have to be in control again. Do you understand?"

Mitla nodded. Of course he fucking understood. Song wouldn't feel right until he'd *controlled* this Fowler individual. Putting it another way, Song intended to cheer himself up by torturing the poor bastard.

Placing his lips near Mitla's ear Song whispered, "Fifty thousand dollar bonus if you see me through everything. *Everything*. You understand?"

Eyes on the chandelier, Mitla sighed. After a few seconds he said, "Just speed it up, all right?"

Song smiled, looking like a child who, after receiving numerous refusals, has finally been told it could go out after all. "One hour," he said. "You and Choi start packing. I'll call the embassy and tell them we've had a bit of trouble. Youngsam has thirty million reasons for coming to my assistance."

Fowler was having a nightmare. In it he lay naked in a lush green jungle, on cold hard ground. A freezing rain beat down on him unmercifully. He had the worst headache of his life. His entire body ached, especially one arm which felt as though it were on fire. He'd been injured but couldn't remember how. Worst of all was the snake. The huge, yellow snake who gnawed at Fowler's hand and sent stabbing pains throughout his entire body.

The cockney opened his eyes and screamed, a cry heard by no one because his mouth was taped.

He wasn't dreaming.

He lay naked in a bathtub, right wrist handcuffed to a faucet. Both ankles were lashed tightly together with a belt. Cold water gushed down on him from a gold-plated tap. The snake was the nude Henry Yue Lan, who knelt outside the tub and with a straight razor was slicing the tattoo from the back of Fowler's left hand.

Though weakened by the beating he'd received just minutes ago Fowler attempted to pull his bloodied hand away from the Korean's iron grip. Song's reaction was to dig a thumb into a nerve inside Fowler's wrist, sending pain racing up the cockney's arm. Resistance dealt with for the moment, Song resumed the task at hand.

But when the agony in the left hand again became too much Fowler again tried to pull the hand away. This time Song pressed the wrist nerve harder, keeping his thumb in place for long seconds. Crazed with pain Fowler whimpered and writhed, splashing Song with blood-tinted water. Meanwhile, from the cassette came the full rich voice of Judy Garland singing, "I'm Old-Fashioned".

Song said to Fowler, "When I remove the tape you will tell me who sent you. I will ask you just once, but I'm sure you'll tell me the truth."

He stared at the cockney through half-closed eyes. "Did you know that everything happens in threes?"

Lips pursed, he dug the straight razor into the back of Fowler's hand, making an incision around the feet of a blue eagle clutching a pink rose in its talons.

9

Seoul, 1961

On a cool April morning an eleven-year-old Park Song entered
a bank in the trendy Myong-Dong district, holding his mother's hand and willing himself to resist a fear which had
him nearly paralysed. If you look frightened, his mother
had warned, then the banker might become suspicious and
her scheme to defraud him would surely fail.

Song's mother Arang was in her late thirties, a slim, dark-
haired woman with a quiet elegance and dominant eyes.
Once a popular *kisaeng* with important political and military patrons, she'd eventually lost the bloom of youth and
been discarded. Utilising her considerable calligraphy skills
she'd turned to forgery, supplementing this with occasional
prostitution and petty theft. Song adored her strong sense of
adventure and the extraordinary energy which drew people
to her.

His father Tae was in his mid-thirties, a slight, handsome
man with a friendly air and a trim moustache. Earlier in his
life he'd spent three years in Los Angeles trying to break
into film musicals as a singer-dancer. Eventually he came to
learn that Asians rarely appeared on American screens other
than as demonic villains or humble and ingratiating servants.
Off-screen their occupations were equally as abject, generally
being limited to those of gardener, pool cleaner and houseboy.
As Tae told his son, an ant could drag an anchor easier than
an Asian could break the colour barrier in Hollywood.

But the American cinema was too exciting and glamorous

to be dismissed merely because it perpetuated bias against non-whites. A fascinated Song listened to his father's tales of stars he'd seen in studio commissaries and restaurants where he'd waited on tables, of glorious parties held at producers' mansions where he'd cleaned pools, of high-stakes gambling at legendary private clubs where he'd tended bar, of being rewarded with a quick glimpse of "the King", Clark Gable, after sitting for long rainy hours in crowded bleachers hastily erected for a film première. For Song's father, what had once been hard to bear had become sweet to remember.

Tae's recollection of Hollywood happiness left its mark on the boy who would share his father's love of film musicals and the belief that movie stars were nothing less than gods come down to earth. Along with his parents actors were those rare people who somehow managed to touch Song's heart.

Nowadays both of Song's parents were confidence tricksters who used their considerable charm and intelligence to fleece marks in a dozen Asian cities. Together with Song, an only child, they lived in a world of fast money, smooth talk and constant excitement, a world where they committed swindles for pleasure and profit. Their cons included stock fraud, phony cancer cures, selling illegal leases on government buildings and operating false schemes to return the personal effects of Korean war dead to their families. Life, as Song saw it, was himself and his parents in a conspiracy against the rest of the world. Everything else was as nothing.

Ordinary existence was for ordinary people, not for him. He had a special life with special parents. His life was entertainment, sport and diversion; he'd never tasted misery. The gods had blessed him with a mother and father who'd brought Song only happiness.

He'd worked his share of flimflams with his parents but nothing like the one they were seeking to pull off at the National Bank of Korea. The sting, a loan against forged securities, was literally a matter of life and death. Arang needed money to bribe a police detective who'd discovered she and Tae were defrauding investors in a non-existent Peruvian silver mine.

The detective was Chun Wonjong, a chinless forty-year-old with a hair-trigger temper and an exaggerated opinion of his own importance. He enjoyed intimidating people and had an unlimited capacity for making them suffer. For the past three days he'd held Tae prisoner in a flat belonging to a crony. If Chun wasn't paid off by noon today he was going to kill Tae and arrest Arang for forgery. Song would be sent to an orphanage or left to fend for himself on the streets of Seoul. The very thought of such a future made the boy shiver.

He'd encountered policemen before but never one like Chun. Things which might annoy other cops brought out an anger and hatred in him which was frightening to see. Chun's life revolved around his ambition. He had no consideration for others and was boorish and rude to those he considered inferior. Despite Arang's forced good cheer Song feared for his father so long as he was in Chun's hands.

Soft-spoken and quick to laugh Park Song lived with his parents in a small flat in Tongdaemun Market near the ancient Great Eastern Gate, the largest market in South Korea. While pleasant and well-mannered he was also secretive, highly sexed and a pathological liar with fantasies of wealth and power. In addition he had a strong fear of his own death which he acted out by killing animals in a substitute death.

Considering himself to be superior Song had decided that he, and not society, was qualified to define what was right. Thus whenever he harmed anyone there was no feeling of guilt or remorse. He was aided in this abnormality by his mother and father who ignored his sexual attitude towards young girls.

A year ago while on a train trip south with his parents for a day's outing in the thickly forested foothills of Mount Gaya, Song left his seat and followed a five-year-old girl to the ladies' room. Minutes later a nun entered the lavatory and was horrified to find Song raping the child. He'd also bitten her face severely enough to draw blood. Later the hysterical girl told a conductor that before the attack Song had given her candy, a new belt and a bit of cash.

Six months later on the grounds of Changdok, Seoul's best preserved royal palace, tourists wandering along the wooded paths of its Secret Gardens encountered Song and a caretaker's twelve-year-old dim-witted daughter having sex in a shaded grove. This was not rape; Song had the girl's consent. He'd given her several presents, among them a bathrobe and a cheap wristwatch. This incident, however, was more ominous than Song's past sexual episodes. This time he'd smeared himself and the girl with blood from a pigeon he'd beheaded. Traces of the bird's blood was on his lips and teeth.

Arang and Tae handled these two episodes as they had similar ones. Police and families of the girls involved were paid off and the incidents spoken of only in private. Being confidence tricksters the parents couldn't afford undue police attention.

His parents knew of his strong sex drive. What they didn't know was how destructive it had become. They didn't know that Song's savage fantasies were now threatening to enter his real life. Nor did they know he'd first imagined himself killing animals before actually doing it, an experience which had left him weak with exhilaration.

This had also brought a sexual satisfaction greater than anything he'd imagined. Lately he'd begun to fantasise about killing a young girl. Young girls were pliable and yielding, easily allowing him to exact obedience and to exercise command over them. The more Song fantasised, the stronger became his desire actually to take a girl's life.

The parents, who'd so often conned others, now conned themselves into regarding their only child as normal. A misplaced loyalty made them reject the idea that his behaviour might be the forerunner of more violent sex crimes. To examine Song too closely meant questioning their permissiveness in raising him, something they refused to do.

Bright and personable he'd been allowed to participate in their cons from the age of seven. A year later when he'd wanted to drink and gamble his parents hadn't objected. He'd been sexually active from the age of eight, something regarded by his father as robust and manly. What others viewed as sin was for Song a way of life.

It was Arang who insisted that Song would outgrow such quirks when he reached the intellectual and emotional development associated with adulthood. She excused her son's behaviour with the observation that the follies of youth were not necessarily the outrages of manhood. As long as his mother was alive Song had no doubt that he would be loved in spite of himself. She was his all-protecting power.

Without Arang to safeguard him the delicate, sickly Song might not have enjoyed more than a few months of life. By the age of six he'd endured operations to correct a curved spine, remove a bowel obstruction and open his throat so that he could eat. He'd also undergone a hernia operation. His mother had placed his welfare before that of herself and Tae, insisting they spend whatever money was needed to hire the best surgeons. It was she who willingly spent long months at his bedside reading and singing to him as he lay in heavy body casts. And it was she who pushed him into tap-dancing and karate in order to strengthen his delicate physique.

As confidence tricksters, Arang, Tae and Song believed in taking as much as possible and giving nothing in return. But what set Song apart from his parents was a callousness coupled with a determination never to let anything get in the way of what he wanted. If one wanted to be rich, one had to be single-minded and unyielding.

Money was more than just bits of paper allowing you to buy tea kettles and jars of mustard. Money was power. Song felt it, knew it, believed it.

Money would save his father from the corrupt Chun. Money and his mother.

In the second-floor office of Mr Khitan, first vice-president of National Korea Bank, Song sat at the banker's desk and toyed with a lacquered red cigarette box inlaid with sharkskin. The cramped room reeked of chilli and garlic. Earlier Mr Khitan, who frequently took lunch at his desk, had stashed today's repast of raw crab legs and sliced raw fish in a desk drawer. The spicy aromas were making a frail Song increasingly unwell.

His mother and the long-nosed Khitan stood out of earshot at a window overlooking a maze of narrow lanes crowded with boutiques, silk shops, beer halls and restaurants. The boy couldn't hear their conversation, but he saw the banker casually reach out to touch Arang's hair. Gently brushing aside the hand she whispered into Khitan's ear, eliciting a smile from the fidgety, bow-legged banker. Her looks might have faded somewhat, but she still possessed the charm that had made her a desirable *kisaeng*. In Song's eyes she'd never stopped being beautiful.

The boy eyed the packet of fake securities which lay on the large oak desk beside a silver-framed photograph of Khitan's wife, a chunky little woman with a hard, unsmiling face. According to Arang the banker had a fondness for the ladies, a weakness which could be used to cloud his judgement. Who best to trick such a man into advancing money on counterfeit stocks but a still beautiful *kisaeng*?

Tae, who'd met the banker two weeks ago at a racetrack, had immediately directed Arang to approach him on the Peruvian deal. While Khitan had shown interest he'd been slow to commit himself one way or another. With Tae's abduction the banker's approval had suddenly become a matter of life or death.

Confident of her power over men Arang was certain she could bring Khitan around. As she told Song, reasonable men were open to persuasion and she knew how to change the most hard-headed man into a man of reason. Hadn't she been trained from childhood to manoeuvre and arouse the opposite sex? Arang could be anything a man wanted her to be.

A frantic Song looked at a small ceramic clock on Khitan's desk. Twenty to eleven. Less than ninety minutes left to save Tae's life. Closing his eyes the boy clenched both fists and gritted his teeth. Rigid in Khitan's highbacked leather chair, he fought a stabbing pain in his stomach. To keep from crying out he bit his lip. Mustn't give into his fears, not when his mother and father needed him so badly.

When someone touched his shoulder Song cried out. Opening his eyes he saw Arang standing at his side and smiling at Mr Khitan who was just leaving the room. A second later mother and son were alone. Song began to weep. Khitan had turned down the loan. Tae was dead.

Song attempted to stand but Arang's slim hand kept him in the chair. Winking, she placed a finger to her lips in a signal for silence. Heart beating wildly, Song stayed put. To calm himself he dug his nails into the arms of the chair. What was going on? He sensed his mother didn't want to talk. Not just now. He'd have to wait a little longer to learn why they were still in the bank.

They remained behind the desk, neither one speaking or looking at the other as they listened to the tick of Khitan's small desk clock and traffic noises from the crowded street below. When the banker returned to the office he was slightly edgy. Leaning against the door he chewed a corner of his mouth and mopped his brow with a monogrammed handkerchief. Then he briskly crossed the room, removed an envelope from inside his jacket and handed it to Arang. An exhilarated Song leaped from the chair.

The boy watched his mother check the contents of the envelope. He'd never seen so much money. Such a beautiful, beautiful sight. Tae was going to live. Thanks to Arang this nightmare was going to pass and the three of them would be together again. Song had never been more proud of his beautiful mother. He wanted to hug her, to throw himself in her arms and tell her how wonderful she was. Instead he watched as she counted the cash, not once, but twice.

Satisfied, Arang drew Song aside to the window, handed him the envelope and whispered in his ear, repeating earlier instructions. He was to leave the bank immediately and wait for her at a corner teashop. She'd be along shortly. She and Mr Khitan had one more piece of business to clear up then she'd meet Song and they'd go and get Tae.

The boy didn't ask questions, not that it was necessary for his mother to elaborate, but as he ran from the office the thought of his beautiful mother with the lecherous Khitan was enough to make Song want to kill.

In a seedy apartment on the top floor of a high-rise facing Yongsan Garrison, the American Army base, a frightened Song and his mother watched Detective Chun count the bank money. Tae was nowhere to be seen. Song had a premonition that something was wrong.

According to the small, thin-lipped Chun, who sat on a windowsill holding the cash-filled envelope from Arang, Tae wasn't feeling well. He was presently in the back room having a snooze. Resting his eyes, you might say. Mr Tae, the man of the family, wasn't going anywhere. Arang and Song could link up with him after Chun completed counting the money.

Chun's two cronies, a scowling bald man with a sightless right eye and a short, bespectacled man with a narrow face, exchanged half-smiles. Song knew enough about policemen to know these two weren't cops. He also suspected they were up to no good. They were certainly more scary than the amiable con men and petty thieves he'd met through his parents. Chun's thugs were crude and unfeeling in their manner and speech. Both smelled as bad as they looked.

When Song glanced over his shoulder towards the back room Arang tightened her grip on his hand. Feeling a growing sense of dread, the boy moved closer to his mother. They were powerless against Chun and his gorillas. All Song and Arang could do was hand over the money and hope for the best.

Money counted, Chun stroked his chin with a thumb. For several seconds he eyed Song, eventually giving the boy a cold smile. Song inched away, but taking care to remain close to his mother. The look frightened him so much it was all he could do not to run away. Finally Chun looked at Arang then jerked his head towards the back room. Song wondered if his mother had noticed the scowling bald man whispering to his narrow-faced little companion. And did she see them smirk as if only they understood the joke?

Forcing a smile Arang bowed, respectfully thanked Chun for his kindness then led Song down a narrow hallway towards the back room. The boy clung tightly to his mother's hand, knowing they were both scared and that she was keeping up a brave front for his sake. Chun deserved to die for what he'd done to Song's family. Was there any escape from his cruelty?

At the back room door mother and son exchanged looks. Both felt the ghostly silence in the room, one which hit them with heart-stopping force. Song, with his sensitive stomach, was on the verge of throwing up. Why was his father so quiet? Song called out to him.

Silence. At the far end of the hallway Chun and his men stared at the boy and his mother with a quiet malevolence.

Arang opened the door.

She and Song saw a small, nearly empty room with unclean bedding on a filthy floor, litter strewn about and a khaki blanket covering the one window. A single dim bulb shone down from a cracked ceiling and the tepid air smelled of perspiration, beer and stale cigarette smoke. Pigeons could be heard cooing outside on the windowsill.

Song and his mother looked around for Tae.

Arang saw him first and screamed.

Tae's bloodied head, barely visible in the half-light, faced them from a low table near the filthy bedding. The eyes had been gouged out and a rolled-up playing card stuck in each empty socket. A cigar had been jammed into his mouth and his hair parted neatly in the middle. Both of Tae's bare feet had been severed from his legs and now rested on a bloodstained pillow. His body was nowhere to be seen.

Arang, hands covering her face, sagged against the door jamb. Song vomited, dirtying his clothes and the floor. Stomach emptied he stumbled to the window, clutched the blanket to avoid falling and continued to heave. As he clung to the blanket it suddenly came loose and dropped on him, covering the boy from head to waist.

Shrieking, he spun round in a panic, desperate to free himself from the suffocating darkness. When he'd pitched

135

the blanket aside he sank to the floor, weeping uncontrollably as he curled into a foetal position beneath the window. Each new second brought with it a thousand bitter and unbearable sorrows. It was impossible to hold back the tears. For the first time in his young life Song hated being alive.

Holding a cigarette, Chun, followed by his grinning accomplices, strolled into the room and stood behind the grieving Arang. "You hooked yourself up with a zero," he said to her. "He was totally inessential, a vain little man who thought he was better than the rest of us because he'd gone to America."

Chun looked at the burning end of his cigarette. "Mr Hollywood. Mr Fancy Man. I had him dance for us. He started to cry, but he did it. Wet his pants, too. Very frightened man you had. That was his final performance. Since he wouldn't be dancing again I decided he wouldn't need his feet any more."

As his thugs roared with laughter the little detective crouched over the weeping Song. He stroked the boy's head then placed a hand on his buttocks. Finally he took a drag on his cigarette and looked at Arang. "My men have heard about you. Heard you were once a special lady. A highly desired *kisaeng*. I've promised them they could have you. You and the cash in exchange for your freedom."

He touched Song's tear-stained face then rose to face Arang. "If you want to live then please my men. Myself, I have no interest in women."

He glanced down at Song. "I find my joy in other pleasures. Your son and I will go into the next room and leave you with these two gentlemen. Your life depends on how well you do. See if you can surpass your husband's performance. If so, then perhaps you will live. We'll see. Meanwhile the boy and I will entertain ourselves. I see by your face that he's never done anything like this before. This is a special day for us both."

He snapped his fingers at Song. "Here, boy."

A tearful Arang stepped to Chun and touched his arm.

"I beg you, a moment with my son. Please let me talk to him. The shock of his father's death has upset him very much. Let me calm him down, then I shall do your bidding."

Chun nodded. He could afford to be generous for a minute or two. Of course this tramp was going to obey him. When his men finished with her, she was going to die and probably knew it. So why not let her say goodbye to the boy. What harm could it do? The detective thought, the length of this whore's life will depend on her passion. As for Chun's passion, it was little boys and in the tramp's son he'd got his hands on a rather attractive one.

He took a couple of steps back, leaving Arang and Song alone at the window. Arang, bending down, took her weeping son in her arms. "Goodbye," she whispered. "I love you very much. Tae and I, we will always be with you. *Always*. Now listen. Say nothing. Just do as I say. Get to your feet then stand to the left of the window. Say nothing. I will save you."

She kissed his cheek then watched as he slowly rose and followed her instructions. Window at her back Arang then faced Chun. "Please come here and talk to the boy," she said. "He doesn't understand why he must leave me. He's used to obeying men. Please talk to him."

Chun dropped his cigarette on the floor, crushed it underfoot and stepped to the window. Hell, he'd talk to the boy. He'd slap the little bastard's teeth loose and make his ears ring. A kick or two in the ass might also help instil the right attitude. That's all the talk the spoiled little brat would need.

Showing Chun the proper deference a tearful Arang averted her eyes, looking down at the floor. Hand raised the detective reached for Song. The hand was still in the air when a shrieking Arang took one step and clasped Chun firmly in her arms. Then before anyone could interfere she hurled herself through the window, carrying Chun with her, the two plunging fifteen storeys screaming to their deaths.

Cool air instantly rushed into the room, tearing at the

137

clothes and face of a hysterical Song. Pigeons, wings flapping loudly, rose from the sill and flew wildly in all directions. Bits of glass glistened diamondlike on the floor and on Song's shoes. Caught in the sudden gust of wind, old newspapers and food wrappings swirled about the room. On the street below the harsh wail of police sirens blended with the blaring horns of drivers caught in the sudden traffic stoppage.

For long seconds Chun's thugs stared open-mouthed at the broken window. Then the man with the sightless right eye caught his narrow-faced companion by the elbow and slowly began backing out of the room. An instant later both were gone and a dazed Song was left alone to look down at the broken body of the mother who'd just given her life for him.

Saigon, April 1975

It was late evening when Song, gripping a Fabrique Nationale 35DA pistol, followed a blood trail along the corridor of a squat office building on the edge of Cholon, Saigon's Chinatown.

Both he and the burly, thick-lipped Kim Shin who was at his elbow wore the uniform of army captains with the collar insignia of South Korea's crack Tiger Division. Close on their heels were three Korean enlisted men armed with AK-47 assault rifles. The man they were tracking was losing blood with every step.

Outside the building his blood had appeared dry. Inside it had appeared wetter and slightly frothy, indicating the bleeding was getting worse. An excited Song licked his lips. He was closing in on Harrison Random, a dwarfish forty-two-year-old CIA agent who'd stolen something from the American Embassy which Song now wanted for himself. Not for the Korean Embassy, where he and his best friend Shin were attached to Intelligence, but for himself. And without the embassy's knowledge.

Random had taken a set of currency plates capable of producing the most authentic-looking hundred dollar bills imaginable. Song wanted those plates more than a drowning man wanted a breath of air. They represented his lifelong dream of becoming rich. To lose those plates was to continue living in an ugly and unhappy world.

He'd endured life in orphanages and youth reformatories, supported himself by labouring in the stench of slaughter-houses and sewers. He'd been imprisoned for petty theft and forgery. To avoid starving he'd eaten out of garbage cans, slept in doorways, tap-danced in sleazy nightclubs and dealt drugs. Eventually faced with a substantial prison term or joining the army for blackmailing a prominent gay cabinet minister, he'd chosen the army where he quickly intrigued and connived his way to a commission.

As a junior officer he played toady and yes-man to his superiors, ingratiating himself with anyone who could advance his career. Ultimately his grovelling and kowtowing paid off with promotions. It also paid off when senior officers conceded him a small share in payoffs received from military contractors and drug dealers. Money didn't console him for the loss of his beloved parents, but it did comfort him for having to endure what he viewed as a lifetime of senseless suffering. Which was why Song believed that Random's plates would guarantee that his life would become what he'd vowed to make it.

Bills from these plates looked real because the plates themselves were real. They belonged to the US Treasury which had quietly authorised their use by the CIA's Saigon station to fund covert operations in South-East Asia. With a private source of cash the Saigon station was able to proceed with certain dubious actions while bypassing Congressional probers, anti-war groups and a hostile media.

This money didn't have to be justified, accounted for, or listed in a budget. Nor did it leave a paper trail that could be followed. Officially it didn't exist. It was unknown and what was unknown could not be inquired about.

To get these plates Song was willing to kill a dozen Harrison Randoms. His desire to own them was a madness in him, an anguish which left his heart and nerves in a constant state of stress. Possessing them would satisfy his lifelong desire for the power and freedom of wealth. He would return to Korea a wealthy man. The future had come, providing he could find Harrison Random.

With Saigon now surrounded by the North Vietnamese Army and expected to fall within days the CIA station chief had ordered the plates destroyed, along with Intelligence reports, dossiers and stockpiles of cash. Under no circumstances were the plates to fall into Communist hands. And they couldn't be returned to Washington where sticky questions might be raised concerning their function and purpose. *They must be destroyed.*

Working round the clock the CIA incinerated mountains of classified material while evacuating Americans and locals who'd worked with the agency. In the resulting pandemonium Harrison Random was presented with an opportunity to which he finally proved equal. Long envisioning life in Hawaii with a younger wife and a fair amount of beachfront property he'd taken advantage of the chaos prompted by America's hasty retreat and stolen the plates.

He'd then approached Jean-Louis Nicolay, a baby-faced forty-year-old French restaurateur to whom he occasionally sold stolen counterfeit hundreds from these plates. This time Random was playing for higher stakes. Did Jean-Louis, a known black marketeer and dealer in contraband, want to buy the plates which made these exceptional hundreds? Price: five million dollars. Cash only, no haggling. Take it or leave it. Nicolay took it.

He acted on the orders of his silent partner in a trio of massage parlours on Tu Do Street, where "yellow fever" – the lust for Asian women – enticed Americans such as Harrison Random. The silent partner was Park Song and as soon as he heard of the plates they became his obsession. Nicolay, who'd met Song by providing him with young Vietnamese and Eurasian girls to be used in appalling ways, was ordered to accept Random's offer at once. He was to agree to the American's terms then leave the rest to Song who intended to get the plates by conning Random or killing him.

The sting. Song began by making sure Random never saw him and Nicolay together. In dealing with Nicolay he let the American feel he was on familiar ground. A new face might make Random too cautious. He'd be more likely to let his guard down around someone he knew.

On Song's orders Nicolay ingratiated himself further with Random by flattering the American's Intelligence skills which were actually very second-rate. The Frenchman also entertained Random at his beach house on Con Son Island, where beautiful young Vietnamese women with eyes and noses surgically revamped Western style did things in bed that Random's Quaker wife had never heard of.

Nicolay never once thought of betraying Song and keeping the plates for himself. He had only to remember the night at the beach house when he'd peeked into a guest bedroom and seen a naked, blood-smeared Song dancing alone, the head of a twelve-year-old Vietnamese girl dangling from his waist. The girl, a war orphan named Lam, had been purchased by Nicolay from her grandparents for twenty American dollars. He'd known she'd end up dead when Song finished with her. But *this*.

The incident at the beach house had inspired a black fear which would stay in Nicolay's mind for ever. Fear remained the source of his awe and regard for the giggling Song.

Meanwhile Song took a more direct hand in conning Random by baiting the trap with a good faith payment, via Nicolay, of ten thousand dollars. Next, he used skills learned from his mother and forged a bank letter which Nicolay let Random read before taking it back. Appearing on genuine bank stationery mailed from Hong Kong the letter credited Random's account there with five million dollars, minus the initial good faith payment. The difference between Random and Song was that while the American wanted to appear clever, the Korean truly was.

A final meeting between Nicolay and Random to exchange the phony letter of credit for the plates was set up at Nicolay's Chinatown restaurant. At the meeting, Song, hidden in the kitchen, heard Random say, to hell with it, I'm going to do this thing my way. As the CIA agent put it, there'll be a short delay while I get a second opinion.

"I want to wire Hong Kong to make sure you're not just blowing smoke up my ass," Random said to Nicolay. Meaning the CIA agent wanted additional confirmation that five million dollars had indeed been deposited in his numbered account. Until then he was holding on to the plates. To punctuate this last remark he opened his jacket to let Nicolay see the Colt .45 tucked in his belt.

The next move was Song's.

Random's wire would definitely expose the con and Song could then kiss those plates goodbye. To avoid this disaster he would have to take the plates immediately. Backed by four soldiers he rushed from the kitchen, goading Random into action. Ignoring his .45, which he'd never so much as test fired once, the terrified CIA agent escaped through a bathroom window, plates taped to his shaven chest. Seconds later he was on the run with two of Song's bullets in his back.

From Nicolay's restaurant Song and his men pushed through crowds, following Random's blood trail for five blocks to the National Police compound on Vo Tanh Street, where Saigon merged into the Chinese suburb of Cholon. Why, Song wondered, had the American fled into the arms of the Vietnamese secret police? Perhaps Random believed he'd lost Song on Saigon's streets which were teeming with refugees, South Vietnamese army deserters and Viet Cong spies. Perhaps Random merely wanted to hide out until he could summon help.

It really didn't matter since nothing was going to save him. Song intended to kill anyone, Vietnamese or otherwise, who got in his way. Those plates were instant wealth. Song was going to have them even if it meant tearing down the compound brick by brick. Driven by memories of his parents' untimely deaths and his own harsh life, he was ready to claim the plates as payment. This was his divine mission. He must not fail.

Home to Intelligence agencies and the secret police the

National Police compound was a series of low office buildings and barracks connected by a network of alleys. Song and his soldiers saw only two plain-clothes policemen and a handful of secretaries, none of whom wanted to tangle with the Koreans whose army was rated the most savage in Asia. Apparently everyone else at the compound had deserted, no surprise in a city under siege. Three days from now Song and all remaining Korean Embassy personnel were due to be flown out of Saigon on American helicopters. If the normally bustling compound was empty it was to be expected. Looking out for number one was the only thing on everyone's mind these days.

The People's Army of Vietnam, as the North Vietnamese called themselves, had a noose around Saigon's neck. The city was expected to fall within the week. Fearful of capture and execution South Vietnamese police and Intelligence agents had refused to remain at their posts and were deserting by the hundreds. For years they'd tortured and murdered Communists, robbed Communist tax collectors and imprisoned real or suspected Reds in the infamous "tiger cages". Every South Vietnamese secret policeman and Intelligence agent had good reason to fade from sight.

Some hoped to catch an American flight out of Tan Son Nhut Airport or be evacuated by helicopter to an American aircraft carrier offshore. The more desperate had fled to the harbour hoping to bribe their way onto the first boat or barge leaving Saigon. Song had seen police throw away uniforms and weapons in an attempt to blend in with the city's civilian population. The Communists were known for thoroughly punishing their enemies, for washing out blood with blood.

Song had even heard of policemen taking special pains not to leave Saigon empty-handed. On the pretext of collecting funds for a last ditch defence of the city they were now looting banks, jewellery stores, wealthy homes and gold shops. Opportunity made for theft. To refuse such an opportunity was to fail for ever. No one understood this better than Song.

Until now fear of the police had kept thieves away from the almost empty compound. Song, however, knew it was only a matter of time before deserters, robbers, refugees and bands of murderous veterans appeared to begin carting off everything that wasn't nailed down. He had to find the plates as quickly as possible.

In the National Police compound Song stood in the doorway of a large, empty office which presumably belonged to a high-ranking officer. Who else but an important man would have rated such thick carpeting and a corner bar stocked with bottles of cognac, Scotch and Pernod. Then there was the huge desk which sported a lamp, appointments diary, office intercom, telephone, pocket calculator and rotary file. The office also had enough space for a small conference table and chairs. Only the wall safe indicated something was wrong. It was open and bare.

The blood trail had led here. Apparently Random had collapsed in the doorway then got to his feet somehow and continued along the corridor. Song lifted one hand in a silent signal to Kim Shin and the enlisted men. *Maintain silence. And find the American.*

Leading the way Song came to a large, empty area that had been partitioned into more than a dozen cubicles. More indications of an abrupt departure. Desk drawers had been pulled out, card cabinets upended, stationery cabinets and coat racks overturned. Sheets of paper were still in typewriters and the soil around house plants was hard and dry. On data display terminals empty screens continued to flicker brightly. The cubicles smelled of fear and despair.

A sudden noise to his right caused Song to spin around, ready to fire until he realised he was aiming at a ringing telephone. The incident frightened him, causing a shortness of breath which made him sway a bit. A sharp pain in his stomach forced him to close his eyes and grit his teeth. Seconds later he opened his eyes and drew himself up straight in a manner befitting an officer. Still, it was a while before he was calm enough to order a search of every cubicle.

144

A search of the cubicles yielded nothing. Song thought, more time wasted. More time for Random to hide elsewhere in the building. It was an impatient Song who picked up the blood trail near a rear cubicle, the trail turning right into a fluorescent-lit grey corridor. Without waiting for the others he took off.

His men caught up with him at the end of the corridor where he was examining a glass-panelled door leading to a staircase. He was looking for wires which might indicate the existence of booby traps. Something signalling that a grenade might have been fastened to a nearby tripwire; that a shotgun had been wired to fire when the door opened; something to suggest that when he opened the door the ceiling was rigged to collapse and bury him.

The Viet Cong used eight hundred tons of explosives a month in booby traps, all taken from American bombs and artillery shells that had failed to explode. Song found it ironic that the Americans should braid the rope used to hang them. As for the retreating South Vietnamese, they were too fixed on saving their own skins to think of guerilla tactics. Since Random had gone through this door without setting off a bang Song suspected the area was secure.

Without touching the door he peered through the glass at a rusted metal staircase leading down one flight to a steel door. Behind the steel door was a corridor lined with small offices and supply rooms. It also contained rest rooms, a small cafeteria and most important of all, two computer rooms. In the course of his duties Song occasionally visited the computer rooms to exchange Intelligence with the South Vietnamese. He'd passed Random in the corridor a few times but neither had spoken to the other. Song suspected Random saw him as just another gook who should have been ironing shirts or playing ping pong. The Korean, in turn, viewed the CIA agent as thickheaded and dull.

Nor was Song any more impressed with South Vietnamese Intelligence which he found to be a reflection of the Vietnamese people themselves, meaning it was incompetent, dishonest and self-serving. The South Vietnamese government was too crooked ever to be straightened out. Without American support it would have collapsed years ago. Even with American money and advisers the South had commanded very little loyalty outside Saigon. It had been a case of the rooster wielding great influence over his own dunghill and nowhere else.

As for the American Army it had been on the verge of collapse for months, suffering from massive desertions, drugs, and the systematic killing of hundreds of officers by their own men. One needn't be a military genius to conclude that such an army was self-defeating and of no use to anyone save whores, black marketeers and dope dealers. Song had been one of several Korean Intelligence agents who'd worked on reports concluding that the United States had not only lost the war but its soul. These reports had also dealt with the negative effects of this disastrous adventure on the American people as a whole. Korea intended to rely heavily on this data in future economic and military arrangements with the United States.

At the door leading downstairs Song ordered the enlisted men through first. Random hadn't set off any explosion but why take chances. Should the door just happen to be booby-trapped then let someone else's arms and legs be blown off. Just because Song wanted the plates didn't mean he had to be a fool. One needed discretion as well as judgement.

Rifles ready, the three enlisted men passed safely through the doorway. By the time Song and Kim Shin stepped onto the landing behind them a sergeant had picked up the blood trail on the narrow rusted iron staircase leading one flight down to the corridor. Eyes on the steel door, Song again signalled for quiet, stepped onto the staircase and took the lead. The idea of owning the plates was so electrifying that he felt like dancing.

Reaching the steel door he decided to go in first. Booby traps were no longer on his mind. The prize waiting in the corridor was his, to be claimed by him and him alone. He had no intention of losing it. He gripped the doorknob, took a deep breath then slowly pushed it open.

Holding his breath he stepped into the quiet, humid corridor. The blood, still fresh and clearly visible, led halfway down the empty hall and into a computer room on the left side. Here an open door allowed Song to hear men speaking in Vietnamese. He also smelled cigarette smoke and heard a Vietnamese male, to whom English was not a first language, singing along phonetically and off-key with Aretha Franklin's "Respect". Song wrinkled his nose in disgust. With the exception of the great black performer James Brown, whom he admired more for his dancing than his singing, Song detested pop music, considering it commonplace, uninspired and vulgar.

Perspiring heavily he walked quietly alongside the blood on the stone corridor floor. Behind him the enlisted men peeked into empty rooms lining the passageway, a safety precaution born of years of caution. At the computer room Song stopped out of sight of the doorway and whispered to Kim Shin. *No witnesses were to be left behind. No one must know what happened to the plates.* Kim Shin nodded in agreement.

Song raised his pistol overhead, holding it up for the men to see. A count of three, then he brought his arm down sharply and leaped through the doorway.

He rushed into a grey, windowless room bursting with computers, terminals, printers, card-readers and disk control units. Song's men quickly trained their weapons on four Vietnamese males, two of whom were standing in front of a central processing unit. One had been singing along with a cassette player at his feet. Frightened by the sudden appearance of the Koreans he accidentally kicked over the cassette which continued to play. A third who'd been walking towards a magnetic tape controller, was so taken by surprise that he stopped in the act of lighting a cigarette, allowing a match to singe his fingers.

The fourth man, whom Song recognised as a lieutenant in the secret police, had just placed the last of four suitcases in front of a printer at the far wall. He started to protest but was shouted down by the Koreans. In these chaotic times one didn't argue with armed men who were pointing guns at you. The lieutenant stopped talking.

Random. Glassy-eyed and open-mouthed he sat on the floor, back against a disk control unit. Beside him a sad-faced young Eurasian woman in bell-bottom jeans and tie-dyed blouse knelt holding his hand. Behind them the Koreans shouted and cursed as they used rifle butts to force the four Vietnamese males to their knees.

Kicking aside empty Coca-Cola cans and old Vietnamese newspapers Song rushed over to Random, yanked the .45 from his belt and slid it across the black linoleum floor towards the Koreans. Then after tossing the woman's purse aside he jammed his pistol under Random's chin. So excited was Song that he could barely get the words out. "The plates," he said. "Where are they?"

As a silent Random stared at the ceiling with unseeing eyes the Eurasian woman pointed towards a nearby folded Vietnamese newspaper dotted with bloody fingerprints. Song reached down for it with a shaking hand. Slowly, almost reverently he unfolded the newspaper. The plates were inside. Two thin pieces of metal slightly larger than an actual hundred dollar bill. *And they were his.*

Giddy with elation he refolded the newspaper, gripped it tightly and stood up. Suddenly he started to giggle. The biggest con of all and he'd pulled it off. If only his mother and father had lived to see this day. Seconds later he began to do a time-step, pistol in one hand, plates in the other. Except for his booted feet on the linoleum and the whir of the computer motors the room was silent. Song was ecstatic and didn't give a damn who knew it.

Forget the gaping enlisted men. And to hell with the frightened Eurasian woman who stared at Song as though he were a madman. They were nonentities, human zeros. He had the plates. The happiness which had eluded him for so long was now his. It was a feeling he wanted to cling to for ever. Across the room a smiling Kim Shin, understanding the meaning of this moment to his friend, hoisted his own pistol in triumph.

Song stopped dancing and smiled at the woman. "Your name?" he said.

She'd turned back to Random and now held him in her arms, her face hidden by shoulder-length black hair. "Constanze Herail," she said in French accented English. "I am his fiancée."

"A middle-aged man's plaything is more like it. What were you and these policemen doing here?"

She turned her tear-stained face to Song. "He was going to take me to Hawaii. We planned to get married there and live by the ocean."

Miss Herail's account of a happy future struck Song as fiction and not the most original fiction at that. Vietnamese and Eurasian women were always being hoodwinked by American soldiers out for a bit of nookie. Still a desperate Harrison Random had turned to Miss Herail as the nearest point of refuge. Who else was he going to press into service? Not the American Embassy, surely. A giggling Song thought, I've kicked away the ladder and Mr Random's feet have now been left dangling.

Feeling increasingly confident he eyed the woman more closely. She appeared to be in her early twenties with a cute little bottom and silicon-enlarged breasts to please tit-happy Americans.

Miss Herail's tears failed to move Song. He saw her snivelling as self-pity, not profound grief. Random had been her ticket out of Saigon, a ticket which had now been cancelled. Unless Miss Herail found another exit she'd end up in a Communist reeducation camp, cleaning toilets and chopping down trees when not listening to lengthy Marxist lectures and being abused by guards.

Song leaned in for a closer peek at Miss Herail or rather at the photo ID pinned to her blouse. She was employed at the National Police compound. Surely, it would have been more normal for her and these four to run off like their spineless co-workers. Had Random told them about the plates? Song sensed there was more going on here than met the eye.

His alert gaze took in the four suitcases and the Vietnamese now kneeling with hands locked behind their heads. They'd been armed with American M-16s and .45 automatics which Song's men had confiscated and placed atop a printer. Since the four Vietnamese had the arrogance of authority Song assumed they were policemen or Intelligence agents. As for Miss Herail she was a secretary or perhaps a clerical worker. It bothered him that these five were still here when everyone else had flown the coop.

He said to Miss Herail, "What sort of work do you do for the National Police?"

She stroked Random's forehead with long fingers tipped in orange nail polish. The American's eyes were closed, his breathing laboured. "He's dying," she said.

Grabbing a handful of her hair Song yanked back hard. "*What is your job?*"

Anxious to relieve the pain she spat out the words. "Records. I work with computer records."

"And these gentlemen with you, what do they do besides travel around with suitcases?"

"Please, you're hurting me. They're policemen. They paid me to help them."

"Help them do what?"

"Gather tapes from the machines." Whimpering, she tugged at Song's hands but failed to move them. Because she was experiencing pain, she suddenly appeared more beautiful in his eyes. Song almost laughed out loud. Imagine being attracted to someone this old. Had she not been in pain, he wouldn't have looked at her twice. It amused him to learn how easily passion could make its way into one's mind.

He released his grip on the sobbing woman's hair, letting her slump to the floor. Song had the picture now. The policemen had come to the computer room to steal files. Not knowing how to work the computers they'd brought along Miss Big Tits to do that for them, to locate tapes and remove information from computers without destroying it. If Song was right those four suitcases across the room were crammed full of tapes, dossiers and other information.

As Aretha Franklin sang "Natural Woman", Song tapped his thigh with the folded newspaper and did some fast thinking. With the war's end just days away the computer room had become a gold mine. If Song hadn't been so occupied with the plates he'd have realised this a lot sooner. And done what these policemen were trying to do.

The Special Police and the CIO, South Vietnam's Central Intelligence Organisation kept files on captured Communists who'd turned informer, collaborator or defector. The files also held the names of spies within Viet Cong and Northern forces, along with those Vietnamese agents the Americans hoped to leave in place after the evacuation. To Communists these were the names of traitors who'd tortured, imprisoned and assassinated their comrades.

Which was why Song knew that the People's Army would empty its purse, if necessary, to buy these files. He did not expect the victors to relinquish their opportunity to be cruel. Victors never did. When you won a war, everything you did was right.

The four policemen kneeling in front of Song's men had to know the value of this information. Otherwise why return to the compound when they could have been fleeing the country? From experience Song knew that in a crisis the South Vietnamese were more likely to fly away than stick it out. That being true, what on earth would keep any sane Intelligence agent or policeman in Saigon at a time like this? For years the South Vietnamese Army had been thinking with its feet. Why stop now?

Unless you were greedy and saw a chance to get rich.

Song's guess: the four policemen had already made a deal to sell these files to the Communists. To protect those listed in the files they should have been destroyed days ago. But the timid doves among South Vietnamese, being devoutly concerned with their own survival, had run off and left the files intact. No surprise. If Song had learned one thing from army service it was that only cowards survived a war. Call it cowardice or half-bravery – fleeing the scene was the one sure way to stay alive.

Meanwhile, fate had presented him with a second opportunity to grow rich. He would take the files and sell them to the Communists himself. Sell them for as much as he could gouge from the comrades. Every man had his day and today belonged to Song. If he didn't make the most of this stroke of luck, he was a fool. And being a fool was worse than death.

Everything happened in threes. As a boy he'd lost his mother, father and his innocence in one terrible day. Today he'd acquired the plates, had valuable files practically handed to him and received a commitment from the shrewd Kim Shin to assist in Song's counterfeiting. After years of struggle fortune had finally fallen into Song's lap. For the first time in his life he felt lucky. And with that feeling came the conviction that he could now have everything.

Walking to the far wall Song placed the folded newspaper on top of the first suitcase then strutted back to stand in front of the policemen. These weren't your usual Saigon cowboys, the slickly dressed draft dodgers or deserters in dark glasses who rode around on motorscooters and earned money by pimping or petty theft. These were tough guys who were used to pushing people around and who'd sell their mothers for a spoonful of rice.

The one Song knew, Lieutenant Dau, was a short, cold-eyed thirty-year-old with a small, gold crucifix hanging from his neck. Song had found him to be pig-headed and obstinate, not interested in any point of view but his own. Dau was too surly and ill-behaved to win friends which was why he'd never been promoted any higher.

Song hadn't worked with him because Dau was a punisher rather than an Intelligence gatherer. As an interrogator in the secret police he prided himself on breaking, by any means possible, those important Viet Cong prisoners and sympathisers who'd proved too tough for other interrogators. Dau was always brought in at the end of the game. The Americans had named him "Relief Pitcher".

Song stepped in front of the boorish lieutenant. "To whom are you selling these files?"

An enraged Dau stared off into the distance, refusing to look at the Korean. "You have no right to hold us at gunpoint. We're here in a professional capacity and it doesn't concern you. If you know what's good for you, you'll stop this play-acting and let us go about our business."

Song giggled. "Aren't you the dedicated one. Steadfast and true under fire. All rats have left the sinking ship save you. Truly commendable. What you've come here to do, my friend, has nothing to do with any *official capacity*. I'll ask you once more. To whom are you selling these files?"

An angry Dau could control himself no longer. Snapping his head forward he discharged a gob of saliva on Song's neatly pressed trousers, hitting the Korean just above the left knee.

In the tense silence which followed Song looked down at the offending stain and shook his head sadly. Then he shot Dau through the left eye.

One step to the right and Song was in front of the next Vietnamese. "The name of your buyer?" he said.

Corporal Manny Decker, M-16 in hand, stood on a landing in the main building of Saigon's National Police compound, staring at the blood trail.

Under his flak jacket he was sweating like a pig. A year in Saigon and he still hadn't got used to the heat. The .45 on his hip weighed a ton and he was starving, not having eaten since lunch. At the moment, however, what bugged Decker most was the blood.

It led down a rusted iron staircase, through an open doorway and into a grey corridor. Decker and Marines Ivan La Porte and Maxey Twentyman, heavily armed and in civilian clothes, were escorting CIA agent Brian Schow to a computer room in the corridor ahead. The Marines were to assist Schow in destroying the computerised records of some eight to ten thousand Vietnamese who'd worked with the South Vietnamese government and the Americans during the war.

The war was lost. Saigon was surrounded by a huge Communist force whose tanks were a mile away from the city and inching closer every hour. America had spent billions of dollars to fight this war, killed nearly a million Vietnamese and suffered over fifty thousand dead.

But in the end it had been defeated by an army in black pyjamas, scruffy sandals cut from old rubber tyres and which was tough enough to march miles a day on a handful of rice washed down with ditch water. An army where villages honoured its men with funeral services before they headed south along the Ho Chi Min trail to fight. By April 1975 this unlikely army had forced America and its Vietnamese colleagues into a hurried and poorly organised retreat from South-East Asia. High tech Goliath had been defeated by low tech David.

First priority on American helicopter flights from Saigon to offshore aircraft carriers went to Americans and their families, Vietnamese VIPs and foreign embassy personnel. This left thousands of South Vietnamese to fend for themselves, to bribe, beg or steal the precious exit visas entitling them to a helicopter seat and possible passage to America.

Of those who couldn't be flown out because their evacuation had been left too late, the ones at highest risk were Communists who'd gone over to the CIA and South Vietnam's Special Police. These were the people described by Schow as a bunch of pencil dicks who couldn't pick fly shit out of black pepper but shouldn't be hung out to dry.

Schow was a plump thirty-five-year-old Californian whose family owned an alligator farm in Orange County and who was known for entertaining at CIA parties by spinning plates on long sticks while whistling "The Sabre Dance". He'd been picked to destroy the files because he'd been running an informant network of important Vietnamese contacts and knew what to look for in the computer room.

Decker had escorted him on past hush-hush jobs and found him something of a busybody who meant well but wasn't too bright. Like many agents Schow was in Intelligence because he didn't want to be in combat. There was less danger in shuffling papers at your desk than in getting hit between the legs by a VC rocket.

Piece of cake, said Schow of their mission in the abandoned

National Police compound. We go in, he told Decker, destroy anything that could identify the locals on our team, then get out. "We owe the gooks that much," he said. "The Commies get those files and everybody listed in them has run his last race. Not to worry, guy. This one's a piece of cake. You heard it here first."

But Decker, a Marine security guard at the American Embassy, had his own thoughts on the matter. The blood in the corridor made him wonder if this mission was going to be the one which got him sent home in a body bag. For openers, whose blood was it? And was the wounded party dead or merely lying in wait somewhere, ready to shoot the first face that turned the corner? Seventy-two hours from now Decker expected to be evacuated from Saigon. He damned sure didn't want to return to the world having joined the body count.

Last week South Vietnam President Thieu had resigned and left the country. At the American Embassy and the CIA compound the air was grey with ashes as incinerators burned classified material round the clock. For South Vietnam it was the end of the line. For Decker it was a chance to go home alive, providing he survived the next three days.

La Porte and Twentyman, also Marine security guards, felt just as strongly about leaving Nam in one piece. Maxey Twentyman, a tall twenty-three-year-old Georgia farmboy who was called Buf, "big ugly fucker", after the nickname of the B-52 bomber, was adamant about not dying over here. As he told Decker, "If I get wasted make sure they send my redneck ass back to Macon County. Don't let them bury me in no country where you can blindfold the people with dental floss."

La Porte didn't want to talk about dying. Talking brought it on, he said. Instead he brooded about dying. He was a slim, handsome Puerto Rican from Brooklyn who'd joined the Marines the same time as Decker but ended up taking his basic training in California. Six months after La Porte and Decker arrived in Nam, La Porte's wife Lucette had given birth to Felix Raymond La Porte, Junior in Brooklyn

Hospital. The closer he came to leaving Nam the more La Porte worried about dying before seeing his wife and son. No more starting the day with the old cry – *the only way to go was home.* A superstitious La Porte had stopped talking about home altogether.

As civilians he and Decker had met at New York karate tournaments where they'd competed as middleweights. La Porte had guts and fairly quick hands, but he couldn't match Decker's hand speed and ability to put together combinations. In three matches against each other Decker had easily defeated La Porte every time.

After basic training both men had turned up at Marine Security Guard School at Quantico, Virginia, each glad to see a familiar face. In those days La Porte had been gung ho, one highly motivated Marine, crazy for the Corps and hot to be a "mustang", an enlisted man who becomes an officer. Decker had nicknamed him F.L., short for Fearless Leader. La Porte was happy in the Corps. Cut open his heart, and you'd find the inside painted Marine green.

Decker'd had one happy moment above all in the Corps and he owed much of it to Gail. She, not his parents, had flown down from New York to Parris Island, South Carolina to share the proudest day of his life, his graduation from Marine boot camp. The ceremony marked the end of eleven weeks of recruit training which had been as sadistic as drill instructors could make it short of flat out killing you.

Goodbye to almost three months of back-breaking, ball-busting hell. Basic training over, drill instructors no longer called you slime, shithead, Communist faggot, or that lowest form of life, civilian. On Graduation Day they called you Marine, something they'd refused to do for almost three months. Marine meant you were unequalled on God's earth.

On the parade ground, in front of a reviewing stand and bleachers packed with relatives and friends, the honour men from each platoon were announced. These were the top trainees, super-Marines of the future. While other graduating recruits wore khaki, honour men were outfitted in Dress Blues, a gift from the Marine Corps Association. Decker had been his platoon's honour man. It was something he'd busted his buns to get.

Before joining the Corps he'd made *nidan*, second Dan black belt in karate, getting the rank by spilling his blood and other people's. He'd racked up more than thirty trophies in competition against the best fighters in the country, taking on all comers, in the process losing a few teeth and suffering his share of broken bones. It had been enough for Decker to do one thing well and that thing had been karate.

Confidence had given him energy and he'd had confidence to spare. Decker believed he could beat anybody. He was king of the hill and if he swaggered through the streets in those days, who could blame him. But nothing had matched the emotion he'd felt when under a fiery sun he'd stood on the parade field with his company and heard his name called as a platoon honour man and he'd stepped forward as a Marine for the first time. The base band had played the Marine Hymn and "Auld Lang Syne". He'd blinked away tears and there'd been a catch in his throat and he'd never loved Gail more.

She'd known how important this day had been to him. When the Manhattan restaurant where she worked wouldn't give her time off from her waitressing job she'd quit and flown to South Carolina to be with him. For Decker there'd never be another time when he'd feel so wholly satisfied with his life.

His mother, a so-so singer who'd never risen above Broadway understudy, and his stepfather, a talent agent obsessed with his glamorous clients, hadn't even considered making the trip. They regarded him as little more than a nuisance. The lives of his ferociously ambitious parents centred round show business. Decker wasn't in show business, which made him a non-person.

Observing his parents in action provided Decker with a first-hand look at how lies, trickery, and other forms of chicanery could be used to get your way. There were no more dangerous people in the world than cunning people. The lesson wasn't lost on him.

His natural father, a veteran of the Second World War, had been recalled when the Korean War broke out and died when a North Korean pulled the pin on a grenade, killing them both. Natural father aside, Decker eventually realised that his family were people he'd never have associated with if he didn't have to. They'd provided him with no emotional security and he'd grown up being on guard against them. Family life was Decker's first contact with the world's dark side.

The one person he'd trusted had been Ran Dobson, the skinny Marine recruiting sergeant from Oklahoma who'd been stationed in New York. Ran, no pretty boy, had been fond of saying that the man upstairs had created him ugly then hit him in the face with a shovel. He'd been Decker's first karate instructor and his only friend, teaching him to conquer his loneliness by becoming good at something.

It was Ran who in five years turned him from a frightened adolescent into a disciplined fighter with the most important weapon of all, an unbendable will. Ran had been the reason Decker had joined the Corps. One of his most treasured possessions was Ran's leather-covered swagger stick which he'd given Decker before flying to a new assignment in Vietnam where he was to die, a victim of "friendly fire".

Ran's death left an empty space in Decker's heart that would never be filled.

After Parris Island Decker was scheduled for Marine Security Guard School where outstanding enlisted men were trained to guard American embassies and consulates. But first he had the two weeks' leave granted new Marines. He spent every day of that leave with Gail in a Hell's Kitchen walk-up she shared with two girls who considerately found somewhere else to stay during that time. He called his mother only because Gail said to, but he avoided the family apartment, a Fifth Avenue duplex in the Village.

His mother telephoned once to say that she and his stepfather were moving to a house in Westchester with a pool, tennis court and two hundred-year-old oak tree. Decker said he'd write and he did, eventually sending two letters his first month in Saigon. Both went unanswered. Gail, meanwhile, wrote him over twenty letters a month. If she was thousands of miles away from Decker, she had let him know that her heart was with him every second.

But Vietnam had changed Decker and those changes weren't going to improve his relationship with Gail. He'd killed for the first time, beginning a year ago when he'd helped beat back a Viet Cong attempt to infiltrate embassy grounds and more recently while bodyguarding the American ambassador on a trip to inspect evacuation proceedings at Tan Son Nhut Airport. Killing had uncovered Decker's dark side, something he was afraid to bring home to Gail.

Over here he'd seen things that couldn't be described. How could he put into words what it was like to go to Graves Registration – the morgue – and see dead bodies of naked GIs sitting in fibreglass chairs, faces stitched after being blown apart, faces more hideous than any horror film ever made.

And there was the Saigon Hospital visit two months ago when he'd gone to see Kevin Lee. Brother K. was a cool black dude from New Jersey who at sixteen had lied his way into the Corps to become the youngest Marine in Decker's Parris Island class. He was a music freak who dreamed of starting his own record company. Gonna be the next Berry Gordy, he said, but better looking, Jack.

During a Cong rocket attack on the airport Kevin had suffered back and leg wounds. However, his recovery was expected to be normal, with little after effects from his injuries. Which is why Decker was stunned when a bulky, full-faced American nurse, who'd been working three days without a break, wearily said he couldn't see Private Kevin Lee because Private Kevin Lee had died only minutes ago. Or rather he'd been murdered.

A crazed, wounded Viet Cong prisoner had left his own bed, stolen a fork and gouged out the sleeping Kevin's throat. MPs had shot the Cong, but it had come too late to do Kevin Lee any good. Kevin Lee had died of a bad paper cut, as they say.

And there was the nine-year-old Vietnamese girl with no legs, a sweet little thing who'd put forth her best effort to kill Decker and nearly succeeded. It happened one night four months ago when Decker, La Porte and Buf had left a bar near the CIA compound. Decker and Buf had been reluctant to leave because the bar was one of the few joints in Saigon where for sure you could meet some round-eyed tail-white women such as nurses, embassy personnel and US dependants. But the homesick La Porte, anxious to make an overseas Christmas call to his family, had insisted Decker and Buf accompany him. It would give them something to do besides getting juiced and looking at broads who'd rather do the wild thing with officers than enlisted men.

As they were walking out of the bar in rolled the legless girl on a small platform, holding a battered tin cup of faded flowers for sale and sporting a heart-warming smile on her little round face. La Porte bought two flowers, saying they were for his Lucette and Felix. Decker said what the hell, and bought one each for himself and Buf. He'd read somewhere that flowers were the language of love. La Porte loved Lucette and little Felix. Question was, did Decker still love Gail?

A block away from the bar Buf, the drunkest of the three, proclaimed at the top of his lungs that he'd rather smear honey on his bare ass and sit on a bee hive than spend another day in this shithole called Nam. Then he playfully threw an arm around the necks of Decker and La Porte, drew them close in a semi-painful grip, and said that he, Maxey Byron Reynolds Twentyman, was a bona fide, certified, verified meteorologist, meaning he could look at a girl and tell *whether*. That's when they heard the explosion.

And the screams. Turning quickly, they saw one big fireball where the bar used to be. Later they learned that the legless girl's platform had been wired with plastique. *Hey GI, my flowers come with a C-4 surprise.* The Viet Cong had put her up to it. She'd killed herself and taken out twelve Americans as well. When La Porte said, I saved you guys, me and my family, he got no argument from a shaken Decker. None at all.

But that night and for nights to come the legless girl came alive for Decker. In his dreams the explosion happened over and over, with the screams of the dying tearing at his brain and the hellish heat of the burning building reaching out for

160

him. He saw his body being shredded by the C-4, saw pieces of his bloodied bones flying in all directions and felt the flames melting his eyeballs, turning him blind, and in a cold sweat he would wake up screaming. What made it worse was knowing that he was terrorising himself and couldn't stop.

Following the blood trail.

In the corridor a silent Decker, flanked by La Porte and Buf, stood a dozen yards or so from the computer room. The blood had dripped its way straight to the computer room with no stops in between. The door was open and what was worrying Decker were the voices coming from the room. Until he knew who they were, it was safeties off and look alive.

He heard male voices but couldn't make out what they were saying. He also heard the voice of "the Queen" herself, Aretha, getting down and dirty.

While Schow was nominally in charge of the detail, when things got hairy Decker would be calling the shots. The Marines knew it and so did Schow. No problem there. In a crisis Schow preferred that someone else make the hard decisions. Schow was so unsure of himself, Buf said, he's probably got twelve-year-old kids he ain't named yet.

A fourth Marine, Private Al Jellicki, had also been assigned to the detail. At the moment he was in front of the building protecting their car, a second-hand Peugeot, from armed Vietnamese deserters who were grabbing everything that wasn't nailed down. Decker touched the hand radio hanging from his belt and thought about sending for Jellicki, the beefy twenty-two-year-old poker expert whose Saigon winnings were said to exceed fifty thousand dollars.

La Porte could change places with him. Outside, La Porte might worry less. Then again, maybe he wouldn't.

Decker looked at the Puerto Rican who appeared calm enough. And seemed to know what Decker was thinking because he whispered, "I'll be fine, bro'. Let's just do it then get the fuck out of here and start packing."

Behind them Buf, a shotgun in his large hands, whispered, "Let's rock and roll."

Decker motioned an uneasy Schow to move further behind

the Marines and smiled when the CIA agent gingerly stepped round the blood. Schow, who wore a flak vest under a summer gabardine jacket, carried two .38s, one in each jacket pocket. When Decker told him to hold the guns in his hands, the CIA agent looked as if he was ready to shit in his pants.

Marines through the doorway first. No argument from Schow, who was more than happy to stay outside until he was given the all clear. This assignment wasn't a piece of cake any more. Not with blood on the floor.

They inched towards the doorway in silence; Decker was the point man. La Porte and Buf were spread out behind him, with everyone taking care to avoid anything on the floor that might make a sound. Near the computer room door, Decker halted and began his hand signals. He'd go through first, then Buf and La Porte.

Decker, heart beating frantically, exhaled. Using the palm of one hand he wiped sweat from his forehead then dried the hand on his jeans. He tried to push the dreams from his mind.

Showtime.

He charged through the door, dived to his right and came up in a crouch behind a metal desk, M-16 to his shoulder and pointing across the room, eyes taking in everything at once. He saw the Korean soldiers. Saw the Vietnamese kneeling with hands behind their heads. Saw two Vietnamese lying on the floor. Forget them. Decker had been in Nam long enough to recognise the eerie stillness and lifeless grace that went with being deceased. He could also smell them clear across the room and see the tell-tale brown stain in their pants. The second you died your sphincter muscles loosened and you crapped in your pants.

Then there was the man sitting on the floor, back against a computer, a woman hovering over him. Decker couldn't see his face; the woman had her arms around him, sobbing as she slowly rocked back and forth. But Decker could see the man's hands. They were white, making him American or European.

"Freeze! Nobody move! Guns on the floor. Now!"

The Koreans froze. Two uniformed soldiers, their backs to

Decker, cautiously looked over their shoulders. Two officers faced him. None of the Koreans panicked, none of them did anything impulsive. They simply stood in place, eyeballing Decker as though he were a toy soldier and they were the real thing. They also didn't drop their guns. Decker didn't like that.

Three Korean enlisted men and two officers, all with enough firepower to make things unpleasant. Decker recognised the officers as Korean G-2, Intelligence, who often put in an appearance at the American Embassy and CIA compound for Intelligence briefings. Neither was a nice guy.

One was Captain Kim Shin, a stocky dude with a volatile temper and a reputation for throwing his rank around. The other was Captain Park Song, the man everybody called Laughing Boy because of his stupid giggling. Song was big on buying stuff from the American PX, especially video cassettes of movie musicals. Decker had heard some weird shit about him and young girls.

Best buddies, Song and Shin were attached to the Republic of Korea's crack Tiger Division which had fought alongside American and South Vietnamese troops during the war. So vicious were the Koreans that whenever possible the North Vietnamese had avoided taking them on. Faced with the prospect of fighting ROKs the NVA often decided that discretion was the better part of valour.

Korean troops had long since left the country. Those few still around were attached to their Saigon Embassy and working with the remaining American advisers. In their day ROKs had been the most feared soldiers in Nam and as tough on their South Vietnamese hosts as they were on the Viet Cong and North Vietnamese Army.

But for the best karate workout in Saigon, you had to go to them. Decker was a Japanese stylist but training with Koreans had kept him on his toes. They were aggressive, in shape and forced you to concentrate every second. They were tough fighters, cold-blooded, and easily provoked. To disagree with them on anything – technique, strategy, conditioning – was a waste of time.

Having seen Song work out a few times Decker had been impressed, especially with his high kicks. The problem with Song was, he could dish it out but he couldn't take it. Hit him once, even accidentally, and he'd clean the floor with you. It was bully boy stuff, the act of a spoiled child who constantly had to have his way.

He'd avoided working out with Decker. The coolness between the two had started with Song being afraid of him, then deciding he just didn't like having an American in the training hall. The relationship had really gone downhill after Decker had learned how Song had set him up for a bad beating.

Decker had more than held his own in any competition against the Koreans. He'd managed to win the respect of a few Koreans who admired his fighting spirit. They were in the minority, however. Most Koreans resented Westerners training with them, especially one as good as Decker. Song belonged to the hostile brigade.

Among many things Decker had learned in the martial arts was that Asians could be racists. Some Asian instructors would keep certain techniques to themselves, teaching non-Asians only so much then no more. Others gave you a hard time until you packed it in and quit.

Deep down most Asian instructors believed Westerners to be physically and mentally incapable of learning the martial arts no matter how long they trained. Decker had learned to be wide-awake around those Asians who detested Westerners enough to discourage them with dirty tricks.

Song may have been forced to smile at Westerners during Intelligence briefings, but he didn't have to smile at them during karate training. He didn't smile at Decker who'd made the mistake of being good at something that belonged to Asians. He had to be put in his place.

Six months ago during a practice session Song urged a Korean fighter to challenge Decker in a so-called friendly sparring. Given the bad vibes between Decker and Laughing Boy it came as no surprise when the fighter, a strong, narrow-faced prick, went upside Decker's head for real.

For Decker, there was a lot at stake in this fight. His pride, the honour of the Corps, and last but by no means least, his ass. Back down, and he wouldn't be able to show his face in Saigon. He'd be better off joining the five thousand GI deserters hiding out with Vietnamese refugees on the edge of the city, all of them living in tents or in shacks made from wood and flattened Coca-Cola cans.

So the fight between Decker and Hatchet Face went on as scheduled. Hatchet Face gave him two cracked ribs, a fat lip and a fractured cheek bone before Decker dropped him screaming to his knees with two kidney punches then knocked him cold with a roundhouse kick to the head. When a bleeding and very belligerent Decker looked around for Laughing Boy, the Korean had split.

The next day Decker went searching for Song with payback in mind. But the Korean didn't show at the training hall or the embassy, not that day nor for a few days afterwards. With news of the fight making the rounds of the American community it remained for Paul Jason Meeks, an anal retentive on the ambassador's staff, to call Decker in for a verbal reaming.

The gravel-voice, square-built Meeks, who parted his hair above the left ear then combed it across a balding pate, laid down the law. Decker was a Marine security guard, making him a representative of the United States government. There any negative conduct on his part could easily become an international incident.

Decker had a choice: he could respect America's allies no matter how much they might provoke him, or he could avoid all athletic contests with foreign nationals effective immediately. Karate was important to Decker, so he bit the bullet and promised to behave himself. He'd stay away from Lieutenant Park Song.

In the computer room Decker, still crouched behind the desk, peered along the barrel of his M-16 at Song and Kim Shin who were some twenty-five feet away. To Decker's left Buf, hidden behind a printer, kept his shotgun on the Korean enlisted men. La Porte was to the right, crouched near a second metal desk, his face almost hidden by the stock of his M-16. On the cassette player Aretha was cooking on "Chain of Fools". Decker was sweating. Something about this setup just wasn't right.

Song, who was standing over the two dead Vietnamese, had a pistol in one hand. Meaning he'd wasted the dead gooks who he figured to be Special Police or Intelligence agents. Maybe he'd been settling old scores, a way of life over here. Saigon was all smoke and mirrors, a place where people threw dust in each other's eyes and nothing was as it seemed. Saigon was quicksand. Decker could live here a thousand years and never understand the place. Meanwhile, the two Vietnamese kneeling in front of a large computer were scared shitless.

Decker said to Song, "What are you people doing here?"

Smiling, Song returned his pistol to its holster then looked at his fellow officer. "Captain Shin had a scheduled meeting here to close out some business. Our embassy was worried about the captain's security. So I was assigned a detail and ordered to escort him back safely. Right now the streets of Saigon are very dangerous. I don't have to tell you that."

Buf said, "You people walk here from your embassy or you take a bus? We didn't see no automobile outside. Unless, of course, somebody relieved you of it."

Still smiling, Song's eyes lingered on Buf for a few seconds then moved to the kneeling Vietnamese. "They shot one of your CIA agents. His name is Harrison Random. That's him on the floor with the woman. We were coming down the hall when we heard her arguing with Random. Apparently he'd changed his mind about taking her to America with him. So she decided to take her revenge, with the help of these four. I'm afraid we arrived too late to save him. These men attacked us. We were forced to kill two of them in self-defence."

Looking over her shoulder at Decker a tearful Constanze Herail shouted, "No, no. Is not true. We shoot nobody." She pointed to Song. "He is the one who shoots because he wants what Random has."

Song's smile vanished. Decker thought, somebody's lying.

166

Somebody's trying to run a game on me. He didn't know the girl but he knew Laughing Boy. Which made Decker want to hear the rest of the girl's story.

He watched Song glare at her. If looks could kill, the girl was dead. Song started to breathe heavily and Decker thought, the guy's hyperventilating. Then he decided no, the little gook's not having problems with his health. He's freaking out. What the hell for?

Suddenly Song took two quick steps, placing him directly over the seated Constanze Herail. Without a word he punched her in the face then kicked her in the ribs, knocking the screaming woman onto her back. When he lifted his foot for a second kick Decker fired into the ceiling over Song's head.

The Korean dropped into a protective crouch, arms shielding his face and head from falling plaster. His men brought up their guns, ready to fire on the Marines and Decker thought, holy shit, it's happening for real. But Song barked an order in Korean and the guns came down at once. Coughing, he stepped forward, hands waving the tainted, smelly air away from his face.

Glaring at Decker, Song removed his hat and used it to brush a chalky powder from his uniform. One day he would kill Decker for this insult. He'd kill them all – the woman and the Marines as well. Kill them for insulting him, for coming between him and the plates.

He refused to blame himself for this new complication. Refused even to consider that he should have taken the plates and left while he had the chance. Why shouldn't he seize *every* opportunity he could? No, he didn't blame himself for this unholy twist of fate. He blamed Decker.

He blamed Decker for making him afraid. The shot fired over Song's head had been horrifying. He didn't want to die in this stuffy, airless room with its infernal machines. Not when he was so close to being rich.

How near had he come to dying? He watched Decker rise from behind the desk, M-16 aimed at Song's chest. "Whatever happens," the Marine said, "you get it first. Now do us both a favour and leave before somebody gets hurt."

Song looked over his shoulder at the suitcases and at the folded newspaper.

Decker shook his head. "Forget it. Nothing's leaving this room except you and your friends."

Song turned to face him. "I outrank you. I want those suitcases."

"It's not nice to beat up women. Might start people thinking you're some kind of weirdo. I don't think those suitcases are yours. I think they were here when you got here, that's what I think."

Hands massaging her ribcage a breathless Constanze Herail sat up. "Those suitcases do not belong to him. Neither does that newspaper. He killed those two men for the suitcases. He shot Harrison to get – "

Song interrupted. "You lying little slut. You'll say anything if you think it'll help you get out of Saigon. The suitcases and the newspaper are mine. I want them."

Buf chuckled. "The man seems awfully interested in one measly old newspaper. Hey, you like the funny papers? Maybe you one of them people if he don't read Batman he gets headaches and can't sleep at night. Me, I dig Wonder Woman. Man, she got those cute little blue panties and – "

"*I want that newspaper.*"

Decker grinned. "Do I look like I give a shit?"

Decker thought, fuck Peter Jason Meeks where he breathes. Time to provoke Laughing Boy. Sneak in a little payback before the big iron bird took off for the world.

He said, "Newspaper stays here with the suitcases. You got a problem with that?" Decker didn't give a rat's ass about the newspaper. He wanted to get under Laughing Boy's skin.

La Porte, still crouched behind the desk, said to Song, "You got your health, man. Don't push."

Eyes almost closed Song stared at Decker who never blinked. Finally the Korean raised one hand, a signal to his men, and without a word walked towards the door. His men followed. Buf said, "Y'all keep in touch, you hear?"

When they'd left La Porte silently stared at the doorway.

Finally he shook his head and looked at Decker. "Close, man. Too close. I got ice in my stomach."

Decker touched the Puerto Rican's shoulder. "Stay cool, bro'. We're going back to the world. Don't even think we're not. Right now, we have to mess up a few machines then we're out of here. This time next week you're back in Brooklyn watching the Mets blow another game in the bottom of the ninth."

But the truth was they'd nearly had their tickets punched and Decker knew it. One wrong move and all of them could have missed the last dance. Meanwhile, the two Vietnamese came over to Decker and started bitching about Captain Song, about how he'd shot their lieutenant and had been ready to shoot them. When Decker asked why, the Vietnamese clammed up.

Suddenly he snapped his fingers. *The man on the floor.* Decker pushed past the Vietnamese and hurried to the man's side. The man literally looked like death warmed over. He was coated in plaster dust, was barely breathing and sat in a pool of his own blood. The woman was picking plaster bits from his hair and looking worried. The man was Harrison Random and Decker knew him.

Random was CIA and Decker had seen him at the embassy and around the CIA compound. He wasn't the brightest member of the Intelligence community. Random might have done a better job if he hadn't spent so much time at the massage parlours on Tu Do Street. At the moment, however, his mind wasn't on getting laid. Harrison Random was about to die.

In addition to an eerie brightness Random's eyes had a vacant stare suggesting he could already see the next world. His chest, thighs and hands were red with his own blood. Decker felt for a neck pulse, finding one so weak he nearly missed it.

Constanze Herail told him that Song had shot Random in the back. Decker was about to ask why but decided it was more important to radio Jellicki for confirmation that Laughing Boy and his goons had actually left the building.

Decker preferred not to have any surprises waiting for him in the hallway. He didn't trust Laughing Boy. The little gook was oilier than a can of sardines.

With the Vietnamese watching his every move Decker unhooked the hand radio from his belt then turned to face the front door. The Vietnamese also snuck in a couple of quick glances at the suitcases. What the hell was in them?

He'd brought the radio to his mouth when he saw Schow barrel into the room, blowing past La Porte and Buf like he'd been shoved hard from behind. The CIA agent stumbled before dropping to his knees, head flopping back on his shoulders. There was blood on his neck and flak jacket.

As Decker watched in amazement Schow toppled onto his right side, head striking the floor. He lay motionless, with Buf chuckling and saying, my, oh my, and La Porte shaking his head, and Decker thinking, the fuck's that all about. And then Decker saw Schow's hands. They'd been tied in the front with his belt. The CIA agent tried to speak, but only a harsh rasp came from his mouth. His throat had been cut.

La Porte saw the blood and sprinted to Schow's side. At the same time Buf spun round to cover the door and that's when Schow literally exploded, the discharge turning most of the room into an inferno. The blast said grenade. One with a time fuse. Someone had pulled the pin, dropped the grenade in Schow's pocket then pushed him in the room.

A screaming La Porte was engulfed by flames. A few yards away Buf was hurled from the room and out into the hall. Decker drew the lucky card. He was in the rear of the room, with the Vietnamese between him and the blast. It was they who took the full impact of the explosion, shielding him unintentionally.

The reduced effects of the blast, however, were still strong enough to knock Decker off his feet and hurt him. He flew backwards, feeling the intense heat and the shock waves, before colliding violently with the disk control unit Random had been leaning against. Bouncing off the machine Decker landed on the floor beside the dying CIA agent and blacked out.

170

Seconds later he opened his eyes and felt a sharp pain in his back. There was a ringing in his ears and he was covered in plaster, punch cards and glass from computer monitors. He smelled smoke and could taste his own blood. He heard the crackle of flames along with the hissing and sputtering of exposed computer wires. And he heard the screaming of people in agony.

Dazed and breathless, Decker moved his arms a bit. Then his legs and hips. Everything was still attached. He felt his balls rub against the floor, meaning he hadn't lost his dick which was the first thing you thought about in fire fights and explosions.

Somewhere to his left Constanze Herail screamed, "I'm blind, I'm blind. Help me, help me."

Decker thought, lady I would if I could, but I happen to be passing out at the moment. Sorry. As the blackness beckoned he wondered how he'd managed to hold onto the radio which was still gripped tightly in his right hand. Didn't matter. He was looking forward to being unconscious, to being out of it.

But instinct said, don't give in. *Don't give in.* Decker forced his eyes open. Again they started to close. He called on all his willpower and forced them open again in time to see Song lead his Koreans through thick black smoke and back into the room. Heart thumping, Decker willed himself to lie motionless. He was afraid, but out of that fear came a hatred so strong he knew his eyes wouldn't close any time soon.

He watched Song, a hand covering his nose against smoke, point to the suitcases with his pistol. They were on this side of the room with Decker and far enough from the explosion to remain relatively unscathed. Slinging AK-47s onto their shoulders two soldiers picked their way through bodies and burning debris to retrieve the suitcases. And the folded newspaper.

On their way out of the room one of the soldiers paused long enough to hand the newspaper to Song. Quickly unfolding it Song looked inside and fingered something hidden within the papers. Satisfied he refolded the paper.

The smoke was irritating Decker's nose and throat. To keep from coughing he bit his lip. Through watery eyes he watched Song speak briefly to Kim Shin and the remaining enlisted man. All three Koreans now held pistols.

When Song finished talking, Shin and the other soldier nodded. Then as Decker watched, the three Koreans began shooting everybody in the room. Alive or dead. The Koreans shot them all.

Decker watched Kim Shin step into the hall, fire two shots into Buf's prone body then furiously yell down the hall in the direction of the soldiers carrying the suitcases.

Inside the demolished computer room Song carefully stepped around a mangled printer to where La Porte, legs blown off by the blast, lay screaming near a metal desk. He shot the Puerto Rican in the head three times. When his pistol clicked empty, he frowned and began to reload.

Several feet away from Decker the Korean enlisted man, AK-47 hanging from his shoulder, shot a Vietnamese who lay motionless behind a computer, hair and clothing on fire. Near an overturned stool the second Vietnamese, his face a blood mask, knelt in the middle of the burning debris and tried to push his intestines back into his stomach. Skirting a burning printer the soldier walked over to him and fired two shots into the back of his head. Then he stepped over the corpse and walked towards Random, Constanze Herail and Decker.

Tightening his grip on the hand radio – shifting his arm to draw his .45 would be too dangerous – Decker willed himself not to move. The soldier drew closer and then he was looking down at Decker, pistol aimed at his head. Suddenly the soldier glanced to his right. Constanze Herail, glass embedded in her eyes, had struggled to her feet and with arms outstretched was now shouting for help.

Decker used the distraction. Pushing himself to his knees he smashed the soldier in the balls with the hand radio, doubling him over. On his feet Decker dropped the radio, gripped the soldier's head in both hands and twisted it hard to the right, breaking the neck. As the soldier slumped to the floor Decker pulled his own .45 and shot him twice in the face.

Song froze in the act of reloading and looked across the room. A second later, eyes wide with horror, he threw his gun aside and sprinted from the room. A groggy Decker swayed then dropped to his knees, the .45 falling from his hand. Crawling over to the dead Korean soldier he pulled at the AK-47 trapped beneath the soldier's corpse. It wouldn't budge. Decker pulled harder. The rifle came free. Aiming the Russian-made gun at the doorway he pulled the trigger.

The noise tore at Decker's ears and eyeballs and he could feel the vibrations through his teeth. But the gun got the job done. No one was going to come near the door. There'd be no more grenades tossed into the room. Not while bullets fed by the thick, plastic magazine tore off the doorframe and gouged eight-inch holes in the corridor wall.

On his feet, Decker continued firing, stumbling towards the door, swearing before God that he was going to kill Song even if it cost him his own life. When he reached the hallway the AK-47 was empty. And so was the hallway. He looked around for another weapon and saw Buf's shotgun, wet with blood, near his corpse.

Gripping the shotgun, Decker staggered down the corridor towards the staircase, bumping into walls and spinning around and losing all sense of direction. He called out for La Porte and Buf, his voice echoing along the empty corridor and coming back to torment him. The black depths of grief drew closer.

He reached the stairs and made his way to the first floor, leaving a trail of his own blood behind him. As he grew weaker the shotgun grew heavier. To keep from collapsing Decker began to talk to himself, to La Porte and Buf and soon they were talking back, telling him to waste that sucker, to catch up to Laughing Boy and wax his ass. *Do it, bro'.*

Ten yards away from the front door Decker dropped to his knees and began to crawl, following the white plaster dust footprints left on the carpet by Song. The shotgun, now forgotten, lay near one of the cubicles.

Inches away from the door Decker passed out.

10

New York, December

Because Manny Decker believed people phoned only when they wanted something he wasn't keen on receiving telephone calls.

But on the morning following the alleged murder-suicide of Max and Gail DaSilva a call came into the precinct which demanded some degree of attention if not courtesy on his part. A woman named Karen Drumman telephoned to say that she, like Decker, believed the DaSilvas had been murdered.

Decker had never heard of Miss Drumman so he said, "That's interesting", thinking, keep it short and to the point. He wasn't in the best of moods, having had only four hours sleep. He also hadn't eaten breakfast and was looking at a twelve-hour work day. And he'd just come from the US Attorney's office where a sullen Yale Singular had reluctantly witnessed his swearing in as a US deputy marshall.

Last but by no means least, Decker felt responsible for Gail's murder because if he'd shown up on time last night she might still be alive. Sooner or later his guilt was going to push him towards some kind of self-inflicted punishment. Some people had one of those days. Decker had one of those lives.

His gut instinct said Gail's killer had known that Decker was going to be late in getting to her place, therefore giving the killer time. Had Gail's phone been bugged? If so, why? In seeking an answer to this question Decker would be poking his nose into someone else's boiling pot – someone who'd gambled he could ice two people before Decker arrived — someone who was slicker than wax on a marble floor.

Miss Drumman had a pleasant voice, slightly husky but precise, as though she'd taken speech lessons at some point. Decker wondered what she looked like. She sounded foxy. Then again she could be ugly.

Karen Drumman said she was Gail's best friend and also Tawny's godmother. According to her she'd known Gail since they'd shared a Second Avenue walk-up back in the seventies, when both had tried for a show business career, Gail as a singer, she as an actress. They hadn't made it. We only lacked three things, Miss Drumman said: talent, luck and the abnormality it takes to go on stage and bare your soul in front of strangers. Decker thought she didn't sound too bitter about failing, leading him to wonder if she'd ever seriously wanted to be an actress in the first place.

These days she was a headhunter, she told him, an executive recruiter who located qualified candidates for high-paying jobs in advertising. She worked for Ralph Sharon Associates on East 42nd Street across from the *Daily News* building. However, Gail's death had upset her so much that she'd stayed at home all day.

On the Saturday, she was in her apartment only three blocks from Gail, and down to her last three Valiums. Decker, with no pity to waste, stayed silent on Miss Drumman's short supply of pharmaceuticals. He had no inclination to give his soul to a stranger, even one with a dynamite voice.

Miss Drumman had got his name from Gail, and while she had him on the phone she wanted to thank him for trying to find Tawny. Decker grunted, wondering if Miss Drumman was who she claimed to be and deciding he'd find out in the course of investigating Gail's murder.

He knew this much: on the phone Miss Drumman sounded angry, sad, and she cried a lot. Decker thought she had a naive charm and was probably too fragile to live in an ugly world. She probably didn't know that in the game of life, you couldn't win, you couldn't break even, you couldn't even quit the game.

Decker was aware that any investigation of Gail's death would be handled by her local precinct which had official jurisdiction. Police department rules said only investigating officers were allowed on a crime scene, meaning Decker shouldn't have been permitted to enter the apartment last night.

However, he'd known one of the victims and was a cop himself, so he'd been given permission to come inside the DaSylva condo providing he didn't get in the way. But should he decide to dig deeper he didn't need to be a college graduate to know he'd better not get caught. Everybody had a scheme that wouldn't work. This could very well be Decker's.

His own precinct wanted him on the Valentin-Dalton homicides while the Treasury Department craved his assistance in nailing Ben Dumas and Laughing Boy for passing funny money. Decker knew he should play it safe, that he should take care of business and stay focused on the task at hand, a time-honoured way of keeping one's career on an upward trajectory.

On the other hand he loved cutting corners. He enjoyed jumping over the fence with the alarm going off. He loved to have fun. So what if he occasionally did something which went beyond dumb and reached all the way to stupid.

As the foxy-sounding Karen Drumman told him that the DaSilvas would never embrace murder-suicide, Decker remained hunched over his desk reading the green sheet, a list each station house received every morning of all crimes committed in the city during the past twenty-four hours. Max and Gail were on the list.

They'd ended their lives as crime statistics, along with a dead three-year-old Hispanic girl found in a burning suitcase on a South Bronx back lot, a pair of human hands found in a paper bag left in an East Harlem apartment lobby, a Brooklyn man struck over the head with a ketchup bottle after an argument over a two dollar debt and the usual dead goats, chickens and cats found by Central Park foot patrols each morning, the carcasses being leftovers from Santeria and voodoo rites performed in the park the previous night. Decker wondered if even planned parenthood could stop crime. He doubted it.

Meanwhile, something Miss Drumman said stopped him from reading the green sheet.

"I have a photograph of you and Gail taken down in South Carolina when you were in the Marines," she told him. "I think it was just before you went off to some special military school. I thought maybe you might want it. Gail never forgot you. She spoke of you quite often."

Eyes closed, Decker massaged the bridge of his nose with a thumb and forefinger. "Could you describe the photograph to me, please?" He took a deep breath, exhaled, then cleared his throat. His heartbeat quickened. He wanted to hear what Miss Drumman had to say about the photograph. On the other hand he wished she'd never called.

She said, "You're both outdoors on a parade field it looks like. You're wearing a formal Marine uniform. She's wearing your Marine hat. It's a white hat. Your hair's cut very short and both of you look so young, so happy."

Decker thought, we were young and happy. We had it all ahead of us. He smiled, remembering how short his hair had been. High and tight like the Corps demanded, sides clipped short so that no hair showed when a cap was worn, the hair on top approximately a half-inch long.

Karen Drumman said, "I let Gail look at some of my wedding pictures and when she returned them, the one of you and her somehow ended up with mine. I never got around to returning it. I'm pretty sure she'd want you to have it."

"Thanks for thinking of me," said Decker whose instinct told him to ignore the photograph, something he couldn't bring himself to say to Miss Drumman. The most painful memories were those involving something you didn't do. This photograph would only remind him of what he hadn't done regarding Gail.

Karen Drumman said, "Any news about Tawny? I can't sleep for worrying about her."

"I'm sorry, but there's nothing to report. I'm not giving

up on her. Not after what happened to Gail." Decker's guilt would devour him if he even thought of giving up.

"I understand," Karen Drumman said, sounding touched by his determination to keep a promise to a dead love. "You know it's strange," she said. "First Tawny disappears then a few days later Gail and Max are murdered. If that isn't bad karma, I don't know what is. You can't call it an accident and you can't call it coincidence, so what do you call it? Doesn't it seem to you as though someone was out to get Gail and her family?"

Decker reached for the dregs of his black coffee. Miss Drumman had a point. There was bad luck and worse luck and there was what had happened to the DaSilvas. Cops and press were floating a scenario which had Gail walking out on Max who didn't want to live without her so he'd shot her twice in the heart before turning the gun on himself. Decker thought, anyone who believed this shit had the kind of head you can see through.

Max may have been a schmuck but he wasn't a psycho, at least not according to Gail. Meanwhile, the press was calling him a disillusioned yuppie whose pursuit of money had left him mentally unbalanced. As one happy-talk newscaster put it, Max had felt unhappy and unloved and so he'd chosen a quick bullet in the head over the slow death of crushed ideals and old age. Decker thought, right, and you're so dumb you couldn't hit the ground if you fell.

As for Gail, she wasn't someone who'd lost control of her life. She was getting divorced, not having a nuclear meltdown. She wasn't dumping Max, they were dumping each other. They'd both been ready to start new lives. People with something to look forward to don't usually kill themselves. Nor do they whip up an elaborate dinner for three, with expensive crystal and silver service laid out on the table and four bottles of Montrachet chilling in ice buckets.

Decker said to Karen Drumman, "You wouldn't happen to know if Max owned a gun?"

"You got to be kidding," she said. "Max was a lover, not a fighter. He'd sooner stick pins in his eyes than go near a gun. Some black kids robbed him at gunpoint in the subway three years ago. Scared him so much he never rode the subway again. Went everywhere by cab or limousine after that. That's also why he owned a car and a jeep. Cost him a thousand a month in garage fees but he didn't care. Gail hated guns more than Max did. Tawny's the reason she'd never have one in the house."

Decker ignored his ringing phone. The switchboard could take messages. Let's say Miss Drumman was correct and Max hadn't owned a gun. Then who did own the brand new Beretta 84, .380 calibre, 9 mm short barrel used to put two bullets in Gail's heart and one in Max's right temple?

In a call to Gail's precinct this morning Decker had learned that no permit had ever been issued for the Beretta. The serial number had also been filed off. The gun was virtually untraceable, a shrewd move on Max's part. Except why go to all that trouble if you're going to kill yourself? And whose fingerprints were on the gun? Max's, of course. Decker thought, whoever concocted this scam was one smooth snotball. He's thought of everything. The man has imagination, not to mention a natural and exuberant sense of style.

There'd been no signs of forced entry, meaning Max and Gail had let their killer into the apartment. They'd trusted him. Why?

Responding to complaints about loud music Ivo Popovich, the building's assistant manager, had used a spare key to enter the DaSylva apartment after Gail and Max hadn't answered the house phone. Mr Popovich claimed to have found husband and wife dead on the living room floor. He then left without touching anything and made a telephone call to police from his office. *Why had Gail and Max let the killer into their apartment?*

"Gail told me Max was planning to raise the reward for Tawny," Karen Drumman said. "Maybe somebody came there to rob them. Could be they thought Max kept big money around the house."

Decker placed the receiver between his shoulder and chin,

then opened his notebook. "Robbery's out. The place hadn't been tossed."

He checked his notes. He'd been right. The apartment hadn't been touched. There'd been loot on the premises which no self-respecting thief would have passed up unless he'd been born without hands and eyes. Such as twenty-one hundred dollars in cash. Or nine credit cards, jewellery, chequebooks, cameras, two fur coats, three VCRs, two home computers and a Proton stereo. Also the keys to Max's two-year-old Mercury and new four-wheel Jeep, both of which were downstairs in the building garage. The shooter had come there to do two people, not fill a pillowcase with stolen property then rush off to the nearest fence.

Karen Drumman said, "Detective Decker, two days ago Gail told me Max was being followed by a black man. He thought it might be someone he'd previously had trouble with. Could this person be a factor? I'm only asking."

Decker rubbed the back of his neck in an attempt to wake up. Earlier he'd gone to the precinct bathroom for a quick shave and looked in the mirror. What he saw looking back at him was like something out of *Night of The Living Dead*.

He said to Karen Drumman, "I can't say more about it at the present time, but the man you're talking about doesn't figure in this at all."

Bulldog Drumman, girl detective. Give the lady credit for bringing up a good point. Interesting that Max had got whacked just before he furnished a description of a spook who'd been following him around for a couple of days. Maybe interesting wasn't the word. Dubious might be a better word.

So Miss Drumman knew about Max's troubles with Rashad Lateef Quai, the black postal worker who wanted to stop selling stamps and switch to making music. Did knowing this make her righteous? No way. She could be anybody; until Decker knew otherwise he was going to be cautious and speak slowly. Cops who talked too much were cops dumb enough to drown on dry land.

After checking out the Beretta, Decker had then checked

on Mr Quai, who Max had suspected of tailing him. Forget about Mr Lateef Quai tailing anybody. For the past seventy-two hours he'd been in jail, charged with stealing forty-two thousand dollars from the post office to pay his phone bill. Addicted to telephone sex he'd spent hours each day in some very expensive phone conversations. Max's black man was not the lecherous and hot-to-trot Mr Quai.

Time to end this conversation with Miss Drumman who talked too much about the past to suit Decker. There were things he didn't want to recall. Recalling them made him feel lonely. Miss Drumman could put the photograph in the mail if she wanted to. End of story.

As though reading his mind she said to Decker, "I don't think I should put the picture in the mail. It might get lost and I'm sure it means a lot to you. It meant a lot to Gail. I could meet you somewhere and give it to you if you'd like."

Decker shook his head. Jesus. What was he going to say – mail the thing and get out of my life? She'd see that as an insult to Gail and she'd probably be right. Besides, she was almost out of Valium so why give her a hard time.

"That would be very kind of you," he said to her.

"I'm having dinner with a client this evening," she said. "Something I can't get out of. If it's not too inconvenient maybe you could drop by the restaurant and pick up the photograph."

"Address?"

"Corner of 64th and Madison. It's called Bougival. It's across the street from my apartment. Gail, Tawny and I used to have Sunday brunch there when Max was spending weekends with his little friend from Switzerland."

"That's nice."

She laughed for the first time, a warm, throaty sound that reached Decker and made him wonder again what did she look like. "Don't worry," she said. "I won't keep you. I know you're busy. I promise to have you back on the street in seconds. Just ask for Brenda. She's the maitre d'. She'll show you to my table."

Decker smiled. If nothing else, he was going to get a good look at Bulldog Drumman, girl detective.

"I have other photographs of Gail," she said. "I'll bring along a few and you can take your pick."

"Thanks," Decker said. This time he meant it.

She chuckled. "Right now I'm listening to Mozart's *Requiem Mass*, which seems appropriate though a bit depressing. Music reminds me of Max and his gadgets, his stereos, computers, tape recorders. I hope they have them where he's going. He was gadget happy. He even dictated memos to Tawny on a microcassette recorder. Imagine dictating a memo to your own daughter. But he dictated everything. Memos, letters, telexes, everything. He kept a dozen recorders in the apartment. Used to drive Gail crazy finding them everywhere she turned."

Decker stopped rubbing his neck. Shit, was it possible? He quickly turned the pages in his notebook until he found what he was looking for. There it was in black and white. Or rather, there it wasn't. He was looking at the list of personal effects found in the apartment, stuff the killer had ignored.

No microcassette tape recorders. Stereo equipment, computers, but no microcassette tape recorders. There hadn't been any in the apartment. Not one.

Decker kept his voice detached. "Miss Drumman, are you sure Max kept microcassette recorders in the apartment?"

"Is there some kind of problem?"

"Just answer the question. Are you sure about the microcassette recorders?"

"I'm sure. Gail had me over a lot lately to talk about her troubles with Max, so I saw the recorders myself. The latest one was a present from a Japanese record distributor Max had just signed with. It was incredible. Gail showed me how it works. It's no bigger than a book of matches and has the most fantastic sound. Wouldn't mind owning one myself, except they're not sold over here."

Closing his eyes, Decker nodded his head. "That's what he did. Son of a bitch."

"Excuse me?"

"Nothing. Just thinking out loud."

The killer had taken something from the apartment after all. He'd taken the microcassette recorders. Every goddam one. When the killer entered the apartment Max had probably been dictating a description of the black man which he'd planned to turn over to Decker. To protect this spook the shooter had taken out Max and Gail.

Decker's smile was unfeeling. He thought, Slick Rick you just made your first mistake. If you'd walked off with only one recorder, I'd never have known. But you're a smartass. You don't trust anybody, so you had to take them all. Ran Dobson was right. Being too clever is dumb.

Turning to a blank page Decker made notes. The killer had been watching Max and Gail. Maybe tapping their phone. Otherwise why hit the DaSilvas just before they were to tell Decker about the black dude. The timing and the missing tape recorders said it all. Someone had wanted to protect this spook in the worst way. Karen Drumman's phone call hadn't been a waste of Decker's time after all. Cops lived by information and Miss Drumman had produced more than her share.

Decker said to her, "All right if I show around eight thirty?"

"Eight thirty's fine."

"Good. See you then."

He hung up, leaned back in his chair, absent-mindedly clicking his ballpoint pen and thinking, Karen Drumman was right. We're talking superior bad karma. But it did seem odd that the DaSilvas should have so much bad karma all at once. Decker wondered if an unseen hand was pushing the pieces around the board.

Reaching for his notebook he wrote Tawny DaSilva's name and the date she'd disappeared. Below it he wrote the names Gail and Max DaSilva along with the date of their deaths. He underlined this date twice.

11

It was almost eight forty-five that evening when Decker and his partner Detective Ellen Spiceland entered Bougival, the East 64th Street restaurant named for a French village seen often in Renoir and Monet's paintings.

The restaurant was a long, narrow room with a small side room near the far end. Both rooms had low white-tiled ceilings, candles on every tiny table and walls of exposed brick hung with Renoir and Monet prints. Decker automatically disliked the place because it was on the eastside, not his favourite part of town.

He disliked the area's phony gentility and the inflated sense of self-esteem on the part of people living there. As for Bougival itself it struck Decker as being no different to a thousand other eastside joints. Look for the raw spinach salad, front doors made of frosted glass and drinks with cutesy names like Fuzzy Navel and Harvey Wallbanger. It catered to a yuppy crowd – young, white, and prosperous, an assembly of wrinkle-free thirty-somethings in the morning of their lives, with minds unshaped by experience. The men wore preppy clothes that were neither in nor out of style, the women wore suits or dresses which stressed affluence over individuality. The one black face in the room belonged to Ellen Spiceland. If this bothered her, she didn't show it.

She was a thirty-three-year-old, beige-tinted woman with high cheekbones, reddish hair and a permanently flattened nose that had been crushed at thirteen when she'd resisted a rape attempt by a Harlem minister. The precinct called her

"Bag Lady" because she entered sinister bars and after-hours joints with a hand in her purse gripping a .38 Smith & Wesson. As she told Decker, coming out on top didn't mean anything. Coming out alive did.

She was heading home but at Decker's request had agreed to keep him company. She lived on the east side, far from the "Silk Stocking" district where Gail and Karen resided. For Ellen Spiceland home was the edge of Spanish Harlem, in a large apartment on a block that was considered safe because it rarely had more than two murders a year. These days she was handling alone much of the case load assigned to her and Decker. Buying her a drink tonight was his way of saying thanks.

For now she was stuck working a dozen ongoing cases alone, but she wasn't bitching. Decker needed help; Gail, Tawny and Willy Valentin were not burdens he could easily shift to God or a shrink. Which didn't stop Bags from realising that she was earning access to future favours. Ultimately Decker would have to pay his debts.

In Bougival she eyed the Renoir and Monet prints, most of which she recognised. She was married to a Haitian artist, her third husband, and a self-obsessed bore to whom she was devoted. They stayed together because her strength reminded him of his mother and because it didn't bother her to give generously to him while getting nothing back. Decker, who stayed out of her personal life, wondered if she was a masochist or just liked a challenge.

When necessary Bags could get down. Two years ago she and Decker, "Black and Decker" to co-workers, had shown up at a West 83rd Street apartment to arrest a Cuban male suspected of having raped an eighteen-month-old baby girl. The Cuban, one Raul Gallaraga, opened the door, a thirteen-round Browning automatic in his left hand and aimed at Decker's throat. Three shots were fired. Decker, who only heard the first, had been ready to die.

But it was Ellen who'd shot Gallaraga three times in the gut, firing through the beaded bag she'd received from Henri on their third anniversary. Decker replaced the ruined bag with a two hundred and fifty dollar Courrèges purse, the best he'd been able to find at Saks Fifth Avenue. And when she told him she'd wanted to kill a maggot like the Cuban for twenty years Decker said, "Thanks for waiting."

Brenda the maître d' who led Decker and Ellen to Karen Drumman's table was in her late twenties, a lean, deadpan blonde in a tuxedo, lengthy blood red fingernails and eyebrows which had been tweezed and redrawn. Ellen whispered to Decker, "Bet she doesn't read on the toilet or pick her nose. You ever see a more icy-looking woman in your life?"

Decker said, "I think she'll tie you up on the first date."

Ellen looked around. "I didn't know Manhattan still had this many white people. I feel as though I'm in a sanctuary for endangered species. Next time I'm bringing my camera."

Decker took her arm. "Behave yourself, Bags. They don't understand you like I do."

"You know, I look at these guys and I think it must be hard going through life not being able to get it up."

Decker was still chuckling when Deadpan Brenda left them at a table off an apparently empty back room and occupied by two people. One was Karen Drumman, a slender, red-haired woman in her early thirties, tanned and dressed in an olive green jumpsuit, matching suede high heels and a studded black leather belt with an oversized gold-plated buckle.

Decker liked the two ivory chopsticks in her hair and the high heels. He liked her eyes which were a clear blue and focused on him without blinking. He liked the fact that when they shook hands, she smiled and held his a little longer than necessary. Truth was, they liked each other on sight.

The other person at the table was Jean-Louis Nicolay, a small, grey-haired, baby-faced Frenchman in his forties who wore a nicely cut, double-breasted dark suit, pale lavender shirt and a yellow silk tie. There was a pink cloth flower in his buttonhole. Decker figured the suit at around fifteen hundred, not including alterations. The cost of Nicolay's shoes probably equalled the weekly take home of a first-grade detective. Monsieur Jean-Louis didn't need company. Anyone loving himself enough to spend this much money

186

on clothes was never alone. Decker disliked him immediately.

From the looks of things Nicolay had been hitting on Karen Drumman and getting nowhere. He had a hand on her knee and his little mouth near her ear, talking trash in anticipation of doing the wild thing. Waste of time. Karen Drumman wasn't buying. Her indifference to the well-tailored Jean-Louis impressed Decker who was suspicious of people in expensive clothes. People like that usually wanted to be seen as more than they really were.

Ignoring the Frenchman Karen Drumman had been slowly tapping a water glass with a sesame seed breadstick. Every so often she'd stop tapping to pick up seeds from the table and drop them in an ash tray. Jean-Louis was making every guy in the room look good.

At the sight of Decker, the Frenchman abandoned his quest to get lucky. Smiling, he sprang from his chair, gripped Decker's hand with both of his and in heavily accented English introduced himself as Bougival's owner. Decker introduced himself but said nothing about being a cop. You had to be careful with citizens these days. They tended to view cops as the custodians of ethical conduct, so telling them you carried a badge usually put a damper on the party. Decker merely gave his name then introduced Ellen as Mrs Spiceland, a business associate.

Jean-Louis addressed Ellen as Madame, kissed her hand and said the pleasure was all his. Head bowed, the Frenchman didn't see her wink at Decker and gently nudge him with her hip. She was being flattered by a pro, leaving her wary but no less charmed. Decker thought, Monsieur's got all the right moves. Monsieur probably didn't make any noise while eating his soup, either.

Decker watched Ellen thank Nicolay for his kind words, doing it in French which she'd learned from her Haitian hubby and which now shocked Nicolay into raising one eyebrow and keeping it up for a count of two. Having experienced French snobbery first hand in Saigon Decker knew Monsieur was surprised to find that an American, a black woman no less, spoke *français* fairly well. Give Jean-Louis credit. In seconds he'd recovered and moved on to the business of being a flirtatious host.

He and Ellen began speaking in French, the language bringing back memories of Saigon for Decker, memories of a letter from Gail which had included the Emily Dickinson lines – *Unable are the loved to die, For love is immortal.* He'd carried the letter around with him until the writing had faded and the paper had fallen apart and he'd got out of Vietnam alive.

Decker enjoyed the fact that Ellen had caught Jean-Louis being a tad condescending. Bags was quick, capable of going from zero to ninety in a second like a cheetah. She could not be easily deceived or imposed upon.

Earlier today she'd stopped Decker from screwing up his investigation of Gail's murder. He'd begun with the Beretta, realising that like many guns it could have been acquired from a gunrunner who purchased weapons in Florida then legally sold them in New York to any deviate who could pay. As a cop Decker didn't view gun ownership as a right. He saw it as a disease.

For now he decided to ignore the Florida-New York firearms connection and play an educated hunch, namely Kennedy Airport. The Beretta was Italian-made, a foreign gun. Gail had been killed by a new one, a piece in mint condition. Decker was looking for a recent import. Kennedy Airport was as likely a place as any to go digging.

OCs, organised crime members, regarded Kennedy Airport as their very own shopping mall, except they never paid for anything. Maybe some wise guys had grabbed a gun shipment from the airport not too long ago. When these slimeballs weren't extorting money by threatening airlines with labour trouble they were stealing any piece of cargo that wasn't nailed down.

Hijacking from Kennedy, the world's richest port, remained one of the mob's most profitable enterprises. Aiding and abetting OCs in this lucrative undertaking were those shipping clerks and loading dock foremen who were habitual gamblers, born losers who paid off debts to mob bookmakers and loan sharks with cargo information on valuable consignments, trucking timetables, airport security. Gamblers ended up betraying everything and everybody. Decker found them to be dimwits who ultimately turned into shitheads.

He'd said to Bags, I'm reaching out for the Bureau of Alcohol, Tobacco and Firearms, which was the branch of the Treasury Department dealing with guns. The T-Boys should know about gun heists at Kennedy. Since Decker was now a deputy US marshal, why not use his new clout. Yale Singular was using him. Why shouldn't Decker return the favour?

"Because it's stupid, that's why," Bags said. "Gail's important to you, but be cool. Yes, he's using you. Take down Ben Dumas, he told you, then get off the set. Stay away from Laughing Boy no matter how much you despise the man. You may not like that part of the deal, but does this mean you should be simple-minded? You want hijacking Intelligence, you know where to go. And I don't mean Fat Boy."

"Safe, Loft and Truck," said Decker, knowing he'd just been reprimanded and knowing he'd had it coming. The police department's Safe, Loft and Truck squad dealt with burglaries, safe-crackers and truck hijackings, keeping updated Intelligence on perps, organisations, informants, fences, arrest records.

"You got that right," Bags said.

Decker had almost made a mistake and all because pride demanded that he do to Yale Singular what Singular was doing to him, namely pull strings and make the other guy jump. Bags was square on target. Yes, Singular was using him but why should Decker compound the problem by passing on his theories about Gail's death to the fat man?

Cops disliked feds and with good reason. Feds usually took whatever you offered and gave you zilch in return. Tell Singular that Decker was looking into Gail's murder and the T-man would somehow use that bit of news on his own behalf. Singular had already made it clear that he didn't think Decker should be out looking for Tawny. In the race to be loved the fat man was bringing up the rear.

Anybody could slip up but only a schmuck persisted in his mistake. Luckily this was one mistake Decker could recall before it cost him anything. That's why he liked Bags. She knew when to rein him in, doing it in a way which didn't make him feel like a retard.

Decker knew several of the sixty or so detectives assigned to the Safe, Loft and Truck squad which dated back to the turn of the century. He reached out for Detective Lowell Chattaway, a red-faced forty-year-old Mick with breath like a drain and a propensity when drunk to crawl under dinner tables and bite diners of either sex on the thigh.

According to Chattaway two cases of Beretta 84, .380 calibre, 9mm short barrels from Milan had been stolen from a Kennedy cargo terminal over Thanksgiving weekend. An informant claimed the heist had been the work of a crew connected to the LoCasio family. To make matters worse, some four hours after leaving the airport the Berettas had disappeared again.

Credit this to the LoCasio sales force which had gone about its job in a pragmatic and businesslike manner. Before snatching the guns Joe LoCasio, the family *padrone*, had customers lined up and ready to buy. The stolen Berettas had been sold in a hurry. Unfortunately, the snitch didn't have the buyers' names. When and if the snitch got lucky Chattaway would buzz Decker.

Progress. And with only one phone call. Decker owed Bags.

At Bougival, Jean-Louis Nicolay ordered complimentary drinks for Karen's table. A gaunt, young waiter with dark, wavy hair and a weasel-like face was assigned to handle their every need. Nicolay himself passed out large, hand-written, one-page menus and described today's specials which included Tunisian couscous, rabbit stew and basboussa, a semolina pastry with almonds. He seemed to enjoy playing host so much that Decker didn't mention he'd only dropped by for a drink and to pick up some old photographs. Take away Monsieur's illusions about being important and you took away his happiness.

As Nicolay and Brenda disappeared into a small passageway leading to the restaurant's back room, a relieved Karen Drumman said to Decker, "My client cancelled at the last minute. Came down with the flu. His whole family's had it and now it's his turn. You two arrived just in time."

She looked over her shoulder then back at Decker and Ellen. "Jean-Louis was inviting me to one of his *special* parties." She shivered in revulsion.

Ellen snorted. "And he smells so nice, too. What kind of party we talking about, as if I didn't know."

"I'm no prude," Karen said. "I've been married and divorced and I've dated a bit, though not all that much I'm afraid. But Jean-Louis's a bit kinky for my taste. We went out a few times after I broke up with my husband. That was two years ago. I suppose I wanted reassurance that I was still attractive. Anyway the relationship went nowhere. Jean-Louis is into life in the fast lane and that's not for me."

She said to Ellen, "You're a cop, too, right?"

"Manny's partner."

"I thought so. I sensed Manny didn't want Jean-Louis to know he was a cop, so I kept quiet. Was it you who was checking up on me today? My office called me at home to say some policewoman had dropped by to ask whether or not I worked there. Are you two always this cautious?"

"Doesn't mean we're not nice people," Decker said, wiggling his eyebrows à la Groucho.

She said, I guess, and smiled at him, making Decker feel he'd said something very funny. Bulldog Drumman was definitely worth a trip across town in sub-freezing weather. In the cab Bags had teased him, saying that Karen was probably ugly enough to scare a dog off a meat truck, that when she came into the room the mice jumped on chairs. Not this time, Bags. Karen Drumman had looks and smarts. Dig the way she'd kept quiet about Decker being a cop.

She had something else, Decker decided. She was sweet and sweet was rare in New York where if a man breathed he could make a woman angry. As a woman said to Decker, if they can put one man on the moon, why can't they put them all there? He suspected Karen Drumman worried a lot, but he was willing to bet she wasn't all that weak. Try to break her and you'd find out how strong she was.

Decker, with an assist from Bags, had learned that Karen Drumman was from Denver, had been in New York fourteen years and lived alone with two cats. She was divorced, earned good money and did volunteer work at a Gramercy Park foundling hospital one night a week. In person she had a sad smile and lines around her eyes that Decker found attractive. She appeared warm and feminine, the sort of woman who aroused a man's protective instinct. Experience, however, had taught Decker that such women could usually take care of themselves.

Ellen said, "Let's hear about this party. We're not going to arrest anybody. I just like to know about those things." Bags was no hypocrite about gossip. She loved it and would tell you so in a minute.

Karen looked down at the table. "Lord help us. Jean-Louis insists the party's very high-class. Only the best people from here and overseas, he says. A select clientèle is how he put it. I'm under no obligation to, you know, do anything. If I go, that is. I can watch or join in, my choice. This is a very unusual party, according to him. Look, what it is, is some kind of orgy."

The table went silent as the weasel-faced waiter brought drinks. When he'd left Karen stared into a white wine spritzer sitting in front of her. "Jean-Louis has some weird ideas about women and sex, which is why I stopped going out with him. There is such a thing as too much, if you know what I mean."

"Define too much?" Ellen said.

Karen Drumman abruptly turned to Decker. "Anything new on Tawny? Stupid question. If there was I'm sure you'd have told me."

Decker said, "Before leaving the station house I checked with the National Hotline for Missing Children and the National Runaway Switchboard. Nothing. Tonight I'll phone a couple more people and see if they've got anything. But to be honest it doesn't look good."

He didn't tell her what a hotline caseworker had said, that because of the growing number of adult males craving sex with children it was more dangerous to be a kid now than it was ten years ago. Pedophiles took pictures of children they'd kidnapped and traded the photos among themselves as you would baseball cards. It was frightening to think about, the caseworker said, but Tawny's photograph might already be in somebody's collection.

Karen said, "Next Saturday Tawny, Gail and I were supposed to see the Christmas show at Radio City Music Hall. We go every year. Tawny just loves it. This would have been our fourth year, the three of us."

She smiled, creating those small lines around her eyes which Decker found very becoming. "Tawny is so special," she said. "She's a bright, bright girl. Has a mind of her own like Gail and dear God, is she beautiful."

Karen lowered her voice. "That was one thing, well of many things, about Jean-Louis which upset me. He thought Tawny was a beautiful woman. Not a child, a woman. This bothered me but I thought, well he's French and I'm from Denver so maybe I'm overlooking something. I never mentioned it to Gail because there was always the possibility I might be reading more into this than was really there."

A quick look over her shoulder, then, "But I *had* to say something when Jean-Louis said there were people who'd pay money for Tawny. People who would actually buy her. Can you imagine? God, was I annoyed with him. Well, Jean-Louis said he was only kidding. Then tonight he turns round and invites me to this slave auction."

Decker said, "Far be it from me to bad mouth anybody, but Jean-Louis appears to be constantly if not perpetually in heat."

Shaking her head Ellen said, "Lord, have mercy."

Karen Drumman said, "I couldn't believe he'd really said slave auction. I'm sorry, sex slave auction. But that's exactly what he said. According to him people are actually bought and sold at these things. He claims it's not a crime because the sex slaves voluntarily put themselves on the market. He says it happens once a year, sometimes once every two years. He could be pulling my leg except Jean-Louis's no choirboy."

Decker thought, Jean-Louis's too free with his hands to be a choirboy. Meanwhile, Bags's knee nudged his under the table by way of saying, I know you like the woman so make your move. Just looking at Karen Drumman made the darker, harder places in Decker's soul feel a bit warmer.

Bags touched his arm. "Mr Nicolay asked me what kind of business we're in."

Decker waited.

"I told him we were systems analysts," she said.

Decker grinned. "You always say that. What happens when somebody asks you what a systems analyst does?"

She and Karen Drumman laughed, both reaching out to touch each other as they shared the particular wisdom of women who'd been scamming men since the dawn of time. For a few seconds Decker felt alone and a bit jealous.

He reached for a large brown envelope near Karen's purse, pulling it towards him, not really in a hurry to examine the contents. Afraid of your own memories, my man? Afraid to behold that which life has taken away from you? Sighing, he reached inside the envelope and pulled out the photographs.

The Parris Island Graduation Day shot. Gaze upon a grinning Manfred Freiherr Decker, named for Baron Manfred von Richthofen, the legendary Red Baron and First World War flying ace. A skinny, shaven-headed Decker in dress blues and sharp shooter's medal and looking pleased with himself. Hell, why not?

And there was Gail with her arms around him, looking luscious in his white service cap, hoop earrings and a black leather mini which showed off her great legs. He thought, we were masters of the future on that day for damned sure. After a while it became too hard to look at the photograph, knowing that Gail was dead. Good or bad, there was no escaping his memories of her.

The other photographs – Decker and Gail at Coney Island where they'd gone on his final leave before he was sent to Nam, Gail and Tawny backstage at a school play, Tawny in ballerina tights and minus her front teeth, Gail, Tawny and Karen in overcoats, earmuffs and boots on line at Radio City Music Hall, Gail and Decker in formal dress on the dance floor with Ivan and Lucette La Porte, the four of them mugging for the camera at Ivan and Lucette's wedding.

Lucette had been three months pregnant when she and Ivan married. To make her eligible for any military benefits Ivan had decided to marry her before going overseas rather than wait until he returned from Saigon. As he told Decker, I don't trust the future. With Lucette I know what I got, but if I wait too long I could lose it. Decker would remember those words long after La Porte was dead and Decker had broken up with Gail.

He returned the photographs to the envelope then dropped it on the pile of menus. Ellen was showing off her knowledge of art, pointing to a Monet landscape and telling Karen the history. Decker reached for his black coffee, not sure if he should go home and get some rest or stay here with Karen Drumman. They were definitely interested in each other.

The weasel-faced waiter reappeared with his order pad. Ellen said she and Decker weren't eating. Karen said, neither am I, and quickly looked at Decker before reluctantly turning back to Ellen. Weasel Face was annoyed; without a dinner order he wouldn't be getting much of a tip from this party of big spenders. On the other hand there wasn't much he could do about it. These were Jean-Louis's amigos so if they wanted to take up space and nurse one drink until dawn what could a poor peon of a waiter do?

Weasel Face, an unemployed actor named Henry Thomas Wilton Agree, had another reason to be teed off. Today he'd had his right nipple pierced, a ploy designed to keep his lover Roger turned on and performing 'twixt the sheets like the lust bucket he was. Roger, a stage hand at Lincoln Centre, loved nipple rings and had paid for the piercing.

But Roger, bless him, didn't have to live with the pain. Henry Thomas Wilton Agree was stuck with that, thank you, and it had him ready to freak out. Brandy and tylenol, Henry Thomas's choice of painkillers, were not doing the job.

He snatched the menus from the table and stepped into the passageway leading to the back room. Far as Henry Thomas was concerned let the frog's amigos eat shit and die.

Touching Decker's shoulder Karen pointed towards the back room. "Better catch our waiter. When he took the menus I think he also took the photographs," she said.

"Can't have that," Decker said. He stood up, thinking, this should be fun. Weasel Face had an attitude problem. Then again most queens had an attitude problem.

He left the table for the back room, feeling Karen Drumman's eyes on him. He'd make his move when he returned. With Bags watching it ought to be some show. Be that as it may, Decker would be dumb if he didn't try to get to know Karen Drumman.

The back room was a smaller replica of the larger one down to the checkered tablecloths, small blackboard listing today's specials and the Charles Aznavour songs flowing from unseen speakers. Only one table was occupied. Across the room three men sat eating and talking quietly near a small wood-burning fireplace. Otherwise the back room was empty except for Weasel Face who stood just inside the doorway to Decker's right washing down pills with Diet Coke. Decker didn't know the number of calories in Diet Coke, but he knew it didn't contain booze which is what he smelled coming from the can.

He was about to ask for the photographs when his attention was drawn to the three men. Two were Koreans, burly and flat-faced in dark suits, skinny black ties and crew cuts. The larger one was in his late twenties, with a bad complexion, and the sizable neck and chest of a dedicated weightlifter. Hired muscle, Decker figured. Earns his pay by protecting his employer in a stern and frightful world.

The second Korean, who also looked inclined to take the hard line, was in his mid-thirties, with thick lips, a wide nose and horn-rimmed glasses. Decker thought, both these dudes look meaner than bears with sore asses.

Jean-Louis was the third man and the only one not eating. He was doing most of the talking, which Decker decided resembled pleading more than it did an exchange of ideas. Nervously fluttering his hands the Frenchman spoke rapidly, apparently anxious to get his point across. Decker thought, he's sucking up to the boys from the Far East who couldn't care less. Jean-Louis's campaign to win hearts and minds didn't seem to be panning out.

Suddenly Decker's heartbeat quickened and his mouth went dry. Dazed, he walked towards the Koreans. He knew the older dude, fucking knew him. And if the guy was who Decker thought he was, it raised a big problem, namely did Decker kill the son of a bitch now or later. A horrible memory, long asleep, stirred within the detective.

First to spot Decker was Jean-Louis who leaned forward and whispered to the Koreans, bringing a quick reaction from the one Decker had recognised. Fork in hand this Korean looked over his shoulder, spotted the detective, and recoiled as if he'd just spotted Freddy Kreuger. Leaping from his chair he stared wide-eyed at Decker, head moving from side to side with short, jerky movements. Decker thought, you prick, it is you. *Why aren't you dead?*

The younger Korean, "Muscles", rose from the table more deliberately, moving with the arrogance of someone who was used to being feared and respected. Fingers clenched into sizable fists, he eyed the detective as though he were the most useless pus head on the planet. Red alert, Decker thought.

But the detective's primary interest, only interest, remained the Korean wearing horn-rims, a man who was supposed to have died in Vietnam fourteen years ago. Decker hated him enough to kill him on the spot. The Korean in horn-rims was Kim Shin, formerly a captain in South Korea's Tiger Division.

Fourteen years ago. National Police compound. La Porte and Buf. Laughing Boy. And Shin. In the back of Decker's mind the grenade exploded again and he heard the screams.

An investigation into the National Police compound killings had been a joke. The CIA and the Defence Department both wanted a cover-up as opposed to another atrocity story. Top priority was keeping the plates a secret. Second priority was hiding Laughing Boy's sale of Intelligence files to the NVA, a sale known to the CIA and which had betrayed Vietnamese it had promised to protect. None of this would make the CIA look good. Unless it managed to shift the blame.

The Korean government wasn't anxious to give up Song or assume any responsibility. America's dead, agents or Marines, was its own affair. As for the files and the plates who was to say they ever existed? Under these circumstances charging Song with war crimes was ludicrous. His extradition on the say-so of a mere Marine corporal was unthinkable.

But a fall guy was needed, someone to take the weight for the missing plates and murdered Americans. Since Decker could be placed at the computer room massacre he was elected. "The Company" was not going to accept responsibility for the missing plates or dead agents if it could lay it off on someone else. Paul Jason Meeks got into the act, contending that Decker's injuries could have been the result of a double-cross by unknown associates. From Seoul, Park Song claimed Decker had lied about him in revenge for Song's having beaten him in a karate match. Unless Decker got lucky he was looking at twenty to life in Leavenworth.

Luck arrived in the form of Gerald Twentyman, a heavy-set, big-nosed Georgia country lawyer who'd helped put a peanut farmer named Jimmy Carter in the state governor's mansion. Twentyman was Buf's father, a former Second World War Marine who'd been wounded on Saipan and whose slow-walking, slow-talking ways hid a steel-trap mind. He wanted to know the truth about his son's death and had been in politics long enough to know when the government was turning the truth, when it was modifying facts to suit its convenience. This whole business, he told Decker, had all the smell of a dead skunk lying in the hot sun.

Twentyman would get to the bottom of this mess, starting with taking on Decker's legal defence. Over CIA objections Twentyman entered testimony from Private Jellicki who swore he'd seen Song and some Korean soldiers rush out of the National Police compound carrying four suitcases. Next

Twentyman had Georgia's senior US senator promise that if the CIA wasn't more forthcoming there'd be Congressional investigation into the matter of the stolen files which had ended up in NVA hands.

Finally Twentyman tracked down Constanze Herail, locating her in a Hong Kong home for the blind. She'd lost her sight when the exploding grenade had propelled flying glass into her eyes. Her deposition linked Laughing Boy to the plates, the murders of the CIA agents and the Marines. Decker was exonerated, receiving an official apology and a belated letter of commendation from the Corps. In Twentyman's words, we cut them Washingtonians high, wide and deep. I think Maxey can rest a little easy now.

Decker walked away from the proceedings convinced that nothing was more dangerous than a government out to cover its ass. As for Kim Shin he'd been reported killed by a Cong sniper on the last day of the war. Decker hadn't wept. His hatred for Shin and Laughing Boy was going to last a lifetime.

In the Bougival's back room he stopped a few feet from the two Koreans, feeling his chest tighten. He also had trouble swallowing. Fourteen years or no fourteen years, there was too much bad blood between him and Kim Shin for something not to happen. He sensed he'd just witnessed a little episode not meant for public viewing. Meaning he'd caught Kim Shin and Jean-Louis with their hands in the cookie jar.

Decker removed his shield from inside his jacket and held it up. He had a duty to try to keep the peace. How would Kim Shin react? "I'm a cop," he said. "Detective Sergeant Decker, Twentieth Precinct. Everybody stay calm. Let's not get excited."

Kim Shin glared at Jean-Louis. "A *policeman*?" he said. "You allowed a policeman here? You stupid fool. When I tell him what you've done, he'll kill you."

A shaken Jean-Louis sprang from his chair. For a few seconds he stood and silently pleaded with Kim Shin. Then a quick twitch of the head and he was hurrying towards Decker. Lower lip trembling, the Frenchman seemed on the verge of tears. Forget about savoir-faire and kissing ladies' hands, Decker thought, the man's scared shitless. Whether it was Kim Shin or a second party, Monsieur was scared of somebody. Then again, one had to wonder why Jean-Louis was hanging out with a dirtbag like Kim Shin in the first place. Monsieur was obviously living wrong.

Arms outstretched with the intention of pushing Decker backwards the little Frenchman said, "Leave at once. Go, go, go. You don't belong here. Return to the other room with your friends. I order you to leave."

Decker stiff-armed Jean-Louis in the chest, stopping him dead. The two made eye contact and held it until Jean-Louis nervously looked away. "Getting physical with cops isn't just wrong," Decker said, "it's loud wrong."

He allowed his words to sink in then said, "If you don't want to be arrested for assaulting an officer get the hell out of my face and sit your little ass down somewhere. Meanwhile, I'd like to talk to Mr Shin who I haven't seen in a long time. I'm interested in how he managed to return from the dead. Maybe he's on some kind of diet I should know about."

Jean-Louis's response was to take two steps backwards, circle right, and run from the room. Kim Shin, eyes on Decker, whispered to the young Korean who nodded but said nothing. After a few seconds of silence Kim Shin shouted at Decker, "Why you come here? Why you follow me? You not suppose to bother us. You go. Out!"

Decker snorted. "Follow you? I didn't know you were alive until now."

"You lie," Shin said. "You follow me. You disobey orders."

Decker thought, am I really hearing this? What the hell was this pudgy little shit talking about? "Orders?" he said. "What orders?"

Cross-examination would have to wait. Decker had trouble. Kim Shin barked a command in Korean and Muscles, clenching and unclenching his fists, strode confidently towards the detective. Up close and personal Muscles was one ugly son of a bitch, with pig eyes and a face like a car bomb. He was ten years younger than Decker, two inches taller and at least fifty pounds heavier. And as Decker knew, Muscles would be good at his trade. A ready for prime time player.

Decker's skin began to tingle. He felt light-headed.

Muscles elected to dispense with subtlety. He started with a sidekick, right knee to his chest as he loaded up for the most powerful kick in karate. But Decker, alert and focused, had looked at Muscles's face and read his moves. The Korean had stared at his target, revealing his game plan, warning Decker.

Muscles kicked sideways, driving his foot at Decker's ribcage. Had it landed, the kick would have broken a number of ribs and the fight would have been over. Tipped off, Decker sidestepped and evaded the attack. At the same time he grabbed a chair by the back, lifted it shoulder-high and swung with everything he had. He connected easily, clobbering Muscles on the left arm and hip, banging him hard enough to crack the chair. Muscles, however, didn't go down.

Decker didn't like that.

The Korean stopped long enough to rub his elbow. Then he punched the palm of one hand, a very loud, very ominous sound. His small eyes got smaller and a trickle of spittle dripped from the corner of his mouth. A quick smile then he shuffled towards Decker.

Still gripping the wreckage of the broken chair, Decker quickly backed up. When he had five feet of space between him and Muscles he dropped the shattered chair on the floor, jammed a foot down on it and pulled at a chair leg. He'd barely freed it when Muscles, arms outstretched, hurled himself on Decker.

Swinging the chair leg Decker banged the Korean across both knees, this time getting more of a response. Muscles stopped, rocked back on both heels and looked down at his knees. Then standing on one leg like a doggie at a hydrant he lifted the other leg off the ground and shook it. Another smile. He felt just fine. Hands up to protect his face he shuffled forward.

Fighting panic Decker swung at the Korean's wrists, putting his back and hips behind the blow, expecting to drop the dude this time. Wrong. With a quickness unexpected in a big man the Korean grabbed the chair leg in midair, yanked it from Decker's grasp then broke it over his knee and tossed the pieces aside. Decker thought, Christ.

The detective backed into a table, fought against losing his balance and that's when Muscles hurled himself on Decker, sending them both crashing onto a wooden floor smelling of lemon-tinged wax. They landed hard, in a tangle of empty chairs and tables, unlit candles, and salt and pepper shakers.

For Decker it was instant pain. He banged his left shoulder and hip. His head bumped into something hard. Instant headache. And he was on his back, a bad position to be in when fighting. Muscles was on top; the sucker weighed a ton, smelled of garlic and he was determined to put Decker away.

Refusing to panic, Decker jammed a thumb in Muscles's left eye, digging into the socket while kicking at the Korean's shins. The Korean's head snapped back. He reached for Decker's hand but before he could grab it, Decker yanked the hand back then drove the heel of the hand into the Korean's nose, crushing it. Without hesitating, Decker gripped Muscles's left ear, twisted and yanked downward, all but tearing it from the Korean's head.

Blood spurted over both men. Muscles didn't cry out but he was hurt. Rolling clear of Decker he flopped back on the floor, to lie beside the detective. Decker sat up first, in time to see Muscles reach inside his jacket for a gun. Muscles's hand was on his shoulder holster when Decker twice punched the Korean in the balls, short, chopping blows which were so quick that Decker himself wasn't aware of what he'd done. Muscles's jaw dropped and his eyes popped out. Cupping his stricken anatomy, he writhed from side to side, bloodying a pile of cloth napkins on the floor around his head.

Decker rose and when the Korean made one more, although extremely weak, attempt to pull his gun Decker kicked him in the head. Muscles fell back and lay still.

The hairs went up on the back of Decker's neck. *Behind him.* He looked over his shoulder in time to see Kim Shin swing an unopened bottle of red wine at his head. Stepping into Shin, Decker blocked his arm inside on the elbow and pushed it down. Then he smashed a forearm into Shin's face.

As Shin staggered backwards Decker, feeling a hot red mist of anger, swung his right leg in a short circle and smashed his shin into Kim Shin's right thigh. Screaming, the Korean sat down on the floor.

Face bloodied, a weeping Shin clutched his damaged leg and slumped to his side. Decker stepped closer, lifted his right leg and drove his heel into the Korean's stomach. He'd just kicked Kim Shin in the stomach a second time when three uniformed policemen, followed by Bags and Jean-Louis, rushed into the room.

It was Jean-Louis who shouted, "Arrest him! He's attacking a Korean diplomat! Arrest him!"

12

It was almost noon when Ben Dumas used his keys to enter
Ken Yokoi's Greenwich Village townhouse. Behind him stood
Oscar who sniffed at Dumas's worn attaché case while wagging a short, nearly hairless tail. Among other items the
case contained a box of mint-flavoured dog biscuits, Oscar's
preferred nosh and a food he regarded as a standard of
perfection.

Also in the attaché case were three hundred milligrams of
an experimental aerosol drug called Pentamidine. A powder
which had to be mixed with sterile water, Pentamidine was
used to prevent a life-threatening type of pneumonia which
attacked AIDS patients.

The Food and Drug Administration had yet officially to
approve the drug but was expected to do so early next year.
Dr Paulo da Sé, the baggy-eyed seventy-year-old Brazilian
who dispensed Ken Yokoi's unauthorised treatments, had
recommended at least three doses a month. Without these
treatments Yokoi would die immediately.

Dumas purchased Yokoi's Pentamidine on the black market, paying twice the list price of one hundred dollars per dose.
Outpatient Pentamidine therapy, which also included doctor
and inhaler machine costs, ran into thousands of dollars.
Money was Dumas's defence against being alone.

Before being stricken with AIDS Yokoi, a small, fortyish
Japanese with a large, square head and sleepy eyes, had been
a charismatic man whose vitality had swept away everything in its path. As a psychiatrist he'd conducted a private

practice from his townhouse where he'd grown prize-winning roses. He'd also found time to mould a slim, muscular physique through bodybuilding, jogging and *kendo*, traditional Japanese fencing.

They had been attracted to one another on sight, Dumas by Yokoi's intellect, Yokoi by Dumas's primitive strength. Both were gay, had a keen sense of order and needed constant excitement which they somehow always managed to find. When their anger was aroused, both could destroy someone and never feel a moment's guilt. What impressed Dumas most about the Japanese psychiatrist was his ability to control and direct others, something Dumas prided himself on doing well.

Yokoi's redbrick townhouse was located on Washington Square South, only doors away from where Eugene O'Neill had once lived. It faced Washington Square Park which guidebook writers continued to call the symbolic heart of the Village long after it had ceased to be true.

Nowadays the park was a hangout for drug dealers, college students from nearby NYU, the homeless, folk singers, break dancers, street magicians and EDPs, emotionally disturbed persons.

In the mahogany-panelled lobby of the townhouse he removed his hat and topcoat, hanging them in a walk-in closet. Then for a few seconds he studied a splendid floral arrangement on a nearby rattan table. It was a seasonal arrangement, one popular throughout Asia. Known as "Winter Promise" it consisted of stark Manzanita branches, azaleas, carnations and leaves of thistle, the mixture representing a promise of spring. The arrangement was one of the best Dumas had ever done.

Traditional oriental flower-arranging was his hobby. Ken Yokoi had suggested it as a means of relieving the stress involved with police work. Before meeting the psychiatrist Dumas had never thought of himself as having a talent for anything aesthetic. But with Yokoi's encouragement he'd demonstrated a gift for arranging fresh and silk flowers.

Still carrying the attaché case Dumas walked through the

living and dining areas which were linked by symmetrical arrangements of rattan and Regency chinoiserie furniture, oriental rugs and Thai tables. Each room also had floor to ceiling bookcases, a fireplace, bleached wooden floors and Japanese folding screens decorated with hand-painted scenes of the four seasons. The beauty of both rooms was enhanced by Chinese Chippendale gilt-wood pier mirrors.

In a large kitchen glistening with overhead racks of brightly coloured utensils Dumas filled a saucepan with water, then opened a door leading to the backyard. Tongue against the back of his front teeth he whistled sharply. Oscar bounded past him, leaping through the doorway and into a small backyard whose space was almost entirely filled by a thriving greenhouse.

Outside a chilly December wind stirred Dumas's thinning hair as he looked around for Oscar's feeding bowl, finding it on top of a coiled-up garden hose lying in front of the greenhouse entrance. After pouring the mint-flavoured dog biscuits into the bowl he placed it and the saucepan of water beside the garden hose. Eat up, Big O, he said to Oscar.

As the three-legged dog greedily devoured his lunch Dumas squatted beside him and stared at the greenhouse. Early in their relationship Yokoi had said to Dumas: "You are more than most men – more intelligent, more truthful, more destructive. By extension you must also be more creative. You're unhappy enough to be creative."

"Unhappy? Definitely," Dumas had said. Years of dealing with mutts, skells and maggots usually made all cops unhappy. But Dumas wasn't creative. He was a cop, coldly self-reliant and unreasonably stubborn at times. Sure he had smarts; he read *The New York Times*, attended the opera and was a member of the Metropolitan Museum of Art. He also collected travel books, a hobby he'd developed during four years in the Navy which he'd joined at the age of fifteen after lying about his age. But as he told Yokoi, this didn't mean he was Leonardo da Vinci.

On the other hand he enjoyed puttering around Yokoi's small greenhouse. The fragrance and beauty of the plants was a new and highly gratifying world, one which fulfilled Dumas in ways he'd never imagined possible. It was far removed from the shabby Bronx apartment he'd shared with a widowed father and uncle, both of whom had sexually abused him until he'd run away from home at the age of fourteen.

The greenhouse, Yokoi realised, touched something too deep in Dumas for him to talk about. That something was buried beneath the wall Dumas had erected as a defence against society's contempt for cops and gays.

"You've accepted your tactile side," Yokoi said. "Now accept the other Dumas, the one who has something beautiful within him."

"Assuming there is another me," Dumas said, "I'd weaken myself if I gave into it. I'd lose the edge I need to survive on the streets."

Yokoi took his hand. "From the moment we admit to being gay we live with an emptiness inside. We're not wretched people and we're not ugly. But society does its best to make us feel worthless if not entirely inessential in the overall scheme of things. We pretend we don't feel this disapproval. The truth is, we do. That's why it's so important for you to accept your total self. Don't go through life like a bird with only one wing. Total self-approval, Ben. That's what you need. That's what we all need."

Encouraged by Yokoi Dumas revealed an interest in classical music, Asian culture, and of course flower-arranging. He'd even begun dressing better. His quick mind allowed him to understand these new ideas and concepts at once. But it was the love shared by him and Yokoi which made this learning process both exciting and pleasurable. Dumas came to rely on the Japanese psychiatrist as he did on no one else.

As for Yokoi he was captivated by the big cop's sensuality and unpredictability. No lover had ever given him as much excitement and pleasure as the man he called "my noble savage".

Because of an enormous sexual appetite Dumas had rarely remained faithful to one lover. The three-year affair with the intriguing and cultured Ken Yokoi represented a milestone in the big cop's life. It had produced a spiritual as well as physical sharing. Not only was Dumas faithful to Yokoi but he never lost his temper with the Japanese psychiatrist. After a lifetime of searching he'd found someone in whom he had complete trust.

They'd met the night Dumas killed India Sabogal, the big-chested thirty-two-year-old Puerto Rican wife of his partner Detective Luis Sabogal. India had been hard-talking, giving Luis, a gloomy-looking, thirty-seven-year-old Rican, some sleepless nights. She'd had enough of his fooling around with other women and wanted a divorce.

To make matters worse she'd threatened to go to Internal Affairs and tell all unless he came up with big bucks as part of the final settlement. This declaration was not to be taken lightly. India Sabogal knew enough to send Luis and Dumas upstate until they were old men and the liver spots were showing through their gloves.

She knew they'd robbed drug dealers of drugs and cash, shaken down Manhattan after-hours clubs, provided drug dealers with information on search warrants and supplied guns, walkie-talkies and police shields to Dominican and black drug gangs.

She knew that gay prostitutes had provided Dumas with sexual services in exchange for drugs and money taken from the police evidence locker, that Dumas and Luis Sabogal had drowned a drug dealer in his bathtub then walked off with a suitcase containing fifty-five thousand dollars and two kilos of cocaine.

Luis Sabogal said to Dumas, "The bitch wants two hundred and fifty thousand cash, tax free, or she gives me up."

"*Us*. She gives *us* up," Dumas said.

"I haven't got that kind of bread and if I did I wouldn't give it to her. Woman's got to go. Soon as possible she has got to go. But I can't do her. She's my wife. Anybody else, I got the balls. But I can't do India."

Dumas said, "And I guess that means me, amigo. I'm just thrilled to be a part of it all. Yes sir, I am really thrilled."

"Look, it ain't all my fault," Sabogal said. "I swear on my mother's grave I didn't tell her everything. Okay, some things I told her. I mean she's my wife. The rest she picked up on herself. India's no retard."

"Let's talk about when and where it goes down. I want to know if India jogs, if she goes to church, if she ever visits her relatives. I want to know if she does drugs. I want it all, partner."

Halfway through Sabogal's rundown on his wife, which included the fact that she was a snow bird, a coke user, Dumas held up one hand in a stop signal. "The ball," he said. "That's where it happens. That's where you get your instant divorce, sport."

"You shitting me? You're saying you plan to walk up to my wife and smoke her when she's surrounded by thirty, forty citizens. And when she knows what you look like. Christ, get real. I been to a couple of these balls and I know for a fact they draw hundreds of people."

"Doing her like that sort of adds to the excitement, doesn't it?"

Sabogal rolled his eyes up into his head, thinking, sure as shit he's gonna do it. Five years partners with this whacko and I should know him by now. He's gonna do it. Thank God I won't be there when this one goes down.

In three days India Sabogal and her brother Danny would attend the House of Grandeur Ball, part of New York's drag scene which held little appeal for the butch Dumas. These balls were combination fashion show and beauty pageant put on by black drag queens who'd been organising them in their communities since the 1920s.

Using a dance style called "Voguing", after the magazine, competitors showed off fashions designed and made by themselves. Harlem dancers had invented Voguing as a parody of the white fashion world which had barred them for years. The House of Grandeur Ball would be held on Hallowe'en. Perfect, Dumas thought. Perfect.

Drag queens competed in these balls as a *house*, a unit. In this sub-culture, with its own rules, language and culture,

India's brother Danny was a superstar drag queen who performed under the name Miss Fleurette. He was a popular singer-dancer at gay clubs and while they'd never met Dumas knew him by reputation. India Sabogal was devoted to her brother, serving as his manager, chauffeur and protector. She also designed clothes for him and the House of Grandeur.

"From now on India's my problem," Dumas said. "You just make sure that on Hallowe'en you're surrounded by a lot of people, say from ten that evening until one the next morning. Now tell me about the ball, especially about backstage or wherever the queens get dressed."

"You might need an invitation. India keeps some around the apartment for family and friends. Whenever her precious Danny's performing she likes a full house. Dude's a highstrung little prick who's always hitting us up for money."

Dumas shook his head. "No invitation. When I show up it won't be at the front door."

Hallowe'en. At eleven twenty-two on a night somewhat mild for the time of year Dumas entered the First Avenue Projects on the Lower East Side, site of the House of Grandeur Ball. Not exactly one of your finer areas, he thought.

Populated by Latins, Chinese and blacks, the First Avenue Projects was a public housing development located in a rundown neighbourhood of abandoned tenements, vacant lots, shattered windows and graffiti-covered walls. Residents included a few elderly Jews, survivors of pogroms in Russia and Eastern Europe, who were now too poor to leave the area. Vandalism and the ravages of time had given the surrounding streets a desolate, menacing feeling.

Dumas wore a black wig, sunglasses, and a scruffy army overcoat purchased at an Eighth Avenue pawnshop. He'd also pasted Band-Aids across the bridge of his nose and stuffed cotton in his mouth between the gum and top lip. Draped over his right forearm was an elegant evening dress made of hand-dyed silk. In his waistband was a .22 Magnum with the serial number filed off and a silencer attached to the barrel. To prevent the gun from slipping down into his pants

Dumas had wrapped three oversized rubber bands around the grip.

Clipping India Sabogal with people around was tricky, but Dumas wouldn't have it any other way. The more pressure, the more he enjoyed himself. He was never happier than when in a crisis. Deliberately putting himself at risk was a process of self-renewal.

On the project grounds Dumas followed a group of people with brightly coloured Mohawk haircuts, leather face masks, chains, spikes, rubber dresses and velcro hightop sneakers. In front of him a chubby Oriental man in a sarong skirt and pearls smoked a joint. To Dumas's left a bearded white male in a hoopskirt held hands with a gaunt black male in a miniskirt and bustier. Dumas thought, either I'm heading towards the ball or I'm marching in some freak and geek parade.

He looked up at the sky. A full moon. Despite the moon the Project grounds remained poorly lit. Vandals and junkies had destroyed or stolen most of the outside lighting, including streetlights, bulbs and a few hundred feet of electrical wiring. Down here they'd saw a cat in half and sell both parts. Dumas, however, welcomed the semi-darkness. It made him that much harder to recognise.

He didn't need lights to know that his size thirteens were crushing empty crack phials by the dozen. Nor did he need to see the faces of local residents and drug addicts who lounged on broken benches and hurled insults. However, he could see black and Latin youths who yelled obscenities from surrounding apartment windows. One of the little bastards threw a D-battery, a lemon-sized chunk of metal which barely missed two bony women dressed in matching white tuxedos and studded dog-collars.

Holding hands the women quickened their pace. The rest of the group, Dumas included, hastily followed. He wasn't scared, far from it in fact. But a sure way of calling attention to himself was to show more balls than his fellow fun-seekers.

On reaching the west wing of the Projects the crowd stopped at the entrance to a basement auditorium. Guarding the door was a thirtyish Latin butch queen in camouflage fatigues who was backed by a snarling Rottweiler chained to the doorknob. Pinned to the dog's studded collar was a button reading, *AIDS is like a balloon – one prick and you're gone*. Just what the world needs, Dumas thought. Dogs as social activists.

Leaving the crowd he walked to the rear of the auditorium, past addicts and homeless men crouched at the building's barred, broken windows. The ball didn't start until midnight so what were these dirtbags staring at? Then from the auditorium came sounds of *salsa*, cheers and applause. The junkies and their pals were enriching their lives by watching a dance contest, a warm-up prior to the main event. For a few minutes the shit world around them didn't exist.

The queens take this stuff seriously, Luis had said to Dumas. The House of Grandeur, composed entirely of Latins, was to compete against other Latin and black houses for cash prizes and trophies. Danny de la Vega, India's brother, was expected to cop first prize in the top categories of best face and best female impersonator, the drag equivalent of two Oscars. Celebrity judges included a famed Italian fashion designer, a celebrated Japanese fashion photographer and two transvestites who sang with a downtown rock group called the Booty Sisters.

Behind the auditorium he stood watching three Latin drag queens walk down a small staircase and disappear into the building. Smoking joints the trio cheerfully hummed "Lara's Theme".

He looked around. Nobody close by, nobody looking at him. Removing the .22 from under his overcoat he concealed it under the silk dress which he'd draped over his right forearm. "Let's do it," he whispered. He felt unruffled, untroubled. His smile was natural and unprompted.

He walked down the short iron staircase leading down into the auditorium. Guarding the doorway was a black bodybuilder in a flat top, and wearing a Trump Plaza sweatshirt, green stretch shorts and white cowboy boots. With him was a skinny Dominican butch queen with dyed orange hair and a nose ring. A folded straight razor hung from her neck on a thin gold chain.

Past them Dumas could see a low-ceilinged passageway with people rushing madly back and forth. Tonight the Voguing contestants were using the area and its offices, supply, laundry and boiler rooms as changing rooms. It'll be total chaos back there, Luis had told Dumas. Confusion up the ass. But that's where you'll find India.

Dumas couldn't have been calmer. Extending the dress towards the bodybuilder he said, "For Danny de la Vega." Under the dress the .22 was aimed at the spade's navel. A reflex action, nothing more. If Dumas couldn't get in he had no intention of icing the spade. He'd simply leave and take out India some other time.

As the Dominican lustfully viewed the dress the body-builder, displaying his cool by wearing mirrored sunglasses, jerked his head towards the uproar inside, a signal for Dumas to enter. The big cop stepped into the passageway. Confusion up the ass was right.

Dumas found the passageway no different from being in the subway at rush hour. The tunnel-like area was crammed with people. Some leaned against graffiti-splattered walls and drank cheap wine from Styrofoam cups. Others pampered themselves with unregistered chemicals. Dumas could have made enough drug busts in this hallway to fill the police property room twice over.

He saw friends calming down nervous drag queens who were suffering from pre-contest jitters. Men and women carrying gowns and women's shoes squeezed past drag queens who were posing for photographers. Dumas stepped on something that appeared to be a small dog but which turned out to be a long black wig. Two queens, make-up and mascara running, held each other and cried. Against his inclination Dumas found the commotion around him exciting.

What he didn't like were the smells – the urine odour found in projects all over the city, compounded by the body odour of contestants and spectators. He also didn't like the heat, the result of too many people jammed in a small space. The sooner he dropped the hammer on India Sabogal, the sooner he could quit this loony bin and take off the overcoat. The wig, which had started to itch, was also a problem. As for the ghettoblasters, forget it. Anyone who liked that noise should have his ears nailed to the floor.

According to a makeshift directory Scotch-taped to the door the changing area for House of Grandeur was to the right, in the laundry room. Dumas began walking in that direction, free arm on the dress to keep anyone from grabbing it and heading south. Down here they'd steal the teeth out of your mouth, then come back for the gums.

As expected the laundry room was crowded with people spilling through the doorway and out into the passageway. Inside, drag queens were having clothes fitted to *salsa* coming from two ghettoblasters. The noise level was nerve-racking. It took Dumas a couple of minutes to get from the hallway and inside where he stood near the entrance and looked around for India Sabogal.

He smiled. She was twenty feet away in front of a broom closet which she was using as a temporary clothes locker. Tonight the pudgy, big-bosomed India wore a hot pink jumpsuit, black satin pumps and a false chignon. Dumas watched her finger a sleeveless blue silk dress being fitted to the prettiest drag queen he'd ever seen. Had to be Danny boy and if so, what a luscious little morsel he was. Curvaceous with an auburn pony tail, Danny de la Vega had slim arms and enticing tits courtesy of hormone injections and silicon. Dumas felt himself getting a hard on.

At least two people in the laundry room could identify Dumas, one being India Sabogal. The other was a young blond hunk who worked as a bartender at a Jane Street gay bar.

Blondie had been one of Dumas's lovers, an association which ended six months ago when a jealous Dumas had broken both of the kid's arms. On the far side of the laundry room Blondie now held hands with a young Latin male who wore a green turban and a gown made from grey drapes. Like everyone else in the room they ignored Dumas.

India Sabogal's back was to Dumas as he pushed through the crowd towards her. Getting past this mob was hard work. At one point the dress was nearly yanked from his arm when he accidentally caught it on some guy's studded leather wristband.

Dumas had almost reached India when she threw up both hands in frustration and walked away. He thought, come back, you stupid bitch. One of her two male Latin assistants pointed to Danny's hemline. Apparently that was the problem.

Danny, meanwhile, was in his own world. Stretching one arm overhead he examined an imitation diamond bracelet worn over a long blue evening glove. He was still admiring his junk jewellery when India stepped into the nearby broom closet in search of something. Hissing at each other in Spanish the two Latins fingered the hem on Danny's dress. Dumas smiled. Time to punch big sister's ticket.

He pressed forward, passing close enough to Danny to smell the little queen's perfume, to see the sweat and pimples on his bare back, to hear his off-key humming.

Four more steps brought Dumas to the broom closet where India Sabogal now knelt with her back to the room. He watched as she impatiently rummaged through a suitcase filled with scraps of dress material. From cursing in Spanish she suddenly switched to cursing in English.

Dumas looked around. Nobody watching. Time to get down.

Keeping the silenced .22 under the dress he pressed it against the back of India's false chignon and fired twice. She fell forward, landing on the suitcase, her chunky body half in, half out of the closet. One bejewelled meaty hand knocked over a pair of green leather high-heeled shoes.

Dropping the dress on India's corpse Dumas shoved the gun under his overcoat and suit jacket and into his waistband. Just one more drug-related killing in Fun City. India had been a coke head, after all.

Turning he coolly made his way through the boisterous crowd, taking his time, not hurrying and feeling more relaxed than he had all day. *A clean hit with a room full of people looking on and he was going to get away with it.* Dumas would risk his life any day of the week for this kind of excitement.

Outside on the project grounds he ducked into the first empty apartment lobby he saw and took off the overcoat. After making sure the pockets were empty he removed the wig, cotton balls and dark glasses, putting them in a jacket pocket. Then he unscrewed the silencer from the .22, placing it and the gun in another jacket pocket. Later he would break the gun down, then dump pieces and silencer into a sewer.

Whistling "Lara's Theme" he left the projects thinking after tonight Danny might need a shoulder to cry on. Dumas could always look up the kid and offer him some consolation.

A block away on Second Avenue he placed the overcoat on top of an overflowing trash basket. Five minutes from now the coat would be the property of some junky or booze hound. Call it a slight atonement for having blown away India Sabogal. Meanwhile, Dumas was hungry.

He began walking downtown towards East Houston Street and a Chinese place which had some of the best *moo goo gai pan* in Manhattan. It wasn't smart to wander around here at night, but Dumas was in a mood to walk. Other than an occasional panhandler or junkies out looking for victims, the area was deserted. Did Dumas fear getting mugged? Anyone who wanted to try was free to step up and take his best shot.

Tonight as Dumas headed towards East Houston he wondered if he ought to charge Luis for having clipped India. Hadn't been for Luis and his big mouth they wouldn't have had any trouble with the woman. Why shouldn't Luis compensate his partner for services rendered? Dumas was still kicking around the idea when he saw it.

Trouble. Which was the last thing Dumas needed while trying to leave the site of a homicide in which he figured rather prominently.

The big cop stepped to his left and stood still, merging with shadows cast by empty store fronts. Eyes narrowed, he stared straight ahead. At the end of the block four males, young Latins, stepped from a battered blue Ford parked half on the sidewalk, half on the street. Standing shoulder to shoulder they waited for two men and a woman crossing the street and heading in their direction.

Dumas thought, what the hell do I do now? The Latins were going to fiend these three citizens, no doubt about it. One spic gripped a length of chain, another had a knife or a screwdriver, Dumas wasn't sure which. A third bore a machete on his shoulder as though it were a rifle.

Oblivious to any danger the well-dressed citizens remained deep in conversation, strolling along with no more concern than backpackers on a nature hike. One was a short Caucasian male with a full head of grey hair and a matching grey suit which Dumas guessed cost a small fortune. Beside him was a tall, blonde woman in a tweed skirt, blue blazer and boots. The third potential victim who was doing most of the talking, was a small Asian male with expressive hands and horn-rimmed glasses. Dumas thought, three chumps begging to be ripped off.

The trio proceeded along a trash-laden sidewalk, past shops which lay filthy and uninhabited behind rusted steel gates, past a filthy, half-naked black man lying at the base of a corner streetlight. Uptown folks out slumming, Dumas thought. Down here to catch an experimental play or attend a gallery opening or dine at some "in" restaurant located off the beaten path.

Like Dumas maybe they'd read *Bonfire of the Vanities* and now wanted to see for themselves how New York's underclass lived. He could only shake his head at the arrogance which had brought these turkeys down here this time of night.

His first reaction was to back off, to let the robbery go down. If these respectable, upstanding folks got hurt, so what.

Let Dumas start playing cop and he'd have to explain to his superiors exactly why he'd been in this area at this particular time. *Detective, would you mind telling us how you just happened to be on the lower east side the night your partner's wife was having her brains blown out at a drag ball?*

Let these schmucks get taken off. Next time they'd think twice before strolling around a shithole like this after dark. If they lived, that is.

But even as he debated his next move Dumas found himself tiptoeing down the block, closing in on the taco benders who'd backed the victims to the corner streetlight. Situations like this brought back bad memories, all tied in with abuse he'd suffered as a kid. Each time he trashed some asshole he was really getting even with his father and uncle. That's why he'd become a cop. That's why he'd never stopped hating those two old men in the Bronx who'd made his life hell.

Dumas kept to his left, staying near the buildings and in the shadows, stepping over empty whisky bottles and beer cans and trying not to tread on syringes discarded by junkies. When he was almost on the Latins he pulled his Smith & Wesson from its belt holster and shifted it to his left hand.

Then reaching into a back pocket he took out a blackjack, a carrot-shaped piece of black leather and black masking tape with a lead centre – a guaranteed bone breaker and life taker. Slipping his hand through an end strap, he tightened the strap around his wrist. The "red buzz", that wild anger for ever in his heart, had made him almost feverish.

Killing India Sabogal had been fun. He hadn't felt the slightest animosity towards the woman. She'd had to go, he'd done it, and that was that. But this little exercise with the four Latins, now that was different. Call it personal. Watching the taco benders swoop down on citizens was a reminder that Dumas had once been a victim. That's why backing off was unthinkable.

Hands behind his back, he stepped into the light of the streetlamp. Spit trickled from a corner of his mouth. His cold eyes never blinked. The red buzz had pushed him into a brief madness. The rage in him knew only the will to destroy.

Like any wolf pack the one Dumas now prepared to confront didn't just want money; it also wanted to exercise power. The tall, blonde woman was the target of a chunky dark-skinned Dominican who used the tip of his machete to toy with a string of pearls hanging from her neck. Rigid with fear she attempted to maintain her composure. Speaking in an English accent, she forced herself to display a calm she didn't feel. "Take what you want," she said, "but please don't harm us."

The chunky Dominican brushed her breasts with the back of his hand. As she flinched he said, "Maybe I want something else. Maybe I take you up on the roof. We get some wine, some dope. We party all night long. I be good to you. Real good."

Eyes closed, the terrified woman shook her head.

As two Dominicans began a search of the two males, a fourth mugger, a tall pock-marked teenager with one end of a bicycle chain wrapped around his fist, sensed someone behind him. He turned and Dumas clubbed him in the collarbone with the blackjack, dropping the teenager screaming to the pavement.

A slender, dark-skinned teen who'd been examining the contents of a victim's wallet never got the chance to turn around. Striking from the rear Dumas whacked him in the right elbow. The kid shrieked, threw the wallet up in the air and clutched his shattered arm. Seconds later he staggered forward, tripped on the curb and fell to his knees in the gutter.

The kid with the machete was caught by surprise. After a quick look at his prostrate associates he eyed Dumas for a second or two before saying, "You fucking crazy or what? I kill your ass, man. I kill your ass." Blade resting on his shoulder he took two steps towards the big cop.

He stopped dead when Dumas's left arm came up and pointed the Smith & Wesson at his face. The Latin turned into a chubby, breathing statue. But he tightened his grip on the machete.

"Want to drop that?" Dumas said softly.

Eyes hot with hate, the Dominican hesitated. Dumas waited, gun hand steady. Finally, the Dominican opened his hand and the machete dropped to the sidewalk. Dumas quickly swung the Smith & Wesson around to cover the fourth mugger, a bug-eyed little crackhead with rotten teeth. Nothing to worry about here, because this one had no *cajones*. Positioned between the two male victims, he hadn't moved to join the combat. Either he'd been scared or he'd had a great deal of faith in machete man's know-how.

As the red buzz subsided a poised Dumas spoke softly. "Turn around and assume the position," he said to the little doper. The crackhead complied, facing the streetlight, legs spread, hands touching the grey metal post.

Machete man, however, was still hanging tough. Still acting hard. "I smell shit," he said. "Must be a cop round here some place. Stinking cop." He spat, narrowly missing Dumas's left shoe. "Had my heat with me, you'd have gone down. For sure, your cop ass would have gone down."

A smiling Dumas said, "There's a time and place for attitude, Chico." He kicked machete man in the balls. Doubling over, the Latin sucked in air and cupped his out-of-order scrotum. Sighing, Dumas returned the Smith & Wesson to its holster. Then almost as an afterthought he slugged the stricken Dominican in the forehead with the blackjack, knocking him unconscious to the ground.

Dumas looked at the victims, thinking, let's hear it. Police brutality, violation of civil rights, racism towards ethnic minorities and all that shit. Surprise. Not a word from the trio. Not a single expression of indignation at this unkind treatment of our Latin brothers.

The blonde woman, in fact, nodded her head in approval. The Asian, he was Japanese, eyed Dumas with an intense, wet-lipped interest. There was something sexual coming from the Japanese which temporarily unnerved the big cop. Talk about a far-out bunch.

He patted down the doper. The little shit had a sharpened screwdriver tucked in his belt and that was it for weapons. Dumas also found a cheap plastic wallet containing a one dollar bill, two subway tokens, change and a single condom. And he turned up three phials of crack which he crushed under his heel, making the perp a bit misty-eyed.

Now the hard part. How to keep this little skirmish from tying him to the murder of India Sabogal.

Still badly shaken the small Japanese, who had a big head and sleepy eyes, stepped forward to assume the role of spokesman. Taking Dumas's right hand in both of his he said, "You saved our lives. I can't tell you how grateful we are." His hands were extremely soft and he never took his gaze from Dumas' face.

The Englishwoman, not as young as she'd appeared from a distance, said, "Had you not come along I dread to think what might have happened. I'm Rowena Ollenbittle. Dear God, I'm still trembling. I've never gone through anything like this before in my life. You were magnificent. Absolutely magnificent."

Dumas lit a cigarette, anything to hide his annoyance with this crew whose stupidity now threatened his survival. However, he did enjoy listening to Rowena what's-her-name speak. She had a beautiful English accent, very upper class, something he heard only on television or in the movies. He could've listened to her talk about anything for hours. If she'd said, I'm third cousin to the Queen of England, Dumas would have believed her.

Of the three, the little man with grey hair and suit to match remained the most frightened of all. Mopping sweat from his brow with a red silk handkerchief, he whispered to himself in French as though not convinced the worst was over. Dumas didn't like the guy's smile. It was too wide. Wide smiles belonged to frightened people and frightened people were also weak people and not to be trusted.

Hand extended, Grey Hair said, "Jean-Louis Nicolay. Thank you, thank you, thank you. So grateful, monsieur, so very grateful."

"You people don't belong down here," Dumas said. "You were only asking to be ripped off."

The Frenchman's wide, nervous smile grew even broader. "Ah, monsieur, we were to go to the First Avenue Projects for a costume show. *Oui*, a costume show. We had dinner at a restaurant a few blocks away. I am thinking of buying it. I am in the restaurant business, you see. Afterwards I thought we could walk to the show. It is not so far away. I thought it would be safe to walk such a short distance."

Dumas said, "You thought wrong." Why couldn't these three clowns just go away and let him get on with his life?

He was pondering his next move when he noticed something odd if not downright unconventional. The three were eyeing each other like people with something to hide. Dumas had been a cop long enough to know when he was being stonewalled. These three had suddenly developed chronic speech impediments. *What were they covering up?*

The sleepy-eyed Japanese stared at Dumas who'd finally figured him out. The dude was gay and watching Dumas kick ass had definitely turned him on. No surprise to Dumas. The Japanese said, "Am I correct in assuming you're a policeman?"

Dumas thought, time to play *Let's Make A Deal*. He'd smelled it coming when the trio stared at each other and had that wordless conversation. For some reason these citizens didn't want cops prowling around their lives.

Dumas smiled. "I'm a police officer, yes. You people want to press charges against this group?" Yeah, right.

Again the trio eyed each other. Silent signals flew back and forth. It was all Dumas could do to keep from laughing out loud. Eventually the Japanese said, "There's no need to carry this any further. None of us was injured, thanks to you. Speaking for everyone, we'd rather not press charges."

Dumas dropped his cigarette to the pavement and stepped on it. "Whatever you say."

The Japanese pointed to the Dominicans. "What about them?"

Dumas smiled. "Looks to me as if they're lost in thought. I think we ought to leave them alone."

Throwing back her head, the Englishwoman let loose with a rousing laugh. "Marvellous. Bloody marvellous. I like this man."

Eyeing the machete lying near her feet she said, "Could we get out of here? At the moment, I haven't the slightest interest in some bloody drag show. The last thing I want to see is some man swishing around in Granny's undies. What I could use is a stiff gin and tonic."

Smiling, she took Dumas's arm. "And you, sir knight or Clint Eastwood, or whoever you are, you shall join me."

The Frenchman looked at the Japanese, ready to follow his lead.

"Perhaps we should forgo the show," the Japanese said. Reaching out he touched Dumas's bicep. "Please forgive me for not introducing myself," he said. "I'm Ken Yokoi. Dr Ken Yokoi."

December, Washington Square. Dumas entered the master bedroom of Ken Yokoi's townhouse in time to see a plump forty-year-old Jamaican nurse with two gold front teeth hook Yokoi up to an intravenous solution. A highly concentrated food formula, the solution nourished AIDS patients who were unable to eat.

Bed-ridden and bald from chemotherapy, a scrawny Ken Yokoi lived connected to oxygen and assorted life-giving tubes. Because he was now powerless and weak he permitted only Dumas to see him. As a psychiatrist he'd controlled everything in his life and that of his patients. AIDS was something he couldn't control.

When the nurse had left them alone Dumas kissed Yokoi's forehead then stroked his cheek. "Can I get you anything, babe?" he said.

Slowly shaking his head Yokoi spoke in a hoarse whisper. "Where's Oscar?"

"In the backyard with his mint-flavoured dog biscuits. I think he's the world's first three-legged gourmet."

"Rowena?"

Dumas took Yokoi's hand. "She arrives from London tomorrow evening. I'm picking her up at Kennedy then we're driving straight to Astoria, right to the house. Auction starts the minute she gets there. Checked out the slaves last night. They're as ready as they'll ever be. As usual I've got extra security on the house until this thing is over."

"And our friend Park Song?"

223

"Laughing Boy comes in tomorrow. Or the day after. You know him. He thinks he's tricky. Gives you an arrival time then switches at the last minute to keep you off balance. He'll show up, though. He's hot for that little blonde kid we're holding for him. And he has to sell enough funny money to come up with Colonel Youngsam's thirty million dollars. Rowena has my final report on the buyers Song's planning to meet here. He should have it by now. Not having heard anything, I assume all's well and he's on his way."

Yokoi took a deep breath then said, "He is one very strange man. Doesn't want women around for any longer than it takes to screw them and kill them."

"You sound like a feminist."

"And you're hung like an amoeba."

Holding hands, they laughed. After a few seconds of silence Yokoi asked about the customers who were planning to attend Rowena Dartigue's sex auction tomorrow night.

Dumas shook his head. "It's amazing how worked up they are for this thing. Spoke to two of them last night. They can't wait. One's Osteros, the Colombian banker who's got this thing about teenage redheads with small tits. Also spoke to that Swedish airline pilot, the one you think looks like Kirk Douglas. He's still into twelve-year-old black boys."

Dumas chuckled. "Takes all kinds, I suppose. Speaking of which, Rowena tells me our friend Laughing Boy can't wait to get his paws on Tawny DaSilva."

Yokoi concentrated. Finally he said, "Tawny. Tawny. Is she one of my patients? So hard to remember. So hard."

A depressed Dumas kissed Yokoi's hand, thinking, nothing prepared you for watching someone you love die of AIDS. Not religion, not years of being a cop, not any philosophy you thought you believed in. Nothing prepared you for this. The suffering dragged you down, made you think, and in the end there was no limit on the pain. Yours and his. It had been years since Dumas felt this inept, this inadequate.

Ken had days on which his mind was as sharp as it ever was. Other days it was painfully obvious that AIDS was getting to his brain more and more. Dumas didn't blame Ken for thinking he'd treated Tawny DaSilva. It was Ken who, from among his more unstable and attractive patients, selected many of the sexual slaves marketed by Rowena Dartigue, apart from those she herself chose from the Lesley Foundation. Occasionally Jean-Louis Nicolay found a slave from among individuals encountered through his eastside restaurant or the Manhattan swing clubs and orgies he attended with great frequency. But it was Ken who worked on the slaves' minds, convincing them to admit they were inherent submissives, to admit they were sexual animals born to obey their masters.

Rowena Dartigue paid for the therapy, the slaves' upkeep and the house in Astoria, Queens, where they were confined until being auctioned off. Other than that rare London sale to a trusted customer, slave auctions were held outside England. As Rowena told Dumas: "I believe you Americans said it best: one doesn't shit where one eats."

She also provided customers from around the world, via the money laundering she conducted through the Lesley Foundation. As Ken told Dumas, Rowena Dartigue's talent was to exploit your needs whatever they happened to be.

Through his detective agency Dumas ran a check on the slaves to ensure they didn't have relatives or friends who might make trouble. His agency also provided security for the Queens house. But in Dumas's opinion neither he nor Rowena was as important to the operation as Ken.

Every so often the tightfisted Rowena bitched about having to pay Ken big bucks. But she was forced to admit that without the esteemed Dr Yokoi they'd each be wearing threadbare clothing and eating cheaper cuts of meat.

Until a month ago, when his respiratory problems had suddenly worsened, Ken had treated submissives from his bed, hiding his deteriorating appearance behind a black satin robe, gloves and a black leather face mask to hide facial sores.

In the bedroom Dumas leaned close to Ken and said, "Tawny's not a patient, babe. She's the kid Nicolay put me on to, the one who used to come into the restaurant with her mother."

Yokoi closed his eyes. "I remember now. You brought her

to see me. Lovely child. She should make Park Song happy even if he isn't into long relationships."

"You got that right," Dumas said. Tawny DaSilva was going to die and all because Nicolay had bought the downtown restaurant he'd been scouting the night Dumas had saved his tush from the beaners. To buy the property Nicolay had borrowed a hundred and fifty thousand dollars from Yokoi at a straight ten per cent interest, a good deal as interest rates went.

But because the Frenchman couldn't hold on to his chef the restaurant had folded within three months of opening. Nicolay then proceeded to ignore his debt to Yokoi, no surprise to Dumas. At Yokoi's request, unfortunately coming after the loan had been made, Dumas ran the frog through the computer.

The cop learned that Nicolay, who was something of a sex freak, had operated restaurants in Nice, Tangiers and Saigon. He'd also occupied himself with such sidelines as gunrunning, pimping and counterfeiting. Luck, political connections, and the timely disappearance of witnesses had so far kept the horny Nicolay out of the joint.

He'd been the one who'd brought Rowena and Ken together. Nicolay and Ken had met at a Manhattan sex club where nightly orgies went on. The Frenchman had met Rowena Dartigue by washing money through her Lesley Foundation. To such a man welshing on a debt was no worse than picking your nose.

After contracting AIDS Ken's need for money became critical. Dumas did all he could financially then demanded that Nicolay pay what he owed. The Frenchman responded by handing over fifty thousand dollars then pleading poverty. He was rebuilding the kitchen in his East 64th Street restaurant, he said. He also had tax troubles and the unions were making his life miserable. All he needed was a little time and he'd produce the rest.

Dumas suspected Nicolay was deliberately stalling, anticipating that Ken's death would cancel the debt. The Frenchman was a calculating little prick who'd lost his shirt more than once because he tried to do too much and never knew when to quit. He also had few qualms about taking advantage of others' bad luck. It was Dumas who freed him from the misconception that he wouldn't have to reimburse Ken Yokoi.

The week before Thanksgiving the big cop made an unannounced appearance at the Frenchman's apartment on Central Park South and delivered what he termed "the final notice". At the close of their dialogue a sobbing Nicolay, looking down at the blade of the Swiss Army knife pressed against his balls, vowed to repay the balance of his loan within the week.

Which was why the next day, a Sunday, he invited Dumas to Bougival restaurant, seating him three tables away from a lovely adolescent girl having brunch with her mother and a slim, red-haired woman. Pointing to the girl Nicolay said: "Her name's Tawny DaSilva and I think she can make us both rich. Ring Rowena and see what she says." The Frenchman's hands shook so badly he had trouble lighting a cigarette. Dumas looked at her for several seconds then returned to his *quiche Lorraine*.

Twenty minutes later, in a trans-Atlantic telephone call from the restaurant office, Dumas described Tawny to Rowena Dartigue. Well done, the Englishwoman said. The AIDS scare had increased the demand among certain prudent adults for youthful sex partners, minors being considered less likely to have the dreaded illness.

Dumas said to Rowena: "I want a bigger payoff this time." His fee for checking out the girl's background and a bonus at the end of the upcoming slave auction wouldn't be enough. Not with Ken's AIDS treatments costing as much as they did. It was possible that little Miss Tawny could bring as much as a quarter of a million dollars.

Dumas demanded half, said demand being non-negotiable. Since Rowena had little choice, she bowed to his wishes. She hated parting with money, but it behooved a sensible woman to know with whom she was dealing. In Dumas she was dealing with a man whose love was mad and knew no limits. Better a fiscal adjustment on little Miss Tawny than arouse Dumas's enmity for refusing to help Ken Yokoi.

In his bedroom Ken Yokoi looked from his intravenous food solution to Dumas and said, "This auction's the first I'll miss since getting together with Rowena. Counting on you to bring me up to date on the gossip. What's wrong? You're looking ultra butch. Means you're brooding about something. What?"

"Manny Decker," Dumas said. "The man's getting closer and I don't like it. He's following Tawny and she's leading him straight to my doorstep. I thought icing her parents would keep him away from me and Russell Fort. Then last night he goes to Jean-Louis's restaurant to meet this lady friend of Tawny's mother and he spies Kim Shin and Jean-Louis having a heart to heart in the back room."

The big cop sighed. "Decker and Shin's bodyguard go at it. Decker not only kicks the guy's ass, he gives Shin a tune-up as well. Since Shin's got a diplomatic passport, this brings the matter to the attention of the police department, the Korean mission and the American government."

Yokoi said, "So what's the problem?"

"The problem is Russell Fort gets Park Song's paper which he passes on to me and Jean-Louis. We then pass it on to Kim Shin at the Republic of Korea mission here and he gets it to Song. Now suppose Decker starts wondering why Jean-Louis and Shin are so buddy-buddy. Suppose he somehow links Jean-Louis to me. That shit at the restaurant last night wouldn't have happened if Decker hadn't been tracking little Miss Tawny, as Rowena calls her."

"Fort still in Washington?" Yokoi said.

"Should be on his way back with the extra paper Song asked for. Kim Shin was bitching that we weren't coming up with the paper fast enough. I figure Colonel Youngsam's holding Park Song's feet to the fire and Song's passing it on. Jean-Louis was trying to calm Kim Shin down when Decker showed up. I might have been there if I hadn't had to go to Astoria and get things ready for Rowena."

Dumas held up two fingers. "My second problem with Decker. Couple days ago he visits DEA and picks up the profile sheets turned in by those two undercover cops who got whacked by drug dealers. I got fifty thousand a piece for fingering them. No regrets, babe. We needed the money and that's that. Anyway, I'm wondering how close Decker is to learning that Fort's lady, Susan Scudder, gave up those two undercover guys."

Yokoi smiled. "This Decker, he's a summer cold. You just can't get rid of him."

"I know all about Decker. He'll keep coming at you and he'll be so smooth about it that if he told you to go to hell, you'd actually look forward to the trip. What happens when he learns that Jean-Louis knew Kim Shin and Laughing Boy in Saigon. What happens if he leans on Jean-Louis and the frog gives me up. By the way, Saigon's also where Decker had a run-in with Shin and Park Song."

Ken Yokoi slowly lifted a forefinger. "Did you or any of those psychopaths who work for you run Decker through your trusty computer?"

Dumas nodded. "The man's squeaky clean. Or maybe I should say he's yet to be caught dirty. Very into the martial arts. Supposed to be good at it. One thing: few years back he quit the cops and went to work for a private security firm. Then after a couple guys at the company got themselves smoked in mysterious fashion Decker resigns and he's back on the cops."

Closing his eyes in thought Yokoi said, "And what does this tell you?"

"There was some talk about revenge, about how Decker had gone to work for the company just so he could get those two guys. He was never accused of anything. To this day nobody knows who did those suckers."

"You think Decker murdered them?"

"The man has his moods."

A smiling Yokoi opened his eyes. "Don't make me laugh. It shakes the tubing loose." He put a finger to his lips in a request for silence. He was thinking. Dumas waited.

Finally, Yokoi said, "Don't kill Decker. Not yet. Not until I tell you to."

"Whatever you say."

Yokoi held up a forefinger. "Check out his support system. Find out who he's attached to. Wife, girlfriend, partner. That's where he's weakest."

"I understand."

"Force him to defend himself on different fronts," Yokoi said. "If you become too reckless and go after him directly, you risk getting destroyed. I know you don't mind getting destroyed, but for my sake please consider this only as a last resort. Position yourself so that you can surprise him. Your helping Colombians to kill cops is one thing. Your killing Decker is another, unless of course it becomes a matter of life and death. Then do what you must. Meanwhile, I want you to outthink Decker, not just react to his agenda."

"You're calling the shots, babe."

"Decker's got trouble. He beat up a Korean diplomat, remember? That's bound to bring a negative reaction from two governments, ours and theirs. For Sergeant Decker, I'd say this means new problems. Problems involving finesse, tact, subtlety."

Yokoi coughed twice and went silent. Dumas looked towards the door and the nurse. Yokoi said, "No. It's okay. Okay. Playing these little games keeps me alive. I love it. About Decker, his most glaring weakness appears to be his sense of guilt. Based on your phone taps of the DaSilvas, I'd say he feels guilty for not marrying Tawny's mother. That's why he wants to find Tawny and whoever killed her parents."

Dumas said, "Had to do it, babe. I had a man on the taps and when I relieved him, I listened in and heard them tell Decker about some black guy who'd been following the husband. They'd have identified Fort and that son of a bitch would have identified me."

"Not blaming you, hon. You did the right thing. Don't doubt it for a moment. Right now, let's talk about Decker. Guilt. That's what's driving him. Let him live, at least for now. But remember what I said about his support system. Be prepared to use it against him. Maybe give him a chance to feel some more guilt. Plan on playing with the man's head."

Dumas patted Yokoi's hand. "You told me when to quit the force. Advised me to open my own agency with only rogue cops. Great idea. I've got eight pros working for me who'll climb all over anybody's peace of mind if I tell them to and that includes killing people. You made the discothèque happen, you got me together with the people who sold me the Bank Street bar and you brought me into Rowena's setup. Wasn't for you I wouldn't have a pot to piss in."

Dumas bowed his head, thought, then looked at Yokoi. "I have to know, babe. Russell Fort and Jean-Louis. Which one can hurt me the most?"

"Fort. Decker's already onto his girlfriend. That's where you could start haemorrhaging."

"And Jean-Louis?"

"How do you put it? He knows the drill. Jean-Louis's been arrested before. All he has to do is clam up, let a lawyer do the talking, then post bail and skip the country. He also knows what you and Laughing Boy can do to him. If that doesn't keep him quiet, nothing will. Still, you never know about these things."

He paused to catch his breath. Then, "Fort and Susan Scudder. My suggestion is you plug these leaks before it's too late. By now Miss Scudder knows you used her to kill two undercover cops. And she knows that Decker's hot on the trail of whoever did the killings. I know you've put the fear of God into Mr Fort, but should Miss Scudder turn out to have scruples or fear for her own safety, you can assume she will refuse to betray any more policemen."

Yokoi paused again. Then, "Mr Fort's gambling will always be a major weakness. No gambler knows when to quit. They refuse to quit because without gambling life is boring and who wants to be bored. As you've already noted, Mr Fort's pathetic attempt to extort funds from the DaSilvas has brought Decker within smelling distance of you and Tawny. You can threaten Fort until the rivers run dry but because of his gambling habit you'll never be able to trust him. Or his little friend. Fort and Miss Scudder can bring you down."

Dumas sighed. "If I didn't need Fort to supply me with

Laughing Boy's paper, I'd seriously consider sending his ass to that big watermelon patch in the sky."

"What's wrong with making your own arrangements with his source? Eliminate the middle man, as they say."

Dumas smiled. "Now why didn't I think of that?"

He was about to say something else when he saw Ken's sunken eyes go to the door. Dumas didn't bother turning around. The Jamaican nurse was efficient. She'd given Dumas twenty minutes. After that she'd return to resume her work and he'd better not get in her way.

Yokoi said, "I think her moustache is thicker than yours."

A smiling Dumas whispered. "Back in a little while. Going to look in on Tawny."

"You know how to handle her?"

Oblivious to the sores on Yokoi's face, Dumas kissed him. "I've had the best teacher."

Four and a half minutes later Dumas, carrying his worn attaché case, stepped from a small, private elevator and into the warm basement of Ken Yokoi's townhouse. After switching on the light he checked the door to a small wine cellar, turning the handle and examining the lock which he'd installed himself.

The wine cellar hadn't been tampered with. A final pull on the doorhandle then Dumas checked the boiler thermostat. Which reminded him: he'd have to make arrangements for the December oil delivery to the townhouse. Ken was dying of AIDS. No need for him to freeze to death as well.

Dumas resumed walking, heading towards the far end of the basement and a light over a green metal door. He'd just passed a washing machine and several metal file cabinets containing the records of Yokoi's past patients when the metal door slowly opened.

A stocky, baby-faced Korean cradling a Uzi stepped through the doorway. He wore a Mickey Mouse sweatshirt, shoulder-length black hair and grey trousers held up with a belt and braces. At the sight of Dumas the Korean relaxed.

As Dumas reached the doorway the Korean silently stepped

aside. Dumas entered a small, concrete room lit by a fluorescent lamp, containing a cot, metal folding chair and a
card table. He frowned at the smell – garlic, cigarette smoke
and innumerable farts. On the floor were copies of Korean
newspapers, girlie magazines, empty pizza cartons and empty
McDonald's bags. A small black and white television set
was tuned to John Wayne's *Sands of Iwo Jima*. The smell,
however, pervaded everything. Dumas thought, it's like living
in a giant douche bag.

Stepping to the rear of the room he rested one hand on a
second metal door and peered through a glass panel. Then he
looked at the Korean. "Everything okay?"

Smiling, the Korean nodded. "Everything okay."

"You touch her, you're dead. If Park Song doesn't kill you,
I will."

Baby Face didn't relax his smile. "Everything okay."

"You'd better hope so, amigo."

Removing a key from a hook to the right of the door
Dumas unlocked the door and entered a second concrete
room, closing the door behind him. Slightly bigger than the
first room, this one also had the same overhead fluorescent
light, cot, blankets, card table, folding chairs. Unlike the other
room it had a private toilet. A closed circuit camera looked
down from one corner of the ceiling. Under the camera Tawny
DaSilva lay on the cot facing the wall.

Hearing the door open she looked over her shoulder, face
almost hidden by her long blonde hair. She was dressed in the
same long-sleeved, cream-coloured blouse, blue pin-striped
skirt and white boots she'd worn when Dumas had kidnapped
her five days ago. After a few seconds she sat up, combed the
hair from her face with her fingers and looked at him with
red-rimmed eyes. He was impressed by her eye contact. The
kid had to be scared, but she managed to hold his gaze. Give
her points for guts.

"I'd like to go home now," she said. Which is what she
said the last time Dumas had looked in on her. She spoke
quietly but firmly. She was making an effort to stay calm, to
avoid coming apart. Dumas admired that. A lot of men would

233

have completely come apart under these circumstances. The kid was special.

Dumas sat on a folding chair and opened his attaché case, keeping the case's cover between him and the girl. Then he switched on a microcassette recorder he'd taken from the DaSilva apartment the night he'd killed Tawny's parents. He lit a cigarette, inhaled deeply, then blew smoke at the closed circuit camera.

After a few seconds of silence he pointed to the food lying on the card table. "You don't like cheeseburgers and French fries? I thought every kid went for that. You have to eat something, Tawny. You really do."

Later Dumas would play this tape for Ken, who'd also look at the closed circuit films and make his recommendations to Park Song. These recommendations would be the first steps used by the Korean in forming the girl into the perfect lover. In the next few minutes anything she said or did, her slightest reaction or response, would speak volumes to Ken. Park Song considered Ken's opinion on the training of slaves to be invaluable.

Tawny DaSilva said to Dumas, "Why are you keeping me here? Why can't I see my mother? You're not a policeman. You say you are, but you're not."

He smiled. The kid had smarts as well. He'd flashed his old police shield to stop her in the street. He'd also used it to get inside her parents' apartment the night he'd smoked them.

Using her sleeve Tawny wiped tears from her eyes. "I don't want to stay here any more. I want to go home."

Sensing someone behind him Dumas looked over his shoulder. Well, well. Baby Face had got tired of watching John Wayne win the war in the Pacific and had quietly opened the door to see what was happening in this room. Munching a Devil Dog he stood in the doorway enjoying the show. Dumas stared at him until the Korean stepped back into the small room and closed the door. If Baby Face was bored with the Duke let him change channels.

The Korean was one of Shin's people, either from the Republic of Korea mission or some local muscle with whom

Shin had a working relationship. Dumas didn't know and didn't care. His own men were tied up working on agency cases or guarding the auction house. Song had reached out for his old pal Kim Shin, presumably a deputy consul with the Korean mission but actually a member of the KCIA. As Dumas had told Ken, this proved you could get good service in New York, providing you're willing to spend thirty million dollars.

Ken's basement, used to put up submissives temporarily, was a good place to hide Tawny. Hiding her made more sense than confining her in the Astoria house where steady customers might be upset to learn they couldn't bid on her.

Ken had also allowed Laughing Boy the use of the townhouse for any deals involving his funny money. If he so chose the Korean could now conclude his counterfeiting and slavery activities at once. He'd earned the privilege of convenience by agreeing to pay a quarter of a million for Tawny.

Dumas said, "Tell you what, Tawny. Why don't we call your mother and see what she has to say about all this. You're here because of her, you know."

Tawny wiped her eyes again. "I don't understand."

"She's given us legal custody of you. Total legal custody."

Fists clenched at her side Tawny rose from the bed. "You're lying. I don't know why, but I know you're lying."

Well, if that doesn't beat all, Dumas thought. Five days in this rathole and she's still prepared to fight back. Kid, you're really something.

"Tawny, it's true. She doesn't want you any more. She's given you to us. Really."

"She'd never do that. Mom would never do that. You're a dirty liar." Her voice rose. "Liar, liar, liar!" *Defiant. And quite attached to her mother. Laughing Boy's going to have his hands full with this one. Turning her out ain't gonna be easy.*

Reaching into his attaché case Dumas removed a cellular phone, extended the antenna and punched several numbers. Then he brought the phone to his ear and listened. As a recorded female voice began to recite the weather report for the rest of the day he said, "Yes, Mrs DaSilva? Ben Dumas.

I'm fine and you? Good, good. Glad to hear it. Mrs DaSilva, I have Tawny here with me and I just wanted to confirm our deal. Yes, I told her but she doesn't believe me."

As he spoke into the phone Dumas watched the girl. Her eyes never left his face. Messy hair, puffy eyes and still beautiful. Amazing. And strong, too. She was an inch from breaking down, but she held on. Held herself together and refused to look away from him. Dumas almost blinked. Almost.

"Yes, that was our deal," he said into the phone. "You've been paid and we now have legal custody of Tawny. Like you told me, this is something you've wanted to do for a long time and – "

"*Mom!* I want to speak to my mother! Let me speak to my mother." *Not afraid to stand up to adults. Watch this one, Laughing Boy.*

Tawny ran at Dumas who quickly said, "Thank you, Mrs DaSilva. We'll talk later." He switched off the phone and pushed in the antenna.

Screaming and weeping Tawny clawed at him and attempted to snatch the phone from his hand. "I don't believe you, I don't believe you."

A smiling Dumas easily fended her off, thinking, everything went down just the way Ken said it would. Then again, was Ken ever wrong? *How would they manage without him when he was gone?*

Stepping back from Dumas, Tawny returned to the cot and sat weeping. Head bowed, she cried aloud. As her body shook with her sobs Dumas closed his attaché case and stood up. He felt no sympathy for the kid. Didn't hate her, didn't love her. Ken mattered, she didn't. Ken was more important than a thousand Tawneys.

Dumas started towards the door. When he turned for a final look at Tawny he found she'd stopped sobbing and sat in a shocking calm. This time Dumas blinked. Was this kid a freak or what? She sat up straight, maybe the way her mother had taught her to do, and used her fingertips to wipe tears from her eyes. Then she placed her folded hands in her lap and quietly said, "You didn't talk to her. I know you didn't."

13

London, December
It was one fifty-eight in the morning when Michael Dartigue, Eddie Walkerdine and two hired thugs began robbing the Shepherd Market deposit centre.

The deposit centre was a plain, windowless room, thirty by thirty feet, with a low ceiling, closed circuit TV monitors, and metal walls lined with safe deposit boxes. Protecting the boxes was a steel vault door two feet thick and seven feet in diameter, equipped with a primary combination lock, time lock and locking bolts. A local alarm connected the door to Fedor SecuriCom which protected the depository.

From a tiny foyer a lone night guard manned a panel of buttons controlling alarms for the front door, vault, floor and ceiling. The centre's owner was Ravi Sunny, a roly-poly, thirty-six-year-old Indian who had been born in Calcutta where he'd worked as a butcher before immigrating to England at the age of twenty-five with a thirteen-year-old wife. In 1980 he had sent his wife back to her family in Delhi, and begun buying slum property in London which he quickly resold at a profit. Fond of London nightlife he regularly made the rounds of trendy clubs, restaurants and casinos, most recently in the company of a black stripper named Helen Bedd. The deposit centre was his sole piece of real estate in a secure area.

Located in fashionable Mayfair, Shepherd Market was a small, exclusive square of little white houses, antique shops, pubs and boutiques. The deposit centre occupied the ground floor of an eighteenth-century house whose remaining floors had been rented out to an advertising agency, a silver-goldsmith and a folk art gallery. Flanking the building were a Rolls Royce showroom and an estate agency.

An edgy Michael had entered the deposit centre first, nose burning from cocaine he'd snorted to give him the guts to go through with the robbery. Front door and vault alarms weren't used during the day, when the centre had its heaviest traffic. Night time, however, was a different story. That's when guards checked all photo IDs before admitting anyone inside.

A lone customer, Walkerdine said, wouldn't arouse the night guard's suspicion. On the other hand four wicked-looking faces at the front door was another story. It was Michael's job to make sure *everyone* got inside.

He'd disguised himself in a dark blue raincoat, brown leather cap and false red beard. He also wore sunglasses, deerskin gloves and carried a small suitcase. His hair had been cut short and dyed red. And he'd shown a phony ID to Joseph Lexy, a horse-faced forty-year-old Irishman who was the night guard.

The ID featured Michael's doctored appearance, left thumb print, and the three-digit number of a fictitious account. Bernard Muir had supplied the ID card, improved upon by Walkerdine who'd added such details as the alias William Henry Pratt, the real name of Walkerdine's favourite actor, Boris Karloff.

Michael had shoved the ID through a slot in the depository's eight-inch thick, oaken front door and into Lexy's nicotine-stained fingers. Seconds later Lexy switched off the front alarm and Michael was inside. To spare Lexy the trouble of searching depository files and finding no matching ID, Michael pulled a .38 Smith & Wesson from a raincoat pocket and pressed it against the Irishman's spine.

This time it was Michael who cut off the alarm, admitting Walkerdine and the two thugs into the foyer. All three wore ski masks, dark trousers, black turtleneck sweaters and surgical

238

gloves. One, a short barrel-chested man with turned-in toes, carried a small suitcase in each hand. The other, a big, thick-necked man, carried one large suitcase.

The barrel-chested man was Patrick Markey, a thirty-two-year-old West Indian and ex-convict whose crimes included arson, computer fraud, and horse theft, the last at a Paris racetrack where he'd been a stable boy. Under his ski mask Markey's fleshy face was missing most of a left ear, courtesy of a razor-wielding sweetheart who'd caught him in bed with her sixty-two-year-old mother.

As Markey set his suitcases down the other man, an over-sized twenty-eight-year-old cockney named Harry Zwillman, joined Michael in wrestling the terrified Joseph Lexy to the floor. Zwillman, a convicted car thief, burglar and strong-arm debt collector, then placed a knee on Lexy's neck, pinning the guard face down. With a quick jerk of his head Zwillman motioned Michael away.

Michael obeyed, backing away three feet to stand in front of a battered green file cabinet. Here he removed his topcoat to reveal a security guard's uniform. As he laid the topcoat on top of the file cabinet he found himself wishing he had more blow. The coke had speeded up his heartbeat and given him a dry throat.

On the upside he was psyched, ready to go hog wild and hit the ceiling. He'd felt this way before. Same high energy level he'd experienced during the last quarter of a game, team down by one, seconds to go, and him bringing the ball up the floor, knowing nobody could stop him from going to the hole for two and the game. There was a lot to be said for going through life with chemical assistance.

Michael had expected to be afraid tonight and he was, but just slightly. Just enough to keep him alert and on his toes. His main feeling was one of excitement at being in on the robbery. It was easy to see how people got hooked on stealing. You didn't thieve just for the money. You also did it for kicks.

Heart pounding, Michael watched Walkerdine go to work on the guard. Taking a cigarette lighter from his back pocket the little Englishman thumbed it into flame. Markey, meanwhile, opened a suitcase and removed a quart-sized orange juice carton. Without a word he poured half of the contents on the neck, back and thighs of a weeping, squirming Lexy. The smell of petrol filled the tiny foyer at once.

Walkerdine said, "You're dead if you don't answer my questions. First, where's the junction box?"

The junction box was the point at which telephone lines and perimeter lines were connected. Walkerdine knew the answer; he'd already got it from Bernard Muir. But to protect Muir that information had to be forced from the night guard, thereby removing suspicion from the Grand Duchess, Walkerdine's name for Muir.

A terrified Lexy struggled to get out the words, his speech being blocked by this latest reminder of the way his life had taken one nasty turn after another. No problems with the nightshift, the Fedor people had said. Bloody liars. Twenty-four hour access to the boxes was necessary, but there were nights when no one showed up for hours. Most guards favoured day hours, preferring to spend evenings with their families. That's why the nightshift paid a bit more.

Lexy had no family, not these days, so he became a bat, a guard who worked at night. The night hid his sorrows – two broken marriages, stillborn children, automobile accidents, failed alcohol rehabilitation. At night he could dream of what might have been had heroin not got in the way of his architectural studies at Dublin's Trinity College.

Now from the floor of the foyer he looked up at fire in the hand of a madman crouched over him. Staring into the flame Lexy found his voice. "Downstairs," he said. "The junction box is downstairs. But you first have to get into the vault."

Walkerdine said, "Right. Now, I need three more things from you. I want you to cut off the vault alarm and open the door to the deposit boxes. Then I want you to cut off the floor and ceiling alarms. Finally, I want you to tell me tonight's code."

"Code?"

With one hand Walkerdine grabbed Lexy's collar and held

the cigarette lighter dangerously close to the guard's nose. "You fuckfaced little twerp. Go feeble-minded with me and I'll roast you alive. Every security company telephones its night guards two or three times to see if anything's wrong. When the call comes in you either say everything's fine, or you give a prearranged answer which indicates you've got trouble. For the last time, what is your bloody code?"

"When they ring me someone will ask, 'Is the new wage to your liking?' If there's difficulty I'm to reply, 'Time and a half won't do. I want more.' The fellow at the other end then says, 'Why don't we let the union decide.' That's it. There's no more, I swear."

Walkerdine stood up. "On your feet, sunshine. You'd better be right about the code."

A shaken Lexy rose and turned off the alarms, allowing Walkerdine, Markey and Zwillman to enter the vault. Michael, posing as the night guard, remained in the foyer. Should depositors appear he was to show them into the vault. There he or she would have their hands cuffed, their eyes and mouth covered with tape. Now cuffed and taped the petrol-soaked Joseph Lexy lay on the floor just inside the vault's entrance. His hands had been cuffed in front, allowing him to use the telephone when his nightly call came in.

With Lexy unable to see their faces Walkerdine, Markey and Zwillman took off their ski masks. Walkerdine and Markey then reached in their suitcases, removing hammers, chisels and small crowbars. From the large suitcase Zwillman pulled out three empty duffel bags. A grinning Walkerdine said, "Merry Christmas, lads. Now let's carve the turkey, shall we?"

Michael had demanded to be allowed to break into his wife's safety deposit box. In his steady pursuit of ready cash, he'd gone through Rowena's handbags, jewellery boxes and private papers more than once. He'd come across her deposit centre ID where she'd hidden it in the closet and filed the information away for a rainy day. In mental matters, she'd always sold him short. Well, he was about to outsmart the bitch.

Rowena's account number was 212. With Walkerdine trailing him Michael found her safety deposit box. Top row, far wall with the larger boxes. Nothing small for Rowena.

Michael could open Rowena's safety deposit box, Walkerdine said, but he couldn't take anything – just dump the contents into the duffel bag held by Walkerdine, who with Markey and Zwillman looked on as Michael went to work on the box with a crowbar. It was nearly five minutes before Michael prised the box open.

Holy shit. *Money.* Tons of it. American hundreds and fifties. An awed Walkerdine whispered, "Bloody Christ almighty." Grinning, Markey and Zwillman slapped each other on the back in congratulations. Michael remained speechless. What the fuck was going on here? *Where did Rowena get this much money?* She'd never mentioned it to him, that's for sure. Well, she could kiss it all goodbye.

Turning to Walkerdine, an overjoyed Michael shoved a clenched fist in the air, shouting, "All right!"

Walkerdine took his arm, glanced at the prone Joseph Lexy then whispered to Michael, "Good work, sunshine, but let's keep our voices down, shall we? Now while I hold the bag, do you think you could transfer all that lovely cash from the lady's account to ours?"

"You got it, dude."

Using both hands Michael scooped Rowena's money from the damaged safety deposit box and dropped it into Walkerdine's bag. How much cash was there? Had to be millions, fucking millions. She'd also salted away some fantastic-looking jewellery which had to be worth a bundle. Michael chuckled. How could stealing be wrong when you could walk away with this much?

Halfway through removing the money Michael came across two black looseleaf notebooks. Walkerdine said, "No, no, sunshine. No reading material for us. You keep them as a souvenir. Just concentrate on the cash."

Walkerdine couldn't stop grinning. "Wonderful woman you married," he whispered. "The look on your face says you knew nothing about this."

"Man, if I had known this much money was in here I'd have paid this place a visit long ago."

"Got us off to a magnificent start, she has. How can you not love a woman like that?"

Markey and Zwillman, meanwhile, went to work with a ferocious enthusiasm, tearing at the boxes in hopes of uncovering a similar bonanza. Feeling generous, a beaming Walkerdine allowed Michael to take a pair of Rowena's fancy earrings for Nigella. One pair shouldn't hurt anyone. Earrings and notebooks to start with. The real payoff would come later, when the haul had been laundered and made untraceable.

Back in the foyer a turned-on Michael took up his position as "night guard", still wondering how Rowena came to have so much bread. Was she dealing drugs or what? Some of the money, but not all, had probably come from Rosebud. According to Walkerdine, who was good at figures, Rowena's stash amounted to between ten and twelve million. Maybe more. You didn't make that kind of money selling handbags and leather belts out of one small store.

And how about all the expensive jewellery? Rowena hadn't picked that up at Woolworth's. Michael snapped his fingers. He knew where she'd got the money. She was stealing from that charity of hers. She was ripping off underprivileged kids. In that case, fuck her. She deserved to get ripped off.

From the foyer Michael looked into the vault where Walkerdine and the others prised safety deposit boxes from the walls before dumping the contents into the duffel bags. The three worked quickly and quietly. Cash, jewellery, coin collections, bonds, securities went in the bags. Everything else was tossed aside. Rejected items included pornographic photos, wigs, personal papers, keys, false teeth, baby shoes, urns containing ashes of loved ones, lacy underwear. Drugs were also left behind. "A small kindness on our part," Walkerdine said. "When the owners see what's happened here they'll need something to soothe their nerves."

In a plan worked out between Michael and Joe LoCasio, the Brooklyn-based Mafia capo was to fence the swag. Sometime this morning all three duffel bags would be sent to New York via air freight for a late night arrival at Kennedy Airport. They would be addressed to a Queens motel, care of a LoCasio underboss registered there under a false name.

By arriving late the bags would be left in the air freight terminal overnight to await morning inspection by customs agents who usually ignored night cargo until the next day. During the night, however, members of the LoCasio family would walk into the warehouse and simply walk out with the bags. Simultaneously the cargo manifest would be changed to show that no such duffel bags had ever arrived.

Immediately after the robbery Michael would leave for New York where Nigella was waiting for him in a Manhattan hotel. Walkerdine was to follow on a later plane, meet Michael and together they'd settle up with the LoCasios. After Michael received his share of the clean money he and Nigella were heading for Miami where the first thing he intended to do was file for divorce. The best part of his marriage to Rowena was the thought of leaving her.

He had thirty thousand dollars from the sale of the Mercedes given him by Rowena which he'd sold to a wealthy Kenyan architect he'd met at Walkerdine's club. Otherwise Michael was leaving England with only one suitcase and the knowledge that for the first time since Miami U. he was a winner.

Coincidentally enough, Rowena was leaving for New York tomorrow on business. Good luck to her. While there Michael didn't expect to run into his wife but if he did, fuck it. Far as he was concerned their marriage was over.

In the foyer Michael kicked around the idea of running off with the duffel bag containing Rowena's millions, the one now lying at Walkerdine's feet. Nice idea, but don't dwell on it. For sure Walkerdine and his boys would come looking for him. Then there was the LoCasio family. With dagos, a deal was a deal. Break your word to them and you'd be lucky if all they did was shove a wrecking ball up your ass.

Michael also had to think about Andres and Nigella, the two people he loved most in this world. For their sakes he couldn't mess up this deal. He'd promised Andres his freedom and Nigella a new life, one which included her own beauty shop in Miami. Money was the only way he could have them with him in the future. Money would set them all free.

Above all it would free him from Rowena. Meeting Nigella at the Belgravia casino where she worked had pushed him into dumping Rowena in a hurry. Nigella was a magnetic force, drawing Michael to her with a warmth and calm completely absent in the harder Rowena. Theirs had been an instantaneous hunger for each other, one filled with sex, genuine affection and a heartfelt interest in the other's problems.

In addition to everything else Nigella had been protective towards Michael without suffocating him. There was a bond between them that had been missing with other women in his life. Like him she'd placed her faith in the wrong people and suffered for it. She'd been too sexually obliging, creating complications she herself didn't always understand. Still, she'd managed to retain a compassion and generosity which drew people to her.

During the three hours they spent clearing out the boxes no customers showed up. Credit an icy rain with helping to keep everybody away. Only one security call came in; remembering Walkerdine's cigarette lighter, Lexy said the right things.

In the foyer Michael passed the time chain smoking and fantasising about how he intended to spend his share. Rowena's notebooks could wait. At the moment Michael was too psyched to read anything. He'd check them out on the plane.

Michael stared through a bullet-proof glass panel in the front door at rain-soaked Shepherd Market. The rain should stop soon. At least he hoped so. Otherwise there could be trouble taking off from Heathrow. Turning, he walked over to the vault. Walkerdine, Zwillman and Markey were busting their guts, stuffing the bags.

He watched a perspiring Walkerdine stop, light up a thin cigar and blow a smoke ring towards the ceiling. Then he walked over to Michael and whispered, "We're packing it in. Be dawn soon. Might as well use the rain and darkness to hide our pretty faces. Come inside and change your clothes. You're leaving for the airport."

Clenched fists held overhead Michael exhaled for a long time. "We did it. Goddam, we did it."

Nodding, Walkerdine touched Michael's arm. "I'd say so. We're bloody tired, the lot of us. Leaving a dozen or so boxes untouched, but such is life. I prefer we leave while God still seems to be on our side."

"That's right, that's right. So, I guess I'll see you in about twelve hours or so."

"My regards to Nigella." Walkerdine handed him a hundred dollar bill. "You two have some champagne on me. Don't worry, my boy. This particular bill happens to be me own hard earned money. You lovebirds deserve a bit of bubbly. Michael, I want to thank you for everything. This whole thing wouldn't have been possible without you."

Michael scowled. "Without me and Bernie Muir, you mean."

Taking Michael's hands in his Walkerdine said softly, "You were fantastic. Held up your end. Did all I asked of you. Didn't fall apart. You're a bit of all right, Michael Dartigue. A bit of all right. Now it's off with you. Mustn't keep our New York friends waiting. Have a safe trip and give Nigella a kiss for me, would you?"

New York, six ten p.m.

Michael leaned against the door of Nigella's Central Park West hotel room, shivering, and held her tightly in his arms. He'd just arrived from Kennedy Airport and still wore his raincoat and leather cap. They'd kissed and his mind had been miles away.

His bloodshot eyes had a vacant, haunted look that went through her. He'd whispered her name, saying, "Hold me, please, please hold me." Taking him in her arms she placed her head against his chest and waited for him to tell her what was wrong.

In a tired voice he said, "The robbery went okay. The bags are on the way here like we planned. It's just that something, something happened." He raised his arms so that she could see what he was holding in his hands.

"Rowena's notebooks," he said. "From her safety deposit box. Baby, I read these things on the flight coming over here and I have to tell you, I'm scared. I mean I am really scared. Rowena is into some very heavy shit."

A concerned Nigella looked at him. "Tell me."

"She's involved with people I don't ever want to deal with. People entirely out of my league. People who'd kill me if they knew I had these notebooks."

"My God."

"Rowena's laundering money for them. Big money. She's washing it through that kiddie foundation she's got. Her customers come from Europe, America, Asia. Something else. She's selling kids to some of these people. Fucking selling children as sex slaves to anyone who'll buy."

"You must be joking."

He clutched the notebooks. "It's all in here. Names, prices, the kind of kids these sick bastards prefer. The charity's a scam. Rowena uses it to launder money and dig up kids for sale. This woman doesn't deserve to live. I'm telling you she doesn't. See for yourself. Here, take a look at this shit."

Minutes later a white-faced Nigella handed the notebooks back to him. "What do we do now?" she said.

"Don't know. I just know I have to get as far away from that woman as I can. I don't ever want to see her face again. Know why she's coming to New York today? She's coming to hold a slave auction, to sell more kids. Some Jap psychiatrist and a private detective named Ben Dumas run the thing with her. Jesus, it's all there in black and white."

Nigella took his hand and led him to one of two twin beds near a window overlooking Central Park twenty floors below. "Get some rest, love. Sleep, then we'll talk about what to do next."

"LoCasio's people are supposed to call and let me know the bags are in the warehouse. Have to set up a meeting with them. Walkerdine's gonna call, too. You know I'm not even hungry. Reading those notebooks killed my appetite."

Nigella removed his cap. "Fine. Then forget food but get some rest. I'll wake you when LoCasio's man calls."

"Wake me when Walkerdine calls too."

"Does he know about the notebooks?"

Michael shook his head. "No. If he did I don't think he'd have let me take them. The guy's a hustler, as you know. He'd have tried to use them to his advantage, I'm sure. Thing is, you don't mess with these people. Man, I'm telling you, you don't."

Nigella said, "Out of those clothes and lie down. I'll wake you when the phone rings."

Three hours later Michael awoke to find Nigella sitting across the room watching television with the sound turned low. Still groggy with jet lag, he yawned and blinked several times before he could focus enough to see what she was watching. She was watching CNN, the cable news network.

"No calls?" he said.

She shook her head. "No calls. The robbery made the telly, though."

Michael brightened. "What they say?"

"You're a rich man. According to Scotland Yard you gentlemen got away with more than forty million dollars."

Michael pressed the heels of his hands to his temples. "Jesus Christ. You're kidding. *Forty million?* Is that great or what?"

He was reaching for his cigarettes on the night table when the telephone rang. One second into the first ring and he seized the receiver, jamming it against his ear, squeezing it with both hands. His heart started flip-flopping.

"You Michael Dartigue?" Male voice. A hard-ass Brooklyn greaseball who's probably been told he looks like Al Pacino and sounds like Robert de Niro.

"I'm Michael Dartigue. Who's this?"

"Fuck's wrong with you? You crazy or what? You know who you dealing with?"

"Zip it, asshole. I don't have time for this shit. Get the fuck off my line."

"You got time for me, cocksucker. I'm with LoCasio. Want to tell me what kinda game you running?"

"I don't understand."

"Well, understand this, assface. No bags. They didn't come in. We checked the flight, we checked the air freight office, we checked the cargo manifest. We even got in touch with somebody at Heathrow Airport. Them bags were never on the fucking plane. They never left England."

Closing his eyes Michael said, "No, no. Can't be. It can't be."

The voice said, "I tell you what can't be. You can't dick us around and get away with it, that's what can't be. We had a deal, hot shot, and you didn't hold up your end. Instead of getting a piece of forty million, we got shit. I think maybe we should all get together and have a little chat."

14

At ten thirty-five on the morning following the fight with Kim Shin and his bodyguard Decker was sitting on a dark green leather sofa in Yale Singular's downtown Manhattan office. He sat with a cup of black coffee in one hand, a folded copy of *The New York Times* in the other and watched as the hefty Treasury agent was chewed out by someone at the other end of the phone. Singular was catching hell because Manfred F. Decker, a newly appointed US deputy marshall assigned to him, had trashed a diplomat attached to the South Korean Embassy.

At one point a red-faced Singular glared across his desk at Decker, who smiled and lifted his cup in a mock toast before sipping from it. Decker assumed Singular didn't appreciate the gesture since the big man narrowed his eyes and began wrapping the telephone cord around a sizable fist. Finally Singular hung up and buzzed his secretary, saying hold all calls. Then he placed both palms down on his desk and stared at fingers gnarled by a collegiate football career which had seen him set a collegiate record for tackles by a middle linebacker in the Cotton Bowl.

At Texas A&M he'd combined sports and scholarship, leading him to believe there wasn't much beyond his ability. In addition to football honours, which included two years first team All-American, he'd also graduated Phi Beta Kappa due mainly to a near photographic memory. But three operations on his right shoulder had kept Singular out of the NFL which hadn't upset him too much since the working life of a pro player rarely exceeded five years.

He decided against following his father and two brothers into banking and it was his football celebrity that solved the problem of employment. It won him a position on the Washington staff of a Texas senator and through him Singular got a close-up look at the Secret Service.

The Secret Service was an arm of the US Department of the Treasury and did more for the taxpayer than merely protect the president and vice-president. It investigated federal crimes such as counterfeiting, forgery of government bonds, theft of Treasury cheques and threats against foreign diplomats, all of which were more interesting than banking. Singular also liked the camaraderie among the agents which he found reminiscent of that among football players. And there was the advantage of having the government behind you, which gave a man power without having to run for political office.

It was the senator, a lanky, beetle-browed man with tiny eyes and lips, who sounded a warning about government service. "You're working for politicians now," he said to Singular, "and with all the power they got goin' for them, it's dumb to expect they ain't gonna use it against you one day. Like LBJ once told me, ain't no good ever come of being around people who'll do anything to get elected."

In Singular's office neither he nor Decker said a word until Singular leaned back in his swivel chair and spoke to the ceiling. "The Justice Department, State Department and US Attorney's office are chewing my balls off because of what you did to that Korean diplomat. Due to your impetuous nature everybody's climbing all over me. Now I get to come down funky on you."

He glanced at Decker from under hooded eyes. "Guys like you really grind my gears. You think you know it all and the rest of us don't know diddly. I told you to walk easy, but it seems the only thing you need to make you go off half-cocked is a warning. Well, city boy, if you're a jackass don't be surprised if people ride your behind into the ground. You been gettin' by on bad attitude for too goddam long."

Decker said, "I guess I should be worried."

"Listen, hotshot, even your own people think you stepped

in it this time. Your precinct commander, the brass down at Police Plaza, they can't wait to put the strap to you and the day ain't even half-gone."

Decker held up the copy of *The Times*. "By the way, I wasn't drinking and I didn't start the fight. Those stories are bullshit."

"Whether you hit the rock or it hits you, it's bad for you. Allow me to explain. I don't give a shit who started the fight, whether it was you or some passing Eskimoes. You look bad which makes me look bad. A deputy US marshall whipping up on a foreign diplomat. Jesus, if that don't take the cake. Goddam it, didn't you hear anything I said? I *specifically* told you to concentrate on Dumas and those dead undercover cops. Forget Tawny what's-her-name, I said."

Decker said, "You also said keep away from Park Song. By the way her last name's DaSilva. And what's she got to do with Kim Shin?"

"Know something, boy? I think it's all getting away from you. There's an advantage to understanding essentials, so before we get to talking 'bout how many inches you gonna lose off your pecker, permit me to expound on life as we know it. This country's forking over three billion dollars a year for South Korea's defence. Despite all the friends them Koreans have in Congress, and they got a lot, some folks say this is too much protection for a country that's enjoying a trade surplus with us. Might be they have a point."

Unwrapping three sticks of Juicy Fruit, Singular rolled the gum into a ball and popped it in his mouth. "At the same time you could say we're caught between a rock and a hard place. Scuttlebutt has it that North Korea's building a nuclear reprocessing plant. If that's a righteous rumour then our troops ain't going nowhere 'cause under those circumstances we can't afford to pull 'em out. We also hear there's secret talks going on between North and South Korea about the possibility of unification. So where does this leave us God-fearing, white Christians?"

Singular shifted the wad of gum from one jaw to another. "It leaves us still wanting to be a player and to do that we need friends. Like it or not, we have got to keep in good with the South Koreans. We can start by not stomping a mudhole in their diplomats. Unbeknownst to you, we've got some very delicate negotiations going on with the Koreans. They pay just one per cent of their defence costs. Uncle Sam pays the rest. That's right, bubba. We're picking up the tab to protect the very people who're putting our workers out of business. Ain't that a hoot?

"These delicate negotiations I mentioned have to do with us trying to talk them into forking over more money for their own defence. But when American policemen start beatin' up on Korean envoys, well, just imagine what this does to the diplomatic process. You see my point?"

Placing his coffee cup on an end table Decker crossed his ankles. "What I see is a man who's jerked me around from the beginning. I see a man who brought me on board to keep me from making waves."

For a few seconds Singular attempted to blow bubbles with his gum then finally gave up. "Detective, your history shows that you're an unhappy man. Unhappy people either think too much or too little."

A grinning Decker said, "The way I look at it, it's a sick world and I'm a happy man."

In spite of himself Singular smiled. "For a man who's sitting on the anxious seat, you don't look all that forlorn to me. You're going around acting like Dirty Harry which only confirms the liberals' theory of cops being assholes. You've also made the federal government's shit list and that is not in your best interest, I can assure you. So why are you sittin' there looking happier than a pig in shit? You know something the rest of us don't? Or could it be you're just not in your right mind?"

Decker said, "Well, let's see how whacko I am. I know the South Korean government's involved with Laughing Boy's counterfeiting."

Singular stopped chewing.

Decker said, "I think our government knows it too. That's why they're pissed at me for clobbering Kim Shin. I think you've been told it's okay to take down Laughing Boy providing you don't make waves. Sounds a bit like the war on drugs to me, the one we really don't want to win. Because if we did we'd never have sucked up to shitheads like Noriega. We'd also stop dealing with ninety per cent of the politicians in Latin America."

"You're pursuing a dangerous line of inquiry, Detective."

"Now why would I do that?"

Singular resumed chewing his gum. "You were saying something about the government telling us to go easy on Song?"

"In Saigon, Shin and Laughing Boy were best friends. They stole the plates together. You know the ones I mean. The ones the CIA tried to send me to Leavenworth for, which they claimed didn't exist and which they don't want anybody to know about."

"Cut to the chase, Decker."

"In Saigon Shin worked Intelligence. I think he still does. These days he calls himself a diplomat but that's standard procedure for the spy business, isn't it? I think we both know he's using his position to help his old friend Laughing Boy."

Decker chuckled. "Well, now. The look on your face says I'm right. How about that? I guess this means you've got a problem. You want to get Song, but you have to do it without provoking his friends in high places. Life's a bitch, ain't it?"

Singular lifted a forefinger. "They say you're a regular Wile E. Coyote. One slick son of a bitch. You fight like a Jap, you think like one and you always come up with a way to outwit the fine print. I think it's time you learned you can't win 'em all."

Decker leaned back, hands behind his head. "Last night at the restaurant the cops kept me in Nicolay's office until they could check my ID. My partner came in and handed me my overcoat. I'm sitting on Nicolay's desk at the time so I dropped the coat on his Roladex. Eventually I got the OK to leave, so I did."

"With your overcoat *and* the Roladex," Singular said. "Makes one wonder who moulded your character."

"I get home and the first thing I do is check out the names

on the cards. Nicolay's got Kim Shin's number at the Korean Embassy and his home number. He's also got several numbers for telephones in Seoul, no names, but I'm checking that out to see if any of the numbers belong to Song. Nicolay's also got some numbers for Ben Dumas and Russell Fort. He's got numbers for people all over the world. France, England – "

Singular said, "Who's Russell Fort?"

"An ex-cop who knows Dumas and who's into the wise guys because of a gambling habit. I found a listing for his aunt, a Mrs Lorraine Buckey who lives in Washington and who used to work for the Bureau of Engraving and Printing. You know, where the money's printed?"

"I can do without the civics lesson. Just tell me about the paper."

"Mrs Buckey's a diabetic. That's Fort's excuse for dropping in to see her whenever he's in Atlantic City. Mrs Buckey's son Arnold. He works at the Bureau of Engraving and Printing. In the department which has access to the paper on which our currency's printed."

Closing his eyes Singular flopped back in his chair. "Drove us up the wall wondering how he managed to get all the paper he needed. How'd you learn about Fort's family so fast?"

"I had DEA fax its Washington office this morning. The minute I read the words Bureau of Engraving and Printing it started making sense. Dumas is Fort's rabbi. I'd say Fort pays for that protection by getting paper from the Bureau of Engraving and Printing then passing it on to Big Ben."

Singular rolled his eyes. "Jesus. We give that little gook the plates, then we give him the paper. And you wonder why the world thinks this country's losing its mind. How do you figure Nicolay?"

"He's second string. He's on the team, but he doesn't have too much clout. Kim Shin was dumping on him and he just sat there and took it. If Fort and Dumas are supplying the paper I doubt if they're leaving it on the Korean Embassy's doorstep. Nicolay could be the drop. There's one way to find out."

Singular toyed with a thick gold wedding band on his ring finger. "Who you gonna turn your magic on this time?"

"Fort. I think he's feeding his gambling habit two ways: with the currency paper and by betraying undercover cops. His girlfriend works at DEA here in New York and has access to information that would appeal to Dumas. My gut says she gave up Frankie Dalto and Willie Valentin. Turn Fort and we plug the leak on undercover cops. And you're a step closer to popping Laughing Boy."

Singular was quiet. Then when he spoke his voice was slightly more relaxed. "We're gonna want to get together with Mr Fort."

"After I nail his ass for complicity in the killing of two undercover policemen."

Decker shook his head. "Dumas still has friends on the force. When I move on him I've got to be sure. I won't get a second chance."

Singular picked up a letter opener and gently jabbed his palm. "Might be a good idea to throw a rope over Mr Fort and drag him into the barn for safe keeping. Maybe convince him confession's good for the soul. I wasn't supposed to tell you this, but I don't want you walking outta here thinking I've gotten used to the smell of politics."

He sighed. "About this little girl you're after, this Tawny what's-her-name. Before Song killed that agent of ours a year ago the agent came up with some information about a Mr Fox – "

The telephone rang. An incensed Singular picked it up. "Goddam it, Nina, I told you to hold all calls. I – "

Frowning, he looked at Decker. "I see. Yes, he's right here."

He held out the receiver to Decker who knew the signs. Trouble. Something was wrong and on a scale of one to ten, it had to be at least a six. Singular looked as if he wished he was anywhere but in the room with Decker. If the news was this bad far away, Decker could only guess how bad it would be close up.

He took the receiver and braced himself. "Detective Sergeant Decker."

The news couldn't have been worse. "Jesus. I'm on my way." He handed the receiver back to Singular.

"Squad car's waiting downstairs for me," Decker said. "My partner's been shot. They're not sure if she's going to make it."

15

Thirty-three hours after the robbery of her safe deposit box a frantic Rowena Dartigue sat in the nearly empty departure lounge at Heathrow Airport and sipped cognac from a small silver flask. Her eleven a.m. flight to New York would be boarding in twenty minutes.

Twenty minutes closer to meeting Park Song. Twenty minutes closer to being confronted by him on the subject of his missing eight million dollars. The same eight million which she'd accepted for safe keeping and which had now disappeared along with her cash, jewellery and notebooks describing her illicit activities in great detail.

Of all her money-laundering customers only Song had money in the box. Only Song.

Rowena had contacted Scotland Yard in hopes the thieves had missed something, only to learn that her safety deposit box had been cleaned out. The bastards hadn't left so much as a paperclip. She specifically inquired about the notebooks and her uncommon jewellery which she described in all its elegant particulars.

Some of the other victims had refused to discuss their losses with the police, preferring to keep certain information out of official channels. Later Rowena wondered if she should have asked about her missing property but this was hindsight. So desperate was she to retrieve the notebooks and the jewellery that she would have talked to the devil himself had she thought he could help.

She'd thought of cancelling her New York trip. But that

would be admitting she had no intention of repaying Song or worse, that she'd been in on the robbery. Avoiding him was an admission that one was never too old to learn new ways of being stupid. Either Rowena contacted him straightaway or she wouldn't live out the week.

Her hand shook as she brought the flask to her lips. At the moment all she could think of was Song's well-deserved reputation for being pitiless and cruel, particularly when he suspected he'd been cheated. Of course he would blame her for his loss. Hadn't the Korean spymaster Youngsam blamed Song when the Frenchman plundered their bank? The thought of Song's rage brought on sharp, agonising spasms in Rowena's back. Fear had left her without an ounce of energy.

She swallowed more cognac, desperately trying to convince herself that Song wouldn't kill her when they met in New York, that he'd give her a chance to repay the money and keep them both alive. Unfortunately, he could be impulsive and unpredictable. Too late Rowena remembered just how easily she had dismissed Park Song's homicidal whims merely because they hadn't affected her directly. She'd closed her eyes to certain unpleasant truths and now had to pay the piper.

Stunned and frightened by the robbery Rowena's initial reaction had been to rush to her bedroom, refuse all phone calls, and devour a bottle of cognac with the intention of rendering herself insensible. Park Song wasn't the only person she had to fear. She also feared what could happen to her should he and the others mentioned in her notebooks learn of their existence. Rowena's fear was such that she considered killing herself before deciding she was much too cowardly to go through with it.

Michael. God alone knew where he was at this moment. Not that he would be of much use in a crisis. He was an eternal adolescent, glib and empty-headed. Supposedly he was working on a deal which could mean a trip to the States to meet with the people involved. Had he been with Rowena right now perhaps his presence might have provided her with some comfort.

Weeping uncontrollably she placed another small log in her bedroom fireplace then crawled under a pair of down comforters. How in hell could she go on with her life after this? *How?* She'd always seen herself as unique and unequalled, far above the common herd. This calamity was a brutal reminder that in the end she was just like other people.

In bed she stared at the fire. Its blaze threw a crimson glow on the parquet floor. It was comforting, a friendly companion inducing her to become solemn and reflective.

As a pretty and outwardly normal adolescent living in the London suburb of Clapham she'd been introduced to sexual abnormality by William Cobden, a moon-faced, fifty-four-year-old vicar and confirmed pedophile. Although Cobden had originated the depravity, the oversexed Rowena revealed herself to be an eager student. It wasn't long before she became the leader in their sex play which included posing in front of Cobden's automatic camera for pornographic photographs.

Nor was Cobden the only grown-up with whom she cheerfully fornicated. An uncle, a police constable and a local rent collector were just some of the older men who enjoyed her precocious favours.

What made Rowena different from other youngsters who were sexually active with adults was a refusal to view herself as a victim of child molestation. From the beginning she endorsed the Reverend Cobden's belief that sex between grown-ups and children was both acceptable and right. As a youngster she found it exhilarating to exercise power over men who were respected pillars of the community and in some cases old enough to be her grandfather.

Eventually her sexual misconduct became too embarrassing for Rowena's pub-owner father who threw her out of the house one day before her fifteenth birthday. Within the week she became the mistress of a fifty-five-year-old West End mobster.

As for a career Rowena had a strong interest in fashion but possessed neither the talent nor the patience to persevere at it.

She grew up alternating between being protected by affluent older men and being so penniless that she was sometimes on the borderline of starvation.

Her disregard for convention was suspended at the age of twenty-two when she became the wife of Roger Ollenbittle, the husky, forty-year-old manager of a sportscar business in Park Lane. Warm and affectionate, the successful Ollenbittle was Rowena's first husband and the only man she would ever truly love.

Two years after their marriage they moved to Cape Town, where he took over as manager of a large American automobile business. The move was traumatic for Roger's sister Finola, a short, skinny, tight-lipped woman and the director of a London children's charity called the Lesley Foundation. Deeply attached to her brother she'd opposed his marriage to Rowena whom she saw as oversexed, headstrong, mercenary and frivolous.

In turn Rowena suspected that at the bottom of the prudish and unwed Finola's drinking problem was a lust for her own brother. For Roger's sake the two women remained civil to one another, though Rowena knew the truce would last only so long as the other wanted it to.

In Cape Town Rowena was the virtuous and loving wife. Her past, which Roger knew of and accepted, was behind them. He provided her with the personal attention her self-centred approach to life demanded, while in bed he was forceful and innovative, delivering all the pleasure she could wish for. In turn a besotted Rowena gave him a loyalty she'd given no other man. With Roger she no longer felt the need to prove she was still the seductress.

While Rowena may have been leading a restrained existence, the same could not be said of all their Cape Town friends. Jean-Louis Nicolay, a French restaurateur whom Roger had backed in a beach front café, periodically invited them to wife-swapping parties, invitations refused by the couple. Nor did they share Nicolay's interest in sex with black and white runaways whom he'd use then casually dispose of. A child, he said, was the magic elixir which kept a man young. If this testimony triggered any response in Rowena she refused to show it.

Neither she nor Roger wanted offspring of their own. Rowena was too possessive of her husband to see a child as anything but a threat, while he preferred having a beautiful young wife to himself. For six years they enjoyed a happy and prosperous life until the day Roger decided it was no longer possible to ignore South Africa's racist system of apartheid.

Against the advice of white friends and business associates Roger openly supported strikes by black workers, and the radical African National Congress led by Nelson Mandela. He also participated in a demonstration in the town of Sharpeville to protest against passbook laws which restricted the movement of blacks in all-white areas. Police brutally suppressed the demonstration, killing seventy people. Roger himself was grazed by a bullet, suffering a minor leg wound.

Immediately after this incident the ANC, the Communist Party and other black groups were officially outlawed. The government also increased its violence against anyone opposing apartheid. While afraid of what might happen to Roger, Rowena admired her husband's willingness to speak out.

"South Africa's a beautiful country," he told her, "but the future has little value here. There's too much hatred and out of that will come much destruction. You mark my words."

A month later the destruction he predicted showed up at their door. On a rainy evening a tall, dark-haired white man dressed as a priest came to their home, rang the bell and when Roger appeared shot him in the chest three times. He died in the arms of a hysterical Rowena without regaining consciousness. An anonymous caller threatened that unless she left South Africa within forty-eight hours she too would suffer her husband's fate.

Taking the warning seriously Rowena called on the assistance of Jean-Louis Nicolay who didn't fail her during this terrible time. He arranged Roger's immediate cremation and Rowena's flight to London with his ashes. Roger's financial affairs, however, were not so easily disposed of.

Rowena and he had lived well, but his death revealed that

he owed back taxes. There was also an outstanding bank loan, other creditors and, of course, death duties. When the estate was finally settled Rowena received barely enough money to live on for six months. She was not only alone, she was penniless once again.

In London Roger's sister Finola proved surprisingly sympathetic to her unhappy sister-in-law. She gave Rowena a job with the children's charity and found her a cheap flat in Bayswater. Grief drew them closer and in understanding each other, they forgave each other. The friendship ended eighteen months later, however, when Finola died. Rowena grieved not merely for Finola but for the loss of the last link with her beloved Roger.

She was now in charge of the charity which had become a losing financial proposition, paying her only a minimal salary. No longer inclined to be a dirty old man's darling she struggled to keep the charity afloat. Public support, however, was hard to come by. People were willing to give away their old clothes and junk they no longer needed, but parting with cash was another matter.

Two months after Finola's funeral she heard from Nicolay who'd come to London supposedly on holiday. He had a favour to ask of Rowena. Would she launder some money, twenty thousand dollars to be exact, through her charity's bank account? It was a simple task and no one need ever know. She could keep the interest and use that for good works.

Rowena was shocked, not by his request, but by the thought of acquiring so much money for so little effort. A bank slip or two, and it was done. The question of legality never arose in her mind. She was three weeks behind in her rent and her landlord, a lecherous Cypriot, had given her twenty-four hours to pay up or start granting him sexual favours. Rowena found Nicolay's proposition infinitely more attractive.

The jubilant Frenchman said this was just the beginning. With future racial conflicts in South Africa a foregone conclusion, smart money was starting to flee the country. During the next few weeks alone Nicolay was prepared to launder several hundred thousand dollars through Rowena's charity. After that he'd be moving to Saigon where he had friends and where the war between North and South Vietnam had created numerous opportunities for profit. If Rowena handled the South African money correctly, Nicolay would send her money from Asia to wash.

Rowena, bored with the charity, had been thinking of walking away from it. There was no money to be made and the children were getting on her nerves. In the light of her new arrangement with Nicolay she would definitely reconsider her distaste for philanthropic labour. That's when the Frenchman told her there was another way of making money from her little charity.

He had a friend in New York, a Japanese psychiatrist he'd met there at a sex club some months ago. Recently the psychiatrist, Dr Ken Yokoi, had been forced to resign from the staff of a small New Hampshire college after a sexual scandal involving a seventeen-year-old male freshman. Yokoi had just opened a Manhattan practice and specialised in therapy for disturbed people who had trouble accepting their own sexuality. Part of the treatment involved putting these patients together with men who were stronger, authoritative and often affluent.

Nicolay told her these particular men were sometimes more comfortable with children than they were with adults. They were willing to pay good money to find the right child. Would she be interested in becoming part of such an arrangement, one which could prove extremely profitable?

A smiling Rowena invited Nicolay to the Ritz for tea and for a further discussion of the way in which the Lesley Foundation could be made more lucrative.

In Heathrow's international passenger terminal Rowena paused with the flask in front of her lips. Behind dark glasses her eyes were hawklike, as though she was about to swoop down on her prey. A frosty smile found its way to her lips. Her nostrils flared. The idea that had just come to her was a daring one, but worth trying if she wanted to live.

She stood up, capped the flask and looked around for a telephone. Her heartbeat was out of control. The excitement now taking her over was almost sexual. At the same time a sense of relief left her much calmer.

A bearded, middle-aged Arab in a *kaffiyeh* headdress and business suit stepped out of her way with exaggerated politeness. Sweeping past him Rowena headed for the duty-free shop. If it had no telephones, someone would certainly tell her where to find one. Her mind spun with the details of the plan she'd devised to save her life.

She would telephone Ben Dumas straightaway and offer him whatever he wanted to kill Park Song. Get the wog before he got her. Rowena was going on the offensive. She would bloody well put out the fire herself.

Ben was knocking off people for everyone else. Why not for her? He could terminate Song when the Korean came to collect little Miss Tawny and at the same time collect one hundred and twenty-five thousand dollars. There would also be a bonus, namely half of little Miss Tawny's new sale price. Rowena intended to sell her to the highest bidder at the slave auction and expected the American girl to bring in one of the fattest fees of the night.

Half the purchase price would go to Ben. Yes, it was a lot of money to hand over to hired help, but with Rowena's life on the line no price was too great to pay for her survival.

As she neared the duty-free shop Rowena allowed herself to feel triumphant. She'd just solved what had appeared to be an insurmountable problem. Her life was about to return to some sort of order. And she wouldn't have to liquidate her holdings, which is what she'd intended to do had Song accepted her offer of repayment.

Liquidate everything in sight, then beg, borrow or steal the rest. The sale of her home and the shop, plus all of her bank accounts might have yielded three to four million dollars. Sending Song on to a better world not only guaranteed her survival but was infinitely more practical. The thought of Song applying cold steel to her breasts had inspired Rowena to think positively.

At the duty-free shop a young Sikh directed her to the telephone. Without thanking him Rowena dashed off in the direction indicated, praying she'd be able to reach Ben. He was due to meet her at Kennedy Airport but she wanted to speak to him this instant.

16

Dumas, cellular phone to his ear, sat on a windowsill in Ken Yokoi's bedroom, staring across the street into Washington Square Park in a light afternoon rain which had cut the number of freaks out doors to a minimum. On a park bench a homeless old Hispanic man eyed a dead, bloodied rooster lying at his feet, the memento of a downtown cockfight. In the centre of a dry fountain a cadaverous blonde woman in a quilted jacket practised Tai Chi with a sombre grace.

Turning, Dumas waved to Yokoi who lay in bed hooked to an IV for his twice daily feeding. The Japanese weakly lifted a hand in reply. A second later Dumas, a wolfish grin on his face, spoke into the phone. "We've got a deal. See you when you get here."

Pushing down the antenna, he laid the phone aside. Then he faced the window again, shook his head and chuckled softly. For a few seconds he watched a tall black drag queen in a white wedding dress, bombardier jacket, and pink parasol skate into the park from Bleeker Street. Then he looked at the cellular phone. Rowena, Song, and God knows who else, he thought. Talk about excitement. What we have here is a bunch of seedy characters with so many irons in the fire you can't see the fire.

Leaving the window he sat on the edge of Yokoi's bed and took the dying man's hand. "You heard?"

Yokoi managed a brief smile. "'O, what a tangled web we weave when first we practise to deceive.' Or as Grandmother used to say, trust everybody but cut the cards. You did fine, just fine."

"Did what you told me to."

"The successful outcome of a conflict sometimes demands you end a relationship. That's why you must be emotionally detached during any confrontation. Otherwise you can't evaluate it properly. You won't know the strengths and weaknesses of any position, your own included. Keep a cool head and you should be able to make people do exactly what you want them to do."

Dumas nodded. "I went after Decker's support system instead of Decker like you said. Shooting his partner has slowed him down. The last few hours he's been out of our hair. Looks like we'll finish the auction and dispose of Tawny without any interference from him."

Again Dumas flashed his wolfish grin. "Park Song and Rowena are supposed to be a couple of deep thinkers but they couldn't carry your jock. They're out in the world thinking they're movers and shakers while you lie here and run circles around them. I love it."

Yokoi said, "Always take the long view, big guy. And once you decide what you want, act quickly. He who hesitates gets fucked. Where's Park Song now?"

Dumas hooked a thumb towards the cellular phone. "He told me he's a hundred miles past Albany which should put him in the city sometime this afternoon. It's raining, but if the roads aren't too bad he should be here before Rowena's plane lands at Kennedy."

Yokoi said, "Dear Rowena. The lady who sees homicide as the solution to her problem. According to her, death is nature's way of saying we no longer have a deal. Looks like big doings in the Big Apple tonight, by golly. We have our annual auction of firm, young flesh, and we're being honoured by a visit from Park Song and Rowena Dartigue, our very own king and queen of depravity. What was that business about Song having trouble in London?"

"Besides losing eight million dollars in the deposit centre robbery, he tells me three phony English cops tried to rip him off at his hotel. Song wasted all three then went after the guy who sent them. Seems the mastermind was the Nigerian,

Katsina Jonathan. I'd already checked him out and he was okay. But apparently at the last moment he got greedy."

"Katsina Jonathan," Yokoi said. "Lovely name."

"He probably wasn't so lovely when Song and his friends got through with him. Song says they worked him over then burned down his travel agency with him in it. But not before they'd broken Jonathan's back and cut out his tongue, leaving him nothing to do but lie on the floor and bake. Our African friend was probably hotter than a goat with two dicks."

Yokoi chuckled. "Goat with two dicks. You're getting worse in your old age. As for Laughing Boy, talk about your morose behaviour. Doesn't pay to catch him on a bad day, does it? You said he hasn't heard from Rowena. So how'd he learn about the robbery?"

"It made the front page of the *International Herald Tribune*. After reading the story and shitting in his pants, Song contacted the London Embassy. It was they who learned that Rowena had asked Scotland Yard if any of her property had been left behind. The answer was no. The lady had a clean box, so to speak. She seemed particularly interested in her missing jewellery and notebooks."

Yokoi smiled. "Clean box. What are you, a gynaecologist?"

"Song told me he wants to ask her about those notebooks which were important enough to have been kept in a vault. My guess is were he to hear something he didn't like Rowena would wish she'd never been born."

"I'd say whoever robbed the safe deposit boxes has those notebooks. I also think those notebooks have something to do with why she's willing to pay you to send Park Song on to his next life. Didn't think she had it in her. Shows you how much I know about women. Does she know about the Nigerian?"

Dumas shook his head. "She didn't mention it when she called from Heathrow. The safe deposit heist is enough for her at the moment, especially with Song out there looking for her. You heard me try to calm him down a few minutes ago. Losing eight million clams at this stage of his life has him climbing the walls. Which doesn't mean he's forgotten Tawny. He's still hot for the kid."

Earlier that morning Dumas had visited Tawny in the cellar, finding the kid increasingly depressed but still a tad rambunctious. Deciding to play with her mind, he said, "Your mother just telephoned to say she's sending over some of your clothes."

"I don't want to talk to you," Tawny said. "You make up stories." She sat on the edge of her cot, schoolbooks at her feet.

"Your mother said she's sending your favourite dress."

"Oh? Which one?"

Taken by surprise a grinning Dumas said the first thing that came to mind. "You know the one. The one your girlfriends say looks so cute on you."

Tawny nodded. "Oh, you mean the yellow one with the blue trim."

"That's the one."

The trap was sprung. But it wasn't Tawny who'd fallen into it.

She eyed him with contempt before lying down on the cot and turning her face to the wall. "Yellow looks like puke. I hate it. I don't own any yellow dresses."

Dumas cocked an eyebrow. Not bad, kid. Not bad at all.

Later Yokoi said, "If you're wondering what's keeping her together, more or less, it's her hatred for you. Song should know this little woman is going to be a trouble and a worry, as the Arabs say."

Now Yokoi said, "The *kisaeng* obsession. Where will it strike next, I wonder? And Song definitely blames Rowena for the safe deposit robbery?"

"For that, and for the problem with the Nigerian as well. Considering how bent out of shape Song is over this thing, I'd say Rowena made the right decision to whack him. In her position I'd probably have done the same thing."

"The end of an era. The bonds that unite are about to be torn asunder. What time are you leaving?"

Dumas looked at his watch. "In a few minutes. I'll return before going to the auction. I want to be on hand when the paper and the counterfeit money's dropped off."

Yokoi said, "Speaking of paper, you haven't forgotten Russell Fort."

"Funny you should mention it. Today's his last day on earth, as a matter of fact. As soon as he delivers the latest batch of paper, he's gone. I've got to make this double hit for LoCasio, so I'm having somebody else take out Fort. After he's extinct I should be able to convince Aunt Lorraine and Cousin Arnold to deal with me directly. If they refuse, there's going to be a family reunion in heaven or wherever Russell's soul happens to be."

"You really have to do these LoCasio hits yourself?"

Dumas nodded. "Joe personally asked me as a favour. He wants it done right which is why he went out and got the best, namely yours truly. This one's a double dip, two for one. It involves his pride so there can't be any slip-ups. After it's over Joe will owe me. I'll be in a position to come to him for a favour. Take the long view, remember?"

They held hands in silence then Yokoi said, "Try not to get yourself killed. If anything happens to you, I'm pulling the plug. You're all I have in this world. No family, really. A few friends, but no one like you. When you go I'm gone anyway, so why prolong the inevitable. Besides, this house wouldn't be much fun without you. Who else is going to make me such great flower arrangements?"

"Stop acting like an old queen."

"I am an old queen."

Dumas kissed him on the forehead. "I'm coming back, I promise."

"There are three ways it could go wrong," Yokoi said. "The Rowena-Park Song thing. The slave auction. And this double hit for Joe LoCasio. Any one of them can be trouble."

He closed his eyes. "Good, bad, everything happens in threes. Anyone ever tell you that?"

17

As Ben Dumas left his lover's townhouse to commit two murders Decker rose from a chair beside the hospital bed of a sleeping Ellen Spiceland and inspected the thermostat. Sixty-five degrees. Too cool, he thought. He turned it up to seventy.

The afternoon rain had caused outside temperatures to drop, chilling the room. Decker preferred warm weather because it eased the stiffness in bones and joints he'd damaged in over twenty years of karate. Warm weather kept him loose which increased the speed and power of his techniques. Cold weather tightened the body, forcing him to increase the pre-practice stretching that was necessary to avoid pulled muscles.

Professionally Decker saw the advantage of cold weather. It kept people indoors, shielding them away from each other and cutting down on street crime. Freezing temperatures, snowstorms and heavy rain sometimes did as much for a cop's peace of mind as a bulletproof vest.

Yesterday morning when Bags had been shot she hadn't been wearing a vest. There'd been no need for one, not when she'd been planning to spend eight hours behind a desk at the precinct. As she told Decker after surgery, she'd stepped from her apartment and was about to lock the front door when someone had shot her in the back three times with what turned out to be a High Standard .22.

One bullet grazed a shoulder, resulting in only a flesh wound. The other two had done more damage, injuring a kidney, piercing a lung and forcing doctors to remove her spleen. In time she would fully recover and be able to return to duty, providing she felt like it. Decker had known cops to recuperate from a shooting then become too frightened ever to set foot inside a precinct house again.

He'd hate for that to happen to Bags, for her sake and his. Their friendship was one of the few things he trusted in life. Her value hadn't really been known to him until he'd heard she was near death. Then he'd almost come apart. The thought of losing Bags had been a sharp reminder of just how much he depended on her. Who else knew everything about Decker and liked him anyway?

She hadn't seen the gunman's face but while lying on the hallway floor after the shooting she'd seen his baggy grey pants and tacky brown shoes as he'd raced upstairs towards the roof. Her husband Henri who'd responded to her screams, also reported hearing someone run upstairs. Once on the roof the shooter had apparently crossed over to another building, then walked down to the street and made his escape. Whoever the bastard was, he'd known his way around.

On their own time a dozen officers from Bags's precinct had joined local cops in combing the neighbourhood for clues. They'd talked to everyone from news vendors, beat cops, whores, winos, storekeepers and street derelicts. At the same time they'd rummaged through garbage cans, dumpsters and vacant lots, hoping to find the gun used in the shooting. They'd come up with nothing. No clues, no witnesses, no motive. All they'd learned was that Bags was a popular lady who'd even earned the respect of local drug dealers.

No, the dealers hadn't tried to smoke her. Killing a cop was bad for business; it brought down too much heat and kept customers away. They pledged their support in solving the crime so that things could get back to normal as quickly as possible.

In the hospital room Decker eyed the flowers and baskets of fruit from Bags's well-wishers. Calls and telegrams had poured in from all over the country, from relatives, friends and cops who didn't know her, all pulling for the policewoman whose near murder had become New York's latest media event. The mayor, police commissioner, borough president and television cameras had come and gone. The switchboard was now holding all calls until further notice and there was a twenty-four-hour police guard outside her room.

Decker, meanwhile, was losing sleep over why someone had tried to whack his partner. Had it been a case of mistaken identity? Maybe a perp from an old bust had tried to even the score. Somehow he didn't think so. Had that been true the shooter should have come after both of them, not just Bags. Unless Decker was next. If someone had planned a crisis deliberately to divert him from his current cases they couldn't have done a better job.

He'd been among the first to donate blood for Bags. Before the day was over more than three hundred policemen and women had come forward to do the same. Most hadn't heard of her until the shooting. All they knew was that a cop had been shot in the back. It wasn't necessary to know anything else.

Decker turned from the thermostat and looked at the sleeping Bags who had tubes in her nose and both arms. She looked so small, so helpless. Who the hell hated her enough to shoot her in the back? Her husband Henri was also in the room, sleeping fully clothed on a cot near the window. He'd dropped his veneer of a world-weary, sophisticated artist and fallen back on his roots, which meant turning to voodoo to save his wife's life.

He'd come to the hospital wearing what he called a magic shawl. Hanging from his neck were three *gris-gris*, small idols, and he'd also placed three peppers under his tongue. Cops working with New York's large Hispanic and Caribbean population knew that witchcraft and cults were more common than the average citizen would believe. So Decker wasn't surprised when Henri excused himself, saying he was going off to hide the peppers somewhere in the hospital. Henri wasn't trying to burn down the place, so why get excited. All he wanted to do was keep his wife alive. Decker didn't have a problem with that.

Without consulting anyone Henri spoon-fed Bags home-made gumbo, making sure the hospital staff never saw him do it. Did any of this make a difference? All Decker knew was that the doctors were staggered by her rapid progress. As was he.

In the hospital room he walked to the closet, found his overcoat and removed several cards taken from Nicolay's Roladex. Then he returned to his chair and bit into the remains of a tunafish sandwich before sitting down. Karen Drumman, who'd visited the hospital, had brought him sandwiches and coffee. At her invitation he'd spent the previous night at her apartment, located within walking distance of the hospital.

He'd slept on the couch, hardly speaking to her, too incensed about the shooting to do more than grunt when she said goodnight and retired to her bedroom. If it took him the rest of his life he was going to learn who'd shot Bags and why. This morning he'd been up, showered and gone before Karen had got out of bed. But not before making a few telephone calls and leaving a note saying to bill him for the charges.

As rain lashed the hospital window he sipped cold coffee and examined the Roladex cards which he'd placed in a certain order. There were Dumas's cards, personal and business numbers and addresses. Then a card for Russell Fort and one for Nicolay, listing lawyers, accountants, apartment and summer home. Then a card for Kim Shin and several other Koreans, most but not all of them at the Korean Embassy here in New York. Decker suspected that some of these names were aliases for Park Song.

Then there was Mr Fox whose card contained several London telephone numbers. Decker had heard that name in Singular's office; the problem was he couldn't remember when and how he'd heard it. Since he didn't know how Mr Fox fitted into the picture Decker placed his card last in the pack.

Decker had telephoned Mr Fox's numbers from Karen Drumman's apartment, learning they were for a clothing shop called Rosebud, a house in Chelsea and a children's charity. All of the numbers had a common link – a woman

275

named Rowena Dartigue who either owned the properties or ran the business. Make that two things in common. Whoever answered the phone had never heard of a Mr Fox.

Singular. What the hell was it the fat man had said? Decker closed his eyes in concentration, breathed deeply and made his mind blank. He relaxed. Waited. Then, *"About this little girl you're after, this Tawny what's-her-name. Before Song killed that agent of ours a year ago the agent came up with some information about a Mr Fox."*

Singular had said something else, too. *"I specifically told you to concentrate on Dumas and those undercover cops. Forget Tawny what's-her-name."*

Then Decker had said, "What's Tawny got to do with Kim Shin?" As usual Singular had ducked the question.

Opening his eyes Decker stared at Mr Fox's card. Song and Mr Fox had been tied together by a dead Secret Service agent. Meaning they'd been in business together. The question was why had Singular mentioned them in the same breath as Tawny?

Leaving his chair Decker walked over to the window to stare down at a rain-soaked Fifth Avenue and Central Park. He relaxed, allowing a wild idea to enter his mind, one which also chilled the blood. Song, Mr Fox and little girls. Dumas, Song and Tawny. Decker began shuffling the cards again. *"About this little girl you're after – "*

Dumas supplied Song with information and currency paper. Had he and Mr Fox joined to supply the Korean with something else? Such as a young girl to be killed. Decker clenched his teeth. That's why the fat man had sent for him. He'd learned that Decker was investigating Dumas *and* looking for Tawny so he had to slow him down. The American government didn't give a shit about Tawny. All it cared about was avoiding an international incident.

Back to the cards. Dumas and Fort. An impatient Decker placed them side by side on the windowsill. A black man had followed Max DaSilva. Max and Gail, Tawny's parents, had been killed immediately after telling Decker about a black man. Fort wasn't just any black man. He was a black man who was being protected by Ben Dumas. Decker, his mind racing, stared out at the rain, not daring to breathe.

The sound of a ringing telephone brought him out of his dark vision. Grabbing the receiver he turned his back to Bags and whispered, "Detective Sergeant Decker. Who the hell put you through?"

"Lowell Chattaway. I thought it was important so I touched base with your precinct and they said go ahead and call. Sorry to hear about Bags. You want help on this, you got it."

"Thanks, Lowell. What's up?"

"You asked me about those Beretta 84s ripped off from Kennedy by the LoCasio crew. I just hope it has nothing to do with anything you and Bags are working on, but you never know."

"Appreciate whatever you have."

"Okay, here goes. Our snitch just reported in. He says the LoCasio people sold three Berettas to the CIA. Not those clowns in Washington, but the Ben Dumas detective agency. You know, *convicted, indicted, arrested*? The guys who can't keep their hands off other people's property."

Decker closed his eyes. He'd just found the last piece of the puzzle. He said, "I owe you one, Lowell," then hung up without waiting for a reply. When he turned around Bags was staring at him.

"How we doing?" she whispered.

Decker remembered that it had been Bags who had put him onto Safe and Loft in the first place. Remembered she'd helped him trace the gun now being linked to Gail and Max DaSilva's killer.

He took her hand in his. "I know who wasted them, Bags. And I know why."

18

Russell Fort sat on an unstable chrome barstool in the cramped office of Jean-Louis Nicolay's restaurant and watched silently as the little Frenchman examined the paper – eight packages of blank notes wrapped in heavy paper and bound with steel strips. Just hours ago it had been the property of the Bureau of Engraving and Printing. The frog had it now. After him, it would belong to a Korean whom Fort had never met and didn't want to meet.

He sat with his back to a heavily barred ground floor window which was virtually opaque with soot and grime. He'd been forced to tuck matchbooks under the stool to keep it balanced on a slightly uneven floor. At the moment Fort was more concerned with cash than equilibrium. He wasn't getting paid for this load which had left him in a bad mood.

He'd owed the LoCasio people a debt which had been paid by Dumas. As a result Fort was getting zilch for this last batch of paper which meant he'd have to come up with five thousand dollars for Aunt Lorraine and Cousin Arnold. The deal was ten thousand dollars a load – half to Fort, half to his Washington relatives. Unless he produced five K pretty soon, Aunt Lorraine and Arnold would turn off the tap, something Fort would have to explain to Dumas. And if all Dumas did about it was slap him bald-headed, as Aunt Lorraine might say, Fort would be lucky.

He lit a cigarette, moving gingerly because he still hurt from the beating given him two days ago by Dumas. His forearm

278

was in a cast and he had two cracked ribs which made it hard to lift his arms or lean to either side.

Fort and Susan Scudder had returned from Washington in a rented Olds, Susan doing most of the driving with Fort nodding out on Percodan in the back seat. He'd taken the wheel in New York where a light rain had slowed traffic to a crawl. Because of the bad weather they'd arrived at the restaurant more than an hour late which caused a jumpy Nicolay to curse Fort out for not being on time. Fort shut him up by threatening to go upside the little frog's head with his cast. Taking shit from a turkey like Nicolay wasn't part of the deal.

The trip to Atlantic City, Fort's cover for the Washington trip, had been a drag. Not only had the blackjack tables gobbled up most of the two thousand expenses money fronted by Dumas, but Susan had turned out to be a problem. He'd had to explain how he'd come to get beaten up so he'd fallen back on the truth. Told the bitch everything – how Dumas had grabbed Tawny DaSilva, how Fort had tried to rip off the parents' reward money, how Decker had become a player. He'd also told her that Dumas had iced Mommy and Daddy.

Susan had freaked out. What the hell had Fort got her into? Wasn't it enough that he'd involved her in the death of two undercover cops? And now this shit. Fort said, that's life, little mama. Fool with the bull and you get the horn. They'd tied themselves to Ben Dumas and now had to live with it.

Susan said, "Live with this, you asshole." With her very dirty mouth she then proceeded to curse the living shit out of Fort for bringing a creep like Dumas into her life. This trip to Washington was the last thing she'd do for these animals, Fort included. He was never to ask her for another thing or she'd go straight to Decker or even DEA and turn them all in. If she had to go down, so be it. But she'd had it with these zero minus excuses for men.

Fort surprised himself by not reacting. He played Mr Cool, coming on as Top Cat and King of the Mountain. Which was how to handle yourself around the ladies if you didn't want to end up looking like chump change. The painkillers helped. They left him so laid back that he couldn't have come on strong if he'd wanted to.

So he didn't slap Susan around for getting in his face. Didn't curse the bitch or make her cry. Why crack the whip when he needed her to keep Dumas off his ass? All he'd said was, we'll talk about it later. Then he closed his eyes and pretended to be asleep, leaving her to drive and think she'd won this round.

Later when he felt stronger he'd sit the lady down and clue her in. Recite the facts of life to her, beginning with the news that you did not say no to Ben Dumas. The best way to get around Susan was to take her to bed and work on that nice, little body until she was tearing at the sheets. Fort was her Sweet Daddy and Lord Right. Get between her legs and he'd bring her around. For sure.

In Nicolay's office Fort slid off the stool, a set of Western saddlebags slung over his cast. No payoff to shove into the bags this time. All he had in there was a ballpoint pen filled with cocaine, a Tom Clancy paperback, a cheap notebook and a fifteen-shot Browning 9 mm. Normally he'd sling the saddlebags from his shoulder but not now. Not with his ribs giving him so much grief.

A smiling Nicolay extended his hand. "Forgive my earlier outburst, my friend. You understand I am under much pressure to have things ready when our Korean friend arrives tonight."

"Well, we all have our problems. See you around."

"Are you absolutely certain you and Susan cannot stay for dinner? Please be my guests. Tonight we are featuring a sea bass guaranteed to melt in your mouth. And for dessert a lemon ribbon cake with home-made lemon ice cream."

Fort shook his head. "Some other time, maybe. We're beat from all that travelling. I just want to crash somewhere and rest this cast. You just make sure Ben knows the paper's here, that's all. Last thing I want is for him to think I fucked up."

"My friend, you leave that to me. I shall call him immediately and say how magnificent you have been. By the way if you want food that is not French I can recommend other restaurants. There are many good ones. You like Italian, Chinese?"

"It's not the food. Susan and me are just tired. We're going to drop off the car, then head straight to her place. I'm hurting all over and besides bad weather always wears me out for some reason. We'll probably pick up something on the way and have an early night."

"Well goodbye, my friend, and I hope Susan feels better. Forgive me if I do not go to the car and say goodbye to her. I must set up for dinner."

Despising Nicolay for his role in Tawny DaSilva's kidnapping, Susan had refused to set foot in his restaurant. Fort had handled the situation by lying, saying she was having her period and preferred to remain in the car so she could get some fresh air. It was a lie which had verged on truth. Susan was sick. Sick of Nicolay.

The Frenchman walked Fort through the empty restaurant and to the door, where they shook hands. He watched Fort cross the street, get into a blue Oldsmobile and chat briefly with Susan who seemed upset. At that time of the month, all women were upset, were they not? When the car pulled away Nicolay returned to his office where he made a phone call.

His end of the conversation was brief. All he said was, "They've just left. No, they're going to drop off the car then go straight to her place. Yes, I'm sure. Quite sure."

When Russell Fort and Susan Scudder left the pizzeria at Broadway and 79th they walked towards a brownstone one block away, where she had a one-bedroom apartment over a Cuban-Chinese restaurant run by a Chinese family who'd immigrated to Cuba then fled when Castro had taken over.

Susan carried a large pizza while Fort carried a plastic bag containing a bottle of red wine and a box of Mrs Fields's pecan brownies. At four thirty in the afternoon it was already totally dark outside. The rain, now a light drizzle, had tied up traffic while reducing the number of pedestrians to a handful. It hadn't kept the panhandlers off the street, however. In the space of a few yards Fort and Susan were approached by

281

three filthy-looking street people, black men holding paper cups and asking for spare change. He gave nothing, insisted Susan give nothing and told them all the same thing – get a job, man, and stop bothering people.

Susan, who loved her food almost as much as she loved sex, was now more relaxed. She spoke of the many Christmas catalogues she'd received this past week, of her intention to take up tap-dancing next year, of her rent having doubled during the eight years she'd lived in the neighbourhood.

By the time they neared her building Fort had an arm around her, remembering how he'd liked her from the moment she'd come into his store for a pair of running shoes and begun flirting with him. Bottom line was, he had himself a sweet lady in Susan. A bit garbage-mouthed at times, but sweet.

At the moment she looked like a kid in that green raincoat and floppy purple hat. A very sexy kid. He was anticipating a mellow evening with just the two of them. At the same time he wondered if he could get a bet down on the Knicks who were two point favourites over Houston at the Garden tonight. Whoever took his action would have to extend credit because Fort didn't have a bean.

At the corner of Broadway and 80th Street they crossed the street and turned left, heading towards Susan's brownstone several yards away. A young Hispanic couple, who'd been on the other side, fell in behind them. The man, small and tough-looking, wore a green wool cap, matching down jacket and carried a Christmas tree taller than himself. The woman, lean with a huge mouth, wore a coat with a fake fur collar which she held tight around her throat with one hand. Neither had an umbrella.

At Susan's building she and Fort started up the single flight of stone steps leading to the entrance. The Hispanic couple continued walking, then suddenly stopped and drew pistols from their coat pockets. Turning they fired at Fort and Susan.

On the top step Fort had stopped and drawn Susan to him for a kiss in the rain, seeing her eyes light up and that's when

282

he saw the shooters from the corner of his eye. Calling on his cop training he attempted to protect Susan, shoving her away and sending her screaming down the stairs. Then dropping the plastic bag with the wine and brownies, he reached for the saddlebags.

He heard *pop-pop-pop*, felt a sharp pain in his thigh and collapsed on the steps, landing on his right hip. A bullet tore the heel from one eelskin boot. Two holes appeared in a ground floor window. His adrenalin was flowing as it had that night on Eighth Avenue when a crazed homeless man had tried to take away his gun and Fort had shot that sucker six times.

Fort shoved his hand into the saddlebags, his senses picking up images – the smell of red wine, the feel of the rain-wet steps hard against his spine, the bright orange of flames from the shooters' guns. He was out of control, crazy to live, to save his life and Susan's.

He took a second bullet through the shoulder and a third whizzed by his ear, gouging away a piece of the stone steps. By then Fort had found the Browning. Thumbing off the safety he fired through the leather, fired four times, hitting the tough-looking Hispanic man in the chest and driving him back into a fire hydrant. Another bullet, this one from the Hispanic woman's gun, struck the stairs between Fort's legs, missing his balls by inches. He returned fire, knocking the hat from her head and sending it flying. With that the woman turned and fled towards West End Avenue, disappearing in the darkness.

Hand still in the saddlebag, Fort limped down the stairs and crouched over Susan who lay on the sidewalk, the rain washing away her blood almost as fast as it flowed from the hole in her neck. Her eyes were open, bright and totally unseeing in the streetlight. Fort shook his head. "Goddam," he whispered. "Goddam."

"Decker. Who's this?"

"Russell Fort. Precinct said I could talk to you at the hospital in an emergency. I didn't tell them who I was."

"I bet you didn't."

"I told them it had to do with those dead undercover cops. They said that you were with your partner. Two of Dumas's people tried to smoke me, but they blew it. They got Susan instead. She's dead."

Decker closed his eyes. "I'm sorry. You said Dumas's people did it?"

"Before we go into that, I want your word you'll get me into the Witness Protection programme."

"Yesterday we might have had something to talk about. But at the moment I don't think you can buy into the game. I know you used Susan to get profile sheets from DEA to learn the identity of undercover cops. And I know you're supplying currency paper to Dumas who's passing it on to Park Song. When the feds pick up your Aunt Lorraine and Cousin Arnold, you can turn out the lights, the party's over. You'll have to give me something else, Russell. Like who killed Gail and Max DaSilva."

Fort was silent. Then, "I think you know, man. If you know this much about my business, then you know the rest. Susan said you were smart."

"I need more. I need you to go into court and testify against Ben Dumas. Otherwise, you and I have nothing to talk about."

"I want a deal then we'll talk. I'm an ex-cop, man. I wouldn't last a week in the joint. Look, I'm not just doing this for myself, I'm doing it for Susan. It's finished for me. The one thing I can do now is see Dumas's ass in the joint for what he did to her. I have an ID from the guy I shot, a Hispanic named Espinosa. He worked for Dumas's detective agency. Look, I don't have all day. I took two bullets and I need a doctor. Also, the cops are probably after my ass for smoking Espinosa. I need protection."

"Give me a reason."

"Dumas got his information on Valentin and Dalto through me and Susan. I'll say that in court."

Decker said, "Where are you?"

"Dumas probably has people out looking for me. And

284

he's gonna get help from guys on the force because that prick is well-connected. The minute you and I get together he'll know about it. By the way, here's something else for you to think about: I can tell you where that kid Tawny is."

19

The knock on Michael Dartigue's hotel room door came
shortly before four forty-five in the afternoon. Whoever it was
tapped twice, not too loud, not too soft. Michael, who'd been
chewing his nails while watching a rerun of *Hawaii Five-O*,
suddenly looked towards the bed where Nigella Barrow, in a
blue silk robe, froze in the act of painting her toenails. For a
few seconds both fearfully eyed each other. Finally Michael
dried his palms on his thighs and went to the door.

Hand on the knob, he closed his eyes, opened them and
cleared his throat. "Yes?"

"I'm from LoCasio." It was a male voice, soft-spoken and
polite. Not like the greaseball who'd telephoned Michael
yesterday with news that the forty million dollars from the
London robbery hadn't been sent to New York as promised. The one who sounded as though he gargled with razor
blades.

Michael opened the door and was greeted by a smile from
Ben Dumas who said, "May I come in?"

"I'm sorry. Sure, come on in. I'm Michael." He reluctantly
extended his hand.

"Fred Hannah," Dumas said. They shook hands as he
entered the room. "I won't stay long," he said.

At the sight of Nigella Barrow he took off his hat and
smiled. Michael introduced them and Dumas took her hand.
"My pleasure."

Then Dumas reached into his topcoat and took out a two
inch phial of white powder, holding it between thumb and

forefinger. His eyes flicked to Michael who, chewing his lower lip and frowning, stared at the phial.

"First things first," Dumas said. "Before you dive into this nose candy let's clear up a few points. Like Joe's guy said over the phone this morning, Joe did some thinking about that little talk you and he had yesterday. He wants you to know he's sorry for coming down on you so hard."

A relieved Michael grinned. "Hey, these things happen. I understand. He did what he had to do."

Dumas said, "Joe understands everybody got jerked around by Eddie Walkerdine so why hold anything against you? I mean the way Walkerdine saw it, cutting you out was a lot cheaper than giving you a third or whatever it was you were supposed to get."

"I swear. No way would I fuck around with a heavy hitter like Joe. I mean, no way. I'd have to be out of my mind to even think of doing a thing like that."

"I know. But you have to see it from his position. You promised him something you didn't deliver, and this made Joe look bad. Not just with his own people, you understand, but with the competition. Actually, it made him look weak, confused, mixed up. Fuzzy-headed, you might say."

Michael shook his head. "Fred, you don't know how bad I feel about that."

Dumas held up a hand in a stop signal. "Like I said, Joe understands. By the way, Walkerdine's turned up in Israel."

Michael's jaw dropped. "Son of a bitch. You sure?"

"We're sure. Joe's got friends all over. With a load as big as this there's just so many places you can go to fence it, especially with all that jewellery. You can't resell stolen jewellery unless you break up the original settings and that takes skill. Men who can do this kind of work are few and far between. Everybody knows who they are."

Michael roared. "I love it. Fucking Walkerdine's going to get his ticket punched. I love it. You guys going to take the stuff away from him, I hope?"

Dumas sighed. "It's not that easy. Depends on how much of it he's got rid of and who he's selling it to. Looks as though he's got some kind of deal going with an Israeli he met in Spain. Anyway, back to you. You realise you owe Joe and — "

Michael put up his hands. "Hey man, any time I can do a favour for Joe, he has but to ask. You want me to be a mule or whatever, you just say the word."

Dumas's smile was wolfish. "Great to be young and alive, isn't it?"

A grinning Michael, one arm around Nigella's waist, nodded. "Fucking A."

Dumas handed him the phial. "Party favours. Joe thought you seemed a little highstrung so that's why he promised to help you out. You two are free to leave New York any time you want. Your problems are over."

Michael swooped up a smiling Nigella in a bear hug and gave her a big kiss. "All right! You hear that? It's over. Man, it's over and we can relax. Is that great or what?"

He released Nigella and took Dumas's hand in both of his. "Man, am I glad you dropped by."

A smiling Dumas said, "If you don't mind, I'd like to stay and join the party." He took another phial from his pocket. "Brought my own."

Michael whooped. "Let's do it."

He ran into the tiny bathroom then returned with Nigella's cosmetic mirror and a single-edged razor blade. By then Dumas and Nigella had placed two straight-backed wooden chairs at a small table near the front alcove.

Since these were the only chairs in the room a gracious Dumas insisted that Michael and Nigella sit. He would stand. He grinned at the haste with which Michael dumped his white powder onto the mirror and used the razor blade to divide it into eight thin lines. At the same time Nigella rolled three one hundred dollar bills into thin tubes. Dumas poured his powder on a small white saucer, using a small penknife to separate it into four thin lines. When Nigella gave him a rolled hundred he smiled and thanked her. Both seemed to warm to him, to relax in his presence.

Anxious to celebrate his reprieve from Joe LoCasio's retribution Michael snorted first. Placing one end of a rolled hundred in the cocaine and the other in his right nostril he inhaled one line, then tucked the bill in his left nostril and inhaled a second. He did two more lines before flopping back in his chair, glassy-eyed and grinning, traces of the white powder visible in his nose hairs. Giggling, he urged Nigella to dig in. This was some dynamite shit.

Dumas watched them for a few seconds then because they were eyeballing him, waiting for him to participate, he went along with the charade. He snorted two lines of his powder, nodded in approval and waited for the drug to take effect. Not on him but on Mickey and Judy, who didn't know they were about to put on a show. No one seemed to notice that Dumas had put his gloves back on.

Suddenly Michael turned red-faced, clutched his heart and inhaled loudly through his open mouth. Eyes bulging, he went rigid in his chair. Nigella, meanwhile, sat with her hands on her throat, gasping for air. She looked at Michael in time to see him fall to the floor where he lay twitching and vomiting.

She started to turn towards Dumas but gagged, her head smashing into the table where she lay still. Seconds later Michael's body stiffened then relaxed, his legs quivering briefly before he lay motionless near his overturned chair.

Dumas had given them one hundred per cent cocaine, pure and uncut Bolivian marching powder with nothing added. They'd indulged themselves on nose candy strong enough to lift an elephant two storeys off the ground and spin him around in the air three times – stuff strong enough to bend steel and raise the dead. Well, it hadn't been entirely uncut. Dumas had added strychnine. Pure cocaine and rat poison. When you care enough to send the very best.

Didn't pay to make a fool out of Joe LoCasio. No, siree.

Dumas thought, Rowena, you sure can pick 'em. This was the first time he'd met Michael face to face. At Rowena's request he'd investigated Mr Dartigue prior to their wedding, passing on his findings which showed the guy to be a stone loser. Rowena, however, had chosen to ignore the facts. She'd got all excited about nothing then gone ahead and married him.

Picking up his saucer Dumas walked to the bathroom where he washed off the white powder – milk sugar – in the basin. After drying the saucer with a bathtowel he left it on top of the toilet. Then he took time to gaze in the mirror and sigh at the continuing loss of his thinning hair before returning to the room.

He found Rowena's notebooks right away, remembering how Ken had said that a man who'd rob his own wife would do anything, including read her most private thoughts. There was always a chance that Michael's accomplices might have the notebooks, Michael not being the greatest brain on the planet. Dumas was to stay alert and if he got lucky he was to bring the notebooks back to Ken for an up close and personal inspection.

Dumas flipped through the notebooks which were written in Rowena's ornate and beautiful handwriting. He wasn't surprised she'd kept such records. She was a meticulous and fussy woman in many ways. The books might simply have been a way of keeping track of sexual preferences, customers and prices. Or it might have been a way of keeping certain financial records away from the taxman, banking authorities and law enforcement.

She could have been planning blackmail at some future date, though Dumas doubted it. Rowena knew her limitations and kept well within them. Her only mistake had been falling for the wrong guy, a guy who would never live long enough to know better.

When Dumas saw his and Ken's names, an eyebrow went up. Can't have people seeing this, now can we? Ken would decide how best to use the notebooks, after removing Dumas's name, of course.

Joe LoCasio knew nothing about these hotsy-totsy tomes. Michael, for his own reasons, hadn't mentioned them. He'd told Joe about the earrings, Rowena's no less, probably in an attempt to win sympathy for having got the shorts from Walkerdine. He'd wasted his breath. Joe had just one thing on his mind and that was to get even with Michael for jerking him around.

Which is where Dumas came in. He doubted if anybody was going to get excited about two coke heads ODing on high-class flake. Things like that happened in Fun City every day.

Dumas looked around for the earrings and found them without any difficulty. Very nice. Typical of Rowena's good taste. He dropped them in a pocket of his overcoat along with his "drug" phial. Rowena would have her earrings back within hours.

Seconds later Dumas exited from the hotel room, leaving a "Do Not Disturb" sign hanging from the door. He really was going to have to do something about his hair.

20

It was seven twelve p.m. when Rowena Dartigue, carrying
a bottle of duty-free brandy in a blue plastic bag, stepped
from the international arrivals building at Kennedy Airport
and followed the dumpy Puerto Rican porter pushing her
luggage cart.

She walked near the building, remaining under the overhang
and away from the curb where a December rain pelted the
taxi and limousine rank. Torrential downpours did little for
Rowena's peace of mind. If she were ever inclined to applaud
the fullness of existence it would most likely be on a warm
and sunny day.

Behind Rowena a dozen passengers queued for taxis.
Shivering, Rowena drew her fur coat around her throat.
Once in the limousine waiting for her up ahead the brandy
should take the chill out of her bones while she and Ben drove
to the slave auction in Queens, a dreary area where an hour's
stay was like a week.

Ken Yokoi and Ben had settled on Queens as the site for the
slave house because its proximity to Ben's detective agency
in the Forest Hills area made security easy to enforce. The
slave house, a private home in Kew Gardens, was owned
by a corporation registered in Panama, the said corporation
being a joint venture of Rowena, Yokoi, Dumas and Nicolay.
A middle-aged Hungarian couple, discreet and trustworthy,
lived on the premises and were the apparent owners on
record.

Sex slaves stayed at the house for varying periods. Those

who came of their own volition, which was to say at Yokoi's recommendation, were rarely there for more than two months. If they weren't sold or paired up in that time by Jean-Louis Nicolay they were asked to leave.

Rowena's interest was with those youngsters from her charity who came over from England in the company of two old queens who'd been her trusted assistants for years. This particular merchandise arrived a week or so before the yearly auction and was invariably snapped up by wealthy customers. Security was maintained by Ben Dumas's men, as ominous a bunch of villains as Rowena had ever encountered. Sales were cash only and there were no refunds. Rowena could expect to take in between two and four million dollars, at least half of which would go towards expenses.

Tonight at the airport a porter bearing a sign with her name had met Rowena at baggage retrieval, announcing he'd been sent by a Mr Dumas to collect Rowena and bring her to a waiting limousine. The gentlemanly and well-mannered Ben, who usually helped her with the baggage, had apparently decided to maintain a low profile for the moment. She was sure he had his reasons. Meanwhile she couldn't wait to get in out of the chill. Nor had she spent ten thousand pounds on a mink coat in order to have it water-logged.

Ahead she saw a silver stretch limousine parked behind a small green bus waiting to transport passengers between terminals. The limousine's trunk was open but there was no sign of Ben. He was probably in the back seat. Give the man credit for having sense enough to come in out of the rain.

As Rowena neared the limousine the back door opened, beckoning her onward. She quickened her step, passing the porter who could handle her luggage by himself which was what he was getting paid for. A relieved Rowena was looking forward to being with the man who would be her safe harbour until Park Song was dead. Ben's fee for the murder was exorbitant but what choice did she have? If life were to go on Rowena would have to dig deep in her purse.

With a sigh of relief she slid into the limousine and opened her mouth to greet Dumas. Instead her jaw dropped and her eyes bulged in shock. Across the seat from her Park Song swallowed the last of his champagne then stared into the empty glass. "Good evening," he said, "I trust you had a nice flight."

He lifted a hand in a signal. In the front the muscular Choi and the Israeli David Mitla left the car. Mitla closed Rowena's door which Song promptly locked by pressing a button on the arm rest. Choi paid the porter, closed the trunk and returned to the car where he immediately turned the key in the ignition. The motor turned over at once and the car began pulling away from the curb.

Rowena took several deep breaths then forced a smile. "Park, darling. What a pleasant surprise. Where's, where's Ben? We were supposed to meet and go on to the auction."

"There's been a change in plans."

"Change? I don't understand."

In the front seat David Mitla turned around to stare at her, his bearded face demonic in the car's dim light. Rowena glanced at him then quickly looked away, squeezing the brandy bottle with both hands. It was only when the limousine passed the parking lot and headed towards the expressway that he faced forward.

Rowena felt ready to pass out. Her throat was bone dry and she had trouble concentrating. Desperate to buy time, she asked Song for a glass of champagne which he politely handed her. She swallowed the chilled liquid in a gulp, thinking, where's Ben? Had something happened to him? Dear God, she hoped not.

"I have a present for you," Song said. He reached into his topcoat pocket and removed something which he then gently placed in her hand. Rowena looked at her hand and gasped. He'd given her the Giuliano earrings.

Rowena said, "Where did you get them? They were stolen from my safe deposit box."

"By your husband, in case you forgot. I got them from Dumas."

"I don't understand."

"You and your husband took my money. I'd like it back."

"You're mad. I never took a penny from you. Why should I, after all these years? Besides, I have more than enough money of my own."

Song's clenched fists came to rest on his thighs. "You also have a husband who's always in need of money. By the way, Dumas told me of your plan to kill me. You'll probably tell me this has nothing to do with stealing my money. It would certainly discourage me from coming after you, that's for sure."

Rowena shook her head. "I never asked Ben to – "

Song put a finger to his lips for silence. "Ben decided that killing me would only complicate his life. As you know, I perform certain services for important people in my country. I spy for them, kill for them, forge documents for them. If Dumas were to kill me, he'd have to answer to these people. He decided this was too risky."

Rowena said, "Park, darling, believe me there's been some sort of misunderstanding. I'm not the type to kill anyone. You know that."

"He taped your conversation and played it back for me."

"Oh God."

As the limousine turned onto the rain-slicked expressway Song gently placed a hand on Rowena's thigh. A second later she cried out as his fingers dug painfully into the soft area around the kneecap. When he took away his hand Rowena sucked in air through her opened mouth. There was no feeling in the leg.

Song said, "You're going to tell me everything. You're going to tell me about the Nigerian you sent to rob me and you're going to tell me more about your foolish husband. Someone has to speak for him since he's hardly in a position to do it for himself. I intend to interrogate you thoroughly. And I intend to take my time doing it."

The limousine hit a pothole, splashing water on the windshield. There was no traffic in front of them and very little behind.

A subdued Rowena said, "What have you done to Michael?"

"I haven't done anything. Dumas killed him."

Rowena covered her face with both hands.

Song shrugged. "Michael had finished his role in the play. It was time for him to leave the stage. He named names, admitted his part in the robbery and to the end remained the amiable loser he'd always been. Had someone not exercised a prior claim I'd have killed him myself."

Rowena stiffened as he again touched her thigh. "Dumas drives a hard bargain," Song said. "I had to pay a pretty penny for my life. Double what I owe for the girl, plus a hundred thousand in counterfeit for him to dispose of as he chooses. I don't believe you came anywhere near that. Then, you always were close with a dollar."

In the front seat David Mitla snickered.

Rowena said, "Is there anything I can say?"

Song shook his head. "Nothing at all."

"I thought as much."

Screaming, "You bastard!" she struck him on the forehead with the brandy, snapping Song's head back and knocking him into a corner of the limousine. In front David Mitla frantically signalled Choi to stop. The limousine slowed but was still moving when a hysterical Rowena unlocked her door and leaped onto the wet highway.

She landed in a large puddle of water, rolling along the expressway, tearing skin from her hands and face and twisting a knee. Painfully pushing herself erect a bloodied Rowena limped away from the limousine, dragging a leg behind her. A quick glance over her shoulder revealed that the limousine had stopped. Taillights blinking, it began backing up. Rowena turned, to be blinded by the headlights of an oncoming vehicle which instantly ran her over.

The driver, a formidable horse-faced woman, braked but was unable to stop. Fighting panic she skidded on the water-logged surface, dragging Rowena thirty feet before coming to a halt on the wet ground bordering the expressway, Rowena's head and shoulders pinned beneath the right front wheel.

21

At approximately the same time as Rowena Dartigue was being crushed by a bus from the Safian Private School for Children, a yellow taxi was carrying Decker past Ken Yokoi's Washington Square townhouse in a rainy darkness.

He had time for a quick look at the residence before the cabbie, an aristocratic-looking Russian Jew, turned left at the corner of Yokoi's block and stopped in front of a store selling occult books, incense, and aphrodisiacs. After paying the Russian Decker stepped onto a deserted, wet sidewalk, yanked down his hat and opened a cheap umbrella purchased minutes ago from a plump-cheeked Senegalese street pedlar near Bags's hospital. When he was certain he was unobserved he pulled his .38 Smith & Wesson from its belt holster and slipped it into an overcoat pocket. Then lowering the umbrella to hide his face he began walking back towards the townhouse.

Two men had been moving about on the townhouse steps and Decker had made them without any trouble. They were Kim Shin and his bodyguard, Shin with adhesive tape across the fractured nose he'd received in the fight with Decker two days ago. The Korean diplomat stood under an umbrella and watched his brawny bodyguard carry suitcases and packages from the townhouse to a Volkswagen van parked in front of the residence. By the looks of things the Koreans were moving stuff out of Yokoi's place in a hurry. Decker had a good idea just what this stuff was.

He slowed down near the townhouse, rain pelting his umbrella as he eyed the very busy Koreans. Decker had no backup, no warrant and he hadn't told his superiors or the Treasury Department what he was doing. Going through official channels would have alerted Dumas. Forewarned, he would have shifted Tawny to a new location. If Tawny was to have a chance Decker had to put his career on the line.

He had another reason for moving fast. Fort refused to give himself up until Dumas was in custody or dead. Given a choice Fort would rather spend a year on a deserted island with Ted Bundy and Charles Manson than two minutes in a room with Ben Dumas. At the moment Fort was somewhere on the street with information that could tie Dumas to Tawny's kidnapping, Gail's murder and Park Song's counterfeiting. His testimony could put Dumas away for ever. But first Decker would have to pop Dumas and give Fort a little peace of mind.

At the base of the stone steps leading up into the townhouse Decker, face hidden by his umbrella, let Muscles pass in front of him. Wearing a yellow slicker and black leather cap the big Korean carried a suitcase in either hand and was seemingly oblivious to whatever Shin was yelling at him in Korean. Decker took a deep breath. Time to rock and roll.

He attacked Muscles from behind. Throwing the umbrella aside he jammed his shoulder into the big Korean's spine, driving him into the side of the van. Muscles hit the vehicle with his forehead and left shoulder, hit it hard enough to drop him semi-conscious into a puddle of dingy rainwater.

Decker spun around immediately, .38 aimed at Shin's head. "You so much as twitch," he said, "and I'll paint the front of this house with your brains. Now ease down the steps, hands up where I can see them."

Lowering the umbrella a shocked Kim Shin clutched at the wrought-iron railing with one hand. "What are you doing here? You have no business interfering – "

"Speed it up, I don't have all day." Decker used the gun to motion Shin down the steps and over to the van where the diplomat looked down at his glassy-eyed bodyguard now on his knees and rubbing his damaged shoulder. Shoving Shin against the van Decker kicked his legs apart and patted him down. Shin wasn't carrying a gun but his bodyguard had a Colt .45 which he appeared reluctant to give up until Decker jammed the .38 into the side of his throat.

Decker ordered both Koreans into the front seat of the van then tossed his cuffs to Shin who sat behind the wheel. "Cuff yourself and your friend to the steering wheel," he said. When Shin finished, Decker removed the ignition keys, throwing them across the street and into Washington Square Park.

Leaving Shin to his dark thoughts Decker walked to the rear of the van and through opened cargo doors examined the vehicle's contents. There was the paper Fort said he'd delivered to Nicolay's restaurant only hours ago. Four pillow-sized packages wrapped in heavy brown paper, bound with steel strips and stamped "Property of the US Bureau of Engraving and Printing". Courtesy of Aunt Lorraine and Cousin Arnold.

Near the paper were five suitcases, two of which Decker opened. One contained new hundred dollar bills while the other held securities, bearer bonds and certificates of deposit supposedly issued by West German and Swiss banks. According to Russell Fort, Song had been planning to sell this shit to a half-dozen buyers and walk away with millions. Fort didn't know all the details but it seemed Song had to raise a ton of money in a hurry or have his ticket punched by some Korean.

Closing the van doors Decker returned to the passenger side and flashed his badge at a surly Kim Shin. "Detective Sergeant Manny Decker. You're under arrest for counterfeiting and for the theft of paper used in the making of United States currency." As rain splashed off the van's hood and into Decker's face he Mirandised the Koreans from memory while suddenly remembering he might be under scrutiny from the house. Nothing he could do about that except press on. Finished, he said, "Dumas inside?"

Kim Shin and his bodyguard stared straight ahead, two statues who'd suddenly lost the power of speech.

"Where's he keeping Tawny DaSilva?"

Keeping his bright black eyes on a Jeep Wrangler parked in front of the van, Shin fingered the tape on his nose.

"You're moving the goods," Decker said. "This mean Park Song's not showing up?"

The Koreans remained silent.

Decker said, "It's really hard to get a word in edgewise with you guys." Reaching into the van he jammed a forefinger into Shin's bandaged nose. The diplomat cried out and pulled away from Decker who said, "Where's Tawny DaSilva?"

Grabbing Shin's coat collar Decker yanked the Korean's head out into the rain. "I owe you for Buf," he said. "Now where's Tawny? And while you're at it, how many men are inside Yokoi's house?"

Kim Shin spat in his face and said something in Korean. Decker used a hand to wipe the saliva from his cheek. Then after drying the hand on his overcoat he said, "No more mister nice guy," and slapped Shin across the nose. The wail of a nearby fire engine drowned out the Korean's screams.

In the master bedroom Dumas sat at Yokoi's bedside turning the pages of one of Rowena's notebooks. "She could have left a lot of people twisting in the wind with this stuff," he said to Yokoi. "She's got all the gory details, not just on Song but on you, me and people who bought sex slaves from her. She's got Song in bed with the Korean government, his embassy connections, the passport forgery, spying and killing he's done for the Koreans. All here. Oh, here's something you'll like. Guess you could call it the chapter on the freaky sexual habits of the rich and famous. Want to hear a bit?"

Yokoi managed a weak smile. "You know I do."

"Me too," said a male voice across the room.

Looking in that direction Dumas and Yokoi saw Decker standing in the doorway, one hand behind his back, the .38 at his side.

A vein began twitching on Dumas's forehead. Closing the notebook he rose and faced Decker. "You're out of here, mister, and I mean now. You're on private property and unless I see a search warrant duly signed by a judge, a warrant specifying exactly what you're looking for, you'd better move."

Decker said, "Front door was open and being a concerned citizen I thought I'd check to see if you've had intruders. May I remind you that police may enter a premise without a warrant if they suspect a crime's being committed. I suspect you've been holding Tawny DaSilva prisoner. Shin says she's been moved to Queens. I'd like you to confirm that for me."

Yokoi started coughing. Dumas glanced at him before turning his attention back to Decker. "Out. And I mean now."

"The shooters you sent after Fort did a shit job," Decker said. "His girlfriend's dead but he's alive and kicking. Need I say he's ready to roll over on you."

Decker brought his hand from behind his back and tossed a book into the room, watching as it landed on a traditional rag rug near the bed. "General Science textbook," he said. "Found it downstairs in the cellar. Has Tawny DaSilva's name on the flyleaf."

Dumas eased into his wolfish grin. "You want to take that to court, hotshot, be my guest. Anybody could have put that downstairs. For all I know you did."

Entering the room Decker sat down on a colonial hardwood chair just inside the doorway and removed his hat, placing it on his right knee. "Your nurse is calling the police but before they arrive allow me to make a few points."

Decker said, "I intend to have the lab guys dust the cellar and I bet they find Tawny's fingerprints which are on file by the way. Gail DaSilva did what a lot of mothers do these days. Had her kid fingerprinted just in case Tawny disappeared and turned up years later. Missing kids get older but their fingerprints don't change. I bet we also find hairs and fibres indicating she's been here. Still think I'm blowing smoke?"

Yokoi pulled weakly at Dumas's trousers. "Ben? Ben?"

Without taking his eyes off Decker Dumas gently touched his lover's hand. "How's your partner, Decker?"

Decker flinched. It had been the last thing he'd expected, this question that wasn't a question. If Dumas had kicked him in the stomach Decker couldn't have been more surprised. And why had Ben the headcase come at him straight on like this? To rattle his cage. And the bastard had nearly succeeded.

For nearly two minutes the two men studied each other in silence, the only sounds being the ticking of a Victorian clock resting on a mantelpiece and rain beating against bedroom windows. Finally when Decker had control of himself again he forced a smile. "So you were the prick who shot her. Can't wait to see Bags's face when I tell her she nearly got wasted by the faggot from hell. By the way, you're going to love this. She tied you to the DaSilva killings. The problem with Joe LoCasio is he's willing to sell guns to any dipshit walking in off the street."

Yokoi said, "God, Ben, he knows everything. What are we going to do?"

Decker said to Dumas. "We both know what happens when a cop goes inside. You won't last a month. The second you step into prison there'll be a contract on your ass and it couldn't happen to a nicer guy. And without you your girlfriend won't last too long either."

Dumas eased towards a night table near the bed.

Decker shook his head. "Makes me nervous when you do that. Just stay put. Even if you could get past me where would you go? Cops, feds, they all want a piece of you. There's federal currency paper downstairs in the lobby, paper Fort says he passed on to you and Nicolay. Anyway, you're not the type to run off and leave your loved one behind. That's why you aren't going anywhere, big guy, except to college."

Using the butt of the .38 Decker brushed rain drops from the hat on his knee. "Fort tells me you're stealing information from police computers and selling it to drug dealers, shyster lawyers, even landlords trying to kick old widows out on the street. You've got cops tipping you about drug raids, investigators in the D.A's office letting you peek at confidential files and you've got court clerks tipping you to grand jury investigations. You also have motor vehicle clerks running licence plates for you. You've been a busy boy. And allow me to point out that you're an accessory in Susan Scudder's murder."

Decker held up a forefinger. "I understand you have a job opening. Fort took out a shooter named Hector Espinosa who I believe was in your employ. Woman with him sounds like his wife Ida. Wasn't she bounced from the force for strip searching women a little too vigorously? She goes both ways, I hear."

Yokoi said, "They're going to put me in some crappy prison hospital with cretins for attendants. God, Ben, I'd rather be dead than manhandled by those fucking morons."

Decker sighed. "The Queen of Mean says she'd rather be dead. Now there's a thought. I had a quick look at those files down in the basement. I wonder what a court-appointed medical expert would make of them? Eight to five they contain more than a few examples of professional misconduct. And what about those video tapes in the cabinet with them? I don't think we're talking Nintendo or the Super Mario Brothers here."

"How'd you get by Kim Shin?" Dumas said.

"I said the magic word. He's in the van, him and his favourite goon. So you shot Bags?"

Dumas grinned. "You asking or telling, hotshot?"

"Did you know that some prison hospital attendants are so scared of getting infected by AIDS patients that they ignore them for days on end? Patient dies and just lies there in his filth, body decomposing and really stinking out the place. Don't you just hate it when that happens?"

A vein throbbed on Dumas's temple. "Put down the gun and we'll see who's scared."

Decker shook his head. "Afraid I can't accommodate you. I'd like to but then one of us would have to kill the other. I need you to lead me to Tawny and Park Song. Besides, I like the idea of you in the joint and your girlfriend having a hard time without you. I like the idea of you worrying about her. How about telling me about this house in Queens where Shin says you moved Tawny?"

Dumas said, "I'm not telling you shit."

"Suit yourself. But you'd better take a last look at Mr Yokoi because after tonight you're never going to see him again. Don't count on exchanging letters or phone calls either. You two lovers have had your last dance. In fact, I will personally see that Mr Yokoi's remaining days on this earth are pretty shitty. He will not receive the best of care, believe me."

Yokoi said, "Ben, what am I going to do without you?"

"Good question," Decker said. "What is he going to do without you, Ben? I'd say he's going to die a lot quicker."

They were suddenly joined by the fat Jamaican nurse who entered the bedroom on squeaky shoes and carrying a thermometer. Just inside she stopped in front of the seated Decker. "Called the police like you say. They be here soon. Now if you will excuse me, I have a patient to attend to. This other business be between you and Mr Dumas. Don't concern me none."

She started across the room and before Decker could say or do anything she was between him and Dumas who seeing his chance reacted instantly. His hand went into the night table drawer and came out with a .38 Smith & Wesson. Decker shouted for the nurse to get out of the way. But she panicked, freezing and going pop-eyed at the sight of Dumas's weapon.

Too frightened to be angry at himself – he should have cuffed Dumas minutes ago – Decker leaped from the chair, landing on the parquet floor and rolling to his right. He needed one clear shot. The nurse was still between them. Still in the way.

Decker yelled, "Goddam it, woman, move!"

The nurse backed up a half-step, then another before turning to flee screaming on her squeaky shoes. Decker had his shot. And so did Dumas who fired once into the top of Yokoi's skull then shoved the .38 into his own mouth and pulled the trigger.

On the floor a stunned Decker froze, telling himself it hadn't happened. It hadn't fucking happened. "No," he whispered. "No, no, no." All he could think was, Jesus Christ. Where the hell did Dumas get the stones to do *that*? As Decker slowly pushed himself to his knees it all came down on him at once: confusion, shock, fear, and above all, relief that Dumas hadn't turned the gun on him. Then he began hating Dumas once more, hating him for forcing Decker to watch him die, hating him because he'd died without telling Decker where to find Tawny.

A kneeling Decker stared at the dead lovers, knowing they'd escaped him and knowing also that he didn't like to be beat by a perp. He was getting control of himself again which is why he saw no reason to pity these two creeps. They'd kidnapped Tawny, killed her parents and sold kids to geeks. Why the hell should Decker feel sorry for these sickos?

At the same time he was goddam happy to be alive. And there was a part of him that knew he'd just witnessed an act of passion, one which would stay with him for a while. In time he'd know whether it was the most terrible or most generous one he'd ever seen. At the moment, however, he was too stunned and angry to decide either way.

Meanwhile, footsteps rushing up the stairs brought Decker to his feet. He heard the nurse shout, *"He got a gun,"* and knew she was talking to cops. He had to work fast.

Leaving his gun on the floor he raced to the bed, picked up the notebooks Dumas had been reading and shoved them inside his overcoat. Then he pulled out his badge, hung it from his neck and turned to face the doorway. He'd just raised his hands when a thickly built Irish cop in an ankle-length black raincoat entered the room and dropped into a crouch, gun aimed at Decker's head. His toothy, long-faced black partner crouched in the doorway, gun aimed at Decker's balls.

The Mick said, *"Freeze, asshole!"*

Decker froze.

At nine forty-two that evening Decker sat in the back seat of an unmarked Buick parked under an oak tree in Kew Gardens, Queens, and peered through a light drizzle at a two-storey stucco house one block away. The house, which had a well-lit exterior, was one of four which formed a snug enclave on a tree-shaded street. It was guarded by two men who sat out front in a red Toyota.

In the front seat of the Buick Yale Singular stopped discussing college football with a slim black agent behind the wheel and shifted his bulk round to face Decker. "We having fun yet?"

Decker said, "What's keeping your guy?"

"Paper work ain't that easy except when you decide to ignore it as you sometimes do. In case you forgot, this can make things sticky when you go to court. You tell me how long it takes to get a warrant. It helps if you get a judge who don't look closely at what he's signing. The judge we wanted was at the opera. We got to go there, disturb his evening and hope for the best."

"Those guys in the Toyota are ex-cops," Decker said. "They might be corrupt but they're damn sure not stupid. Sooner or later they're going to make us."

"You done good by finding the paper and Song's funny money," Singular said. "Now don't go getting hysterical on me. To enter that house and get your little girl we need a warrant. You didn't have one when you encountered Dumas. The fact that he went and swallowed his gun took us off the hook. Catching Kim Shin with his hand in the cookie jar don't mean he'll do time on account of you didn't have no warrant. Shouldn't have to tell you that. Now since you come to me for help this is how I choose to go about it. We wait for the warrant."

Decker said, "If I didn't need backup I'd have gone in there alone."

"And maybe got your head blown off. From what I hear you almost did get your balls shot off."

"This address is all over Yokoi's records. A nice house in a nice neighbourhood. Just the place to sell sex slaves. Want to tell me how Dumas, Yokoi and Rowena what's-her-face got away with it for so long? Shin says Tawny's here. Son of a bitch better be right. Dumas didn't confirm it, but it makes sense. Where else could they have taken her on such short notice?"

"South Korean Embassy, maybe," Singular said.

"That's a possibility. Except that Shin was also bringing the counterfeit money and paper out here."

Singular said, "If Laughing Boy is on the premises it's gonna be like I died and went to heaven. I do want to pop that sucker so bad. Heads up, folks, I think this is the man we've been waitin' on."

Blinking its headlights a yellow cab slowly approached the unmarked car. Singular said, "That's him. Let's get it on."

Decker, Singular and the black agent stepped out into the rain. As Singular spoke into a hand radio the black agent raced towards the cab which braked to a quick stop. Seconds later he trotted back to Singular and handed him an envelope. The big man brought the radio to his mouth. "Move out!"

Secret Service agents and cops hidden in nearby parked cars rushed into the wet streets, kicking up water as they sprinted towards the stucco house. Three cops, pump shotguns trained on the Toyota, remained outside. Decker, gun drawn, stayed close to Singular who despite his bulk moved quickly and gracefully. With Singular running interference Decker was able to push his way through a dozen armed lawmen and reach the house first. *Tawny.* Decker's torment was about to end. He was going to find her.

Ignoring a small mounted television camera set up to screen visitors Decker and Singular barrelled through the doorway and into a pink-lit foyer where a short-haired young Cuban in a yellow leisure suit quickly touched his shoulder holster before throwing up his hands. He'd been sitting on a metal desk and talking to a tall middle-aged male Hispanic whose opened purple robe revealed he was wearing nipple clamps and a studded black leather dog collar. In between checking customers' names on a small personal computer the Hispanic had been reading the Cuban's fortune with a set of tarot cards.

The Hispanic started to ask Decker and Singular for IDs and then he spotted their guns. At the sight of the weapons and badges he dropped screaming to the floor on all fours, the robe riding up to reveal his hairy ass. Singular kicked him in the butt, sending him flying to the red-tiled floor.

Because he wanted to reach Tawny as quickly as possible Decker ran ahead, racing along a carpeted hallway lined with erotic prints and smelling of incense and marijuana. At the end of the hallway he stepped through a beaded curtain and into a large room decorated as a medieval dungeon. He was in a sexual supermarket. The glitter ball in the ceiling and the sound of Vivaldi coming from hidden speakers couldn't hide the fact that this scene was as sick as anything he'd seen in his years on the cops.

In the dungeon two dozen well-dressed men of various races were examining a collection of naked youngsters who'd been shackled to the walls. The youths – black, white, Latin, Asian – were being inspected as though they were canned goods on a shelf. A quick look told Decker that Tawny wasn't on display.

To his right a naked black teenage girl, mouth taped to hide her screams, hung upside down on a fake gallows. Some of the adults had newly purchased slaves sitting at their feet, the cowering youngsters naked except for a dog collar and leash.

The buyers saw Decker coming. Saw his gun along with the badge dangling from his neck. Saw other law enforcement officers rushing into the dungeon. Panicking, some buyers decided to flee which didn't stop Decker from grabbing one, a slick-haired, squat Arab with a spade-shaped face. Holding onto the Arab's collar Decker dragged the frightened man back before elbowing him in the face hard enough to knock him to the floor. Then he resumed the search for Tawny.

In a room just off the dungeon Decker found a bondage cross, bondage post and a wall hung with chains, paddles, whips, nipple clamps, dildos and leather face masks. He also found customers who'd been examining cages containing naked adolescents. Jean-Louis Nicolay, in a white suit, green tie and dark glasses, had been auctioning the youngsters to the highest bidder. At the sight of Decker he began hyperventilating. The buyers around him began looking for an exit. Too late. More cops and Secret Service men now entered the room, shouting and cursing as they roughly herded buyers and slaves towards the walls.

Making his way to the heavy-breathing Nicolay, Decker grabbed him by his expensive tie. "Where's Tawny?"

"Tawny? I do not know what you are talking about."

Decker twisted the tie knot, increasing Nicolay's breathing difficulties. "Dumas and Yokoi are dead," Decker said. "This leaves you and Rowena Dartigue or Mr Fox as she calls herself, holding the bag. You two are in it alone now. We've got Yokoi's files and we've got Russell Fort who's ready to give you up. Start telling me something good while I'm still in a mood to listen. Like where's Tawny and Park Song?"

Gasping for breath Nicolay said something Decker couldn't hear. "Louder," Decker said.

"I said it's too late. They're on their way to Korea."

22

Forty-eight hours later, on the first day of the month without rain, Decker and Karen Drumman entered Yale Singular's office carrying small suitcases. A nervous Karen gnawed her lower lip and kept one eye on the door. She and Decker remained standing, waiting for Singular, seated at his desk, to acknowledge them. A formidable English secretary with throaty tones had been told to hold all calls and to put through only the secretary of the Treasury and the president of the United States. Singular didn't want to be disturbed while talking to Decker.

Sipping cranberry juice from a Fred Flintstone-embossed glass the big Texan examined five pages taken out of Rowena Dartigue's notebooks. Decker had photocopied the pages then sent them to the Treasury Department, the South Korean Embassy and the US State Department. The copies were only samples. Decker had hidden the notebooks because they were his only chance of getting Tawny from Park Song.

Along with the sample pages Decker had included an ultimatum: if South Korea didn't instantly turn Tawny over to the US Embassy in Seoul and allow Park Song to be extradited to America, Decker was giving the notebooks to the press. South Korea had forty-eight hours to comply. After that Decker was going public with Mrs Dartigue's shocking disclosures about counterfeiting, money laundering and child prostitution in high places. Decker didn't need to be reminded that in threatening the Koreans he'd caused the odds on his survival to take a considerable drop.

Learning of his attempted blackmail, the New York police department started proceedings for a departmental trial on charges of suppressing evidence. As an added bonus the department also promised to kill his pension. Next came the State Department which promised to bring him up on federal charges of interfering with foreign policy. And as of yesterday, the FBI had begun watching his every move. Win or lose, Decker was under no illusions about the enemies he was making.

On the other hand certain people in law enforcement kept him informed of every move against him. They were offering their help anonymously because they wanted to see Tawny saved and Park Song doing hard time. Yale Singular, who had two daughters, had joined this private early warning system. But like other members he insisted that Decker neither acknowledge his help nor mention his name.

"Backin' your play at this point in time," said the Texan, "is like driving on the wrong side of the road."

Decker had made the Valentin-Dalto case, solved Gail's murder, learned who'd shot his partner and stopped Dumas from tapping into police computers. He'd also cut off Park Song's paper supply, confiscated most of his counterfeit money and exposed the South Korean government as Song's partner in crime. What he hadn't done was find Tawny DaSilva.

He drew his courage from guilt, from the inability to forgive himself. There were times when he knew this guilt wasn't rational, that it twisted his reasoning and sent him racing down dark roads. But it served a purpose. Guilt was the witness who reminded Decker that he owed something to someone other than himself. Guilt suggested that if moral precepts were sometimes inconvenient they were still necessary.

In taking on South Korea Decker was asking for trouble. They were a tough people, shrewd, uncompromising and extremely patient when it came to getting their revenge. Decker had his work cut out for him.

When it came to Decker's ultimatum Singular had expected the Koreans to hang tough, to save Song's ass in return for all his services over the years. As for Tawny, the Texan said that neither the Koreans nor the Americans were ready to jeopardise important military, trade and political considerations for the sake of a thirteen-year-old girl. Singular hated to say it but the kid was history.

Which was why Decker couldn't believe it when an elated Yale Singular told him that the Koreans had agreed to Decker's terms. They would return Tawny and approve Park Song's extradition to the US for trial. What's more the Koreans would throw in the plates as a bonus. Decker had won and won big. Or so it seemed.

Instinct, however, told him that something was going wrong. He hadn't read the fine print on the Koreans' offer and when he did, Decker didn't like it.

"They want you to go to Seoul to pick up the girl, Song and the plates," Singular said. "You and nobody else. You're to go unarmed. No weapons, no backup."

"You got to be kidding."

"That's how it came down from the State Department. The Koreans specifically asked for you. You're to come alone. And empty-handed."

Decker shook his head to clear it. Was he hearing correctly? "We have marshalls who do that shit, who go round the world bringing back wanted felons and they do it with guns."

"You could refuse. Guess it all comes down to just how badly you want that little girl."

"This whole thing sucks. Why me? A half-dozen marshalls or Secret Service agents could go over there and bring back Song with no trouble. And Tawny? All the Koreans have to do is turn her and the plates over to our embassy in Seoul."

"Listen up, crime-fighter. The Koreans want to save face on this thing. They don't want to admit they even heard of Tawny, let alone know where she is. Same thing with them plates. They don't want no big to-do, no reporters, no government people with high profiles moving in and out of their country. One man – you – goes over there, picks up everything and everybody, then hops a plane heading west the same day. Short and sweet."

312

Decker said, "Except that nothing's ever that simple, especially with Asians and I speak from personal experience. China, Japan, Korea, it's the same. To them any man who tells the truth is a fool. Believe me when I tell you the Koreans are nobody's fool."

"You learn that in the martial arts?"

"What I learned is you never do the obvious. The martial arts have taught me there's more to this Song business than the Koreans are letting on. They want me over there for a reason. I'd like to know just what that reason is."

Singular said, "Be easier for Song to kill you on his turf, that's for sure. Which would leave him with the girl and the plates, not to mention a much happier frame of mind."

"Why drag me over there to kill me? Why not take me out here?"

"I ain't no soothsayer. I'm just a humble civil servant who knows that nobody in our government wants to go near this one. Our embassy in Seoul has been ordered to stay away from you when you arrive, which I understand is a concession to the Koreans. You're gonna be isolated over there, I'm sorry to say. But if you want your little girl, you got to go there and get her. You ever been to Korea?"

Decker shook his head. "No. When I was in Nam I went on leave to Hongkong, Tokyo and Thailand. But not Korea. From what I hear I didn't miss much. Jesus, whose idea is this? I'm supposed to go to a strange country, pick up a psychopathic killer and do it without backup or weapon. Am I the only schmuck these people know?"

Singular said, "I've been told to tell you that if you bring back Song and the plates no action will be taken against you on account of them notebooks. State Department, your own police department, they both gonna back off. Gives you an incentive to travel, don't it? You got everything to gain and you got everything to lose, 'cause as sure as a fish drifts with the tide Song's not gonna go quietly. He's gonna try and kill you."

Decker said, "No shit."

"You ain't got a level playing field on this one, Bunky. They don't want no publicity, by the way. One line in the papers and the deal's off. When you get to Seoul you've got just six hours to get Song, your little Tawny and yourself on a plane outta there. After that the Koreans will stop cooperating. Comes down to that little girl, don't it? Like I said, how important is she to you?"

In his office Singular looked up from his desk, took in Decker and Karen, then leaned back in his chair. Aiming his chin at Karen he said, "You have any idea what you getting yourself into?"

Decker said, "I need her. Tawny's going to be frightened. Seeing me isn't going to make her any less afraid. To her I'll only be one more man who wants to harm her. She has to see a familiar face, preferably a woman's. Her mother's dead. That leaves Karen as the next best. Without Karen I couldn't deal with Tawny. The Koreans approved her coming along. I don't know what I'd have done if they hadn't."

"I'm glad to help," Karen said. "She is my godchild. I don't mind telling you, though, I'm frightened to death. I've never been to the Far East and with what I've heard about Park Song, I can't say I'm looking forward to the trip."

Singular pointed to a white envelope on his desk then looked at Decker. "Your extradition order. Signed by all parties concerned. I'm really looking forward to having Song on trial over here. Too bad we ain't got capital punishment. Love to see that bastard fry for killing an agent. It goes without saying you ain't got a friend in Korea or Washington, but I assume you know that already. Them notebooks are a source of worry to a lot of people. The way you waved them around has folks thinking you're as common as catshit and twice as nasty."

Singular stroked the side of his nose with a thick forefinger. "Don't suppose you care to tell me how you come by them. No, I guess you don't. First you grab Nicolay's Rolodex then you steal Mrs Dartigue's notebooks. Anybody ever tell you that stealing is wicked and unprincipled behaviour? Poor old Miz Rowena. Ends up gettin' squashed on some expressway outside Kennedy. How'd you like to finish your life as a road pizza? I tell you, God does have a sense of humour."

He looked at the pages on his desk. "This stuff could shake up the Korean government no end. Counterfeiting, money laundering, sex killings. And the man who did it all also did dirty little jobs for the government, like spy, kill people, forge passports and wash stolen money. This here's the kind of information that sets people to milling about in the streets and stormin' the palace. And we only got a few pages."

Decker said, "You get the rest when I return."

"*If* you return. That's what's bothering a lot of people. You just might not come back. What happens to the notebooks then?"

"I've left instructions for the notebooks to be turned over to you if I don't get back."

"I suppose they're ensconced in the safe of some shyster lawyer."

Decker held up three fingers. "Three copies, each in a different place." He'd left one copy with Gail's parents in Baltimore and one in the safe at Karen's office. The third was with Bags, locked in the hospital safe with her valuables. When he returned to America Decker was to hand the notebooks over to the South Korean Consulate in New York. Whether all would be forgiven at that point, well, he'd just have to wait and see. Koreans weren't big on mercy or leniency.

As for Kim Shin he'd come up smelling like a rose. He and his bodyguard were now on the way back to Korea. As part of the Song deal no charges had been filed against them. What's more the State Department had written a note of apology for the disrespectful treatment accorded Shin by New York police. The capacity of politicians to connive and scheme never ceased to amaze Decker.

In his office Singular looked into his empty Fred Flintstone glass. Finally he said to Decker, "Song's gonna try and kill you."

Decker said, "In his position I'd do the same thing."

A horrified Karen covered her mouth with both hands.

"Be you and him over there," Singular said. "One on one.

315

Except that it's going down on his turf. Ain't nobody gonna come to your assistance either. Some of us talked about maybe hiding a gun at the Seoul airport for you but we couldn't figure out how to do it without gettin' caught. Man in charge at that end is Colonel Youngsam, head of the Korean CIA. A real hard-ass and as smart as they come. Over the years he's been Song's rabbi. Kinda odd him giving up Song without a fight."

Singular looked at Decker. "There's something going on with this business that I can't put my finger on. A hidden agenda of some kind. Wish to hell I could figure out what it is. Got to be a reason why all of a sudden Youngsam and his pals agreed to let us have Song and the girl. It goddam bothers me. Aggravates me when people knows somethin' I don't know and should know."

Decker said, "We've got a plane to catch. Thanks for what you tried to do about the gun."

Singular looked at him. "I'm gettin' the feeling somebody is hoping you and Song kill each other. Be a lot of happy people if you two guys upped and died."

The fear on Karen's face made him realise what he was saying. "Goddam, I got a mouth big enough to bite myself in the neck. Sorry, Miss Drumman. Sometimes I forget there's more than just us boys in the world."

She forced a smile. "That's all right. I just don't know what Tawny and I would do if anything happened to Manny."

Decker said to Singular, "What if I don't bring Song back? What if I come back with just Tawny and the plates. Let's say Song's unable to travel. What then?"

Singular turned the calendar page back to yesterday's entries. "We lost a damn good agent to that little bastard. Nice young man with a wife and a son less than a year old."

Leaving his desk the Texan stood at the window and looked down at Broadway twenty storeys below. "It's your call, crime fighter. You're on the firing line so that makes you entitled to do whatever's necessary to stay alive. By the way, you and I never had this conversation. Have a safe flight, Miss Drumman."

316

23

Seoul, December

At noon on the day he was scheduled for extradition to America, Park Song was tap-dancing on the polished, black granite floor of his living room to a video cassette of *In Caliente*, his favourite Busby Berkeley movie musical.

As a frightened Tawny DaSilva watched from a tapestry-upholstered armchair Song added his wobbly tenor to the song "Muchacha". Dancing past Tawny he patted the heads of both large bronze Art Deco lions flanking the fireplace before tapping his way back to the oversized television screen displaying the cassette. Dancing was fun again. The headache induced by the blow from Rowena's brandy bottle had vanished.

However, there was a purplish bruise in the centre of his forehead, making Song look like an East Indian with a stupid caste mark. If Rowena hadn't died beneath the wheels of the American school bus, he'd have killed her as painfully as he knew how. She'd expired before Song could ask her about the notebooks which currently figured so prominently in his life. As of now they were Colonel Youngsam's problem. Let that bullet-head fool worry about them.

And worry he should since the Korean government was holding him responsible for their recovery. The Razor's political survival, not to mention his very life, depended on whether or not he could outwit Decker and get the notebooks away from him. Given Youngsam's recent treachery, Song didn't know just who to cheer on.

He closed his eyes, visualising himself dancing with Dolores del Rio, *In Caliente*'s breathtakingly beautiful Mexican star. How could she have sunk so low as to have appeared in an Elvis Presley movie? Shouldn't be too hard on her since she'd made *that* film towards the end of her career when good parts were few and far between. As Simone de Beauvoir, his mother's favourite writer, had put it, "Live long enough and you'll see your victories turned into defeats."

There wasn't going to be any of that victory-into-defeat stuff for Song. The fact that Decker had just landed at Kimpo Airport and was heading here to collect him and Tawny didn't make Song a beaten man. He wasn't returning to America with Decker or anyone else. And he wasn't giving up Tawny, his exquisite *kisaeng*. He was going to pull through this mess because he knew the secret of surviving: there was no such thing as a thousand ways to fight. There was only one and that was to win.

In New York the Korean Consulate had given him the shocking news that his "goodies" had been confiscated by Decker, an irritating piece of shit who just wouldn't go away. Song had vomited, wept and literally banged his head against a wall. He'd have given anything for the chance to kill Decker who was sabotaging Song's plans to repay Youngsam.

Nor had there been anything cheery in the news that Dumas had shot Yokoi to death then turned the gun on himself. The unnatural and the unexpected had entered Song's life with a vengeance. His attempt to grasp the clouds had failed. It would seem that his life had been little more than an attempt to write numbers on water.

And as if his luck wasn't bad enough, Song also learned that Russell Fort intended to betray him to the police in hopes of saving his own neck. For all of his macho posturing Mr Fort was so stupid he made a pig look brilliant. He was born to be a dismal failure with no more chance of success than of learning how to fly by flapping his arms. Unfortunately, Fort knew enough about Song's counterfeiting operation to get him thrown in prison until stars fell from the sky.

318

Forced to flee New York with his tail between his legs, Song had returned to Canada where he'd taken a hastily chartered flight back to Asia. He was a dead man, an impending victim of the Razor's wild rage. Song could no more raise the rest of Youngsam's thirty million dollars in time than he could empty the ocean with a sieve.

All he'd taken with him from America had been little Tawny who was every bit as beautiful as her photographs and who represented his one victory over Decker since Saigon. With Tawny and his bodyguards a desperate Song had headed towards Seoul, the only place he knew which offered him the slightest chance to avoid extradition. He'd considered fleeing elsewhere but no safe country came to mind. Where could he go to avoid the Americans who were closing in on him like hounds after a fox? Halfway between the Philippines and Hong Kong, he'd nearly come to blows with David Mitla over whether or not they should continue to Seoul or change course for somewhere else.

And then like a happy ending in one of his favourite films Song had received a thoroughly unexpected but highly welcomed reprieve from the hangman's noose. Using the plane's radio the Razor himself had personally passed on the extraordinary news: Song's entire debt to him had been paid. *Paid.* Unable to help himself Song had broken down and cried. Cried like a baby. Then watched by the co-pilot and navigator a wildly delirious Song had broken into a time-step before rushing to the back of the plane where he picked up a sleeping Tawny and spun her around while his bodyguards eyed him as though he were a madman.

His debt to Youngsam had been paid.

And how had this miracle come about? It seemed that KCIA agents in Tel Aviv had located an Englishman named Eddie Walkerdine who had gone there to dispose of money and valuables plundered from a London depository. To obtain the full story behind this crime the agents had removed four fingers from Mr Walkerdine's left hand. No further persuasion had been necessary to get Walkerdine to turn over the robbery's proceeds which were in excess of forty million dollars.

The Englishman was now a permanent resident in Tel Aviv, having been buried alive at the base of a sand dune north of the city. There appeared to be little reason to mourn his passing. Not only had he double-crossed his associates but he'd hired professional killers to murder two of them, a depository guard and a black ex-convict.

The KCIA had also wondered if Walkerdine had been involved in the death of Rowena's husband Michael, who'd been one of the depository thieves and who'd passed away in New York under dubious circumstances.

Walkerdine had smuggled the depository swag out of England aboard an El Al flight to Ben Gurion International Airport southeast of Tel Aviv. It was ironic that the loot had included jewellery belonging to Rowena Dartigue who'd gone to great lengths to protect her property from her roguish husband. An hour after she'd reported the missing jewellery to Scotland Yard its description was known to the KCIA. In an attempt to recover his money Youngsam then ordered the description wired to his agents around the world.

Seoul. With Youngsam off his back Song had assumed that life would go on as normal. For the first time in weeks he could breathe easy. He could sleep without being tormented by thoughts of his own death. He could eat without worrying about keeping his food down. The Razor was out of his life, out of it for ever if Song had his way. From now on he'd stick to counterfeiting and his *kisaengs*.

But he'd barely shown Tawny to her room when his world was shattered by a telephone call from his nemesis and saviour, the Razor. Song, he announced, could stay in Seoul for just thirty days. *Thirty days.* After that he would have to leave South Korea permanently. This decision was final and not open to debate.

A stunned Song tried to protest only to have Youngsam hang up on him. *Thirty days.* Was Youngsam mad?

In desperation a terrified Song telephoned further government contacts but failed to uncover the reason for Youngsam's sudden cruelty. Some claimed they had no idea what was going on. Others knew but refused to get involved. This particular affair was a hot potato; no one wanted to touch it. At once Song picked up on the signals he was getting: there was more shit to come.

Less than an hour after the first phone call Youngsam telephoned again, this time with even more horrifying news. *He had approved Song's immediate extradition to America.* Decker, of all people, would be coming to Seoul to take him and Tawny back to New York. Song was speechless.

A nightmare. That's what it was, a nightmare. A disgusting dream that would end the instant he awoke. But it wasn't a dream. Before the day was out a copy of the official extradition, signed by Youngsam and other officials, was hand-delivered to Song's pavilion. He'd been victimised by the same type of police treachery that had killed his parents. Because of it he now faced a lifetime of imprisonment in America, an idea so frightening that it caused him to black out, temporarily losing consciousness in front of a stunned Tawny. Had Youngsam been in the room with him that moment Song would have kicked his fat skull into a thousand pieces and fed them to a dog.

His extradition, Song learned, could be blamed on Rowena's notebooks. Damn that snobbish whore. Decker was using the notebooks to pressure the South Korean government into turning over Song and Tawny. The notebooks, it seemed, contained embarrassing data about Song's counterfeiting, his sex life and his relationship with the KCIA. This information, officials felt, could easily result in negative press which would then harm trade and defence meetings with America. Rowena's scribblings, it seemed, were more important than Song's freedom.

The notebooks, went the official line, could only be blamed on Song. Hadn't he and Mrs Dartigue been business associates? Furthermore his obsession with adolescent girls, also mentioned in the notebooks, had brought Detective Sergeant Decker into the picture, leading to the arrest of agent Kim Shin. In Youngsam's words, how many more agents would the KCIA have to lose because of a tap-dancing fool?

The Razor's treachery had sent Song racing to the medicine

cabinet for sedatives but there had been one aspect of this foul business which had bolstered his spirits. His admirers in the KCIA, young agents who idolised him for his flair and cunning, had been angered by Youngsam's throwing him to the wolves. Why should Song, a loyal Korean, be sold out just to please the Americans?

These young agents disliked the Razor whom they found imperious, stubborn and vicious. He was also tightfisted, refusing to share with them his considerable monies from corruption, bribes and other graft. The young Turks had long sought a reason to knock the wily spymaster from his lofty perch and in Song they'd found it. His forthcoming extradition was all the motivation they needed to defy openly the hated Youngsam.

Led by Kim Shin, who'd been plucked from Decker's clutches and returned to Seoul, these KCIA hotheads had contacted Song and pledged their help in any escape. At Song's urging Shin had worked the rebels up to a fever pitch. Were they ready to take on the Razor? They were indeed.

According to Shin the rebels, brimming over with youthful spunk, couldn't wait to get back at Youngsam and dispose of the troublesome Decker. This assistance, however, was not being offered gratis. Admiration for him aside, Song's deliverers expected to be rewarded for their efforts. These helping hands came complete with itchy palms.

Song wasn't surprised. As Americans were fond of saying, there was no free lunch. In any case money wasn't a problem. He had bank accounts and property in Hong Kong, Taiwan and the Philippines. There was no chance of selling off his beautiful home since Youngsam had already claimed it for himself. He'd be moving in after Song left for America, a piece of dismal news given Song yesterday when Youngsam had dropped by to confiscate the plates. Just another reason why Song was determined to see this egocentric prick, this so-called saviour of the nation, in his grave before the week was out.

If Song no longer had his beautiful home he did have

Tawny. And a plan to escape from Korea which included killing Decker and Youngsam.

As Song tap-danced in his living room, Cha Youngsam prepared to leave his third-floor office which overlooked the low two-storey building that was the Republic of China's Embassy. His departure had been interrupted by two men, high-ranking government officials who'd showed up unannounced to discuss Song's extradition. While unwanted and unwelcome, this pair of pen-pushers was too important to ignore. When it came to being devious and sly Youngsam was their superior. These two, however, had the president's ear and could make trouble if they wanted to. Better to hear these idiots out even if Youngsam would have preferred to slam the door in their smug faces.

The senior of the two was a small, watery-eyed man named Rhee who had a talent for distancing himself from power struggles and who this afternoon did most of the talking. It was Rhee who led off with what he saw as a tough question. Youngsam saw it as a waste of his time, an attempt to undo what could not be undone.

"Do you still feel you have made the correct decision to abandon Park Song?" Rhee asked.

Youngsam spoke to the ceiling. "Song's presence here threatens the stability of this present government, one which I am sworn to uphold and serve to the best of my ability. Furthermore he's been identified as one of my agents which makes his personal life and criminal pursuits a state matter. As you well know, this could affect our trade and defence negotiations with the Americans. It might also encourage Western inquiries into our country's alleged government corruption not to mention so-called human rights abuses. I prefer not to have this happen."

Bloody fools, he thought. The kind who want to save a burning house by pissing on it. This twosome could very well be on Song's payroll. If so, Youngsam intended to keep a close eye on them.

Rhee said, "Song has long been a valuable servant of the

Korean government. Some of us feel that by approving his extradition you have acted too hastily. Is it possible that you want him out of the country merely to avoid being personally implicated in what you claim he's done? If this is true then it's apparent your own survival takes precedence over that of our beloved Korea."

Youngsam's face did not betray his anger. His dark eyes, however, virtually closed and his breathing became nearly imperceptible. To calm himself before speaking he steepled his fingers under his chin. "This matter has been cleared with your superiors, so with all due respect any further discussion seems pointless. I safeguarded Song for the good of our country. For this same reason I choose not to safeguard him any longer. I will not allow a scandal to bring down this administration and that is final."

A frowning Rhee gnawed at his lower lip. Youngsam thought, so the little pen-pusher isn't quite so sure of himself after all. Rhee whispered to his companion, a squat man named Paik whose moon face sported a natural scowl and whose government position had turned him into a strutting peacock lacking any sense of humour. The silent Paik nodded but said nothing, letting Rhee do the talking.

Seconds later Rhee turned to Youngsam. "You have Song under guard, I assume?"

"Around the clock. He'll be at home when the American comes for him and the girl. I've also arrested Song's bodyguards. They'll be released after this business is concluded. The American policeman has already landed in Seoul, a bit of news which I'm sure has reached your ears before now. It would seem Song's extradition is proceeding on schedule."

Rhee sighed. "Over the years it was inevitable that Song would learn a great many government secrets in your service. I would think you would find this reason enough to keep him out of an American courtroom and away from Western journalists."

Rising from behind his desk Youngsam walked over to his coat closet. These damn cretins had wasted enough of his time. They'd come here, probably on their own, hoping to bluff him into changing his mind about Song. Well, they could all go piss up a rope. Youngsam's plan for dealing with Song had been approved by men who outranked these two fidgety imbeciles.

Obviously, Mr Rhee and Mr Paik hadn't been told the plan's every detail, perhaps because they weren't meant to have them. Perhaps Youngsam didn't have to be quite so polite to Mr Rhee and Mr Paik after all. In any case it was time for him to leave and get on with his job.

His visitors were as feeble-minded as those insolent young Intelligence agents who'd appointed themselves Song's protectors, who'd *dared* imagine themselves Youngsam's equal. Bureaucrats or would-be rebels, they were all little more than self-destructive buffoons with a taste for high drama. They built their lives around outlandish dreams which were doomed to failure. Youngsam saw them as eventual victims of their own confusion.

He slipped into a coat made of bear fur, offering Rhee and Paik his iciest smile, delighting in seeing the bastards flinch. "Song cannot stay in Korea and that is final," he said. "On the other hand, it is not to our benefit to have him appear in an American courtroom. So how do we deal with this extraordinary complication? Well, that's my job, isn't it? It is up to me to do the impossible, to make the sun rise in the west and set in the east. And that's exactly what I intend to do."

Youngsam reached into the closet for his fur hat. "Gentlemen, thank you for stopping by. Now if you will excuse me."

In his living room Song said to Tawny, "Do you like to dance?"

"Yes." Her voice was barely audible. She'd caught a cold on the flight from America and still wasn't eating properly. She'd soon get over that, of course. As part of her training Song would withhold food until she followed his sexual instructions to the letter.

"I will teach you Korean dances," he said. "You will learn them perfectly and then you will dance only for me."

"I thought I was going home," Tawny said. "The man who came here yesterday said I was going home to my family. He said somebody from America was coming to pick me up."

In yesterday's appearance at Song's pavilion the Razor, in addition to promising Tawny her freedom, had warned Song that an escape attempt would be unwise; the guards had orders to shoot to kill. As if Song wasn't astute enough to figure that out for himself. Youngsam also warned him not to have sex with Tawny. Should she return to America without her maidenhead, Song would make that same trip without his balls. Fingers or testicles, the Razor couldn't resist menacing Song's extremities.

Not content with threats Youngsam had also ordered the arrest of Song's three printers who worked in the pavilion basement. Throughout this abominable display of trickery Song had remained composed and seemingly detached, knowing he'd soon be free. Knowing also that he'd soon get back at the Razor and do a lot more than deflate the tyres on the bastard's golf cart.

Song pointed to the large television screen and said to Tawny, "See how Busby uses the camera? Look at those overhead shots and the way all dancing girls' movements are synchronised. They don't make movies like that any more. It's a shame, really."

Tawny's eyes welled with tears. "Why did you bring me to this place? I don't want to stay here. I want to go home."

"This is the big number. Everybody sings 'The Lady In Red' then the dancers do – "

He stopped talking and looked towards the front door. Well, well. Song smiled, hearing the guards shout as they converged on a car which had just entered the driveway. Now who could that possibly be? Rubbing his hands together Song giggled. "Welcome to you, o visitor from across the sea."

The thought of killing Decker practically made his mouth water.

He said to Tawny, "I think your friends from America have arrived. Time to embark upon our little adventure. Wear that lined denim jacket I bought you during our stopover in Hong

Kong. I'll buy you many things in the future. We'll have a wonderful life together, you and I."

In the black and white entrance foyer of Song's pavilion, Decker searched Laughing Boy for weapons.

He worked in silence, seeing no reason for small talk. What could you say to a man who was going to try and kill you within the next couple of hours? Edgy and with little sense of location or direction after his long flight, it was all he could do to keep his hands from shaking.

Watching him were three Korean guards in fur coats and hats, tiny-eyed, round-faced gorillas stinking of garlic and packing Kalashnikov rifles. This crew was big on giving him dirty looks, no surprise since Koreans disliked anyone who wasn't Korean.

Behind him a shaky Karen tried to calm down a near-hysterical Tawny, the two of them standing against a dark-toned wall painting of a windblown cherry tree with blossoms scattered over a second wall and the ceiling. Decker had met Tawny for the first time only minutes ago; instantly his heart's memory had made him see Gail in her face. Tawny was a reminder that his memories of Gail were becoming increasingly painful because of all he hadn't done.

As for Song, the little prick hadn't changed much over the years. He'd added a bit of weight but there wasn't a line in his face and he didn't have a single grey hair. The vicious counterfeiter of today and the young army officer who'd tried to kill Decker fourteen years ago looked the same. *Fourteen years.* Had it been that long since the gook had tried to waste him? In Korea Decker had found his past again. Given a choice he'd have preferred it remain a memory.

Song's giggling indicated that he was still the same loony-tune he'd been in Nam. For a guy facing the maximum sentence, Laughing Boy was too cheery for words. Meanwhile, all Decker found was five thousand dollars in counterfeit hundreds and credit cards under four different names. He pocketed the funny money and phony plastic then waited for Song's reaction. The smile never left the Korean's face. Something was definitely wrong with this picture.

Decker also checked out a small brown leather valise Song was bringing with him, finding two shirts, jeans, a pair of sweat pants, a pair of tap-shoes, some toiletries and several video cassettes of old Hollywood musicals. It all looked innocent enough.

During the flight from New York Decker and Karen had discussed her options should he be imprisoned or killed while in Korea. The truth was she only had one which was to get to the American Embassy and contact Yale Singular who'd promised to help in case of an emergency. He'd also promised to return Decker's corpse to the US. "So shines a good deed in a naughty world," Singular said.

The other crucial matter discussed by Decker and Karen had been the best way of telling Tawny about her parents' death. Decker didn't think there was an easy way but he agreed with Karen that she was the one to do it. The child would need someone visibly moved by her sorrow, not Decker who would have held back his tears, who would have let no one know that Tawny's tears could only revive his pain over Gail's death.

In the foyer an uneasy Decker finished checking Song then said, "Let's go," expecting the Korean to have a shit fit, to blow his cool finally and make trouble. Instead, Song calmly stepped to a wall mirror, slipped a grey fedora on his head and smelled the carnation in the buttonhole of a tailored camel's hair overcoat worn over his shoulders like a matinée idol. A last look in the direction of his sumptuous living room and at an antique cut-glass chandelier overhead, then he smiled at Tawny and strolled towards the front door like a man without a care in the world.

Outside on a cold, grey day the snow had started to come down heavier. Breath steaming from his nostrils and mouth Decker checked his watch. He was booked on the first flight from Seoul to the island of Guam, America's nearest territory in the Pacific. Here he'd turn Song over to Singular and a dozen US marshalls. Then it was off on a charter flight to New York and goodbye to the Far East. Singular was coming along because he wanted his share of the credit for bringing down the Treasury Department's most wanted man.

Decker's Guam flight took off from Seoul in three hours. Unfortunately, the snow would make getting to the airport a bit harder. It might even ground his plane. Christ, that's all Decker needed.

Ordering Song and the women to remain near the pavilion, he slipped on leather gloves and began searching the car which had brought him from Kimpo Airport. A green Hyundai with tinted windows and a telephone, it was parked in the snow-covered, circular driveway. Parked behind it was a black Toyota containing four Korean Intelligence agents assigned to bird-dog Decker until he left Seoul.

Decker knew he had been inside the pavilion long enough for someone to have hidden a gun in the back seat of the Hyundai, tampered with the brakes or wired a half-dozen sticks of dynamite to the engine. At least ten people had access to the car – Decker's watchdogs, plus the five guards outside the pavilion grounds and Kang Jung Hee, the frog-faced Korean who was Decker's assigned driver. Song could have bought any or all of them.

At Kimpo Airport Decker and Karen had been met by Colonel Youngsam, the bull-like chief of Korean Intelligence. Though the subject of blackmail hadn't come up Youngsam did manage to communicate his instant dislike of Decker through an unpleasant manner and a beady-eyed stare. Decker hadn't felt this fidgety around anyone since Nam. Immediately he knew he was at the mercy of this man's moods, that the only way he'd get out of Korea alive was if Youngsam wanted him to.

According to Singular the colonel had the reputation of being a seriously unpleasant man. And if he was giving up Song after all these years, he also didn't warrant too much trust. Singular had warned Decker to proceed with extreme caution around the colonel, a man who was not out to win friends.

On the colonel's orders both Decker and Karen were searched for weapons. Neither was armed. Decker wasn't even wearing a bulletproof vest, figuring if the Koreans were determined to take him out they'd find a way. He was, however, tossed so thoroughly that he knew Youngsam had to be looking for the notebooks. Meanwhile, the search, which lasted over an hour, contributed nothing to Decker's peace of mind. And it ate into the time he'd been allotted in Seoul. He sensed the delay was deliberate. Youngsam was increasing the pressure, tightening the screws.

Decker couldn't stop wondering about the truth of Youngsam and Song's relationship. After all these years why had the spymaster and the king of funny money come to a parting of the ways? Maybe they hadn't. Maybe this so-called extradition was just a scam to lure Decker to Korea so that Song could easily kill him.

As Singular had warned, no one from the American Embassy had come to the airport to meet them. Decker and Karen, strangers in a strange land, were on their own. When Youngsam's armed guards finally escorted them to their car, Karen was so indignant over being strip-searched that she vowed to file a complaint with the State Department. Decker thought they'd be better off taking evasive action, such as turning around and getting on a plane leaving the country.

Decker finished checking the Hyundai. Finding no weapons, he ordered Karen, Tawny and Kang into the front seat. As for Song, the man was enjoying himself. He waved goodbye to the guards who smiled and shoved their rifles in the air, calling out to him in Korean. Laughing Boy looked more like a candidate for political office than somebody with his ass in a sling.

Decker cuffed himself to Song – left wrist to the Korean's right – then slid into the Hyundai's back seat, Song on his heels. The guards peered in at Decker. They'd stopped smiling now. Their high-cheekboned faces were now primitive stone masks, showing no pity. Decker had seen that same remote look on the face of out-of-control killers. His jaw tightened; his mouth and throat suddenly went dry. Cold weather or not, he could feel sweat on the back of his neck.

A sharp command from Kang and two guards rushed to slam the Hyundai's door on Song's side. Jittery and cold, Decker bit his lip while Kang turned the ignition key then switched on the heater and windshield wipers. The Hyundai slowly rolled out of the driveway. *They were heading for the airport.*

As the Hyundai circled Kyongbok Palace Decker checked the map on which he had marked his return route. Kimpo Airport was southwest of Seoul. Allowing for traffic and bad weather the trip should take between one and two hours. This should put them at the airport an hour and a half before takeoff, barely in time for the required security check on international flights. It was cutting things close.

Leaning forward, he whispered to Karen, "How is she?"

Karen stroked Tawny's hair. "Scared. And hungry. She's eaten very little the past few days. Tawny, did you know that Manny's a friend of your mother's?"

The girl turned around to look at him. "She talks about you sometimes. You were in the Marines."

Decker nodded. "That's right."

"How come my mother didn't come to pick me up?"

With the back of his free hand Song stroked the tinted window on his left. "Your mother's dead."

"You're lying," Tawny said. "All of you are lying. You, that man in New York who pretended to be a policeman, you're all liars."

"Am I? Ask your friends."

In the silence that followed Tawny looked at Karen then swung around to stare at Decker. At the sight of their faces she shook her head in fierce denial. "It's not true. My mother isn't dead. She's at home waiting for me. She's – "

Throwing herself into Karen's arms, she buried her head against her chest and wept fiercely. Karen wept with her.

"Daddy's out of luck, too," Song said.

Grabbing the cuffs Decker yanked Song closer. "Son of a bitch," he said, "I ought to wax your butt right here and now. You say anything to Tawny again and I'm tying you to the rear bumper and dragging your ass to the airport."

"Manny!" Karen had leaned across the front seat and was pulling on his coat lapel. "Don't. Please don't. It isn't good for her to see this. Please."

An enraged Decker looked away from Song who now hummed "The Lady In Red", keeping time by patting his thigh with his free hand. In the front seat Karen clung to a weeping Tawny. No one spoke. Kang politely kept his eyes on the road while Decker, grateful for the silence, stared out the window.

The traffic was bad, Korean drivers worse. Construction, excavations and the snow didn't make travel any easier. It took nearly ten minutes for the car to make its way through a large open-air market packed with shoppers on foot, bicycles and pulling handcarts. A strong smell of fish and powdered red pepper found its way through the closed window. Squid slithering about and a supposedly dead octopus hanging from a hook made Decker feel queasy. What nearly brought him to the point of nausea was seeing a pile of dog carcasses. The dead dogs would be used by restaurants for spicy soup, an Asian delicacy.

The sight of American servicemen with Korean women brought back past memories of his own good times in Saigon with Asian ladies. Decker also allowed himself a brief smile when he saw a theatre marquee advertising the Korean version of a Neil Simon play. The whole world laughed at the same things, apparently.

The sun popped out briefly, hanging around long enough to reflect off the high-rises lining the Han River before disappearing. By the time the Hyundai crossed the river Decker had begun to think they might make it to the airport without incident.

As the Hyundai passed through the last of the city's crumbling medieval walls it was overtaken by a small blue bus containing nearly a dozen singing men dressed in Alpine garb – windbreakers, backpacks, caps with feathers and hiking boots. According to the guidebooks seventy-five per cent of South Korea was hills and mountains, making mountain-climbing a popular pastime.

When the bus was in front of the Hyundai its driver honked twice before speeding up along a newly constructed and fairly empty highway. Kang tooted back, smiling at Decker in the rear-view mirror as if to say, we're all brothers in this grand and glorious land. In seconds the bus had vanished.

The froggy Kang, meanwhile, eyed the left-hand wing mirror. Deciding to check out the escort car himself Decker looked over his shoulder and felt a chill. *The Toyota had disappeared.* In its place were a pair of dusty GM vans. Behind the vans was a long, flatbed truck stacked with small cars. The hairs on the back of Decker's neck went straight up. Beside him, Song giggled.

Decker turned in time to see Kang make a hard right off the highway. And then the Hyundai was speeding along a gravel road leading into an empty snow-covered park of low wooded hills, frozen ponds, pavilions and small bridges. Both vans followed the car into the park. Behind the vans came the flatbed truck.

Fear brought pain to Decker's bowels. His heartbeat became so rapid that he thought he would pass out. His hands and feet suddenly turned cold. Instinctively, he reached inside his overcoat for the gun that wasn't there. Finding no weapon he suddenly felt weak and exhausted. Seeing the look on his face Karen peered over Decker's shoulder. At the sight of the vans, she paled. Whispering "Oh, my God," she reached out for Tawny.

Ahead of the Hyundai the mountaineers' bus had blocked the road. And as Decker watched, the singing mountaineers, carrying automatic rifles, quickly piled out into the snow. He looked over his shoulder to see the vans and the flatbed truck close to within fifty yards of the Hyundai.

The trap was sprung.

Braking suddenly, Kang sent the Hyundai off the road and skidding towards a low icy foothill leading down to a frozen lake. At the top of the foothill the car halted suddenly, rocking briefly on its axles before coming to a complete stop. Without hesitating Kang reached inside his overcoat.

Karen shouted, "Manny, he's got a gun!"

Decker leaned forward to grab the driver.

Song, however, lifted his cuffed hand and tried to elbow Decker in the face. Feeling his cuffed hand rising Decker leaned away to protect himself, evading most but not all of Song's attack. The Korean's elbow caught him just behind the left ear, blitzing the back of his head with a sharp pain. At the same time Kang, PPK Walther in his hand, twisted around for a clear shot at Decker.

Karen clawed at Kang's face, gouging his cheek and ear. Shrieking, the driver jerked his head away, spoiling his aim. His gun hand went up and he fired twice at the roof. Tawny screamed.

In the back seat Decker jammed his left heel down on Song's instep. As Song yelped Decker threw himself forward and quickly punched Kang in the throat. Eyes bulging Kang fell back against the steering wheel, setting off the horn. As the horn blared he clutched his throat, coughed up blood, and thrashed violently in the front seat.

Decker wanted Kang's gun. But before he could yell for Karen to give it to him, Song threw himself on Decker, free hand grabbing at his balls. Decker caught the hand. Break the little finger, he thought. Then break the bastard's neck. Kill him and die happy.

But again Song struck first. He bit Decker in the face, digging razor-sharp teeth into his cheekbone, grunting and salivating, head twisting wildly in an attempt to tear away flesh. Decker nearly spooked. He tried to claw at Song's throat but the Korean knocked his hand away, then quickly leaned back and head-butted him, cracking Decker's left eye socket and cheekbone.

Inside Decker's skull a bright red light exploded repeatedly. His brain threatened to burst through his skull. He fought to maintain his concentration. But even before the red light subsided Decker knew he was blind in the left eye.

Groggy and desperate, he embraced Song, hoping to smother the Korean's attacks until his head cleared. Song, however, sensed Decker's weakness. He clawed at his eyes, missing as Decker twisted his head wildly. A second later he

334

tried to knee Decker in the stomach, but Decker was too close. The knee struck him in the hip, harshly jolting his spine.

Suddenly the car door behind Decker opened and he tumbled out onto the snow, dragging Song with him. Karen had opened the door, a break for Decker who was being taken apart by Song's infighting. Both men now rolled about in the snow, flailing at each other with their free hands.

A horrified Karen, Tawny at her side, backed away as Decker and Song slid down the icy foothill, heading for the frozen lake. Ahead of the two men a pair of wild ducks hidden near the lake's edge quacked wildly and took to the sky. Trailing counterfeit money Decker slid down first, dragging a screaming Song behind him. Near the lake's edge both came to a stop in knee-deep snow. Rising to their knees they continued attacking each other.

Decker threw a short right hook to Song's face. Blocking it with his left hand, the Korean then shoved the heel of his palm at Decker's right temple. Decker shifted his head to the right and the blow grazed his head. It worsened his headache; the full blow could have knocked him out.

The handcuffs were a terrifying hindrance. They eliminated Song's kicking skills as well as Decker's speed and superior strength. Once when Song tried to get to his feet Decker yanked on the cuffs, pulling him face down in the snow. In a flash Song scooped snow into Decker's face, blinding him in his good eye. Then quickly scrambling to his feet the Korean kicked Decker in the ribs.

Decker's overcoat absorbed some of the kick, but not all of it. The kick hurt. Weight on one leg Song readied a second kick. But Decker threw himself backwards, tugging on the cuffs with both hands and pulling Song off-balance – pulling them both into the lake.

They crashed through the ice, landing in waist-high freezing water. First to rise, Song pushed Decker's head down below a layer of counterfeit bills now floating on the water's surface. Desperate for air Decker twisted wildly, painfully wrenching his bad knee. Worse, he nearly lost his balance. He finally freed himself but not before swallowing foul water.

On his feet and inhaling through his mouth, Decker stumbled backwards. He felt Song pull on the cuffs. To avoid falling, Decker pulled back. Suddenly Song released his grip, hoping to drop Decker back into the water. But by stepping back and continuing to pull, Decker kept his balance. But the mud sucked at his feet.

He and Song, tiring quickly, were now in deeper water. Water-logged clothing and bitter cold made every move a struggle. Attempting to stand Decker realised he and Song were too exhausted to dominate the fight and too restricted in their movements to win easily. Each was experienced enough to take advantage of mistakes. First man to fuck up was dead.

On the other hand, the first man to gamble could win the fight.

Worn down by the freezing water, a weary Decker backed away through ice and counterfeit hundreds floating around him, inching towards deeper water. He had decided to take a wild gamble.

His left eye ached terribly and he had cracked ribs. His right knee burned with pain and it barely supported his weight. He kept most of his weight on his left leg, barely touching the lake bottom with his right. Twice he backed onto a rock and nearly went down. Step into a hole and both he and Laughing Boy could drown.

And then he was in water up to his chest, unable to stop the shivering and feeling so cold he could hardly move. For Song, the water was now shoulder high. His arms were underwater. His hand techniques would now be slower.

Suddenly realising the danger to himself Song frantically pulled on the cuffs, trying to move back towards shore. Decker resisted with all his strength. Song then brought his cuffed hand to his mouth and sank his teeth into Decker's thumb, drawing blood. The pain was excruciating. It was all Decker could do not to cry out.

Again he pulled against Song. In retaliation the Korean dug his left thumb into a nerve on the inside of Decker's left wrist. A stinging, burning hurt raced along Decker's arm and up his left side. He nearly dropped to his knees in an attempt to escape. But that would have been useless because he would have drowned. And he needed to stay close. With no choice, he endured Song's torture.

A jubilant Song saw this as Decker's weakness and pressed his advantage. He bit down harder with his teeth and dug in deeper with his thumb. He was going to kill Decker and escape.

He never realised his mistake. His hands were tied up and he could not mount another attack. And his head was within Decker's reach.

Decker threw himself at Song, wrapping his legs around the Korean's waist. A deep breath then Decker sank underwater, taking Song with him. Below the lake's surface Decker, in a grey, frozen world, concentrated on killing Song.

He felt his thumb being released. Song had opened his mouth to breathe. Which is when Decker unhooked his legs, grabbed Song's head and leaped upwards, ignoring the pain in his bad knee.

Both men simultaneously burst through the surface of the water, sending counterfeit hundreds rising into the air around them and in that instant a screaming Decker, still in midair with Song's head gripped tightly in both hands, broke the Korean's neck.

They fell back into the water, Song's corpse dragging Decker down. Struggling to his feet Decker fumbled in his overcoat pocket for the handcuff key.

The pocket was empty.

During the fight he'd lost the key to the handcuffs.

He tugged at Song's corpse trying to pull it on shore. But the Korean was deadweight. Decker fought against panic. Hearing splashing, he turned and saw Karen wading in his direction. When she grabbed his elbow he shouted, "Pull!"

But she couldn't pull two men. When Song's corpse began dragging them both into the water she screamed.

In death Song had not stopped trying to kill Decker. The lifeless counterfeiter tugged at him relentlessly until Decker found himself under water. Stumbling to his feet, he looked over his shoulder. Jesus. Standing at the top of the low foothill was Colonel Youngsam, backed by uniformed Korean soldiers armed with AK-47s. More soldiers were climbing out of the small cars stacked on the flatbed truck. All silently watched Decker's battle with the dead Song. Watched without moving a muscle.

Other spectators included the men in mountain gear, four Korean guards from the Toyota and Koreans who'd been in the two GM vans. But they had their hands in the air.

Unless a miracle happened Decker was going to drown. He wasn't going to get any help from the colonel and his boys.

He heard Tawny yell, "Karen, here! Take this!" Decker looked over his shoulder. Tawny was holding out Kang's pistol. "The cuffs!" she yelled. "Shoot them!"

Stumbling out of the lake Karen snatched the gun from Tawny then ran back, nearly losing her balance. As she rushed towards him Decker, now in water up to his chest, used his fading strength to lift Song's corpse out of the water. Staggering under the dead man's weight he planted his feet apart and held out his cuffed wrist. Song began to slide from his arms. In seconds Decker would be underwater again.

"Do it!" he shouted to Karen. "I can't hold him much longer!"

When she was beside him Decker said, "Hold the gun with both hands. Point it away from me. Away, away. Barrel against the chain. Now pull the trigger. Go, go!"

Karen fired once, splitting the chain. Dropping Song's corpse Decker fell backwards into the water. A hysterical Karen threw the gun aside, grabbed his arm and helped him to his feet. Together they staggered out of the lake and onto the shore where Decker shivered uncontrollably.

Unable to stand he dropped to his knees in the snow, coughing up water. To keep his hands from shaking he tucked them in his armpits. Finally he sat down in the snow, prepared to sit there for ever. He'd never been so cold in his life.

He stared at Youngsam. The man with the hidden agenda, the man who'd orchestrated Song's death to protect his country. The man who preferred to see Song dead rather than

338

spilling his guts in an American courtroom, who'd saved face by having someone do his dirty work for him. And do it in secret because what had just happened in the park would never see the light of day. Decker had just gone through an exercise in damage control.

And the man who'd planned it was staring down at him from a hill in a country where Decker could be down to his last few breaths. Decker was staring at the man who'd outfoxed every player in the game.

Youngsam was about to ring down the curtain. Eyes hidden behind dark glasses he casually lifted a hand in a signal to the soldiers. Karen quickly grabbed Tawny and turned away. Somehow pushing himself to his feet Decker limped to a position in front of them and waited, his body between the women and the soldiers. He looked up at the sky, at the softly falling snow. Still no sun. He tensed to receive the bullets.

The soldiers fired, killing the mountaineers. Killing the Toyota guys. Killing the Koreans who'd been in the two GM vans, Kim Shin being one of this crew. The powerful AK-47s lifted the dead and dying men in the air, turning them into bloodied rags, sending them rolling and sliding down the hill. As a stunned Decker watched, wondering if he was still alive or what, Youngsam lifted his hand again.

This time three of the firing squad started down the incline towards Decker, Karen and Tawny.

24

New York, December

It was noon on Christmas Eve when Decker, Karen and Tawny and several thousand other ticket-holders entered the grand lobby of Radio City Music Hall. While Karen and Tawny gazed up at a pair of two-ton chandeliers hanging from a sixty-foot-high ceiling, Decker looked over his shoulder. For the past week he'd been followed.

Whoever was doing it was good. Decker had yet to spot the bastard. But he'd followed enough perps to know when someone was sitting on him. The question was who and why?

What did Decker see in the Music Hall crowd of happy campers, all looking forward to a good time? Zilch. How much could he see with one eye anyway? Behind dark glasses he was wearing an eyepatch; he'd have to wear it until the blurred vision cleared up which should be in another two weeks. Meanwhile in the Music Hall he saw nothing to explain why he'd been ready to jump out of his skin.

Outside in front of the theatre a homeless black man, built like a dust mop with lips and wearing a button reading *Free James Brown*, had hit on Decker and Karen for a "contribution to the United Negro Pizza Fund". The guy's rap had tickled Karen who'd decided to reward him. As she dug in her purse for change Decker suddenly felt as though he could reach out and touch whoever had been tailing him. And hurt him until Decker got answers.

But when he looked around all he saw were *faces*, New

York faces flushed with cold, or half-hidden behind scarves or tight-lipped against a twenty-one degrees temperature or maybe just pissed off because they hadn't finished Christmas shopping. He hadn't seen *the enemy*.

He'd studied these faces, looking for something in someone's eyes and finding nothing. Then he'd stopped looking because Tawny had wanted to tell him a joke. And he'd listened because it was important to pay attention to her.

"What did the man say to the waiter in the restaurant? He said, give me an alligator sandwich and make it snappy."

Karen, a great audience, had laughed. And so had the skinny homeless dude who'd been dressed in a plastic shower cap, two different running shoes and the tackiest looking army blanket since cloth was invented. Decker had smiled, telling Tawny the joke was very funny, but he'd kept his eyes on the crowd. Whoever was following him had backed off. But he hadn't gone far.

It had been Karen's idea to invite Tawny back to New York from Baltimore, where she was living with Gail's parents, and take her to the Christmas show as in previous years. For Decker it had meant cancelling a trip with Karen to Bermuda, something they'd both needed. Both, however, had agreed that it was right to cancel. Tawny needed them. And Decker owed the kid his life. Besides, Gail would have wanted them to do it.

Except for a handful of people Tawny was now suspicious of adults. Karen said she cried a lot at night and no longer made friends so easily. Gail's parents were bending over backwards to make her life comfortable but weren't having much luck. Decker wasn't surprised. Tawny had been a victim and often victims never recovered.

Sometimes Tawny went days without speaking. She'd just started back in school but wasn't making good grades. Whether she'd ever lead a normal life again was anybody's guess.

In the lobby Karen said to Decker, "You bought the tickets so I'm buying the popcorn. Tawny and I'll do the honours. Wait here, unless you want to battle that hungry mob."

Decker shook his head. "No way. I'll be here when you guys get back." He waited until Karen and Tawny had disappeared in the crowd before taking a position with his back to the wall. He thought, Son of a bitch you're out there. Edgy and annoyed, Decker still looked forward to playing the game.

It couldn't be Dumas's crew. The agency had had its ticket yanked. Anyone who hadn't been arrested at the sex slave house had faded from sight. Decker could handle those maggots. Bad cops were predictable. They turned bad and stayed that way until somebody killed them or they ended up in the joint. What Decker found hard to handle was what he couldn't see.

He touched the bandage on his face. Being bitten by Song had meant getting a series of tetanus shots. This was Decker's first week without them; he didn't miss that nasty needle at all. His thumb was healing but his cuffed wrist was still raw and two cracked ribs were healing in their own good time. As for his knee, he was strengthening it with weights, not that it would ever be strong again but weights would help.

All three – Decker, Karen and Tawny, had colds. The Sniffle Sisters, Plus One, Tawny had called them. No surprise.

He'd been granted a week's leave by the precinct where for the moment he was no longer regarded as dogmeat. How could the entire department not love him? He'd recovered the plates, plugged the leak in the undercover programme and whacked Song. Everybody loved a winner.

But if Decker was a winner, why was he being followed?

When Karen and Tawny returned the three of them entered the huge theatre which sat six thousand people and was the largest in the world. As Decker ate popcorn he found himself actually looking forward to the show which he'd never seen before. A dumb thing for a New Yorker to say, but what the hell.

The entire audience seemed to be in a good mood. Joys of the season – New York was a great town at Christmas. As the lights dimmed the audience applauded. Spotlights suddenly found singers dressed in colourful Dickensian Christmas gear arranged along the walls like living decorations. Another spotlight picked up the big organ which boomed out the first chords of "The First Noel". Decker could feel the organ's vibrations coming up through the floor. The singers joined in. As usual the black singers had the best voices.

Sitting between him and Karen, a happy Tawny bounced in her seat with excitement. Her eyes lit up. It was the first time Decker had seen her smile. Reaching out, she touched his arm and grinned at him. Seeing Gail in her face, he smiled back.

But after she looked back at the stage, he glanced over his shoulder, peering into the darkness.

Seoul

Late the following evening Cha Youngsam locked the door of his office then returned to his desk where he opened a file folder marked "personal" and which he kept in a floor safe in his closet. As he studied a recently received report he tugged gently at the hairs in his nose as he usually did when thinking. Occasionally he stopped toying with them to sip from a glass of snake's blood which he drank to keep himself fit and virile.

By allowing Song's "escape attempt" to proceed uninterrupted Youngsam had solved two problems. He'd silenced Song, of course, and recovered the embarrassing notebooks. He'd also lured his agency enemies out into the open where they'd been terminated without difficulty. He smiled, remembering their arrogance. To laugh at the elderly was to laugh too soon.

He'd figured correctly that the young Turks would rush to Song's side as a way of getting at him. And so they had, paying for this tactical error with their stupid lives. The Razor had indeed cut swift and deep.

More than most men he was aware of life's changes and chances, aware that one had to be eternally vigilant in order to survive in a world where treachery lay around every corner. Life was a harsh reality and it was necessary to conquer it every day.

He put down the report and picked up a photograph of Tawny DaSilva, subject of the report. After another sip of snake's blood he stroked the photograph with his fingers.

Fingers. Song had sent him the fingers of the last *kisaeng* he'd slaughtered, an insult Youngsam had avenged as promised. As for the DaSilva girl she'd caught Youngsam's eye with her bravery in the park. Had it not been for her Decker would have certainly died at the hands of a dead Park Song, a wicked bit of irony to be sure.

Tawny DaSilva was unique. The more Youngsam thought of her, the more he had become obsessed with this child. Lovely, yes. Unspoiled. And brave, an attractive quality in and of itself. Just looking at such a unique child made a man feel younger.

How exciting it would be to possess this little treasure and enjoy her before time and circumstances turned her into a lying mask of an old woman. It was a pleasure Youngsam had promised himself that day in the park when he had seen her rush towards Decker carrying Kang's pistol.

He had always found courage in a woman to be the most sensual of qualities.